THE PIT AND THE
PENANCE

A TWIST OF POE MYSTERY

Also By

VELDA
BROTHERTON

TWIST OF POE MYSTERIES
The Purloined Skull
The Tell-Tale Stone
The Pit and the Penance
Masque of the Rising Moon

THE VICTORIANS
Wilda's Outlaw
Rowena's Hellion
Tyra's Gambler

THE MONTANA SERIES
Montana Promises
Montana Treasures
Montana Dreams
Montana Fire
Montana Destiny
Montana Legacy

OTHER TITLES
Beyond The Moon
A Savage Grace
Once There Were Sad Songs
Stoneheart's Woman
Wolf Song
Remembrance

THE PIT AND THE
PENANCE

A TWIST OF POE MYSTERY

VELDA
BROTHERTON

LAGAN

OGHMA CREATIVE MEDIA

www.oghmacreative.com

Library of Congress Control Number: 2018944180

ISBN: 978-1-63373-292-6

Interior Design by Casey W. Cowan
Editing by Gil Miller

Lagan Press
Oghma Creative Media
Bentonville, Arkansas
www.oghmacreative.com

This book is dedicated to the countless volunteer Rural First Responders and EMTs who give hours and hours of their time, both for training and responding to calls.

These men and women are tireless in their efforts to rescue those of us who live in the rural areas of the Ozarks.

ACKNOWLEDGEMENTS

I would like to acknowledge the many people who were with me along the way from the beginning of my writing career. These *Twist of Poe* mysteries are based in a large part on the nine years I spent as a feature author and city editor for *The Washington County Observer*. Though we never investigated a murder like Jessie West and Dal Starr, we met so many marvelous characters who now walk through the pages of this series.

In particular, I'd like to recognize Parker Rushing, my editor and the owner of the paper. Parker hired me though I never had a day's training as a journalist. He guided me through every facet of my job from photography—we still used black and white film developed in a darkroom on site, and 35mm cameras—to conducting interviews and telling the stories. He gave me opportunities I'll never forget, and was with me when I learned my first book, *Goldspun Promises*, was to be published by Penguin. Parker has passed on now, but he will always remain in my heart.

I'd also like to give a special thanks to Casey Cowan, Venessa Cerasale, Gordon Bonnet, George Mitchell, Gil Miller, Dusty Richards,

Amy Howk, and Cyndy Prasse of Oghma Creative Media. Keeping a small press afloat is an overwhelming job even at the best of times, yet they always somehow manage to find time to keep me on track with my writing.

1
CHAPTER

Fur on end, the growling pit bull stood spread-legged in front of Jessie showing a mouth full of teeth. Even a dog person would've been wary, which meant she was terrified. He wasn't about to move out of the way, and he couldn't chase what wouldn't run. Or at least she hoped not. Yet, he stubbornly barred the way to the dorm where Nikki Bracken waited to be interviewed. It wasn't an exciting assignment, but what the heck? The latest recipient of a full scholarship to Bailey Junior College had one of those poor but highly-intelligent backgrounds. The kind of story Jessie's readers ate up.

The lousy mutt's barking added to the clamor of what was called music today blasting from the dorm. Both were about to get on her nerves. With each bark his front feet left the pavement. She was tempted to throw a rock at the ugly animal who dared her to take another step. Better yet, she might pitch her brand new purple Adidas through a window. Shut up that blasted racket.

Sent by her boss to get what should be an easy interview with Nikki, she hadn't expected to have to deal with the snarling, drooling, ugliest dog in the world. One ear lopped down with a tear in it, a lower tooth pinned a corner of his upper lip into a permanent snarl, and one of his eyes peered in the wrong direction.

She shook a fist at him and shouted, "Git on out of here."

He bounced once more on his front legs and curled the rest of his upper lip to show gleaming incisors. There must be some way to dissuade him from gnawing off her left foot, which he eyed with slobbering delight.

"Just try it, mister, and I'll kick those silly teeth down your throat. Why don't you go on and find another dog to chew on? Maybe a Great Dane."

Again the bounce and bark. This time loud enough to rouse the interest of someone inside the place. The door cracked open and a burred head poked out, looking like a body-less entity.

"Snout, shut up that racket. Who you wantin' to see?" Though the ear-ringed head continued to face the dog, it was obvious he was addressing Jessie.

"I'm looking for Nikki Bracken. Is she here?" Hard to be heard over the rap or whatever the kids called that racket.

"I think so. Come on in. That dog won't hurt you none."

"Are you sure? Cause I think he favors my leg for supper."

"Go on now Snort, before I find me a shoe."

The dog, Snout or Snort, or whatever might be his name, turned, cast a disgusted look over one shoulder, and trotted down the sidewalk, butt swaying high like a stripper.

At least the dog noise was gone. "Well, does Nikki live here, or not?"

"Last I looked, she did. I'll try to holler her up. You wanta come in or wait out here?"

Considering the cacophony, she preferred to remain outside. "Perhaps

I could wait here. I'm with *The Observer*. I'd like to talk to her for a story about her scholarship. But it would be nice if we could hear each other."

The boy emerged from behind the door proving he had a body, but one of those skeletal kind she was seeing more and more of. Honestly, some of these kids looked about to starve. He put one hand over his mouth and widened his eyes.

"Oh, my goodness *The Observer*? You want to write a story about Nikki? I'll go get her."

She'd definitely impressed him. Despite her preference to remain outside, he urged her to come in. Pushing the screen door wide open, he stepped out on the stoop and stood back to make room for her to slide by.

Nothing exciting had gone on all summer, but now that students were returning to the college for the fall semester, action would pick up some. No doubt there'd be a few snatch and grabs, more gas station drive-offs, and the usual he said—she said scuffles between husband and wife, boyfriend and girlfriend, and other mismatched couples. She never wished for murder or mayhem, just a little excitement now and then. Occasionally something really bad happened, even in small Grace County.

The kid kept talking while they waited. "She's really smart, our Nikki, but to tell you the truth, we never thought she'd win. Only one student a year gets a full ride from the Walmart Scholarship fund here in Cedarton." He had a habit of running one palm over his cropped sandy hair. Without warning, he leaned his head back and shouted. "Shut up that fucking music."

Ears ringing, Jessie glanced around the living room. It wasn't dirty, but stuff lay scattered everywhere in what her grandma always referred to as a right smart mess, which also applied to a plate of beans and cornbread. A gigantic pair of shoes, several school books, two computers, one open and flickering, and on the table in front of the plaid covered couch, a half-empty pizza box. Just generally an unpleasant room. The noise ceased, the silence so unexpected she staggered and caught herself on a chair back.

Instead of going to find Nikki, the boy stuck out his hand. "I'm Dylan, one of Nikki's roommates."

Dylan, huh? No surprise there. Every other kid in school carried that name. "Glad to meet you, but do you think you could find Nikki? I'd like to ask her some questions, maybe take her photo for the newspaper."

"Oh, good luck with that. She don't like her fucking picture taken, shuns it like she might be fucking ugly. But she's really not. Far from it. She's real bad."

"Well, Dylan, could you fetch real bad Nikki for me?"

"Sure, guess I can." The boy must've realized she was growing impatient because he let go with another shout that rattled the windows and included what was clearly his favorite four-letter word. "Nikki, you got company. From the paper. Nikki. Git yore fucking lovely butt down here. You're gonna be famous."

Well, at least this was a different beginning to her week. The long, lazy summer days were coming to an end. The last week of August brought students back to town for fall semester at Bailey Junior College, and things had a way of perking right up. Traffic, football games, tail-gating, and minor crimes all seemed to go together.

With Dallas off in Little Rock learning some new CSI tricks, she had the crime scene to herself. He couldn't stand over her and grunch about reporters tromping all over the place. The other deputies were stretched thin to patrol the entire county so she sometimes got first go. But all remained quiet. Sheriff Mac had put in for a new deputy, but so far nothing.

A pretty blonde bounced down the littered stairs, dodging piles of clothing, shoes, and backpacks with ease. If Nikki was bad, then it must mean gorgeous. Blonde hair, blue eyes, a complexion to kill for. And she didn't belong in the skeletal group. All that and intelligence as well.

Jessie introduced herself. "Could we maybe go out on the porch or in another room to talk?"

The girl, prettier than Jessie expected because the smart ones usually had a different look than this one, nodded. "I didn't know there'd be a story in the paper about me. I'm so excited, though. Even if it is only a two-year college, I'll get a head start on getting my degree over at the University of Arkansas. And it won't cost me near so much." She swept a pile of clothing off the couch and sat down, patted the empty spot beside her.

Okay, so they'd stay inside. Jessie dropped beside her, took out her pad.

"Now, you said cost you. Does that mean you're paying for your education?" This could be a good slant. Girl working her way through school wins scholarship.

She finished the interview in good time. Turned out it was a girl plus single mother, both working to keep her in school. Background struggles, hopes, dreams kind of thing. A real tear jerker, something she could do in her sleep. She thanked Nikki and went out the door.

Dylan followed her onto the porch and told her goodbye, with an offer she could come back sometime if she wanted to fucking party. The dog was nowhere to be seen. She headed down the street away from the dorm buildings and back toward the square and *The Observer* office. A clicking sound followed along. She turned. The pit bull stopped and barked.

"You following me?"

He barked as if replying. Stared at her. Damn if he didn't look like he wanted to actually speak. She stared back. "One for yes, two for no."

He barked again. Once.

"It figures. You'd better scat back home. I don't like dogs. And especially not pit bulls. I've seen your wanted pictures online. All bloody and torn up from fighting. Go on home."

He sat down and panted.

Satisfied, she went on her way again. Toenails clicked behind her on the concrete sidewalk.

"Snort or Snout, or whatever your name is. I hear your mom calling. Now git." She stomped. He jumped, bounced on his front legs, and barked twice. Two for no.

Best to just ignore the beast. He hadn't bitten her yet, he probably wasn't going to. Surely he'd get tired of her if she paid him no attention and didn't feed him or pet him.

Since it was Thursday no one was at the newspaper office. It was the one day she could be alone and concentrate on writing her weekly historical column and any stories she might have picked up. Monday and Tuesday were the busiest days getting the weekly laid out and ready to send to Harrison to be printed. She fingered the door key from her pocket, turned it in the lock, and stepped inside. Something furry rushed between her legs, nearly knocking her down. Switching on the lights revealed Snort/Snout, legs spread, head cocked, tongue lolling out one side of his mouth.

"You are, without a doubt, the ugliest critter I've ever seen."

He replied with two barks and she laughed. The damned dog was arguing with her. "Go on home."

No, he barked, and stood his ground.

Rather than confront him and perhaps get chewed on, she propped the front door open. If she ignored him maybe he'd leave. At her desk she dropped the backpack on the floor, sank into her chair, and turned on the computer. The scholarship interview would make a good enough story for a small rural weekly newspaper. And everyone who knew Nikki would buy a copy. The only thing better would be finding a body floating in Grady's big pond south of town.

The phone rang and she picked up, identifying the newspaper.

"Gotcher police radio on?" Tinker, a dispatcher and deputy at the sheriff's office.

"Well, friend, I don't need it, seeing as how you keep me up to date."

"Is Dal ever gonna be pissed. Listen to this. Mister Ledger went out in his backyard to find out, as he put it, 'what the consarned hell smelled so bad,' and he found someone had set fire to his shed. Fire department is out there, but I figured you might want a picture cause I know how much Parker likes fires on the front page."

"Oh, good. A real story." Jessie yanked up her backpack, stumbled over the damned pit bull lying in her way like he owned the place or something, and finally made it out the front door and to her car.

Across the road from the office one of the fire engines took off, sirens screaming and red lights flashing.

Treman Ledger lived a couple of miles away on the west side of town, in a run-down house on a few acres filled with old rusty cars. The owner, a man by the unlikely name of Spider, had kept tires there till the law made him get rid of them. For some reason broken down cars were perfectly okay. To replace the scant income from the recycled tires, he'd let this Ledger fellow move in a few months earlier. Why anyone would pay rent for the rundown shack, she didn't know. A tent would have been more comfortable. From that direction a spiral of smoke rose into the still morning air. Snout/Snort made it into the seat of the Jeep before Jessie backed out and raced down the street after the fire truck.

"You, buddy, need to find another home. You have no business chasing ambulances and fire trucks. And settling on a name wouldn't hurt."

He watched her in silence.

"What's wrong? Can't think of anything to say?" This was turning into an unusual kind of day with her talking to a dog, a real live story instead of stuff taken from the AP wire, and now a fire. Wow. Might fill up the whole front page if she took some good pictures. Most of the summer had been so quiet she and Parker had been forced to work hard to turn nothing stories into something readable every week. Dallas had even taken to playing checkers at the First Methodist Church Senior Citizen Activities Center and Sheriff Mac took up fishing, which he'd always hated. His catches made for a grand Friday night outdoor fish fry at his place. Most of the town turned out to eat at the picnic tables in the sheriff's back yard, several of the ladies boiling hush puppies and fries in vats of oil set out under an old oak tree.

A couple weeks ago Dallas had insulted her when she showed up to write a story about some escaped snakes from the Snake Man's collection. Herb & June Melone kept exotic reptiles which they showed during a summer tour all over the south. They'd returned in early August and one of their pythons decided to take a slink into the woods. Jessie showed up to write a story and Dal made some remarks about her letting him take care of it cause she'd probably holler so loud if she came upon the poor snake that it'd either have a heart attack or run away and they'd never catch it.

She might've taken that okay if she hadn't been pissed over some comments to Parker about a story she'd written the week before. She dared air complaints received by the school board and interviewed a few letter writers who claimed the public was not being informed properly. Seemed it stirred up certain members of the board to the point they showed up at the office to complain. Said she had no business revealing that sort of information. Parker told her not to worry about it, she should know she was doing something right when people rose up in arms. Besides, what she'd written had legally been public knowledge if anyone had cared to check it out. Considering her past though, their comments irritated her some. To be truthful, Dallas took the brunt of her upset and she'd pitched a hissy fit over the snake comment. She hadn't spoken to him since.

Brushing aside regrets concerning that issue, she silently thanked whoever or whatever had started a harmless fire out at Spider's place. So would Parker, who was out at his farm trying to breed his mare with yet another stud. A third try at making it take. Yep, it had been that kind of summer.

At last, a story worth following up.

She skidded sideways in the dirt road that wound its way through Spider's junkyard and came to a halt behind the red fire truck. The pit bull flew off the seat into the floor and objected with a yelp.

Dust kicked up beneath the firemen's boots while they rushed around to put out the fire. One of the men had dropped the hose in a nearby pond because the water truck hadn't yet shown up. A less than effective spray arced onto the blazing shed. Clearly it was a total loss. His renter, Treman Ledger, wasn't home. Spider paced back and forth, waving his arms, mouth going a mile a minute. You'd have thought the old shack was a million-dollar mansion, the way he carried on. Whatever he had to say was lost in the men's shouts and roar of the truck. A terrible stench filled the air.

Jessie snapped a bunch of photos on the new camera, the best of Spider scratching his butt through slouching overalls. The only exciting thing to happen this summer at the newspaper was Parker giving up the darkroom and 35 mm Nikon in favor of a digital camera. One for the office, which everyone shared, and one for himself. Said if he liked the results he might give in and buy one for each of them.

A new young ad man muttered something about just using their iPhones, but Parker ignored that remark.

"Hey, someone ought to call the sheriff." One of the firemen stood near the smoking heap that had once been a shed and waved his arms. "Git back, no one go in there."

No one had tried, but he must want to look busy.

The sheriff wasn't really needed, but she didn't say anything.

Water puddled in low spots around the heap of smoking timbers, making mud holes. She tried her best to avoid them while closing in on the scene. Had to be something good, the way the guys were standing around pointing and gabbing. And it was. The remnants of a smoking leather shoe pointed into the sky. A rank odor gagged her and she stumbled back a few feet. The smell of burning human remains was unpleasant, to say the least. Or maybe that was only when you knew what was making the stink. At any rate it wasn't true that burning flesh smelled like a good barbecue. The shoe most definitely held a burned foot.

Something scurried between her feet and bounced up and down close to the foot, barking like mad.

"Get that damned dog out of here." The new young fire chief, a fella by the name of Ken White, had a voice that boomed as if on a loudspeaker. Snout/Snort took offense, tried to take a bite out of his boot, and was shook loose to fly several feet through the air and land in a mud hole. He rose, shook himself, and ran to Jessie's Jeep where he climbed in and hid on the floorboards, mud and all.

"Hey, where you reckon that come from?" This from Spider, who had finally spied the subject of everyone's interest. He dropped both arms to his sides, gaze locked on the foot.

Chief White, a bit flustered by the find, hollered, "Did someone call the sheriff? Jessie, why don't you do that? And might as well call Doc Weston while you're at it."

Probably be a good idea if she did, even though any one of them could. None were very happy with her bringing a dog to the fire though, so she ran to the jeep, plopped her backpack in the seat, and pulled out her iPhone. Imagined how much fun it was going to be to report this to Sheriff Mac. Before he could answer on the other end, she had another thought. She would get to write a story on this unusual occurrence before Dallas returned from Little Rock. He'd be madder than a hen caught in a rainstorm at missing being first on the scene.

Mac answered, his voice wavering in and out. Uh-huh, he was out on the lake fishing. "Mac, I reckon you'd better get on in here to the Grafton place. There's been a fire and there's a dead foot sticking up out of the ashes."

"A what? A dead root? Nothing unusual in that."

"Not a root, a foot still in its shoe. They've sprayed so much water all over the place you'll be lucky to find any clues at all."

"Go ahead and let Doc know."

"The very next call I make."

"Well, Jessie, I'm sure time I get there you'll have it figured out how it got there, who built the fire, and who the foot belongs to."

"You keep bad mouthing me and I'm going on back to the office. You can just figure it out all by yourself. The only man who can really solve this sort of weird stuff is off in Little Rock. Course the spirits may have got in touch with him already and have him on his way home."

Mac had hung up somewhere during the course of her spouting off. She didn't blame him. He put up with a lot from her, considering he'd been her grandpa's best friend and felt he owed her something when she crept back home from California, tail between her legs, looking for a job. He probably still regretted asking Parker to put her to work writing those cute little gossipy morsels, as Mac referred to her articles in the paper.

After summoning Doc, she plopped down in the seat of the Jeep to await Mac's arrival so she could get more information about the foot.

Dallas Starr pressed harder on the accelerator, zipping the patrol unit through traffic along I-40 as if on his way to a fire. He never drove any other way if he could help it. A perk of being a deputy in Grace County, Arkansas. Leaving Little Rock as fast as he could seemed a damned good idea. People who lived mostly sitting in their cars in traffic befuddled him. Course, it wasn't quite as bad as Dallas, that sprawling Texas city his mother had named him after. But then he'd finally got good sense and left that place like his tail was on fire.

All this thinking about fire should tell him something, and when he concentrated it did. Some poor soul dead in a fire already needed him to figure out exactly what had happened. The gift inherited from his sha-man Cherokee grandfather never failed to keep him up to date on this sort of shit. He fingered up his radio and hailed Mac, dodging around a semi crawling along at seventy-five.

"Hey, Mac. What's going on up there? Got yourself a fire?" Fun to show off every once in a while, though his abilities still made Mac and the other guys antsy. He'd hated touching spirits involved in violence when he worked undercover narcotics in Dallas, but out in the boonies it wasn't so bad. Even spirits didn't get up to as much mischief in the country, though he'd already had his share of murders to solve.

"Where you at, Dallas?"

"Um, Clarksville. Be there in a few minutes." He laughed and Mac joined him.

"Way you drive I wouldn't doubt that much. Reckon you know about the fire."

"Just some poor guy caught up in something he didn't have much control over. You dig out the body yet?"

"You're gonna like this one. There ain't a body." Mac paused and Dallas could just see his crooked grin, thinking he'd pulled something over on his deputy.

"Ought to be. You look all around real good?"

"Yep. Just a shoe and a left leg from the knee bone down. Still digging up the shed floor, but don't think he's all here. It's quite a mess, too."

"Course it is, after all those idjits got through stomping around and spraying water everywhere. I'll be there in a little while. See what you can do about keeping them off it, would you? The rest of the poor fellow is nearby."

A long pause, and Dallas waited. Mac probably trying to think up a smart aleck remark. Instead, "Jessie's here."

"Of course, she is. Tell her to stay the hell off my scene."

"Will do, for all the good it'll do." Mac clicked off.

No sense in expecting protocol from the old man. He'd been around a long time, and pretty much made up his own rules where the law in the small Ozark county was concerned. That included allowing that nosy reporter in on just about everything that happened, even ongoing investigations. Dallas had got so he put up with her presence sometimes. Right now she wasn't speaking to him, but that wouldn't last much longer. Not the way she liked his loving.

He grinned, pressed the pedal down some more, and blipped the siren to get past a double lane of slowpokes. Jessie was still mad at him over a misunderstanding a few weeks earlier, so things were way too cool between them. Maybe if he finished poking around early enough, he could talk her into going to supper with him. Or not. She was still plumb pissed. Be good if while he was at it he could find out why. It might've been the snake deal, though he wasn't real sure. Women were too complicated to figure out most of the time.

He turned north on Highway 23 and cut his speed a tad. The Pig Trail was not a road a fellow wanted to do ninety on unless he had a death wish, or was a redneck driving a dually. A big chunk of an outside curve had caved off into a deep ravine during some hellacious rain storms in May. There was still some work being done so only one lane was open to traffic. He took it easy, despite his desire to get home. Cedarton was truly his home, more than any other place he'd lived. For the most part people there treated each other with friendly respect, even welcomed strangers as long as they didn't pull any fast ones. None of them liked the new highway from Tulsa to Branson that had opened that spring. It wasn't the highway so much as it was the one exit into their town that they resented. There was some talk about rigging up a gate on the blamed thing. True to their fears, it had allowed in all sorts of crime the town had never had before.

Though in a hurry, Dal slowed enough to enjoy the scenery along the two-lane shortcut between I-40 and northern Arkansas. Dumped him right in the middle of Grace County. He drove directly to the scene of the burned foot. They'd left it there in the mud and ashes so he could do his thing. Several deputies drifted in from their regular patrols and joined Doc Weston to stand around waiting for his exam and deductions. Treated him like a high school football game they couldn't stop watching. A dead foot was a big thing in Cedarton. Watching Dal work was just about as big a deal still yet.

Out of uniform, dressed in tight jeans and a tee shirt he'd picked up at the convention that read "*I Find That Humerus*" with a picture of an arm bone, he made his way through the churned-up mud around the remnants of the burned shed. Neither Jessie nor her Jeep were to be seen. Damn. Still mad at him. If this lasted much longer he'd actually have to apologize for whatever it was she figured he'd done. Cause he missed the hell out of her. To tell the truth he was addicted to her gift for surprising him with unusual sexual liaisons. And he sure didn't want to be celibate much longer. It was annoying.

Though he didn't think he'd done anything wrong, he'd have to come up with some way to make it up to her. Teasing had never bothered her before. Tinker kept urging him to get to the bottom of the whole thing before it got any worse, and he agreed he should. Just wasn't sure how to go about it.

If all else failed, he might have to take her dancing.

Vaguely disappointed Jessie wasn't there, he herded everyone back away from the leg, dug it out of the mud, but left it right where it was. Hopefully, he could get something, though a piece of a leg might not hold much in the way of spiritual connections. The small crowd, mostly deputies, but firemen too, hushed when he stood over the appendage. Accustomed to what he did, but still a bit wary, they waited in silence.

He squatted, placed the flat of his hand on the mud, fingers touching the unburned portion of the leg that had been buried. Bits and pieces of angry conversation floated to him, but nothing he could make out. The fire and the water and so many feet tramping around had pretty much squished out any good information. He remained that way a while longer, then dragged his hand up over the cold, stiff flesh.

A man hollering, followed by the words *the bastard will pay* resonated like a distant radio broadcast riddled with static. Though he waited no more words were spoken. He rose, brushed his hands together, and scanned the crowd.

"Doc, you here?"

The short, paunchy, white-haired old man stepped forward. "Yep. Couldn't park nearby so I walked up. You done, I'll get the poor soul, or what's left of him, over to the mortuary so we can send him on down to Little Rock." He glanced up at Dal, hazel eyes glistening. "That is after I take a good look at him."

"You have room for him in the cooler?" Dal smiled at the old man. "I figure we can come up with the rest of him shortly and you can send his pieces all at the same time." He turned to the crowd. "Any of you know of anyone missing from the area, come on down to the sheriff's office so we can get the information. And I'd appreciate it, so would Doc, if y'all went on about your business and moved your vehicles so he can get the hearse up closer."

Some joker in the crowd hollered, "Yep, that there's a might heavy load to have to carry any distance, ain't it?"

Everyone laughed including Dal and Mac, but Doc frowned his disapproval. A retired ME from Kansas City who had taken over the mortuary when Doc Bean retired, he took his work a mite too serious. Sometimes laughter went a long way during the worst of circumstances. Firemen and lawmen understood that very well. But Doc was serving as an undertaker till the body could be sent to the Medical Examiner in Little Rock.

Doors slamming, engines revving, tires slipping and sliding, trucks and deputies' units worked their way out of the parking jam and country silence descended. Dal and Mac walked the area hoping for something helpful, but all they found were footprints in the mud, a few cigarette butts, and tobacco juice splatters. Dal stood near while Doc removed the leg and laid it in a body bag. No more response came from the limb.

"You thinking the rest of him's nearby? No sense you coming on in this evening. I take it he ain't going nowhere." Mac waved a hand dismissing Dal. "Time enough to start in fresh in the morning."

Dal returned the wave and folded long legs into his SUV. The deputies all drove four-wheel drive SUVs because of the rough roads, many still unpaved, in the county. Butt weary from sitting so long at the conference, then driving home, he headed for his trailer to shower and poke something in the microwave.

When he drove around Ina Mae's wilting, end-of-summer garden he spotted the tail end of a red Jeep parked near his trailer. Jessie. With a satisfied sigh he pulled in beside her, already imagining taking her to bed.

Looked like she might want to make up, and he sure as hell had nothing against that. Not at all.

2

CHAPTER

When the car door slammed outside the trailer, Jessie moved from the windows and the view of the creek across Dal's back yard to peer through the front glass. He unfolded his long legs from the SUV and stretched both arms above his head. One gorgeous man, and her ready to make up with him, if he'd have it. She wouldn't much blame him if he didn't. Maybe the oven filled with his favorite supper, reheated from the Deli at the Walmart Neighborhood Market, would help. If it didn't he was likely to toss her out. He was never one to mince words. And she'd been a real bitch lately.

Fingering strands of hair off her face, she waited for him to step inside and see her before moving toward him. Just in case he felt inclined to less than politely kick her out.

A spark in his deep green eyes and that lilting Cherokee voice when he said "Hi" caressed her in parts that ached to be touched.

"Hi yourself."

He paused, sniffed the air. "Smells good. You surely didn't cook."

A standing joke between them. She didn't and couldn't cook. What else she couldn't do was stand that far from him any longer. He was definitely open to making up and she reached for him. "Walmart. Buffalo wings, French fries, and a cherry pie. It'll keep warm."

At the invitation his grin widened and he lifted a hand, their fingers twining. "Will it? You not pissed at me anymore? I didn't apologize, but I sure will if need be. Just tell me what I'm sorry for."

She could neither speak nor swallow, just shook her head. His touch sent a shiver through her and she turned, led him through the small living room into the smaller bedroom. There wasn't space for much more than the two of them side by side. He shifted so they were belly to belly and unbuttoned her shirt real slow, his burning, sensual gaze never leaving hers.

Going for his belt, she made short work of getting his pants down around his knees. By then her heart thudded so fast she could barely breathe. No man had ever affected her the way he did. And she'd gone without him just about as long as she could. All he had to do was look her up and down and she felt beautiful and special. A passionate desire for his mouth, his tongue, his fingertips, nipping, licking, kissing, exploring, went all over her, leaving shivers like tiny footprints.

She ran her palms inside his jockeys, caressed the warm tight muscles. Gaze fastened on his, she rolled the underwear down, freeing his erection.

He hissed through his teeth and fell to his bottom on the mattress, fumbled with her jeans, uttering Cherokee words under his breath when they didn't come off right away.

"It's anticipation, sweetheart. Enjoy." She helped him peel her jeans down, straddled his thighs, and pushed him flat on his back.

Hands spread on either side of his broad shoulders, she hovered above him, barely brushing his naked flesh with hers in a carnal touch-and-go as performed by a butterfly.

"Good God, woman." He stiffened, shuddered beneath her.

Lowering her mouth next to his ear, she said, "Hush now and enjoy that anticipation." The entire misunderstanding forgotten, she would now make up for it.

"Trouble is, I been anticipating for a couple weeks now."

"Sixteen days, to be exact." She nudged a bit closer so he poked stiffly against her. "Doesn't that feel wonderful?"

"I'll give you wonderful."

Raising up a bit, she laughed at the tortured expression. "Anytime."

Pushing her hands aside, he slapped both palms against her bare behind and writhed to find entrance, then slipped inside her, oh so very slowly, stealing her breath away. "That, *wesa*, is wonderlust."

Lights flashed behind her eyes. He'd called her that before. It meant literally cat, often used for pussy. The heady fragrance of honeysuckle floated on a night breeze that cooled her fevered cheeks. If only she could remain in that time forever, captured by that fiery passion, yet it might be enough to drive her mad. Deep inside her soul his spirit tangled with hers. A coupling that would forever unite them.

With a gasp she clung to him and they rode as if mounted on a winged creature until neither could draw breath and they collapsed in exhaustion. At last she stirred, touched him to make sure he was real. All around her fanciful beams danced, ethereal as fairies from another world. A place so pure tears of wonder poured down her cheeks.

"What did you do?" Her gaze locked with his.

"It was mind blowing."

Something in his tone worried her. Mind blowing? It was divine. Like inhaling the breath of angels. "I don't understand what just happened." No way could she stray from his touch, as if they were molded together.

"I didn't intend… I mean—*dammit.*" He touched her cheek, pulled away. "It was nothing. Don't be frightened."

"I'm not, but how can you say it was nothing? I'm bewitched."

Sharp laughter of dismissal sent chills through her. "I'm sorry, that won't happen again."

Why was he acting this way? "Please don't apologize for something so glorious. But what was it?" She wiggled against him, trying to tease him out of this funk.

He refused to look at her, stared instead across the room at nothing. "Our souls—our spirits if you'd rather—linked."

"You're kidding. No, kidding is by far not the right word. Dallas?" She tilted his head so she could look him in the eyes. Emerald eyes that held a deep-down fire. "What exactly is not supposed to happen? This is some Indian thing, isn't it? One of your tricks, like conversing with the dead. Their spirits. Tell me the truth." Not sure what she wanted to say, her tongue twisted over the words.

Something was way wrong here.

"Never mind, Jess. You're right, it's just some dumb Indian thing. Nothing to it at all." His tone, his very actions, appeared contrite as if he wished it had not happened.

The feeling, or whatever the hell it was, fell away and darkness replaced it. He was no longer there with her, but somewhere else.

Pulling on her jeans restored some sort of reality. What had happened wasn't real. It couldn't have been. She'd just been way too glad to be in his arms again, to make love to him, to be with him. But that didn't explain his reaction. Was she losing him? Fear of that possibility sent a deep-down shiver along her spine. Bending to pick up the shirt, her fingers brushed his leg giving off a spark. Startled, her glance met his.

He blinked. "Don't worry. It's okay. I was only teasing." But he didn't smile and she didn't believe him for a minute.

Could she have done something terribly wrong or was he having trouble getting over their earlier spat?

The aroma of the wings tickled her nose. Supper warming in the oven. She buttoned the blouse while hurrying in to put food on the table. Avoiding her touch he helped.

They sat across from one another and after they filled their plates with the hearty supper he broke the silence. "It smells good. Where'd you get it again?"

"At the Deli in the Walmart. The one they just opened."

He nodded. "It's pretty good."

"Yes, it is." They spoke in sentences as stiff as wood. This was crazy. Whatever had happened was beautiful, not something to be embarrassed by. Yet what could she say to make it okay? Because he obviously hadn't wanted it to happen and wasn't about to explain it to her.

Souls touching, spirits tangling.

What could that mean in his world? In *hers*?

All along, ever since they'd met he'd backed off when things became too personal. He wanted nothing serious and she'd known that all along. He still loved his wife, suffered when he recalled her death with a needle hanging from her arm and all that followed for his career as an undercover narc on the streets of Dallas.

She could hardly blame him. Besides she had her own bad memories to live with. Maybe two people carrying so much baggage ought not to attempt to have a relationship. Yet they were drawn together like magnets.

And all along her believing that she could make him love her, make him forget the wife he'd loved so tragically. Obviously she'd been a fool. The realization planted a sadness within her. A fear that she could never have him, that she might have lost him. Or because she expected too much.

But he was the one who initiated what happened. God, she could still feel that joining of their souls. Wished he would perform the magic again. Just the thought of it caused the beginning of an orgasm and she clenched her thighs and trembled.

She left soon after cleaning up the leftovers, acting like a virgin who wished she'd said yes. What a fool she was. He wouldn't touch her or meet her gaze. Usually he kissed her goodbye, but not this time. Perhaps what was wrong would be settled the next day when they were brought together. She for a story on the foot and the fire, he because he had to investigate the bizarre crime scene. The buried body part could hardly have been an accident.

Fists gnarled, Dal leaned against the door until the sound of her Jeep faded into the night. What in the hell was wrong with him? The woman crawled under his skin until he lost all control. Even now, if she were in the room, he'd have her rammed up against the wall, fucking her. That was acceptable, fucking he could handle. This had been something else entirely. Allowing his inner wraith loose like that was inconceivable.

He hammered the wood facings until his knuckles bled, then leaned his forehead there and took several deep breaths to clear his mind of the snakes slithering through that haunting void. He did not want to love Jess, or any woman, nor did he want to lose her. What was wrong with him? And why in hell didn't he just stay away from her? But that would mean leaving this place he'd grown so fond of. The people here were just what he'd hoped for when he left Dallas.

Grumbling he went to the fridge, took out a packet of frozen corn and held it on first one hand then the other till the worst of the pain in his battered knuckles receded.

Staring at the floor between his feet brought him back to the crime scene. That's where his mind should have been all along. Who cuts off a leg and buries it with the shoe still on the foot? Good question. There was a message there somewhere, but he'd gotten very little of it. Odd.

Better question. Where was the rest of the body and why bother to separate them before burial? First, he had to admit that someone so crazy was in his town. Then he had to face something worse. Were they on a rampage and was this only the beginning? He had to hope it was a one-time thing, which meant someone close to the dead guy. That left only one problem. Who the hell was the dead guy?

Fetching the phone, he dialed Doc's number. If Dal knew Doc Weston, he'd be with the body—correction, *foot*—until he puzzled those questions out. He might not legally be the ME, but he always did his best to figure out what happened before he readied the body and sent it down to Little Rock. That was an immense help to Dal because the wait could be weeks for results from the official ME down south.

This one would especially challenge Doc.

Dal waited for him to answer. It was probably gonna challenge him, as well. So far the bone itself had little to say.

"Haven't had much of a chance to do anything." Doc seldom said hello, just picked up and started talking. "Blamed phone keeps ringing."

"Sorry. What's your gut tell you?"

"Aside from too bad I ate so much barbecue sauce on that steak dinner? Someone cut off his lower leg, probably with a hand saw of some kind. Quit calling and I'll figure out what kind of blade did it."

"Okay, will do. I'll want to know his name, sex, age, where he was from and what he did for a living." Anticipating Doc's expletive, Dal laughed.

"Well, shit fire, boy. Why don't I let you know what he had for breakfast and how many times he's been married?"

"If you can, Doc. If you can." He hung up on another spout of cuss words that would've made a sailor proud.

The conversation with Doc sure did cheer him up, considering how he'd felt over the mix-up with Jess. Having such a mystery to solve was just what he needed to get his mind off her. And working with Doc Weston was usually a pleasure. When the old man came into town six months ago, bought the mortuary, and announced he was a retired ME from KC, Dal figured he'd be trouble, but it was just the opposite. Plus, they hit it off from the get-go. And Dal didn't hit it off with very many people. Occasionally they got together to play cards or chess or watch a game on TV. Just like old friends.

He'd been that way with Jess too. They'd fought like badgers, but it was always with a sexual undertone, an attraction that began at the first crime scene where they'd tangled and just kept on keeping on. No matter how much they disagreed, they always ended up in bed, or having sex in some other convenient or inconvenient location. He'd have loved her except for one person. Leann. Always Leann. He'd failed her and had no right to find happiness, or love, or serenity.

Sitting there staring at the wall was doing no good. He let out a gusty breath, rose, and grabbed his belt from over the back of the kitchen chair. Strapping it on, he fastened the Velcro strap around his thigh to hold the .45 in place, hooked the walkie to his shoulder, touched his pocket to assure himself that his keys were there, and shoved out the door. Cool night air hit him in the face. It smelled of cedar and pine trees and water drenched soil. He sucked at it to renew his spirit. Damned stupid Indian.

All the way across town to Treman's place, his mind clicked off possibilities. There was no reason in particular for cutting off a dead man's leg. The killer had done it to send someone in town a message, otherwise they'd have just buried the body deep and forgot about it.

So why be so obscure about the message? Worst of all, why wasn't he getting anything much from the stiff, muddy limb?

Probably needed the entire body. That had to be it. He'd never read a piece of a body before. Grandfather Lone Bear Stands hadn't taken much time to explain things to him. Evidently thought he'd figure it all out for himself. Eventually. Maybe he would, but the old man who'd handed this gift down to him could've saved him a lot of trouble.

He parked near the smoking remainder of the shack. A light burned in a nearby shed, leaking through wide gaps in the walls. No doubt a kerosene lantern since the man didn't have electricity to his place. Said it tended to flow from the plugs and make his sinuses ache. Dal never laughed when anyone claimed such weird beliefs. For all he knew they were right. Especially when you considered some of the things he ran up against.

To keep from getting shot at, he helloed the shack and waited for Treman to open the door, shotgun hanging down at his side.

"Deputy Starr out here, sir. Wanted to take another look around. Okay by you?"

"Fine by me, sheriff."

People tended to call all the deputies *sheriff*, and he didn't bother to correct them.

"You reckon the remainder of that feller might be laying around out yonder somewhere?" Treman gestured with the shotgun and sounded worried. Dal didn't blame him. Some mighty odd occurrences had a way of happening out here in the boonies.

"I'll do my best to find him and get him out of your way. I'll be using a flashlight out here for a while."

"Okay. Would you let me know when you leave?"

"Sure will, sir."

Dal turned to go back to the burnt shell and a huge bird with a wide wing span swooped low enough to topple his hat to the ground. A god-damned owl. A sign someone would die… or maybe *had* died. Or a sign of wisdom, depending on who you talked to. He hoped for the latter interpretation. Some shaman's grandson he was. He leaned down and picked up his hat, hands trembling from being startled.

In the moment it took him to rise, something caught his eye in the darkness. A shimmering that stood out against the black of night. Accustomed to such oddball signs, he studied the apparition, waiting for a message of some sort. What he'd come out here for. It wanted to tell him something, but he couldn't get it. It wasn't here for no reason, or even to scare him. He moved across the field and into the edge of the woods, intending to touch the thing. Instead, he was knocked backward on his butt and the glow disappeared. Didn't float away or fade, but simply turned off like a light bulb. The air smelled of a coming thunderstorm but there wasn't a cloud in the star-filled night sky.

He returned to the scene of the fire. Though he walked a grid back and forth, he sensed nothing more and came away more disappointed than frightened. If the damn thing was going to appear, the least it could do was say something to him. All it had done was show him where the rest of the body was, which he'd have to be content with. As he'd promised, he went to the shed and tapped on the door, hollered and told Treman he was leaving.

The door swung open.

"Find anything, didja?"

"Not really." Better to lie than to stir the man up some more. He'd return in the daylight.

Apparitions didn't appear out of nowhere for no reason. In the daylight he'd have some digging done. It wasn't going to be easy to find, or to identify, but it was out there all right. No use asking himself how he knew, he just did. Something creepy crawling around inside. He'd follow it, deal with the strange visitations, maybe even solve the murder before the ME sent his report up.

Eventually they'd have DNA, even if all they had was the leg. Funny, people thought DNA was a magic potion that told the name of every person on earth. Course that wasn't anywhere near true. Down in Little Rock he'd learned a lot more about using DNA to build an airtight case, but one thing he knew for sure. It wouldn't tell him and Doc who this guy was. Not by a long shot. Not unless for some reason his DNA was on file somewhere. Or they picked him up for something else and could get permission to test his DNA.

Might come a time, they'd told their audience down at the conference, when everyone's DNA would be on file somewhere. That day would be a long time in coming and that might be a good thing. As a lawman, he hadn't ought to think that way, but he did.

Back home he stripped down and showered, then dropped onto the mussed bed. The linens smelled of Jess and he couldn't help nuzzling the pillows before closing his eyes to go to sleep.

The damned dog settled himself inside Jessie's cabin, under the table back in the corner. He'd ridden around with her all day, but no amount of coaxing would move the critter. Even shaking a bowl of Cheerios didn't draw him out. Maybe dogs didn't like Cheerios, but it was the best she could do. The idea of going to bed with that ugly little cur in the house scared her. Pit bulls liked to fight, didn't they? And bite people? She'd seen the pictures. With no animal control closer than Fayetteville, there was no one to call. Be damned if she'd call Dal or any of the other deputies. They'd never let her live it down.

Along about eleven o'clock she gave up and crept to bed, not taking her gaze off the cowering dog until she'd closed her bedroom door and propped a straight-backed chair under the knob. The handgun she'd obtained a few months earlier had lain in the dresser drawer ever since, even though she had a carry permit. She took it out and stuffed it under the pillow. If the dog broke in, she'd have to shoot him. She dreamed a passel of dogs chased her down the road and clear through town right to the door of the sheriff's office where all the deputies stood around pointing and laughing. And Dal hovered back in the shadows as if he didn't care. She awoke with the sheet wrapped around her so tightly she almost didn't get out of bed in time to make it to the bathroom, considering the chair she'd used to bar the door.

Such was her need that she forgot all about the dog and bounded out of the bathroom and into the kitchen to put on a pot of coffee. Turning from the counter she let out a scream. Lying crossways of the door was that ugly Snort/Snout dog, curled around one of her shoes. His eyes flared open, he grabbed the shoe and ran back under the table.

35

"Some mean dog you are." She hunkered next to the table. "How about you come out and I'll share my bacon with you."

Ears perked and the tail wagged.

"Oh, you like bacon, do you?"

He crawled on his belly toward her, stopped just short of her reaching him. "I guess you want the bacon before you'll come on out, huh?"

Again the tail wagging and ear wiggling.

"Good God, I'm actually talking to a dog. I don't even like dogs."

The dog growled. She covered her mouth. "Oops, sorry about that. Bacon, bacon?"

That did it. The ugly thing leaped to his feet, ran out carrying her shoe, and planted his round butt right next to her. "Okay, but just till I can find out who you belong to. No longer."

She shared her breakfast with the dog, who turned out liking fried eggs covered with gravy with his bacon. She let him vote whether he liked Snort or Snout for a name, learned he liked neither and so they settled on Brad, a fitting name for a pit bull.

"But I'm not keeping you, Brad. You do understand that?"

He wiggled his butt and licked her hand, not fit actions from a pit bull at all. "First thing we'll do is take your picture and put it in the paper so whoever owns you can come get you. Let's hope. Meanwhile, you can stay with me provided you behave yourself."

All through her speech, he watched her with intelligent brown eyes, as if he understood every word.

"And give me back my shoe." She reached for the sneaker, but he was faster. Grabbing it, he ran to the other side of the room, lay down with it between his paws. She headed that way, but he darted into the bedroom and under the bed. At least it wasn't one of her purple Adidas, but rather one of the pair she kept by the back door to slip bare feet in when she wanted to run outside.

"Oh, so you want to play?"

For the next few minutes she chased him, laughing each time he got the better of her. "Well, I have to go to work, now, so you can stay here with your shoe and guard the place. I'll be back after a while."

Showered and dressed, she picked up her backpack and headed out the door. Brad caught up and jumped into the Jeep ahead of her. He looked so cute sitting there with her shoe in his mouth that she took out her cell phone and took a couple of pictures. Someone would probably claim him when the paper came out Wednesday.

She had time to check out the crime scene, then try to find out if anyone was missing. Best place for that was the Red Bird, which she'd hit for a grilled cheese and a piece of lemon meringue pie for lunch. If anyone was missing, someone there would know about it.

She parked near Treman's shack, dug out the digital camera cause Parker didn't like phone photos for the front page. Go figure. She had no idea. Leaving the bag because she planned on circling about through the nearby woods, she went to the shack and hammered on the door. No one came. She hollered.

"It's just me, Jessie West, taking some pictures. Don't shoot me."

After another moment without a reply she shrugged and kicked her way through empty tin cans outside the window and took several shots of the crime scene tape fluttering in a morning breeze. It was hot and the air smelled of wet smoking wood. She peeled off her sweatshirt and draped it over the stub of an old wood fence. Someone had raised stock and built a split rail fence to hold them in. Had to have been many years ago.

The firemen had made a real mess of the surrounding weed-choked yard, but she was careful not to leave any footprints near the numbered markers where the foot had been discovered. The morning was so quiet with the exception of red birds singing that the click of the camera sounded clearly. After about five or six shots, she took a few steps back from the spot and stumbled right into someone.

Startled, she squealed, heart doing skips and beats.

"Whatchoo doin, Missy?" A slight man in sagging dirty clothing and needing a haircut and a shave stood spraddle-legged, gripping her shoulders with dirty fingers. He smelled of something worse than body odor. A stench she remembered from somewhere. "Out here taking pitchers. Ain't no one tole you you could come on this place."

"Turn me loose. Who told you you could come here? This is Treman's place. Who are you, anyway?"

"Don't belong to no Treman. Belongs to me, Spider, who lets Treman live here. Again, whatchoo doin here?"

"I write for *The Observer* and I'm taking pictures for an article."

He waved a filthy hand in the air above his head. "Git on out. You gonna take pitchers, then you need to pay for them. You cain't just go around taking pitchers of anything and ever'thing. Don't belong to you anyway."

"You're crazy as a loon. Leave me be before I call the sheriff. He'll come out here and run your butt off to jail."

"Ain't no phone out here, Missy."

She lifted hers from her pocket, held it where he could see it and pushed the number programmed for the sheriff's office. "I'd suggest that you leave before one of the deputies gets here. You're batshit crazy."

He launched himself at her, ramming his shoulder into her midsection. She went down, him sprawled on top, knocking the wind out of her. She whoofed and so did something or someone else. She opened her eyes to see who had joined the fray. Brad, who'd been asleep in the Jeep, was on top of the man with all four feet, had the back of his ragged shirt in his mouth and shook it so hard the material shredded.

"All right, that's enough." The familiar voice immediately quieted things down. Broad hands had the dog by the nape of the neck and the old man by the back of what was left of his shirt. "What's going on out here?"

Jessie scrambled up off the ground to face a scowling Dallas. He flipped a glance her way. "You hurt?"

"No, I don't think so."

"You?" He held Brad up, gazed at him, then darted back as if expecting to be bitten when the dog lunged forward. Instead he received a friendly lick across the nose. Frowning, he set the dog at his feet, grabbed the man's shoulders, and turned him around. "Don't you know men don't go around knocking women on the ground? What's going on out here? None of you belong here."

Jessie held up a hand. "Excuse me, but I can come for pictures as long as I don't disrupt the crime scene."

"It's private property. Ain't none of you'ns belong here."

Dal sighed, turned the old man loose. He scurried away and disappeared in the woods. "Who is he?" Dal stared at her.

"I have no idea. Said his name was Spider and that this place belongs to him. I never heard of the man. I thought Treman Ledger lives here."

"He does." Dal scuffed a boot toe toward the dog, who sat there staring up at the deputy as if in love. "And this one?"

"That's Brad, the pit bull."

"Well, aren't we all having one hell of a happy morning?" Still playing gruff, he made every effort to stifle laughter.

She had no such luck, and when she lost control so did he. Brad whined a bit, then barked, dancing on his front feet, alternating between Dal to Jessie, then back again.

After a while Dal was able to sober up and study the scene in silence.

"Hush, Brad," she said when he kept dancing around making playful sounds. The little dog was really quite cute when he was having fun. She glanced at Dal. Same went for him, but he was back to business and acting like he'd never held her in his arms.

"Since when is there someone in this town you don't know?"

"Lots of strange people living deep in these woods. I don't especially know dirty old men who come at me like he did. He scared the crap right out of me. I'd guess he lives way out in the woods and cooks meth, the way he smells."

"Well, that describes half the old coots in Grace County."

"Yeah, good thing it's not against the law." She squared off, daring him to start something.

"My job is to solve this murder. You want a narc, you'll have to go elsewhere." The words held a bitter remorse and she was sorry she'd even brought it up.

A long silence, during which time they stared at each other. All she wanted was to step into his arms, kiss him, hold him close. Make everything all right for him. Hell, for both of them.

"Could I take a few more pictures?"

"Go ahead."

"Get you in one? You know how Parker is."

Without replying, he knelt as if inspecting something on the ground and she snapped off a few.

"Now leave me be. I've got work to do, and I'll bet you do too."

He was really pissed at her, so she started toward the Jeep.

"And take that mutt with you. Brad the pit bull, indeed."

A very small opening, but an opening nevertheless.

When she drove away he was walking slowly toward the woods, taking in the surrounding trees as if he expected something to leap out at any moment. It gave her the shudders.

CHAPTER 3

A wavering figment lurked in the trees. An oddity so peculiar Dal stared at it a long while. A spirit with a message. Whatever it was, he was getting nothing. He pushed through low growing huckleberry bushes stirring dust and insects from the leaves, turning red and gold. In his memory the taste of Grandmother's pies mouth-watering. He glanced up and a large pale green katydid smacked him in the corner of his eye. Burned like the very devil. He dug around in his pocket for a handkerchief, and stumbled to a sawed-off stump to plant his butt there so he could see to the eye.

Never had he been buzz-bombed by one of those iridescent flying bugs. A Cherokee myth told that the katydid warned of death, as today many people believed they foretold when winter would arrive. Their job was to sing in the late summer and predict when the first frost would come, not try to blind him. He mopped at the closed lid, lowered his head and sat there a moment with both eyes squeezed shut.

When the burning finally subsided, he took a cautious look at the ground. Everything was sort of blurred. A small white button nestled in the grass between his feet. He reached down to pick it up. A tatter of attached fabric emerged out of a covering of dried fall leaves.

His insides shuddered, sending a jag of pain up his spine.

Okay, he got the damned message.

Slowly, carefully, he laid the flat of his palm over the spot. Was shaken to the core by a long, low moan that rose all around him. It was like being doused in waves of anguish. Once, twice, three times. Then utter silence. No birds, no insects, no noise whatsoever. Damned bug was sent to get his attention but it was a bit of overkill.

He slowly counted, kind of like how he had done as a kid when lightning lit the sky to see how long it took to hear the thunder. Must've been at least ten seconds before all returned to normal. Wind in the trees, cardinals singing, frogs croaking along the creek bank, even a blue-striped lizard scurrying through dried leaves.

Nature and the apparition had done its job, attracted his attention and shown him what he needed to see.

The ground was too hard to remove whatever was under there. But he knew, by damn he knew exactly what it was. He needed a digging tool. Tying the white hanky on a branch nearby so he could find the spot again, he thrashed through knee-high brush to the patrol unit, pulled out a folding camp shovel, and hurried back through the woods to where the white cloth fluttered in a slight breeze. With care he cleared away the top layer of grass and leaves, then dug a shallow trench out a ways from the exposed cloth.

Damn, he had to stop digging and get the Spaceys out here. They knew how to uncover this without destroying evidence. Whatever was down there had something to do with the leg and foot, but it was older.

His cell phone had no service, same with the walkie, so back he trudged to the car, muttering under his breath, and keyed the mic on the radio.

"CSI One, I need some help." Every time he used those call letters he had to chuckle. CSI One? He was the only CSI, but in the hopes of building up the Crime Scene Investigator unit, Mac had insisted on giving him the number so the department would get accustomed to using it when he hired CSI Two. If that never happened Dal would be happy.

He requested the Spaceys and gave directions. While he waited, he used the radio to touch base with Doc.

"Glad you called, Dal. You'll never believe this."

"Try me, I tend to believe just about anything."

"You know our leg? Funniest damned thing. The leg and foot have crystals in the flesh."

"It's been frozen?"

"Exactly."

"Can you tell for how long?"

"I doubt it, but another even funnier damned thing. The shoe?"

Dal chuckled. "It's brand new."

"How do you do that? It was soaked in mud and old hog piss. You couldn't have told by looking at it."

"Doc, how did you find out?"

"The numbers inside this particular brand of shoe? Tell when it was manufactured. But you didn't see that, so how'd you figure it out?"

"Doc, I think you're gonna want to come out here pretty quick. That is if you want to see what the Spaceys are gonna dig up." Easier to dodge the question than try to explain. Besides, new shoes weren't exactly a viable clue to anything. Or were they?

"Do you know?"

44

"I've got a pretty good notion, but I don't like to second guess my hunches. It's not my style."

"Hunches? Is that what you call them? I never knew."

"Got a better word?"

"Probably. I'm going to be out there in about thirty. Don't let anything really fascinating happen till I get there."

He laughed. "I'll do my best."

Back to the tree stump, he plopped down feet planted on the side away from the button and shirt, and had a short conversation with Grandfather.

"You know, you could just simply tell me what's going on. The bug in the eye was a bit much."

"Grandson, that would be no fun at all."

"And this is, I suppose." He swept an arm around to include his surroundings that had acted up to get his attention.

A chuckle that faded with the words. "Oh, yes, indeed it is."

"Wait. You come back here. That can't be all there is."

The fading chuckle blossomed into laughter. The spirit, or *asgi`na* in Cherokee, wavered, then moved through the shadowy woods. That beat the hell out of the evil ones, the *anasgi`na*, screaming and shaking him up till he couldn't stand. Grandfather had developed a sense of humor.

The crunch of tires on gravelly soil dragged his attention away from those thoughts. The Spaceys couldn't have arrived so soon. The reflection of light off glass flashed across the ground nearby. A car door slammed.

"Hey, what's up?"

Shit.

He gritted his teeth before looking up. There she was, that slash of sunshine cutting through her hair so it glowed like a halo. Her smile urged him to envelop those lovely lips with his own. She strode through the weeds, her jeans stirring up a cloud of bugs. Always lugging that damned backpack over one shoulder everywhere she went.

All he could do was climb to his feet, try his damndest to stay right where he was, with little luck. God, she was beautiful. But it was way more than beauty. Something spiritual that locked on to him. Hell, he couldn't explain it.

"Hey," he uttered from down in his throat. In a few steps he stood over her. Removed the backpack, lowered it to the ground. Wrapping both arms around her he gathered her close and nibbled at those tasty lips while she encircled his neck in a strong hug.

When he could speak, he did. Mouth against her cheek. "Are you okay?" Had to ask because he'd mistreated her earlier, fool that he was.

She kissed his earlobe. "Perfect, and so are you. Anyone out here yet?"

"Nope. Kathy and Dave on their way."

She rubbed a hand down his shirt front, tugged it out of his pants. "How long do we have?"

Holy hell. "Enough."

He unzipped her jeans and yanked them down, ripped at the thong panties she'd taken to wearing recently. He'd figured out why, so didn't bother to ask. By the time he got that done, she had his belt unfastened and his britches down. About then he wished he was wearing thong jockeys. Reckon they made them?

He shoved her backward a few steps. "Standing or on the ground?"

"Now. Oh, God, Dal right now."

He lifted her. Both legs snaked around his waist and he plunged inside her. She answered his joyous shout with a long drawn out moan. Palms on her butt, he pulled her close, shoved deep, pulled tighter, shoved deeper till the top of his head threatened to fly off.

She came the very moment he did, both holding on so tightly their bones cracked.

Her warm, moist tongue licked his neck, she sucked his ear lobe, wiggled and squirmed and situated herself tight against him. "Once more. Can you?"

"Hell, yes."

And he did. Even though his legs trembled, his back muscles tensed and held on while he lost all sense of where he was. She kept nuzzling him and making contented purring sounds. Finally, in his ear so soft he almost didn't hear. "You are truly something, yes you are."

He could've done it again, but a horn sounded not too far away.

Kathy and Dave. He laughed. The two of them had seen her car and absolutely knew what went on when they got together alone. Especially in the woods. Especially anywhere that they could get caught. It ramped up the sensation of making love, doing it where they might get caught.

By the time the Spaceys hiked in, clothes were back precisely where they belonged and the two of them stood far enough apart to appear casual. It didn't fool Kathy. Maybe it did Dave, you never could tell what he thought.

Kathy had the nerve to wink at Dal, and he flushed, and she made that tinkly sound that passed for a laugh. "Well, what do we have here? I know it must be something crazy weird."

"And how do you know that?" Dal walked over to the shirt mostly covered with dirt, stared down at it.

"Why else would you be here?"

Jess removed the camera from her pack and stood back out of the way while Dal and the Spaceys checked out the find and discussed how to go about digging it up without losing any evidence.

"It's going to be an old body."

Kathy eyed Dal. "How old? How do you know that? Spirits?"

"A little bit. Anyway, it's minus part of one leg. Probably several months." He told them what Doc had learned about the partial limb that now lay in the mortuary. Thawing.

"Doesn't necessarily mean—"

"You know it does." Jess cast Dal a sideways glance. "Okay if I take some photos while you dig? Mac will want them."

"You go ahead, honey. Don't you let this big old grunch stop you." Kathy glanced at Dal, then led Dave back to the SUV where they gathered their equipment to begin the dig and lay out a grid for evidence. They were going to be there a while.

Doc arrived in time to lend a hand with the final careful uncovering of a slightly withered body with part of a leg and foot missing.

"I'll be double damned." Doc stared at Dal with admiration. "You're a hell of a hidden body detector. You know, boy, I wouldn't believe this if I hadn't seen it for myself. Any place else, you go around finding dead bodies like this, we'd know we had a serial killer pretending to be a lawman on our hands. I'll swear, I'd heard the stories, but I wasn't sure I believed 'em, the way Arkies like to pull the legs of newcomers."

After Jess took the requisite pictures of the corpse and some of the dig in progress for the paper, she placed her camera and notepad in the backpack and slung it over one shoulder. "How come Mac didn't show up?"

Dal answered without looking up. "He's checking out a call. someone stole a lawn mower, one of those big fancy dudes. Mac said he'd be more useful there than traipsing around out here. He just doesn't like ticks and chiggers, is his problem."

Chuckles came from everyone. Doc scratched up under the cuffs of his trousers. "No one told me that was the way to get out of woods duty. I'll keep that in mind for next time."

"Lye soap is good for those bites." Kathy paused to pick a tick off her arm and mashed it between thumbnails. "When you get home, jump in the shower with a good stiff brush and a bar of lye soap. Scrub all over really good and you'll maybe come away with just a few bites."

Doc stared at her hard. "You pulling my leg?"

"Nope, not at all."

They all pitched in, assuring him Kathy was right.

"Okay, then. Just one question. Where do I get this lye soap?"

"Craft shop up on the mountain," they said in unison.

"Unless your grandma makes it." Droll comment from Dave. They all stared at him. He rarely said much of anything.

Still smiling, Jess left them. Nothing like a good fuck to make the day worthwhile. One of these days, he'd make love to her, but until then she'd given in to calling it what it was. That business the day before had come darn close to being classified as loving before he pulled the plug, so to speak, and ruined it.

Wonder what Mac had learned about the stolen mower? Not something that happened around here, stealing. She'd left Brad with the sheriff before coming out to cover the reported body find. No use in letting a dog near any digging. Her planned visit to the Red Bird hadn't worked out because of Dal's call-in about the discovery he'd made in the woods near Treman's burnt shed. So it was still a mystery who the body might belong to. Right now she had to get back to the newspaper office and put together a story on the body. Maybe someone would come forward with a missing person's report after the story hit Wednesday's edition.

Parker's old beat up truck was parked in front of *The Observer*. He must've heard about the find. He usually didn't come in on a Thursday. It was his day for taking a special interest in his horses. He showed them around Oklahoma and Texas occasionally, but never won anything. Not that he cared, It was his passion. Right next to stirring up trouble with his editorials in the paper.

Like the time he insulted not only every church in town by making fun of the sign out front of the First Baptist Church, but he also angered the friends of the volunteer fire department and several members of the city development society. All in one editorial. Claimed getting all the incensed letters to the editor went to show how many people read the paper. It was a scientific experiment.

Barking greeted her when she opened the door of the office. Brad raced across the room, nails slithering on the slick flooring.

"I thought you were with Mac." She shoved her way around his happy, twisting, leaping butt.

Parker came to the door of his office. "He was, but the old devil brought him over here, shoved him through the door grumbling something about the damn mutt gonna get the entire department sued. Think he tried to lick someone to death. I thought this was a pit bull. Expected him to gnaw my hand off or something."

She lowered the backpack to the floor next to her desk and scrubbed at the ugly dog's ears. "That's what I thought too, but he sure is a friendly one. I guess all those stories about how vicious they are might be exaggerated. What are you doing in here today?"

The dog nuzzled her while she removed the camera from the pack and set it on the desk.

"Was up at the Red Bird peacefully having me some lunch when Theron asked me about the dead foot that was found out at Treman's shed. Well, there's not much would get me in on a Thursday but a dead foot unless it'd be a live one. Couldn't resist. So spill."

"Guess you were in the barn without the police scanner turned on."

He nodded. "Yeah, that young mare foaled in the night and I thought I ought to stay with her and the little one to make sure nothing dire occurred."

She filled him in on what had happened during the fire and later when Dal went to the woods and found what him and Doc both thought might be the rest of the chopped off foot and leg.

"I sure hope you got some pictures."

"Did. Seems you're overworking me the past couple of days. Got pictures of Nikki Bracken and a story on her winning that scholarship. Turned out to be a pretty good story."

"Personally I welcome a good old murder compared to that kind of stuff anytime. Makes for a much better series of stories. Do as much as you have and we can update Tuesday before we send the paper to print."

"There's plenty of meetings and city stuff going on to fill the front page around the dead foot." He was back in the office before he said her name.

"Uh-huh?" She kept typing.

"Nearly forgot. This was in the mail for you this morning when I came in." He stood in the door, holding out an envelope. "It looks personal, but guess it could just be something from a reader, though we don't have that many subscribers out in Oregon."

Her fingers froze on the keyboard and for a moment she couldn't move, couldn't even look up or take the piece of mail. He tossed it on her desk and returned to his office.

Couldn't be. Not after so long. But still, Steve always said he'd find her. When she left California after she got him fired from his job, he went to Oregon. She learned that from an ex-friend who also said she hoped he found Jessie and paid her back good for what she did.

For a while after she'd returned in disgrace here to her hometown, she'd expected to see him everywhere she looked. But now, well, now, she hadn't thought of him for nearly a year. She spread her palm over the letter in an effort not to check the handwriting or the post mark. Squeezed her eyes shut. Tears trailed from under the lids. In anger she swiped them away, went back to the keyboard to write the story. But the words wouldn't come. Every effort to ignore the envelope failed and her gaze continued to slip and slide in that direction.

Well, shit. She grabbed it up, ripped it open using the end of a pen and spread the single page with trembling fingers. Get it over with. Find out what he had to say. Take what she deserved, then burn the damned thing and forget about him. Again. If she could. Goddamn him, anyway. Easier to curse him than herself, though she deserved it more. Deserved his threats and the fear that gripped her stomach till she gagged.

Through tears she made out the blurry words. "Be careful. I know where you are, but haven't made up my mind what to do about it."

She wadded the paper into a ball and stuffed it in her backpack. It wasn't signed. Didn't need to be. How in God's name had he found her? She closed her eyes and saw him. Tall, lean, blond hair in a burr cut, blue eyes squinting into the California sun. How she'd loved him. But not enough, not nearly as much as she loved that job. If she'd really loved him, she could never have betrayed him and used pillow talk to write a story that ruined his career.

He would never forgive her, but hell, she hadn't forgiven herself either.

A hand dropped onto her shoulder and she jerked.

"You okay?"

Parker. He was the only one who knew some of the story. No one else did. How could she bring herself to admit such a hideous secret?

She slipped her hand over his. "Um, I'm fine."

"Bad news?"

She nodded, unable to say more. Now she'd be afraid again.

"Need to talk? Go home?"

Placing her fingers back on the keyboard, she shook her head vigorously. "Nope. Work, that's what I need."

A split-second later she let it all flow out. Sitting there in her chair, chin on her chest while he kept a hand on her shoulder. Her renewed fears, a need to run fast and far away. How she deserved whatever Steve did to her. Parker knew some of the story, now he had it all.

He studied her for a long moment, then reached for her hand. "Don't know about that. Maybe running back here was a fine idea, but I can't see you running to someplace where you don't know anyone. None of us should ever be flat out alone, no matter what. You got plenty of friends here, folks who'll help you out, if and when you need it."

All the while he spoke in that low, soft voice that drove her nuts, and held her hand in both his. When she finished he turned loose, grabbed a handful of tissues from a box on her desk, and held them out.

She mopped her face. "That's enough of that. I know you're right. For all I know it's a prank." She tried out a smile, which he returned.

"Get to work on that story." He patted her shoulder and returned to his office.

The story of the severed leg and the body still being dug up, though there'd be rewrites there when Mac sent the official release, flowed onto the screen. Her stomach growled and Brad replied with a sharp bark. She hadn't eaten all day and neither had the poor dog. Swallowing the last taste of fear because she couldn't live with it always on the surface, she rose and leaned through the door of Parker's office.

"Want something to eat?"

"Sounds good. Ham sandwich?"

"Okay. I'll be back in a few. Wanta dog watch?"

Parker eyed the animal staring up at Jessie. "Looks like he wants to go with you. I don't think he likes me."

She glared at Brad. "Stay here, you little fart. I'll bring you a hamburger."

He bounced on all fours and barked up at her. "Be quiet, you. What I always hated about dogs. Barking. All the time. Cats, they're quiet."

"Yeah, but they stare at you. Can make you feel guilty as hell if you don't let 'em lay in your lap every minute of the day. Or on the keyboard. And you never know what they're thinking. Jessie, you sure you're okay? You look sort of peaked."

She waved away his concern. Somehow she'd handle this. Besides, it might be Steve was just using scare tactics. He'd told her he never wanted to lay eyes on her again. Maybe it wasn't even him. She could keep thinking that way till she convinced herself.

Car keys in hand she slipped out the door and closed it before Brad caught on and followed. How in the world had Steve found her? And why had he bothered?

While waiting at the Red Bird for sandwiches and Cokes, she talked to a few of the afternoon crowd. Mostly guys getting refills on their coffee thermoses and buying break snacks. None of them had any idea that anyone was missing from the area. All the talk was about the dead foot found in Treman's burned shack. Didn't seem like anyone had heard about the body that was still being dug up out in the woods. Wouldn't take long before everyone in town got the word. She slipped in a question about anyone seeing any strangers in town, as if it were connected to the body. No one had, which was a relief. Strangers didn't come to Cedarton without everyone knowing it, real quick like.

One of the guys doing some electrical work on high lines along the highway had a theory that someone had fed a body to the hogs that were kept in the lot near the shed before Treman's time.

"You know hogs likes to eat us about as good as we like to eat them. They'd not leave very much. Good way to get away with killing someone."

His friend jumped right on that idea. "I don't reckon there's been any hogs there for several years though. Looks like that leg woulda rotted plumb away by now if that were the case."

The first guy chuckled. "Yeah, but you gotta admit it's a fascinating thought. Hey, maybe it was a serial killer passing through, you know in one of them white vans, and he just tossed that leg by Treman's shed in the dark of night and went right on his way."

"It ain't exactly like he lives on a thoroughfare." The second fellow tightened the lid on his thermos and the two of them left, each one carrying a huge cinnamon roll from the morning offering and arguing about the leg.

Norma, the waitress, watched them out the door, shaking her head. "Now there you go, Jessie. You've got your story. I vote for the serial killer and the white van." She handed her a bag with the sandwiches in it and two large foam cups. "Is strange though. No one's gone missing around here in a while. How long do they reckon that foot's been there?"

"Didn't hear. Guess you'll have to read it in the newspaper."

Jessie left without saying anything else. Probably hurt Norma's feelings, not staying around to talk, but she wasn't in the mood. The note gnawed at her. It could be from someone else who had a mad-on at her for some story she'd written. When she got back to the paper she'd check the records and see who all subscribed from Oregon.

Every vehicle parked on the square near the Red Bird could belong to Steve. How would she know? Fool. Her nerves were a-jangle for no good reason. She had to settle down before she turned into a basket case.

When she got back with lunch Parker didn't bring up the note and so she said no more about it. She followed him out the back door and sat across from him at the picnic table he had put there a few years earlier. He objected to workers eating while they worked, saying everyone needed to take time off for lunch. Besides, keyboards didn't need crumbs and spilled Coke accidents.

When they returned to the office there was a message from Mac that he had a release ready for the stolen mower and she should call him.

She dialed and Tink picked up. "Girlfriend, you okay? Wanta go to a movie Friday?"

Not really, she didn't, but she'd put Tinker off several times lately and felt guilty about shunning her. "Thought you'd be going out with Burt."

"Am for sure, but that's Saturday all day. We're going to a car race, spending the night and gonna go to Lake Fort Smith Sunday, rent a boat, all that fun stuff."

"All night, huh? Sounds promising. Don't do anything I wouldn't."

"Leaves an open field, doesn't it?"

Dammit, why didn't she and Dal do something like that? All they did was play grab ass when they were together. It was like he didn't know how to have a date. Back to the business at hand.

"Mac left me a message he has a release. Is he available?"

"Yep. So the movie? Which one and what time?"

"I don't care. You pick and let me know what time to be there." Tink had never been cured of her fear of the dark so things were always arranged so she was not left to drive home alone in the dark.

Silence. Tink must've transferred her to Mac. Yet she came back in a serious voice. "Jess, what's wrong?"

"Nothing."

"Not nothing. You decide when you wanta talk about it, but why don't you stay over Friday night? We can have a real girl to girl talk about it."

"Not feeling much like a slumber party. Maybe. I need to talk to Mac so I can finish up here and go home."

"Sure, sweetie. Whatever you need. Putting you through. See you Friday at five. We can eat first. Okay?" Tink didn't wait for her to agree, and Mac was on the line.

"Ready?"

She put the phone on speaker, laid it down, and got ready to type Mac's release. No matter how many times she and some of the deputies tried to get the old man to use email, he refused. "Like putting it out there for the whole world to read," he always said, or words to that effect.

She didn't even bother anymore. He read the release, she typed it, thanked him, and hung up. The story was ready in twenty minutes for Parker to put his spin on.

A theft in town demanded the front page, especially one that would produce a laugh. And this one would. Old man Harris had been walking down the street, saw the mower idling in Mr. Plunkett's yard while he ran in for a drink, hopped on and took it for a ride all over town, then forgot where he found it. His son loaded it up and took it to the sheriff's station. It would be credited to Observer Staff. Didn't look too good for all the stories to be written by the same person.

That evening she drove slowly down the lane to the cabin, checking out the pastures and trees surrounding it. No one anywhere. Living in the country had always pleased her, but last year she'd bought a revolver and got a permit to carry when her life was threatened by someone after she'd written articles about two murders. Since then she'd kept the gun next to her bed when she was home and in a side table by the front door when she was out.

Brad leaped from the Jeep and ran up on the porch as if he'd always lived there. Wrestling with her backpack, she carried keys in her hand. Since the time of the earlier threats she'd taken to locking the house up, though she hated the idea. The empty yard offered no hiding places, but still she checked all around before unlocking the door and nearly tripping over the silly dog who skidded between her feet like he was afraid he'd be locked out.

"Make yourself right at home, you ugly beast." She took the time to relock the door behind her, then opened the drawer and lifted out the small .38 and went through the small rooms to make sure everything was okay. Brad went right along with her, sniffing everything.

"You silly mutt. Guess if you're sure, it must be safe."

Despite that, she took the gun back to the living room and replaced it in the drawer where she could get to it quickly.

When she'd obtained the revolver Dal took her out to practice shoot before she took the course to get her permit. When they returned she'd emptied it. He shook his head, reloaded the weapon, and placed it in the drawer.

"Keep it loaded. What do you think you're supposed to do with it? Beat someone over the head?"

Remembering his words, she ran her fingertips along the gleaming silver barrel, doubting she could shoot anyone, even if they came after her. A cold shiver climbed her spine and she glanced down at Brad, who whined and licked her ankle.

"Your job is to bite their leg off. Got that?"

He barked once.

She rubbed his head. "Guess I've got myself a dog. Let's go find something to eat."

4
CHAPTER

Dal stood back while Doc, Dave, and Kathy placed the partially decomposed body in a black bag and zipped it up.

Kathy dragged her fingers over the thick plastic. "Been under there a while, looks like."

"Leg is missing from the knee down." Doc sucked through his two front teeth and stared off into the distance. "Don't know yet if it'll match up with what was in the shed."

"You're kidding, of course." Kathy grinned at the old man. "You honestly think we've got two murder victims out here somewhere with one leg partially removed? This ain't Kansas City, you know."

"Well, now it just could be. You never know, what with that new highway and everything. We may have ourselves a boom in interesting homicides around here."

She and Doc had become great buddies after the old man was appointed as the local coroner. Both delighted in joking around.

She joined Doc laughing, then sobered.

"But Dal knows." She turned to him. "Don't you?"

"Not yet, I don't. Y'all get on into town and leave me be a while, I might come up with something." Something about this bothered him and he studied the empty hole.

"Spirits not liking our company?" Doc chortled, trailing along after Dave and Kathy, who carried the sagging body bag between them.

The three formed a somber parade paying homage to the corpse wrapped in black. Who in hell wanted to be around dead people all the time? Bad enough he had to deal with them occasionally. It seemed like some folks would rather work with the dead than the living. He wasn't a bit happy to have another murder on his hands. This was supposed to be a peaceful place where nothing much ever happened. Should've been a day of fishing, broken only by arresting some drunk for pissing on the cornerstone of city hall.

He squatted near the hole dug out close by the sawed-off tree and stared into space. No bugs nor shimmering visitors. Nothing but a quiet summer's evening on a serene Ozark mountainside. He touched the disturbed soil with a welcome sense of relaxation like whoever had lain there was happy to have his life ended. But by who and why? Finally he rose, stretched, and strode back toward the SUV, barely favoring his bad leg. What if he couldn't solve a murder without the help of Grandfather? Lately he'd been feeling odd, like something was missing in his life. Didn't know what it could be. He was exactly where he wanted to be, doing exactly what he wanted to do. He liked a woman who appeared to like him back. So why did he feel like he was perched on the edge of a cliff, ready to dive off? Didn't make sense.

For a few minutes before climbing in the unit, he checked out the surroundings slowly and carefully. Once leaves were off the trees this spot would be visible from Treman's place. He needed to find out for sure the time of year the body was put in the ground. Even in the summer with foliage heavy old Treman's hound dogs wouldn't have put up with something like that without howling their fool heads off. But would he bother to check it out? While there was definitely something out of kilter about this place, he got no vibes of violence, even from the body.

That told him that the killer may have snuck up on the victim, and with no remorse killed him somewhere else besides here, then cut off the leg. It was the peace that dug at him. Someone surely had to be furious or violent or both to commit such a crime, yet he got nothing like that. It was more like something planned, carried out with satisfaction at a job well done.

And why hadn't the victim's spirit kicked up a fuss? That could only mean that this was not the crime scene and the victim welcomed his own death. This was his final burial with no one to mourn his passing. Blood seeps into the ground, disappears when it rains, so that couldn't always be counted on.

Doc would know if the leg was removed postmortem, but he'd bet his bottom dollar it was. At least he'd learned something. How and where a crime was committed could often point toward suspects, and that's where they needed to start.

The sun sank toward the horizon, the fading light walking shadows of trees across the clearing where he'd left the SUV. A breeze lifted, smelling of rain. They could use it. Late summer had been hot and dry, leaving a crackly feel in the air and underfoot. Thunder rolled lazily overhead and the sky darkened, almost as if clouds had appeared out of nowhere. His people believed that thunder was caused by supernatural beings, but then they believed a lot of things he put no credence in.

By the time he turned the vehicle around and headed back to the main road, darkness crept over the land.

The first splatters of rain hit the dusty windshield when he turned onto the pavement. He clicked on the headlights, ran cleaner over the glass, and turned on the wipers. The classic western radio station played "Blue Eyes Cryin' in the Rain."

"Oh, clever." The small station, unlike most larger ones, still kept a DJ who chose music, played requests, and talked to his audience as if he knew them all personally. Living in Grace County was like life should be, but in most places wasn't. Even with an occasional murder or crime, it was a safe place to be.

Damn, he was getting sentimental. He hummed along with the song and drove home feeling better than he had earlier. A rainy night was made for listening to music and sipping bourbon and branch water, not mooning over the past. Had to be careful with that bourbon sipping, seeing as how he was on duty 24/7. Didn't do to have liquor breath going out on a call. This night he'd take the chance with one drink to mellow down. The itch he had he couldn't scratch, not without taking a chance he didn't want to take. Going by Jessie's cabin, just to see if she was awake. Nope, not this night, not the way he felt. Like he could allow himself to melt into her, become one spirit.

Lights were on at Ina Mae's when he drove into the trailer park, tires swishing through puddles standing in the twin tracks. One of the curtains lifted and he smiled. The old gal checking to see who was coming in. Good for her. Hadn't been for her and her shotgun he'd have bought it last year right in his own yard. Still embarrassed him to think about being rescued by a gun-totin' grandma.

He blipped his horn and she dropped the curtain. At the end of the lane the trailer waited in serene darkness. Back in Dallas going into such a dark place would've set his heart to racing, the hairs on his neck rising. Here, he leaned back in his seat till Willie stopped singing, then turned off the ignition and climbed out into the late summer rain. The drops cooled his face and dampened his shoulders. Ducking inside, he took off his hat, hung it on the hook beside the door, and flipped on the switch. Light spread through the tiny kitchen nook and splashed out the back windows to shimmer in the rain. A creek separated his back yard from a small area where kids liked to park and swim in the summer, and neck behind steamed up glass in the winter.

One car sat there this night, and he spared it a glance before closing the blinds. By rote he removed his utility belt, hung it over the back of the kitchen chair, and opened the freezer. Pulling a Mexican dinner from the shelf, he slit the box and set the plastic container in the microwave. Instead of going for the bourbon, which he might have later, he lifted a beer from the fridge. He set everything on the table and using a hot pad took the burbling dinner out of the oven.

His wife always made a pan of cornbread to go with Mexican food, especially when she cooked up a pot of chili. Those were early days in their marriage. Damn, best to stop thinking about all that shit. Just eat the refried beans, rice, and tamales and forget the memories. They led to nothing but heartache. If only he could let them all go, he might be able to treat Jessie better, maybe even love her. Every time they made love he saw that goddamned needle hanging out of Leann's arm. Felt the self-hatred that he couldn't save his own wife from the drugs he struggled to take off the streets of Dallas. Loving someone like he'd loved her and not being able to save her put a box around his heart and he couldn't open the lock. Dared not try for fear of what it would do to him.

And that, my friend, explains a lot. So get on with it. Easy to say.

With the beer, he washed down the last of the rice, tossed the can and container into the trash, and went to sit in the recliner. Boots kicked off, he wiggled his toes and stretched out. Felt so good. Maybe he'd read a while before taking a shower and going to bed. He closed his eyes… awoke sprawled in the chair, clenched fists swinging. He rubbed the flat of one hand down over his face to clear his mind of striding through a dark alley being stalked by an armed drug dealer. The clock read twelve-thirty. It had stopped raining and frogs sang up their kind of storm out in the creek.

He rose, stripping out of his clothes on the way to the bathroom, took a shower and paraded naked into the bedroom, filled with a king sized bed. He fell across the mattress on his face.

Something licked his bare butt. A dream. He smacked the spot. Teeth grabbed his fingers. Growling. He hunched upward with a grunt. Something like a banshee hollered and hit the floor with a little squeal.

"What the hell?" He shoved off the bed, stumbled into the wall, smacking his nose.

"You okay? Is it broken?" Hands patted his back, took him by the shoulders, and guided him to sit on the edge of the bed. "Wait. I'll get a wash cloth. Hold your head back. You're bleeding all over the place."

A tongue lapped his feet. His bloody feet. He kicked out, shoving the fucking vampire through the door.

"Go on, Brad." A sweet voice, one he knew too well.

At last he could see, and he peered into bars of sunlight coming through the window. Glowing, shining in her hair. Gorgeous. Shit, that hurt.

"Jessie? What's going on? What the hell?" His nose throbbed. Both hands were covered in blood.

"Tilt your head back, honey." She washed his face with the cool rag. "I'm so sorry. That silly dog came rushing in, leaped on you, and started licking. It was like you exploded out of the bed or something. Anyway, before I could say or do anything you were smack up against the wall. Blood everywhere. Put this on the back of your neck. It'll stop the bleeding."

He took whatever it was, a bag of something freezing cold, and eased it over the back of his neck. What the hell good would that do?

"Stops the blood from flowing so fast through your head to your nose." As if she'd heard him.

"Bullshit." The rag over his mouth muffled the expletive.

She chuckled. "What I thought, too, but it works. Already slowing down. Just keep it there a while longer." She kissed his fresh washed cheek. "I'm so sorry. I had no idea Brad would cause such an explosion."

For a few minutes everything went quiet. Her breasts pressed against him while she cleaned his face. They felt so good, she smelled so delicious he wanted to take a bite. Funny how he could still smell through a broken nose.

"There, it's stopped. Just sit still for a while." Pause while her breath fanned over him. "Do you realize you're naked?" A whisper that ran down his spine like a troop of barefoot lizards.

"Yeah." His voice sounded weird, like he had a mother of a cold.

Her fingers moved on either side of his nose. "Is it broken?"

"Probly."

She scrambled away, gathering the bag of garden peas and the wash rag. "I'm calling Doc. He can fix it. Can't he? I mean he knows about fixing live people, doesn't he?" She giggled. "I'm sorry, I can't help it. The whole thing, well, it was pretty funny."

"Didn't feel like it to me."

"You just wait. This time next week you'll be telling everyone how it happened and laughing about it."

"Don't think so." He gently fingered his face. "Ow. Call Doc, I think it's broken."

"Don't be a baby. Men have such a low pain threshold."

She had some nerve and he glared to show her what he thought of that.

"Okay, I'll call him. We wouldn't want that gorgeous face marred by a crooked nose."

"Make that dog stop licking my feet. He's a fucking vampire."

"Come on, Brad." She scooted the little fart out of the room. "It's no different than you using a piece of bread to sop up the blood from your rare cooked steak."

"Good grief, Jess. You say the most godawful things sometimes."

"I can't understand you, sweetie," she called from the other room.

But she could. She damned well could. He muttered all the time it took to drag on his britches. To hell with a shirt or boots.

In a few minutes she came back in with a plastic dishpan full of water and cleaned up the blood on the wall and floor.

An hour later Dal tried to show her how he could take pain. He sat on the couch while Doc ground the bone back in place, added some plaster across the bridge, and left still chuckling over the story Dal had told him and Ina Mae, who followed Doc to the trailer when she saw him arrive in the coroner's wagon.

"Was a-scared you was dead or something." She told this to Dal while she examined his face. "You're gonna be swole up and black for a while."

"Go ahead and laugh." His voice sounded muffled.

But Jessie was right, it was already pretty funny. Ina Mae wiggled her fingers and stomped out the door and across the porch. When the old woman walked in those sturdy black shoes you could hear her a mile off. Down the steps and she was gone.

Jessie turned from the stove and slid scrambled eggs and sausage into Dal's plate. Even with the swollen face, he looked scrumptious in the early morning light with no shirt hiding his copper skin.

"She cooks." He picked up a fork and gently stirred the food.

"A bit overcooked, but I didn't burn them, and that in itself is a miracle. Maybe I'll learn to cook yet."

Without replying he scooped up a bite, chewed carefully, and swallowed. The nose crackled a bit and he grunted. "Are there taste buds in your nose?"

She took a bite, made a face. "Could use something."

"Pepper." He added some. Butter too, but he didn't say so. Instead he glanced at her as she slid into the chair opposite him. "Thank you."

It came out of his mouth at the same time she said, "I'm sorry." And she was. Brad sat at her feet, uttered a little woof. She set her plate on the floor for him to clean off.

Dal sipped gingerly at his hot coffee. "Hope you're gonna wash that. You gonna keep the mutt, I guess."

"I don't know. Maybe. He makes me feel safe at night."

His eyes flashed in her direction. "Didn't know you don't feel safe."

Oh, shit. She didn't want to tell him about Steve and the note he'd sent her. He was too quick to feel protective. Just his nature, nothing wrong with it. Except she didn't want him worrying about her. He only knew a little bit about what had gone on between her and Steve out in California before she ran back to Cedarton to lick her wounds. Truth be told, it was only mostly her side of the story.

"It's just that there are so many strangers wandering through since they opened the highway. I don't trust people I don't know." Don't look up, just keep playing with the eggs so he doesn't see the lie in your eyes.

"Hmm, hadn't noticed more than the usual. Students coming in for Fall semester."

"It's the highway. People I don't know in cars I've never seen. Just driving through town. Staring at everyone on the street. Makes me feel like I'm on display."

She was saying way too much and shut up.

He nodded, his expression telling her he wasn't in the least satisfied with her reply. "Where do you keep the gun?"

"In the table by the front door."

"When you come in at night, if you feel scared, get it and carry it into your bedroom. Put it in the drawer by your bed. Then put it back by the door before you leave. That would make you feel more protected."

She could kiss him for allowing her to think she could protect herself so she didn't say she knew to do that. Let him feel like he was taking good care of her. Men liked that. He'd stayed with her back after she got shot. But that was as much to make himself feel better, and she understood. He'd been so damned scared he almost said he loved her.

He pushed back his empty plate and stood. "Well, I'd better get dressed and get in to the station. By the way, what brought you here this morning? Surely it wasn't to sic that ugly mutt on me and watch me break my nose."

"Keep calling him ugly he's liable to attack you again. I completely forgot why I came. Must've been good, though." The look she gave him sent a message, but she turned it off, shoved back her chair, rose, and went to his side. Had kept her hands off him as long as she could. That bare chest needed touching, even if only for a moment. Placing the flat of her hands on his warm skin, she slowly raised them to his shoulders, curled her fingers around his neck, and kissed the tip of his chin.

He smiled down at her. "This is what you came for?"

"Not exactly, but it's not a bad idea. Wanted to ask if you learned anything about our murder victim we can put in the paper. Last minute stuff."

"Haven't put a finger on anything yet. Will let you know when and if I do."

"Not sure I believe you, but…." His eyes batted when she went for his mouth. "It's okay. I'll be real careful."

"Maybe you will be, but I'm not sure I can."

"Sure you can." She feathered her lips over his. He had the nicest lips she'd ever kissed. Sexy and warm and gentle, though they could go all urgent real quick. Demanding, searching. With a shiver she opened her eyes and let the vision fade. Touched his mouth with the tip of her tongue, then backed away.

"Just as it was getting interesting."

"Go, put your shirt on while I can still resist you. It's Friday and if I don't get to work I won't have a job."

He headed for the bedroom. "Yeah, as if Parker would ever fire you. He's in love with you, you know."

"No he isn't. We're just very close friends."

Without a word he went on into the bedroom. She stared after him. Parker wasn't in love with her. Sure, they liked each other a lot, understood each other, worked well together. That didn't mean anything. Did it?

Oh, God, she hoped not. That kind of complication in her life would be way too much. The relationship between her and Dal caused enough problems without that. And now this note from Steve. What in the world was she going to do about that? Just sit and wait for him to show up and try to hurt her? Maybe it wasn't Steve. Maybe she'd written a story about someone that had made them angry enough to retaliate or try to scare her. The note wasn't signed.

God, don't let it be Steve here to make her pay for what she'd done.

While she cleaned up the breakfast dishes Dal came out of the bedroom and disappeared in the bathroom. Later they walked out together, Brad running between her feet on the steps till Dal grabbed her arm.

"Be careful, that dog could make you fall. What will you do with him today while you work?"

"Why, you wanta dog sit him?"

"Hell no. Keep him away from me. I don't like his appetite for blood."

"He'll be fine. I'll put him out back."

"Okay, as long as he doesn't attack someone, suck their blood."

She smacked his arm. "Will you hush up about him and blood?"

"You saw how he is." He grinned down at her, gave her a soft kiss, and opened the door of his SUV. "Stay out of my way today, lady. I've got a murder to solve."

"I'll do my best. You have any clues you'll let me know?"

"You go on and write your stories and leave me to mine."

She straightened, gave him a mock salute. "Yes sir." She waited till he backed out before climbing in the Jeep and starting it. Out back of the trailer across the creek sat a car. Odd. Funny time of the day to be making out. With a shrug she drove off to deliver Brad to her backyard and get busy.

Friday was like most Fridays. Last minute ads and stories. Engagements and anniversaries, obits, city council meeting, arrests, all fitted into the eighteen pages with the front left for the fire at Treman's, leading to the story of the dead foot and the body, using Mac's release and a couple of photos Jessie had taken that were cleared for use. She got on the phone and talked to Kathy to work up some vague quotes about the body to add to Mac's. Dal did not do interviews or give quotes. She dare not even think about using anything he said. It came too close to what she'd done with Steve, though him being undercover made her trespass more dangerous.

She did a sidebar from an interview with the new fire chief Ken White, who was much more pleasant to deal with than Harold Smith. He'd asked that the paper print a warning to residents of the dangers of a fire getting out of hand as dry as the woods were. The alert was high and there should be no outdoor burning. The previous night's rain hadn't made a dent in the arid conditions of the woods. He went on to tell her more about the fire at Treman's and how it got started. Maybe and could be. Vague stuff to keep from putting the arsonist on guard.

By five-thirty she was more than ready to meet Tink for supper and a movie. They preferred to rent a DVD for their frequent get-togethers rather than drive all the way to Fayetteville to a movie theater. And this night they opted to stop by Backyard Burgers for one of their heart-attack meals they could carry to Tinker's.

Jessie followed the patrol unit Tink drove, even though Mac still hadn't let her in the field. She parked under a maple tree in the yard of the apartment she rented over the garage of the hundred-year-old house turned into a bed and breakfast by its new owners, Betsey and Bob Black. They named it The Five Bees. Everyone in town thought that a bit too cutesy, but then the Blacks weren't from Arkansas. That excused them a lot of weird behavior.

At the Red Bird, comments had flowed the day the sign went up out where the lane turned off the road.

"Who wants to stay where bees are everywhere? Gimp Johnson did a good job painting those bees on the sign, but good gracious. Bees?"

"You gotta admit it's different." Wanda stacked a row of plates up her arm and carried them behind the counter without dropping one.

"I ain't gotta admit that at all. It's plumb dumb, if you ask me. Jest cause of all the Bs in the names."

"But then they didn't ask you, did they?"

Someone rapped on the window, breaking Jessie's reverie. She grabbed the bag containing the burgers and hopped from the jeep.

"Where were you?" Tink reached for the drinks.

"Just lint picking. I'm starved and these burgers smell delicious. Let's go in and eat. What movie did you get?"

"*Gravity.* Thought it was about time we saw it."

"Be better on the big screen, but we missed seeing it there. Remember why?"

Tink squinted her eyes shut in thought. Raised her shoulders. "Nope, guess not."

Jessie studied her a long time, waiting, not willing to give any hints.

Tink flushed. "I remember. It wasn't my fault, though, they tied me up and threw me in that dark cellar. I thought I was going to die."

"And?" Jessie raised her brows.

"I refused to leave the house for two weeks after. Had to take my vacation time and everything."

"And so by the time I dragged you out, kicking and screaming it had gone from the big screen to DVD, so I'll just suffer through watching Clooney in less than gigantor size."

"Okay, mea culpa, mea culpa. Now let's eat. The smell of these hamburgers and french fries is killing me."

Toward the end of the movie a knock came on the door. Muttering, Tink hit pause and went to see who it was. Jessie strained to hear but could only make out two women's voices. Tink returned, cheeks flushed.

"It's Betsey Black. She's worried about one of her patrons. He hasn't been back in a couple of days and some of his clothes are still in his room. Let's go over and check it out. I've always wanted to run an investigation and Sheriff Mac is adamant that women can't go in the field cause it's dangerous. I heard him say once it was unseemly too. Come on, Jess, it'll be fun."

"We can't go messing about what might ultimately turn into a crime scene. Are you crazy? I could lose my job and Dal would be incensed."

"Then you stay here. I'll go over as a deputy and take a look. If I think anything bad has happened I'll call the station and get a 'real' deputy over here."

"I don't think you should do this. Mac will not be happy. Suppose you mess up a crime scene?"

"I'm just going to take a quick look. I won't touch anything. Betsey is glued to the floor out there and isn't going away till I do something. If I call it in someone will maybe have to get out of bed to come over. It's nearly eleven o'clock." While she talked Tink searched for her shoes.

"You're wearing a sleep shirt. What kind of deputy does that?"

Tink glared at her. "I'm just going to see if it's something that needs to be reported. It's just down the hall. I'll be right back."

Jess shrugged, gesturing toward the door. "Be my guest."

"Oh, cute." Tink disappeared through the door.

Thirty minutes later, when Jessie had almost given up and gone to fetch her friend, deputy Tinker Mattawan rushed into the apartment, eyes sparkling. "I think we have an honest to goodness missing person."

"Did you call the station?"

"Not yet."

Jessie rolled her eyes, held up a hand.

"No, wait. I can solve this. I know I can. And if we turn it in to the sheriff I won't get the chance. If I figure it out, maybe he'll see I'm a good detective and let me go on calls."

"Sweetie, Mac's not going to let a woman go on calls if you figure out what happened to D.B. Cooper and all that money."

Tinker tilted her head. "Who's D.B. Cooper?"

"Never mind. I can't be a part of this."

"Why not? Just let me tell you about it. You're good at this stuff. Dal lets you help him."

She snorted. "Lets me? Not on your life. I butt in is what I do, and sometimes I figure things out. With him hollering at me the whole time."

"Well, I don't care. If you won't help me, the least you can do is not tell them. Give me a chance to figure this out."

Jessie sighed and shook her head. This was exactly the kind of thing she had to avoid at all costs.

"No, listen. Just listen. Don't you owe me that?"

"Why do I owe you this?"

"Remember when I said I'd come stay with you when you were getting all those threats? And—"

"And you had a meltdown on the way out and deputies had to go out looking for you cause I thought you'd been kidnapped or something? Is that what you're using to blackmail me into this?"

Tinker nodded vigorously. "Even though I was terrified of driving to your place in the dark I tried and it was awful."

"Okay, I'll do this much. I'll go home, not aware of what you are going to do, and give you tomorrow without saying anything. But so help me, if you rat on me and tell Mac I knew, or God forbid breathe a word to Dal, I'll strangle you. I'll never speak to you again. You get me?"

"First, let's watch the rest of the movie," Tinker said. "Then you just go home and don't worry. I told Betsey I'd get dressed and everything and be back to check things out more thoroughly." She plopped down on the couch, picked up the remote, and gestured toward Jessie.

"Good grief." She fell down beside her friend and watched the rest of the movie.

In the Jeep, she backed away from The Five Bees, grumbling under her breath. How had she let Tink talk her into this? Nothing good could come from it. Nothing at all. She ought to drive right out to Dal's and tell him what was going on. He was sure to find out about Tink's wild-ass plan, and right soon after he'd know she was in on it.

Maybe she ought to check with Betsey, see who this guy was and learn if it sounded dangerous or like it might be a crime. Hell, the guy could be on a bender, or maybe he went fishing or was visiting friends. Any number of reasons for not returning to the B&B for a couple of nights.

Nope. Stay out of it. Do that, then she'd be involved as much as Tink was. Just stay in touch and make sure her friend wasn't in any danger, or that she wasn't walking all over a crime scene. Surely she'd know better than to do anything stupid. Yet, she wanted to be a real, honest-to-goodness deputy so much, she'd do about anything to convince Mac she was good enough.

In the end, Jessie decided to wait the weekend, then press her to turn it over to Mac if the guy didn't turn up. How much damage could her friend do in two days?

5

CHAPTER

Saturday morning early, Dal woke and stared at the wall for a while, then switched to gazing at the clock. Hands hadn't moved more than six clicks. Five-twenty. Eyes closed, he thought of Jessie taking off her shirt. Thirty minutes crawled by and all he got was a hard-on. Shit.

Grumbling, he pulled on a pair of jeans left on the floor the night before, then the wrinkled tee shirt under them. Brushing his teeth, he studied his reflection. Two black eyes and a swollen nose. Maybe he could say he'd been in a fight and you should see the other three guys. From the hall closet he grabbed his fishing gear. Boots sat by the recliner where he'd left them last night and he pulled them on. He made a pot of coffee, watched birds fluttering to the creek for a drink and his glance drifted past the parked car.

Hell, that car was there yesterday. Odd. Well, maybe someone liked that spot for meditating and they'd come back for more. The view wasn't bad if they didn't look his way. Who wanted to stare at a bunch of trailers hunched under trees? Necking kids wouldn't stay all night, surely. He got nothing from the stare, so gave it up. His receiver was broke and he really didn't give a damn.

Coffee finished, he filled the Thermos, fingered a honey bun from the cookie jar, remembered to get his weapon, and went out to the patrol unit where he locked the .45 in the glove box. A peaceful morning on the lake was just what he needed. Waiting around for information on the body from Doc or the Spaceys would drive him nuts. These things took time, and the crime scenes weren't telling him anything. Maybe Grandfather had deserted him. That might not be so bad, except it was one reason he had this job.

Forty-five minutes later he sat on a huge boulder above the quiet surface of the lake, bobber floating deathly still. Labor Day Weekend and the lake would fill fast once folks got the camp and camper ship-shape. Around the shoreline, trees and mountains hung upside down in the deep green water. A canoe glided silently through the glint of early morning sunlight. A man in the front faced a woman in the back, each languidly dipping an oar over the side. Their conversation and laughter lingered in the sweet morning air.

Dal leaned against the rough bark of a tall pine propping the back of the boulder up, and closed his eyes. Out of the serenity grew the roar of an outboard motor. Moving too fast. He came alert, leaned forward. The fool was going to swamp the canoe. He leaped to his feet, shouted. It did no good, they couldn't hear him, but they heard the boat, paddled fast and hard to get out of his way. The guy would slow down. Surely he would. At the last minute he cut the engine, swung the boat in a hundred eighty degree turn, the stern forcing the waves into a huge wash that filled the smaller boat. It went under, dumping its yelling passengers, then popped upside down to the surface.

Neither passenger wore a life vest. Maybe they could swim. The woman screamed, thrashed about in the classic action of panic. He kicked out of his boots. What in the hell was she doing out there without a life jacket? The water was a good fifteen feet below the boulder, but he jumped in feet first. When he came up everything happened at once. The man floated around shouting, the guy in the boat fired up the motor and ripped away from the scene, and the woman disappeared in the depths, hands reaching for the sky.

Dal memorized the numbers on the hull of the fleeing boat, while taking long strokes toward the upside down canoe. The man kept diving and coming up without the woman. Dal joined him and dove deep into murky water. Like an apparition, she hung midway between the surface and the bottom, one foot trapped by branches of an old tree long since swallowed by the damming of the White River that formed the lake.

As if reaching for the sky, her arms floated above her head, long blonde hair strung out around her. He grasped her ankle, wrestled the foot loose from the clinging fingers of the dead tree, and hauled her toward the surface. Lungs aching for air, he surfaced and sucked in a loud breath. The man must've caught sight of him. He swam with some dexterity to help get her to shallow water. The two of them dragged her out by the arms to the gravelly shoreline. Without a word, Dal began compressions while the man breathed in her mouth. Nothing. Another round and this time she spouted water from her lungs in a great noisy gasp and they turned her on her side.

She probably coughed up a quart of water before the man took her in his arms and started rocking back and forth. Still not a word. Damn fool. Taking her out without a life jacket when she couldn't swim. And her too. She ought to've known better. Not only stupid but illegal.

Fury kept him silent as it often did, for he feared losing his temper and taking the fool's head off. Without waiting for useless words, he stood and shuffled away from the couple, sock feet taking a beating on the rocky ground. Let them figure out what to do next. He had no sympathy for stupidity.

Yet he had allowed Leann to lose her life to drugs. A danger he well understood. All the while running around saving total strangers from the same fate.

"Hey, mister. Wait. Thanks. Wait." Calling out from behind him.

Idiot had finally come to his senses. He stomped on, but the man caught up with him, grabbed his arm. He swung around, fists clenched, ready to do battle. The guy took a few steps back, held up both hands.

"Just wanted to thank you. You saved my wife's life."

Then his eyes grew wide. One mad Indian with a busted nose and two black eyes, was more than he'd bargained on. For all the poor guy knew Dal might scalp him. He held open palms up, reversed, and ran off toward the woman, who remained sitting on the bank coughing.

Dal's anger bled away. No sense taking it out on the two of them. You couldn't fix stupid. Been a long time since he'd been that close to losing it. As always, he went around saving other people. But not Leann. Now he spit out that fury at someone he didn't know, would never see again. Last time he'd lashed out was the day he fought the barbed wire after a set-to with Jess over the danger of drugs.

He hadn't even known her at all then, and she took him home and bandaged his bloody hands. That'd been two years ago. She'd never once been afraid of that temper of his. Somehow knew he would never hit her, or any woman. One thing he'd never do, no matter the anger.

At the incline above the shoreline he pulled himself up holding on to saplings, then followed an animal trail, bruised feet protesting. When he reached the boulder, his finest, newest rod and reel were gone, the tackle box open where he'd left it. A damned fish must've pulled the pole right into the water. And he didn't even have anything to show for his fishing trip. Except that his feet were cut up from the walk. Carrying the boots 'cause he didn't want to bleed in them, he limped back to his unit, tossed his gear in the back, and climbed in. Some fishing trip that was. He had the number of the offending boat. For two cents he'd turn him in to the park rangers, but at best all his trouble would only end in a ticket with a small fine for the boat owner.

"To hell with it." The guy could spend some sleepless nights worrying over how he'd almost got her killed. The woman he loved. They'd been lucky.

He drove the dirt track back out to the road and headed for home, feeling like the day had been wasted. It was barely noon when he tramped inside the trailer, and he was starving.

Changing out of his wet clothes, he pulled on dry jeans, a clean tee shirt, slipped his sore feet into a pair of moccasins, and headed for the Red Bird to get something to eat. When he walked in, Jess was sitting in a booth devouring a hamburger and fries and yakking with Theron and Fudge. The two were often together, both being bachelors. Sometimes Fudge worked for Theron on his farm. They sat together at a table near her.

She waved at Dal. "You look like you've got a thorn in your paw, deputy. Sit with me only if you wipe that glower off your face."

He plopped down opposite her. "I like my glower, thank you. I believe I'll just keep it."

"Suit yourself. You're walking like you got a corn cob in your britches."

She glanced down at one long leg stretched outside the booth. "And no boots. I hate to mention it, but your tee shirt is inside out."

Wanda sidled up about then with a cup of coffee for him. "Your usual, sheriff?"

"Why does everyone insist on calling me sheriff?"

"Well, you're in one heck of a good mood. But that could be expected from a man who wears his clothes inside out. Looks like someone cleaned your plow, too." Wanda dealt with all sorts of customers and none of them could faze her with a bit of shouting. "Want me to go away and come back when you're ready to be civil?"

He deserved that and mumbled he was sorry. "Give me what she's got. And it was a dog."

She raised her brow and stood beside the table, fist doubled on one hip.

He looked up at her. "What?"

"I already know the story. Jessie beat you to it. One little dog? You know, saying please wouldn't hurt you, deputy." She accented every letter of the title.

"I guess I'll have a hamburger and fries, please, ma'am." There, that ought to do it.

"That's only a tiny bit better, but looks like it'll have to do."

"What's got your tail in a knot?" This from Jessie.

"Ah, shit." He leaned back in the booth. What? Tell her he just saved a woman from drowning and almost decked her husband? Admit why was he so angry over that? It was best left unsaid.

Jess touched his fist doubled on the table, enclosed it in her warm hand. "Bad night?"

He glanced at her, wanted to kiss her right there. "Something like that I guess. I'm okay, just being my usual ornery self."

She nodded and went back to devouring the huge hamburger. He liked watching her eat. She had no self-consciousness, just lit into her food like a lumberjack. Like making love. A piece of onion escaped her lips and she pulled her hand away to capture it and poke it back in. Even that she accomplished with grace. He grinned liked a damned fool.

She put down her burger and covered her mouth, swallowed and grinned back. "Stop that. I'll bet I have mustard on my teeth."

"Nah. Well, maybe. But I have my tee shirt on wrong. Besides, I can't help it. You bring out the best in me, if there is any best left in there."

"There is. Believe me, there is."

"You two ought to get a room." Wanda stood beside the booth, a platter filled with a two-ton hamburger and fries. "Like your mocs, deputy."

"Thanks, Wanda. And you may call me Dal when I'm out of uniform."

She threw her head back and laughed. "I'll call you jackass if I please."

Everyone in the diner roared with delight. Dal joined them.

It was a beautiful day after all. Maybe nothing bad would happen and the three-day weekend would reel out easy like.

Jessie wanted to crawl under the table and do all sorts of things to Dal, right there in the diner. When he flashed that dimpled grin at her the way he had a moment ago, her insides coiled like snakes. Turned into mush. Tied into knots.

Get a grip, girl. Watching him watch her. Eat. Pick up your hamburger, take a bite and chew. Don't go all gaga and choke. Why had she allowed this to happen? She'd tried so hard to fight with him when he got angry. Instead she turned all maternal and soothed away his sour moods.

And he let her. That was amazing. A big, strong, self-assured man like him usually fought back when a woman got all lovey-dovey to smooth out a temper tantrum. Not him. He ate it up. The only time he fought with her was when she did her job. Hung around a crime to get a story. That incensed him.

It was the other side of their relationship. He hated reporters and never let her forget it. Because of what had happened to him in Dallas. What had happened to his wife.

He peered at her over his mug of coffee. "Whatcha thinking?"

"Me? Nothing. Why?"

"You went all sober and thoughtful. Want to go dancing tonight?"

Out of the blue, without warning. She'd rather dance with him than eat or sleep. The way he held her, like she might break, yet tucked ever so tenderly against his chest. His muscles contracting against her breasts. Good grief, stop it. Must be something in the air. She cleared her throat and took a huge drink of Coke.

All too often something happened to take him away at those moments when they were the most intimate. That's one reason she grabbed unusual times and places to seduce him.

"Where's Tink? Did you and her get your night out?"

She set down the Coke. "Yes we did. We watched *Gravity* and ate BackYard Burgers. By the way, Dave and Kathy are having a Labor Day barbecue Monday. We're all invited. I mean Tink and Burt, you and me. Can't miss one of their cookouts."

"Sounds exciting."

"It was and it will be. Laid back, good company, and better food. Our jobs are exciting enough, though Tink would sure love to do some real police work."

"Wouldn't miss the cookout, but too bad Mac's not gonna turn Tink loose in the field. If I were sheriff that little ball of dynamite would be promoted to a unit overnight. First dark night she had a stakeout, you can bet your bottom dollar she'd freak out and that would end that. Mac ought to realize that would be the easy way out."

"That's not fair. She's got a mind for solving crimes." Telling him that Tinker was looking into a missing persons without reporting it was on the tip of her tongue, but he would feel wrong about knowing it without warning Mac, so she kept it locked up inside. If he ever found out she knew and didn't say anything, he'd be pissed. But too bad.

"If they take place in broad daylight."

Jessie held her tongue. There was no changing other people's minds and she'd given up trying.

"Don't you have anything to say to that?"

She shook her head no and buried her teeth in her burger.

Fudge, who had finished his meal and was digging in his pocket for money, spoke up. "Ain't no chance of Mac retiring, he'll be sheriff here till he's found at a crime scene, stiff and cold. He won't ever quit his job."

"No chance I'd want the job, either." Dal glanced at Jessie, then looked away. "Just saying about Tink. Women ought to understand their limitations. Nothing against the finer sex, you're just different from us, thank goodness."

He didn't dare look at her and say something like that. Ought to kick him under the table.

"Thank God for that," Wanda echoed. "Reckon we need to stick to fetching and toting, washing, soothing bruised egos, having babies—"

"Okay, okay. I give." Dal lifted both hands above his head as if being arrested. "I apologize with all my heart. Go on, do anything you damn well please, and when you get in trouble, some big strong man will rescue you. And if it's me, I won't even remind you of this conversation. I'll just smile and kiss you and go on about my business."

Jessie tapped her fingers on the table. "You're a misogynist. Plain and simple."

"Now you've gone and insulted me. I do not hate women, I do not resent women. I protect women, I take care of women, I adore women." He smiled wide and wiggled his eyebrows. "Why just this morning I dragged a woman out of the lake too dumb to know that when you can't swim you wear a goddamned lifejacket."

Jessie studied him. Wait, he saved a woman's life this morning? Really? No wonder he looked so wiped out when he came in. And now he was furious, turning his anger inward.

"Dal, you saved a woman's life? And you just walk in and order a hamburger? Where is she? Who was she? How did it happen?"

"I have no earthly idea. I was so pissed I didn't get their names or anything. For all I know the two of them are sitting on the lake shore waiting for someone to miraculously show up and give them a ride. Hell, don't ask me about it. She goes out in a canoe on that deep lake without a life jacket with a man too weak to rescue her when the boat swamps. Idiots."

"And you jump in and save her life?" Jessie stopped the finger drumming. Smacked him on the arm. "Hell, you shoulda let her drown, dumb as she was. She doesn't deserve to live. Damn. Tell me where she is and I'll go hit her in the head with a rock."

Eyes glistening, Dal stared at her a minute.

She glared back. And then it hit her, too late. She reached for his hand, but he jerked away. "Sorry," she whispered.

He turned his head to gaze out the window, raised his shoulders in a big sigh. "Okay, smartass. I give. I take it all back, except the part about Tink going in the field. I agree with Mac. One of us would get hurt saving her from her own fears. You know that, Jess. Perfectly well."

She nodded and went back to her hamburger. If he ever stopped beating himself up over what could not be changed, he'd be much happier. However, he was probably right about Tink. Still, she deserved a chance to prove herself somehow. Let her investigate this missing person. That would show Mac Tink could do something besides answer the phone and stand guard at the jail. It would be worth the trouble that would fall on her head, cause Tink was her friend. She would back her up where she could.

She nodded at Dal, took the last bite of her burger, and grabbed her Coke cup. "Can I get a refill? Want to go home and clean house and wash dishes. Have to do some writing for the paper. Taking Monday off means working yesterday and today. Good thing I don't have a man waiting for me, or I'd be fetching for him too."

Dal laughed. "Hush up and get out of here before I run you in for annoying an officer of the law."

When she passed him she patted his shoulder. "Pick me up at six and we can eat first."

"Oh, figgered you wouldn't want to dance with a misogynist."

She hammered on his arm. "I make exceptions when a man looks like you, cutie. Besides, I have a feeling I can change your mind before the night's over. About women, that is. 'Course, you ought to do something about those black eyes. I can loan you some makeup."

When she went out the door everyone in the Red Bird was still laughing at her final remark.

Finally the place quieted down and Dal turned to Theron, who was eating fried chicken in the next booth. "You know of anyone gone missing around here lately?"

"Naw. Far as I know no one around these parts has come up missing." Theron wiped bread through the last of his gravy and stuffed it in his mouth. "Must not be from around here. We'd know he was gone. So you got no name for this unfortunate fella yet?"

"Nope. Doc didn't find much." He couldn't really tell them any more since it was an ongoing case. 'Course the grapevine had pretty well passed the story everywhere. Fingerprints were being run. The body had to go down to Little Rock for anything else, including the autopsy. All Doc could do was prepare it to be transported. He would turn over any personal belongings to the sheriff's department and they could run the prints, but anything else had to come from down there.

Dal sat in the patrol unit for a while before taking off. He'd come close to making a damned fool of himself inside there today. Somehow Jess had dampened his fury. He needed to go home. Best place for him to be. He could do some cleaning, maybe have a beer and kick back. He was headed that way when Mac hailed him on the radio.

"There's a car on fire out near your place. Thought you might be at home and could fill me in."

"I'm about halfway there. Where's it at?" He craned his neck to see smoke.

"On Dye Creek Road back of Ina Mae's. Not sure exactly where, she must not be to home or she'd've let us know. Someone called on a cell phone and hung up without identifying themselves. You shouldn't have any trouble spotting it. I'm clear on the other side of the county serving a warrant. Thought it was a purty day for a drive." Mac laughed and hung up before Dal could accuse him of just that.

Because he enjoyed it and thought it might work off some of his anger, Dal turned on the siren and floor-boarded the Ford, sliding sideways onto Dye Creek Road and sending gravel and dust spiraling into the air. The tires left the road crossing the bridge and adrenaline set his heart to thudding.

Ahead, a cloud of black smoke rose straight up in the windless sky and he slowed to keep from flying over the water and through the windows of his trailer. A car parked in the same location as the one he'd spotted the night before and again this morning was burning down to the tires. Sure to be the same one. Twisting the wheel, he slid to a halt a good distance away to avoid the heat pouring off the blaze.

No point in trying to put it out, but he leaped from his SUV to watch. A wall of rage nearly knocked him down. A rage that set his blood to boiling, as if from the heat of the fire. Teeth grinding against a shudder of fear, not his own but that of one of the men arguing while they poured gasoline over the vehicle. Well aware of that feeling from crime scenes, he staggered, reached out to support himself by his car door. Dealt with the drama in his mind.

"Why the hell'd you leave it setting here, anyway?" the one in charge shouted. "I told you to run it off in a holler or something. Last time I'm working with an idjit." He set to hitting the other one with the empty gas can. Thunking, thudding noises and yelling.

Pure hatred from one of the struggling figures, some of the worst emotions he'd ever come in contact with. He staggered from the violence that burned him worse than the heat from the car. Sweat poured over his face and soaked his shirt. Hatred and a devastating terror reached out and enclosed him so he lost his hold on reality and sank to the ground, arms wrapped around his knees.

In the distance a siren sounded, breaking through the emotional assault. He crawled to his car, managed to haul himself to his feet before the Grace County Volunteer Fire Department arrived. He shook off the debilitation as best he could. No good having them catch him like that. There was enough talk about him and his often weird behavior without being found groveling on the ground like a maniac. What the hell had happened, he had no idea. Bad as his reaction to violence had ever been, it had never hit him like that. He felt as if something evil had crawled inside him and wrestled with his soul.

Chief White hustled out of the truck and strode over to Dal, heavy boots dragging their heels in the gravel. "Hey, Dal. Get 'er out, did you?"

"Yeah, pissed on it." He gritted his teeth and forced a grin. Keep up the banter, maybe no one will notice you feel like you've been hit by a ten-ton truck.

"Tangle with a perp, did you?" He gestured at Dal's face.

That didn't work. "A dozen of 'em."

White chuckled. "Gotta watch the dirty dozen."

Time to change the subject. "Might be a good idea to furnish us deputies with a fire extinguisher since we seem to arrive first."

"A better idea would be to have a paid fire department, getting a paycheck like y'all do."

"That too. I'll talk to my boss. Maybe we can split our big ole check, seeing as how we make so much."

White laughed, twitched his nostrils. "Smells like gasoline."

"Yeah, I figure they doused it good. Don't know why yet, though. I'm thinking it might be connected to the homicide."

"Wouldn't be a bit surprised." White rubbed a hand over his crew cut. He was retired from the army and had only moved here recently. Not a surprise that he'd been elected chief when Harold Smith retired. He was big, in his mid-forties, and full of the get 'er done mentality. Worked at a lumber yard on the edge of town. Tough guy. Despite himself, Dal was beginning to like him. First thing you know, he'd be liking everyone in town.

"You want us to stick around and help you look for clues?"

"Nah, you can go back to playing poker or whatever it is you boys do in your spare time."

White grinned and hollered, "Let's go home, boys. Law's taken charge."

Dal waited till the truck went out of sight before he sank back to the ground. All the while he'd visited with White, the niggling feeling in his gut would not let up. Like a huge fist squeezed his insides.

"Well, hell, Grandfather. What now?" Just 'cause he accused the old man of abandoning him? This was a bit much. He sprawled on his butt, stared at the dying fire, the shape of the car growing more distinct through the fading smoke and flames. Sort of killed his appetite for cleaning or a beer. Mac would want him to hang around till he could dig through the remains, though nothing much would have made it through such heat. Not even a read from the guys doing this. Once that monster or whatever it was, reached out for him, he lost all ability to read the crime.

Been almost a year since the last homicide in Grace County and that'd been a double, both connected to stolen diamonds. Seemed like killing was about a once-a-year thing in these parts. Rest of the time it was rustled sheep, cattle or horses, meth and related drug arrests, family brawls, and the occasional fisticuffs out at the beer joint on highway 23.

He was still sitting in the dirt watching the last of the smoke when a car pulled up to his trailer across the way.

Oh, shit. He'd promised to take Jess dancing and here he sat stinking of smoke and gasoline and sweat. He hauled himself to his feet, leaned in, and beeped the horn a couple of times to get her attention.

She emerged from the front of the trailer, saw him, and waved. "What happened?"

"Car fire. Looks suspicious. I'm gonna have to look it over."

"May I join you?"

"Sure. Bring your camera. Good photo-op." Damn, wasn't that nice of him? What was up with that? Sometimes he thought he was losing it with her. Still, her presence had a soothing effect on him. And he wasn't sure why that was, either. Oh, well, at least he smelled so bad she'd keep her distance.

Camera in one hand, she ran down to the creek bank, took off her shoes, rolled up her britches legs, and waded carefully through the slick rocks. She was dressed for the evening out. Jeans and western shirt, huraches, and a red bandana tied around her head like a headband. She looked good enough to eat and she came at him as if ready to allow it. Halted. Studied him closely. Too closely.

He held up a palm. "Better not. I smell bad."

She tilted her head. Managed a weak grin. "What happened?"

He swung his arm around, indicating the burned-out car. "Fire."

"Something else."

How did she do that? "Nope. Just got too close to the fire."

For some reason, she caught on. Didn't push. Changed her tactics. "You look pretty good to me. All sweaty and hot. I could take your shirt off. Or we could get in the creek. Or—"

Again he signaled her to halt. "Get your pictures, I'll poke around a bit, then we can go to the trailer, I'll shower and we'll go dancing." He glanced at his watch. "It's not too late."

She nodded, strode around taking plenty of pictures, then moved away so he could check out the car. It didn't take long to realize that there was nothing but ashes and a metal frame. He called a wrecker to have it towed in so they could go over it more thoroughly, but he didn't have any hopes. Besides, he needed to be with her. Let her do for him what she was so good at. There was plenty of time Monday to go back to work.

Jessie watched him climb into his SUV. Whatever had happened out here had knocked him for a loop. Probably read the crime scene and was still reeling from what he learned. It must be awful to allow the terrible things some people do crawl around under your skin.

He waved out the window. "Catch you on the other side. Be careful on those slippery rocks."

She headed back toward the trailer. Would it be worth it to take off her clothes and crawl in the shower with him? It would mean losing her 'evening look' and going dancing looking more like a country girl, a well-satisfied country girl, at that. Ah, hell, what difference could it make? Besides, he looked like he could use a lot of TLC, and she so enjoyed giving it to him.

Heading up the steps to his door, she took the bandana from her hair and unbuttoned her shirt. By the time he came in, she had the shower running hot and reached for him when he stepped in the small cubicle.

A while later, she sat in the corner of the tiny space trapped there by his intense presence. Water beaded in his black hair, he knelt between her splayed legs, lazily running a finger over one breast and circling the nipple. Pinning her with green eyes that glazed with passion, he slowly lowered his mouth to hers, licked her lips with his tongue, one direction then the other.

The orgasms had barely faded from their earlier lovemaking, yet she sensed a feverish desire fed by a part of him she'd never seen. A wild lust that excited her libido, sent heat surging to the depths of her being. A place no one had ever been before, and he opened it up with one move. His mouth, his tongue, his hands lifting her to go deeper and deeper. Tasting her like a predator with prey. Growling like an animal, while she uttered feral sounds and clamped her hands on either side of his face to keep him there while she came in hot libidinous waves.

A pain so exquisite as to render her unconscious crawled up her insides from between her legs to the pit of her stomach, spread to attack her breasts till they throbbed in agony. When she came to he was laying her on the bed, saying her name in a guttural murmur. Over and over. Fingering her drenched hair back from her face, cheek touching hers.

"Are you all right?" His whisper trembled with fear.

"What happened? Where am I?"

"I think… I'm afraid the evil, the dark part of me, escaped. I'm so sorry."

His expression of terror engulfed her. "No. No, we just got carried away is all. That's all, Dal. Things like that don't happen." She reached to touch his face but he pulled away.

"Don't. I'm not sure what happened. It could hurt you. That I do know."

"That's not possible."

He rose, shaking his head. "I don't know all I should about that part of me that drives me to do what I do. Something comes over me and I become someone or something else I can't control. You've seen it, you know. It was worse this time. It scared me."

"You would never hurt me, or anyone else for that matter."

He turned, left the bedroom. Threw over his shoulder, "You don't know that. You don't."

From down inside where the orgasms dwelt, came a vibration that sent her into spasms. She pulled her knees up to her chest, squeezed her thighs together, and rocked until they faded to nothing, leaving her so spent she panted. For a long time she lay like that, hoping, wishing he would come back. Talk to her. But after a while the door slammed, then a car door thudded shut, an engine revved and faded into the night.

Tears filled her eyes. "What the hell?"

Much later she crawled weakly from the bed, picked up her clothes off the floor in the living room and dressed. Something dreadful had happened to Dal, and it had to have done so between when they were together at the Red Bird and when she arrived here at his trailer to find him standing near a burning car.

And she would find out what that something was. He was a weirdly possessed man, believing in some of the spiritual teachings of his people. Ghosts of victims of violence and death came to help him solve murders. Supernatural beings that were all too real to him. It was bound to affect him in other ways. Had he experienced one of those possessions out there by that burning car? If so, what could have happened to cause him to go all crazy while they were making love? Worse, what had come over her?

6
CHAPTER

Dal gripped the steering wheel till his fingers went numb. A fist squeezed his gut. No matter how he struggled, his foot would not rise off the accelerator, just kept pushing harder and harder. If he drove fast enough maybe he could escape the raw terror that pursued him. Mail boxes and driveways whipped past. His head throbbed. An occasional double set of lights rushed toward him, horns blaring in a drawn-out bellow. The violence, the threat of flinging him into oblivion, fumed inside him and he couldn't escape. He was going crazy.

Speed overtook the high beams and he barreled into a sweeping curve. He was going to crash. Fly off the edge of the mountain. Sail into the night and burst into a thousand fiery pieces. Time slowed down. Seeds of evil sprouted in his soul. A voice screamed obscenities, pummeled his every thought. Letters with no meaning, syllables strung together like glutinous strands of mucous. Every spirit he'd ever encountered babbled thoughts too ludicrous to understand.

Grandfather had failed him. He wanted to be free of this curse forever.

Time chased him, caught up. The car slewed, changed ends, sent the surrounding darkness into a whirl of confusion. All he could do was hang on to the wheel, plant both feet on the floor, and wait for his fate. Bits of gravel pinged onto the roof.

The car rocked to one side, hung there for an eternity, dropped back down on the tires with a thud. His teeth clacked together. At last he dragged in a deep breath, then another, sagged in the seat. His mouth parched. Had he gone over the bluffs into the valley below, died, and passed into the land of the stars? Several more breaths tainted with fine dust assured him of one thing. He was not dead. Such pain was for the living. Blinded by a headache, he coughed, sneezed, bailed out of the car, and staggered down the side of the road. Stopped, bent forward, hands on knees, and spat out the grit.

"Grandson, you must think on this."

"No, I will not." He could scarcely speak. Cleared his throat and tried again. "I want no more to do with this foul spell. I want you gone. This is my life not yours, not theirs."

No reply. Around him, only the sound of critters chirping, sawing, clicking their tongues. He rose straight and tall, peered through the darkness, shouted in Cherokee, "To run from fear is to fail as a man."

As if smothered, the night sounds shut down. Sudden silence, a haunting lack of noise.

"Grandfather?" The whisper trembled from his lips, echoed from the surrounding woods as if he had shouted.

Grandmother's hands soothed his fever, her voice calmed the child he had once been, and a peace settled over him. Freedom from the evil of others. But he would be alone without Grandfather.

Head tilted back, he gazed at the stars scattered so thickly in the dark sky they burned away the night. His ears roared with the sound of nothingness. All life muted as if the earth had settled into a death-like slumber. His heart thumped, his breath whooshed. He trudged back to the SUV, canted crosswise in the road. Gravel gritted under his boots. A sound alone in the void.

Slumped in the driver's seat, he leaned on the headrest, allowing his heart to slow, his breathing to ease. What in the hell had happened? Though definitely alive, he was strangely purged. Would he ever feel the same again? Earlier he had hoped not, now he wasn't so sure. Something had entered him while he stood beside that burning car. Something black and terrifying, the wicked violence of the man who had attacked his buddy and set the car on fire. Now it was gone, leaving him unsure. What if in purging that evil he had somehow lost his ability to do the one thing he was good at? What if he had lost Grandfather? He would be useless to himself and others.

He drove back to the trailer at a much slower pace. If Jess was still there he would rather not go in, yet he had to make sure he hadn't hurt her. Or frightened her.

There was no sign of her car in the drive, but all the lights blazed, as if she'd torn out of there so fast she hadn't bothered to shut them off. He cut the ignition and opened the door. A sweet night breeze touched his cheeks, dried the tears. Funny, he hadn't known he was crying. Not like him at all. But did he really know who he was? He became someone else when he dealt with the violence of killers, but never before had he taken on the persona so completely. It had scared all common sense out of him.

His footsteps crunched on the scattered gravel of the drive and scuffed up the three steps. Hand on the doorknob, he paused, felt for any remnants of the spirit that had invaded him. Nothing there. Just his own heartbeat and the growling of his stomach.

That easily his life became normal again. Or as normal as it had ever been. Hunger gnawed at his empty stomach. He checked the refrigerator, found some ham and cheese, a jar of mustard and another of dill pickles. On the shelf, a few cans of beer, and he snagged one. Sat at the small table and built a sandwich from the last two slices of bread, one the heel.

Jessie drove home from Dal's trembling so violently she could barely hold on to the wheel. The porch light she'd left burning lit the way up the steps, across the porch, and to the door.

Brad rose from his rug on the porch near the door and rushed to her, wagging his tail and making a funny chuffing noise that passed for his friendly bark. Ignoring the ugly little brute, she dug the key from her purse. But the shaking of her hand kept it from fitting in the slot. She sagged against the frame and breathed deeply. Brad pushed against her leg and whined. Damned if she wanted to think of Dal out there in the dark, fleeing his demonic spirits.

Get it together, girl.

Another try and the door opened. Brad scurried inside as if sensing her turmoil. For a long, scary moment she leaned against the wood panel, shaking her head. What had happened to Dal? When he first arrived here he'd been pretty mixed up and once or twice had gone off the rails, but nothing quite as bad as tonight.

The phone rang. Brad barked. On trembling legs she took three steps to the table and picked it up. Tink, whose voice sounded shaky.

"What's up?"

"You know the guy who's missing?"

"From the bed & breakfast? Yeah. Did you find him?"

"I'm afraid he might be a killer for hire."

"Aw, Tink. Your imagination is running away with you."

"No. Listen. I found some really strange stuff in a drawer of the bedside table."

"Strange? What sort of strange?"

"Well, it's, uh—I think maybe you ought to see it. Make sure it's not my imagination."

She sank onto the couch. The little mutt joined her, his warm body curled up against her thigh. The last thing she needed tonight was a trip back into town. And Tink would not drive out here after dark. Damn, she wished the girl would get help with this fear of the dark crap.

"Can it wait till morning? I'm so tired I can't see straight."

"Jessie, listen, you need to see this. It's an article. A clipping from a newspaper. I—it's got your byline on it. And then there are some scribbled notes. Locations around town, a few names. People we know."

Despair gripped her. Article? Hers? Crap. She swallowed a few times. "Hang on a minute, Tink. I just got in and I need a drink."

"I hope not something alcoholic."

"I was thinking water, but perhaps yours is a better idea." Okay, think of some ways anyone besides Steve might have a copy of that article. Published in Los Angeles three... no... almost four years ago.

She opened the fridge, took out a bottle of water, laid the phone down to open it, and drank noisily, all the while thinking a mile a minute. Could it be an old friend from those days? No, how would they find her? Gone back to her real name after using a pseudonym all the while she wrote for the *LA Times*. God, dear God. Someone wanted her pretty badly.

It had to be Steve.

Right. So, let's be rational. Fake it. Lie, for God's sake. That's all she'd done for these close to four years. Lived a lie.

She cleared her throat, picked up the phone. "Hi, Tink. Still there? You know this is not unusual. I've written tons of articles."

"Well, maybe. But this story you wrote. I mean, it's about some sort of crime out in California. And he's written down some names. Parker and Sheriff Mac and Rick Granger and Dal."

Her throat clogged and for a moment she couldn't draw her breath. When she could she croaked out a question. "The article. What does it say?"

Silence, then Tink came back on. "All of it?"

Dammit. "Where are you?"

"Home."

"Okay, I'll be there in thirty. Don't go anywhere and don't let anyone in." She hung up before Tink could say anything else.

Steve. Damn him. He was in Cedarton. But staying at the bed and breakfast? She could only think of one reason for the names. So he could damage her reputation. Was she finally going to have to pay the price for what she'd done? As if losing her career hadn't been enough. He'd promised she'd pay someday, but at the time she hadn't believed he'd actually come after her. Or at least, she'd tried not to believe it. They loved each other once.

Bigger question. Why had he disappeared after arriving and registering at the bed and breakfast? Maybe he gave up and left. Let that be true.

She dragged herself off the couch. Brad followed, danced around his food dish, a battered tin she'd dug from her seldom-used baking pans.

Scolding him for being such a pest, she poured a cup of Kibbles for him, filled his water dish, another discarded pot, grabbed a Pepsi from the fridge, and headed back out. This business with Dal would have to wait.

But that didn't happen.

Headlights cut the darkness before she could turn around and start out of the drive. The glo-paint on the door of his unit announcing Grace County Sheriff gleamed when he barred her way and he was out of the car, his figure outlined by the lights from both vehicles.

Thank goodness he was safe, but if he was still so out of kilter…. He reached her door and she locked it, powered the window down. He gripped the open frame with both hands and leaned down to gaze in at her.

"You okay?" His voice not its usual firm tone.

"Yes. You?"

"I was worried about you. Wanted to make sure you were all right."

"Sort of the same, right back at you. What in the world happened?"

He grabbed the door handle. "Open up. I'm sorry, it's just that—"

"I have to go over to Tink's."

He straightened, hammered both hands against the window frame, then backed off. "Okay. See you later." Back stiff, he limped away.

"Dal, you sure you're okay?"

He lifted a hand and waved without turning around or looking back, climbed into the SUV, and backed up to let her out.

On the way down the lane, she glanced into the rearview mirror, but could only make out his silhouette. Something about his actions added to the fear she'd felt when he was so rough with her in the shower earlier. There wasn't time to worry about it now. What Tink had said was far more terrifying. Dal often came out of his funks without help and he'd never hurt her. She'd thought the same about Steve, until now.

At the B&B, she took the steps two at a time up the outside of the garage and tapped on Tink's door. She must've been standing inside, for it swung open instantly. Her friend stared at her with wide eyes, face as white as bleached flour. Without a word, she held out the newspaper article. Jessie took it, a black dread filling her like boiling water.

One glance told her what it was, what she'd been afraid of for a lot longer than this one terrible night. The headlines she'd never been able to put out of her mind. ***Undercover Cops Plan to Raid Drug Traffickers.*** It was the article that brought about the most damage, though. Revealing in detail how Steve and another undercover cop had infiltrated the Los Angeles Drug Underground, and put together a dawn raid to take down some top men.

Trouble was, the story came out the day before the planned raid. Members of the drug cartel hit Police Plaza, wounding eight cops and blowing the back out of the station house with C4. Steve was one of the wounded. Thankfully no one was killed.

Where had she gotten the information? Pillow talk while lying in bed with her lover, Steve Wainwright.

"Are you being blackmailed?" Tink's question interrupted her reverie, her tone sounding as if she already knew the answer. But no way she could. It was much worse than blackmail. Much.

Steve was here to kill her.

"Of course not." She didn't have to read the damnable thing. The story had haunted her ever since she'd written it and revealed facts that had almost gotten the man she loved and a few others killed.

"Then what's going on? What's this guy who has mysteriously disappeared doing with your story? How does he know Parker and Mac, and why do you look like you just swallowed a frog?"

Jessie shrugged and dropped into an ugly orange recliner. "What name did he register under?"

"John Brown, obviously an alias. Do you think he's a killer or something? Girlfriend, you can't get away with silence. Not with me. This man has been missing for several days now. He could well be dead, and you right in the middle of it. What if he turns up in a ditch somewhere? How will you explain this?"

"He's not dead. He's after me and he doesn't want to be found yet."

"You said you weren't being blackmailed." She waved the article around. "After you for this? Anything else?"

Jessie covered her eyes with one hand. What a mess. She was not that woman anymore. Out for only one thing and that was the story at all costs.

Damn you, Steve, what are you trying to do to me?

"Come on, Jess, you know you can trust me. Is this the past you'll never talk about?"

"Let me see those slips of paper you found."

Tink reached in the pocket of her uniform and pulled out several wadded sheets, placed them on the coffee table and smoothed out the wrinkles. "These were in the trash. See how he's made a tick mark after Rick Granger's name, but not the other three? And these places. Diamond House and Lover's Leap. What do you think these mean? Isn't Lover's Leap that place out on South Mountain where the bluff hangs out over a deep canyon? Where they say some woman jumped after her lover left her? Never heard of the Diamond House, though."

Jessie studied the list. Too much going on and she couldn't bring up a memory just out of reach. Annoyed, she tossed the sheaf of papers back onto the table. "Means nothing to me. This article, I wrote it while I was still in California working for the *LA Times*. It means nothing either."

Could Tink guess that was all a lie? Every single word?

Not yet ready to explain, she jumped up. "I gotta go. Been gone all day. I'm starving."

"I thought you and Dal were going dancing tonight. You look all dressed up for it."

"We were, but we got distracted." This she muttered while headed for the door. If she didn't hurry, Tink would have more to say about that.

Oddly enough, she didn't. Instead, she poked some more at the stranger. "Wait. What should I do about this missing guy?"

"Why ask me? You're the deputy. You're the one who wanted to handle this case."

"Aw, come on. You're so good at figuring this stuff out."

"Maybe, but I didn't take on the case."

"If Dal was working on it, you'd tag along and make suggestions right and left."

Jessie stepped out onto the small porch a story off the ground. "Yeah, but that's Dal and you're not as cute as him. Don't forget the Spacey's Labor Day cookout Monday."

Tink's objections followed her down the stairs and out to the Jeep but she ignored them.

All the way home she carried on an argument with herself. Should she run, should she stay and stand up to Steve? Either way, she was done for. The Diamond House and Lover's Leap. What had she told him about those two places that would lead him to add them to his list? Parker and Mac were understandable, but Rick Granger?

As a kid she'd run around with Bud Granger's son, Rick, but hadn't seen him since her parents had brought the family back for a visit when she was sixteen or seventeen. Bud was sometimes at the Redbird, but what the hell? Rick was all grown up and surely married by now. She had no idea where he might be. Had she ever told Steve Rick's name? She didn't think so.

Oh, dear God. Rick and the Diamond House. Now she remembered, but how could he know that? How could she have forgotten? Life sometimes did stuff to you, though. This was getting plumb scary.

Back home, she made as little noise as possible unlocking the door and getting inside. For all the good it did. Brad jumped around chuffing and wagging. The little scrapper wouldn't let anyone in the house without taking a bite out of them. All the same, she slipped the table drawer open, removed the .38 revolver, and went through the house holding it down at her side, with the safety off and her finger outside the trigger.

Dal had drilled that into her head when she insisted on obtaining a permit to carry the gun. Though she seldom carried it, she felt better with it in the drawer when she came home to an empty house. There was no one there, nor did it appear anyone had been.

Tink had spooked her, and she laid the revolver down on the kitchen table while searching around in the fridge for something to eat. A slice of leftover pizza from the day before looked a little the worse for wear, but she pulled a heavy cast iron skillet from the cabinet, turned the electric burner on high, and heated it enough to make the cheese soft.

Brad seemed to think he ought to share and she sat on the couch feeding him bites while she nibbled at it. The mutt ended up scarfing down the crust, which she didn't like anyway.

"You're gonna get fat living here with me." She scratched at his lopsided ear and he gazed up at her with canine adoration. He was getting cuter by the day.

And here I am talking to a dog. Don't even like dogs, but here he is.

Leaving Brad to his own devices, she fetched a pad and pen and wrote down the scribbles from what she was now convinced were notes made by Steve. She had to presume he was here for payback and act accordingly. The phone rang while she was contemplating the meaning of the items on the list.

It was Parker. "Can you come in tomorrow?"

"Sunday? Well, sure I guess. What's up?"

"I'll meet you there. Nine too early?"

For a moment she hesitated. What was going on?

"Uh, no, I guess not."

"See you then." He hung up before she could reply.

Now what the hell? He rarely went in on Sunday. Probably had some work to do before taking Monday off. It meant a long day Tuesday too. Obviously something important was going on. What if Steve had already made contact? And Parker was going to fire her ass. And worse, Steve would be waiting to apply the double whammy.

All night Dal woke over and over to stare into total darkness, finally rolled out of bed before daylight hit the valley. Mountains kept the rising sun hidden till nearly nine o'clock, so it was hard to judge the time. He picked up the alarm clock, squinted to read the hands. Six-thirty. Hell, the only time he ever got up this early was when Mac had a wild hair about sending him to the other side of the county for some reason. Last night's headache was gone, leaving his temples sore like someone had beat on him.

Perched on the edge of the bed, elbows propped on his knees, he contemplated his feet, one bare, the other in a sock. Surely he hadn't been on a bender the evening before. With thumb and middle finger he massaged the sides of his head. What had he done last night? Be damned if he could remember.

Best thing was to dress, have some coffee, and sit out on the back deck for a while, get his thoughts straight. While he accomplished that, his mind wandered about trying to put in order what had happened the day before. All he could draw was a blank. The last he remembered was making a date with Jess to go dancing for last night or the night before. Or maybe tonight. He didn't know. If they did go out he had no memory of it. Shit, he hoped he hadn't gotten drunk and made a fool of himself. After Leann died he did that for a while, but not lately.

In the bathroom, a glance in the mirror revealed his two black eyes and swollen nose. He remembered that well enough. No wonder his head hurt.

Back in the kitchen hot water hissed through Mr. Coffee and did its magic. He stood at the sliding glass doors and stared across the creek at a large patch of burned grass. A vision of something on fire... a car maybe. Nothing there now. Heat and pain slashed through him and was gone. What the hell? The coffee finished and he poured a cup, stepped out into the crisp air of early morning. Fall was coming on. Not his favorite season, though the turning of trees would soon cloak the mountains in a colorful patchwork quilt of gold, red, and orange. The mountains turning brown, everything going dormant, the leaves falling, reminded him of death, somehow.

A hazy movement across the creek dragged his attention away from the coffee. He peered over the rim of the mug. Nothing. Must've been mist rising into the warming air. But, no, again there was something hovering around the burnt area. A figure, maybe two. Blurring in and out of tendrils of fog.

Above the chattering of the water words reached out to him.

"I warned you about this. I tole you not to put him in there. They kin find blood and skin and hair jest like that. You damned idjit. Now git to it 'fore I kick yore butt."

His skin rippled as if he'd been struck and the cup fell to the deck floor, bounced, and sloshed the remaining coffee over his boots. A shower of violence wrapped around him, drove him to his knees. Hugging himself, he swayed. Collapsed under the agony of being struck over and over on the head and shoulders. Heat and the stench of smoke sucked away oxygen till he could barely breathe. Gagging, spewing, he crawled from the attack, scrambled to the other side of the deck and gasped for air.

Damn. He had gone back to the moment when two men had burned a car. The vehicle was gone, dragged to town to the garage where it would be kept untouched until he could get there and go over it. Or so he hoped. Maybe he'd already done that yesterday. He sure as hell didn't know. Despite the distress, he struggled to return to that moment, at least learn some names. But birds sang, a clean breeze blew, and the creek burbled. It was over, leaving him slumped against the corner posts of the deck.

So that was it. Two men, one beating the other and yelling at him, forcing him to set fire to the vehicle. Cursing him for leaving clues from what must've been a dead body, probably hauled either inside the car or in the trunk. Stupid fools didn't realize they were burning evidence within sight of a deputy's home. A deputy who could read violence long after it had occurred at a crime scene. A deputy who right now wished to hell he couldn't.

Was this connected to the severed leg and body they'd found? Why couldn't he remember anything but remnants of the previous day and night? Something had happened later. Maybe Jessie could tell him. She was always around crime scenes and she'd have been at this one as well.

Using both hands, he dragged himself to his feet, fumbled his cell from a pocket, and punched in her number. Waited impatiently while the phone rang and rang and rang.

She finally picked up, mumbled something unintelligible.

"Oh, sorry, Jess. I forgot what time it is."

"Dal. Honey, are you all right? I've been worried sick about you."

"Uh, as a matter of fact, that's why I called. Could you…? I mean, I know it's early."

"Give me thirty minutes. I'll be there." Dead air. She was gone.

He stared at the phone for a minute. What the hell had he done to get a response like that? And at seven o'clock in the morning too. Never knew how she was going to react. Guess that's what made her so damned intriguing. Another time she would've taken his head off for waking her.

While he waited he mopped the spilled coffee from the deck and poured himself another cup. She arrived twenty minutes later. He let her in. For an instant she studied his face, then reached up and cupped his jaw in the palm of her hand. Like always, her touch went through him like rainbows and thunderstorms. On tiptoes, she planted a feathery kiss on his mouth.

"You okay?"

Numbness crawled all over him. "What did I do? Last night."

"You don't remember? Dal, what's going on?"

"I'm not sure, but I'd appreciate it if you'd fill me in on what you know about yesterday."

"I'll need a cup of coffee first, and if you've got any stale honey buns. I'll take one of them too."

He nodded toward the coffee pot, fetched two of their favorite breakfast rolls while she poured a cup and refreshed his. Together they went out on the deck and sank into chairs next to each other.

The morning sky shone a robin's egg blue. Trees on the mountaintops glowed gold from the sunlight's first touch, but cool damp shadows still hung around their shoulders. He turned to gaze at her. The muss of her hair, the way her azure eyes sparked when she looked his way, that determined set of her chin. How had he found someone so attuned to his needs? Why did he keep pushing her away each time they drew close? What a damned fool he was. How often had he decided to tell her how he really felt, then let something stop him? He had no idea what.

"Dal, you're scaring me. Why are you looking at me like that?"

"After the fire, what happened?"

"You don't remember?"

"Would I ask you if I did? I woke up this morning and could not recall a thing about yesterday, hell, maybe the day before for all I know. It's as if I went on a quest."

"You remember finding the leg in Treman's hog pen after the fire?"

He nodded.

"And the rest of the body?"

"We dug it up." He frowned. "Did we go dancing last night?"

"No, we didn't get that far."

He smiled. "Don't tell me I forgot the good part."

"Well, at first it was good, but then you went…. Let's just say you ran into a barbed wire fence."

She was referring to the time soon after they first met when they had an argument over the danger of marijuana use by some people.

"I didn't, uh, do anything to hurt you, did I?"

"No, you were a bit rough with the lovemaking, but we've been there a few times before. You know I don't mind red-hot passion. It's just you were so upset or angry or both." She managed a wry grin but he couldn't respond in kind.

"And that was all it was? Nothing worse. Tell me the truth, if I ever hurt you I'd—"

"No, nothing like that. You acted really weird and that scared me, but not for myself. I was worried about you. You bailed out of here like your tail was on fire, and so I went home. Best to leave you alone, I've learned. You been having a hard time about Leann and that mess over in Dallas again?"

"No." He stared toward the burned patch across the creek. "It's something else, but whatever happened last night, I don't remember. This morning I had some visits with whoever did that." He gestured vaguely. "Everything sort of back to normal."

"Yesterday you did, too. In fact, it hit you pretty hard. You never said much about it, though. Figured you didn't learn anything useful."

He finished off his coffee and rose, reached down to take her hand and pull her to her feet. "Not till this morning. I think I'd better go talk to Mac while it's all fresh in my mind."

"Hey, that's not fair. Can't you tell me anything?"

"You know better than that. Mac will get a release to you soon as we know anything we can share."

She pretended to pout, but it was an obvious tease. He leaned down and kissed her and she kissed him back. Nice and sweet. Sometimes, in her company, all he wanted to do was grab her up and ride off into the sunset with her, just like in some corny cowboy movie.

This time, though, he sighed and grinned. "Gotta get to work."

"Hmm, me too. For some reason Parker wants to see me this morning." She appeared more worried than such a summons should cause. What was going on there?

"Everything okay?"

"What? Oh, I'm sure it is."

But she didn't look like it. Still, she touched him briefly, then left. Too bad. He wanted to question her further. But it would have to wait. He put his worries about the loss of time behind him. For the present.

7
CHAPTER

Before going to town to meet Parker, Jessie stopped by her cabin. When she unlocked the door Brad darted out. Poor dumb dog. Attaching himself to someone who did well to remember she might have to pee, let alone tending to his urges. He'd be better off to find himself someone else to love.

She shed the clothes she'd hurriedly donned when Dal called. In the shower. body wash in hand, she stood under the rain showerhead, one of the few recent additions to the cabin. It was nice when two showered together.

Dal looked terrible, like he'd been through hell and back. Whatever was going on, he might tell her in his own time, but it would do no good to push him about it. That didn't stop her from worrying about him, though. He had some weird hang-ups, but who wouldn't who had to deal with visits from spirits? Especially violent and angry ones. Being raised by grandparents in the old ways, the beliefs sometimes didn't mix well with modern ideas.

Later, dressed and headed out the door, she remembered the scribbled notes Tink had given her from the missing man, and dug them out of the pocket of the jeans she'd worn. Stuffing them in her backpack, she looped it over her shoulder. Maybe she could take some pictures or something on the way in. Parker liked to use unrelated photos on the front page when he didn't have any to go with breaking stories.

What if she took some shots of Treman's place, what remained after the fire? Maybe talk to him and get his thoughts on the entire affair. He might have some things to say that would make a good follow-up story while they waited for the press release. She glanced at her watch. There was time before Parker expected her.

At the highway she turned southwest instead of heading into town. By eight o'clock she was parked near his place. He'd found an old trailer somewhere and it now sat catty-wampus to a ramshackle shed that remained standing. No electric lines ran to the property from the main road. Some folks who lived in these hills deliberately shunned modern facilities of any kind. That she could almost understand, but why pile all their trash and discarded furniture around till the yard looked like the county dump? That she'd never get. According to what she'd heard, Treman hadn't been here but a few months. It probably looked like this when he moved in. Which begged the question, who would move into such a dump? Someone hiding, that's who.

With a great deal of care, she picked her way between a pile of old tires, two broken kitchen chairs and various cushions with the stuffing poking out. A skinny hound rose from beneath the trailer, issued one groan of a bark, and lay back down.

"What you want?"

She jumped and looked up to see Treman in the doorway. He wore blue work pants so dirty they'd stand alone and a ragged shirt with the sleeves ripped out to reveal well-muscled arms. His hair was badly in need of a wash and comb. A pair of gray eyes peered from the dirt-smudged features to pierce the air between them, sharp as a dagger.

"Good morning. I'm Jessie West with *The Observer*. Would you have some time to talk to me about all this?" She swept a hand around. "I'm sorry to drop in without calling, but—"

"Don't have a phone. Why don't you wait right there a minute?" He disappeared into the gloom behind him, returned with two steaming mugs of the blackest coffee she'd ever seen. He placed one cup on the rail of the stoop and carefully closed the door. Odd behavior, like he didn't want her to see inside.

"Let's sit out here where it's nice." He retrieved the mug and led her around the pile of tires to a wooden bench that resembled the pew from a church. Sitting on it would put their backs to the piles of trash. Handing her one of the coffees, he took a handkerchief from his pocket and wiped the seat for her, then lowered himself on the other end.

She dropped her pack between them, eased down, and took a timid sip of the hot brew. Hopefully, the heat would kill any germs. It was so strong it would have supported a spoon, and she shuddered.

He laughed in such a pleasant way that she studied him closely. Beneath the surface, he was not at all what he seemed, and this was an interesting turn of events. Though he spoke with an Ozark hill drawl, something about him appeared citified. That business with dusting the pew with his hanky.

"You're lucky you caught me. I'm off today unless I get called in."

How could he get called in if he had no phone? Another sip gave her courage to go on. "Where do you work?"

"At Greely Cannery. You say you're with *The Observer*? I don't want a story about me in the paper."

"Well, actually my story is about the fire and how you are reacting to it. Do you think someone set fire to your house, and if so, why would anyone do that?"

"Some folk are naturally turned wrong is all." Those sharp eyes, gleaming like slate under water, stared at her over the rim of his mug and he gulped two or three swallows. "Can't think of anyone who'd be that pissed at me, though a feller never knows. Please don't print that."

"Did you know the man who was killed?"

"You mean the man whose leg was dug up out of my hog pen? Wouldn't know if I did by jest looking at his foot. Did they find the rest of him yet?"

"Yes, weren't you aware they were out there digging up his body?" She pointed toward the edge of the woods where yellow crime scene tape hung around trees. That would be a good camera shot. She took the Nikon from her pack and snapped a quick dozen angles of the view.

He remained silent until she was finished, like his talking might interrupt her concentration. Then he spoke. "Must've been when I was at work. Or off getting this trailer hauled out here. Done that yesterday. Didn't want to sleep in that shack any longer than I had to." Another slurp. "Who was he?"

"I don't think they've identified him yet. No one seems to be missing, so he must not be from here." She lifted the camera and centered him through the lens. "Would you mind?"

"Afraid I do mind." He blocked his face with a surprisingly clean hand, the nails well-trimmed.

She put the camera down on the bench, said nothing.

"Hard to get too het up about him without knowing who he is."

A gust of wind carried the lingering scent of burned wood and decomp, like it had hung around just long enough to remind them what had happened out here.

Secretive too. Very strange. "Were you home when the fire started?"

"No'm. I was at work. I'm there much of the time. I keep their electronics running."

She stared at him. Must've misheard what he said. "Sorry, did you say electronics?"

"Yes'm. Somehow comes natural to me, understanding how all those components work. What keeps 'em running. One place I worked I fixed stuff when it broke till they took notice and run some tests." He shrugged, favored her with that expressive grin. "Guess I passed."

White teeth. Hadn't they ought to be sort of stained or something? An alarm went off in her head. This guy was not who or what he pretended to be. But if not, who was he?

A cell phone rang and he dug in his pocket, pulled out the latest in iPhone technology and spoke his name. Listened for a while, then nodded. "Sure, tell Leroy not to throw a hissy fit. Have him set the blue box breakers, then reboot the main computer and I'll get there soon as I can." He slipped the cell phone back into his pocket. "Better git. They pay me over a thousand a week to keep them gadgets running. Welcome to come back if you want." He touched his forehead with a two-finger salute.

All she could do was stare at him. He said he didn't have a phone. What did he call that thing he carried in his pocket? Anticipating her curiosity, he grinned. "It don't belong to me. Hate the things, but they make me carry one to keep in touch. You'll have to come back another time."

"I will definitely do that. I'd like to know more about you, if you wouldn't mind. Off the record of course." A thousand a week was a lot of money for Cedarton. He was probably lying about that. Trying to impress her, but that was way out of character. Why the deception then? His reply to her request only served to confuse her further.

"I expect you would. Sometimes I'd like to know more about me as well. If you'll excuse me I have to go now."

Surely he wasn't going to work looking like that. She picked up her pack, turned in time to see him unbuttoning his shirt on the way inside the trailer. The shirt slipped off his muscular back. From inside sunlight gleamed on something that looked strangely like a computer screen, but the door slammed before she could get a good look. Well, at least he was going to change clothes, and hopefully take a bath. How he would accomplish that she wasn't sure. Wow, the phone wasn't his only well-hidden secret.

A savant living in the woods. What a story that could make, if she could talk him into it. That is if he wasn't lying about the job. He did have the iPhone and knew how to use it. She spared the trailer another quick glance, hoping to see more, but all was silent. If she didn't have to meet Parker she'd hang around, see if she might learn more about this mysterious Treman whatever his name was. Like how in heck did he manage to take a bath without running water or electricity?

Meanwhile, she had to get to town and find out what Parker wanted.

She parked in front of the newspaper office beside a car she didn't recognize. On the bumper was a sticker for a local car rental place. Her heart jumped into her throat. Steve? Hunting her down.

Oh, cool it, for God's sake. How would he have found her, even if he was really here looking? Still, her hand trembled when she opened the door and stepped inside. No one at the front desk, but it was Sunday, and technically they weren't open for business, though when Parker was here he left the place unlocked. Liked to have people drop in just to talk.

From his office came the hum of low conversation. She deposited the pack on her desk, stuck her head inside his door, which he never closed, and announced her presence.

With a knot of fear in her throat she glanced at the back of the visitor's head. Neat blond hair. Broad shoulders above the chair back. Could easily be Steve. She hadn't seen him in nearly four years, but still-....

The man glanced at her. Nope, not Steve.

"I'll be right with you, Jessie." Parker turned back to his visitor. "Sorry to interrupt. Go on."

Properly dismissed, she backed out of the room, relief so strong her head swam. Sitting at her desk, she couldn't help but eavesdrop on their conversation. Well, actually, she would've moved closer if she couldn't hear them. That's just the way people in her profession were. Always had to know everything that went on, even if it was none of her business. So she listened.

And what she heard nearly knocked her out of the chair.

Still troubled by his loss of memory on the previous day, Dal drove into Cedarton at nine o'clock to catch the sheriff before he took off on his daily meanderings. Mac liked to spend at least one day each week driving the entire county, just "keeping an eagle eye on my county," as he put it. This was that day. Labor Day Weekend was no exception for the law. He left after church let out, when many people were eating dinner out and paying visits. He'd only begun the habit last year after two murders and all the hoopla surrounding stolen diamonds. He decided he needed to keep a better eye on Grace County and its population. Checking for suspicious goings on, like meth cooking, cult gatherings, anything that didn't set right. Previously he'd relied on deputies to spot something out of the ordinary, or deal with complaints during their weekly shifts. But those two murders last year just plain got under his skin in a big way.

The parking lot behind the station wasn't crowded, but that wasn't unusual, since there were ten slots back there, and deputies off duty took their units home with them. He snagged the slot right next to Mac's SUV, locked the vehicle, a new regulation after Aidan Smith from out on Sugar Mountain had come along and stolen one of the unlocked units, taken it for a joy ride and left it parked on the overflowing spillway at the lake. As punishment the boy was put to work detailing and washing all six of the deputies' cars, plus Dal's and the sheriff's, weekly for three months. The kid never did reveal how he managed to start the car without a key. It was supposedly not possible.

Dal went in search of Mac, who wasn't in his office. He wanted to get his investigative report on tape before anything else came up. Or his mind forgot it. They were usually on a murder site together and Mac taped his experiences for the record.

The sheriff was in the tiny kitchen making a pot of coffee. "Tink off today or did you just get tired of weak coffee?"

"Girl called in sick this morning. Odd for her. She never misses a day and it is her week to pull Sunday shift. Gonna need somebody to sit at the desk and help with bookings. Ain't too worried. Probably won't have any. Have to pull Jeff, I reckon. What's up?"

"Had some information about who burned the car. Thought you'd want it recorded."

Mac nodded. After the coffee made and they each had a cup, Dal followed Mac into the interrogation room where he could most easily record what he'd experienced this morning out on his deck. When they finished, Dal told Mac he was going back out to the two crime scenes.

"I don't expect much from the spirit of a leg, but the gravesite might yield something. You didn't come up with anyone missing yet, did you?"

Mac scratched under the back of his Stetson. "Nope. Sent a statewide BOLO out this morning. Maybe we'll get something from that."

"I'll check in later, then."

Mac nodded and left to drive his weekly county route.

Out at Treman's, Dal cruised past the trailer and parked near the burial site. Sure didn't take Treman long to get himself another place to live. Though that little thing didn't look like much, it was an improvement over hunkering in a damn shack with wide cracks in the walls. Come winter, the trailer would be warmer. Looked like a small generator out back of the place. Musta got tired of living without electric.

There was something about Treman, who had moved into the run-down farm about six months ago, that had always puzzled Dal. Too bad he couldn't figure out what it was. The man was off-putting, was the only thing he could come up with. He'd never gotten close enough to him to actually probe his mind a bit.

He spent some time pacing around the spot where the leg had appeared out of the fire like a phoenix rising. A more careful search of the ground yielded nothing, but he wasn't surprised. Firemen's boots and tons of water tended to wipe out what clues there might have been.

Since Treman's vehicle, a beat-up Nissan pickup of indeterminate color, was nowhere to be seen, he didn't bother to knock on the trailer door, but hiked across the pasture to the wooded area and the grave of the unfortunate man. Squatted beside the dig, he prepared himself for the worst, but the woods remained devoid of any spirits.

Grasshoppers fled his path through the dried out grass, their buzzing filling the otherwise quiet air. The man had not been killed in a fit of rage. Remnants of that plus terror would have clung to the body, been deposited in the soil. At least enough for Dal to sense. Maybe the victim had been passed out prior to the murder. Maybe drugged by someone he knew. That would leave no trace for Dal to pick up on.

After a while, with nothing else showing, he hiked back to the car and drove in to see Doc at the mortuary. He would still have the body, but not for long. Dal wanted another look at it.

Doc led him into the morose silence of the morgue. From the chapel in the next room, a voice was raised in preaching, backed by soft organ music. Someone's funeral. Must be old Mrs. Cooper's, who had passed a couple of days ago. He wasn't particularly comfortable in these surroundings. It wasn't the service so much as the spirit of poor dead Clementine Cooper, remarking on the funeral that bothered him. She wasn't at all pleased with the choice of music and very unhappy with her son's wife.

"The slut would wear bright red to celebrate my demise." Her ancient voice declared that with some vigor.

Damned clear he hadn't lost the ability to hear spirits, in spite of his experiences of the night before. He tamped down her complaints to concentrate on the body Doc uncovered. A body that now had a few stern words for his killer or killers.

It was more disgust than fear or fury that assaulted Dal when the body bag unzipped to reveal the dead man. "Never thought I'd go this-a-way. Drinking was supposed to be my undoing. Some joke, sticking my poor leg in all that hog shit. If I wasn't dead I'd blow that idjit's brains out."

Not quite sure he understood what was going on with this one, Dal shook his head. Stared down at the peaceful countenance of the dead man.

"Doc, what kind of saw you think was used to sever this leg?"

"Well, I took a cursory look. Figgered the boys down in Little Rock would want to come back with an idea. It's fairly ragged, no hesitation that I can see, just whap, hacked right through it. Done postmortem. Why in thunder, who knows? I'd say some kind of handsaw by someone accustomed to using one, but I doubt I could give you the brand name." His eyes twinkled with the final comment. "Not like them 'ol boys on the TV."

"Okay, I think we're fairly safe to say someone went to a great deal of trouble to make sure we found at least the foot. Someone sending a definite message. To my way of thinking it was something like 'this is what you get for running.' Took two men to clean up afterward."

Doc angled a curious glance at Dal. "Two?"

"At least when it came to disposing of the body."

"So you're not getting any more than that from your magic act? Is your mojo out of whack?"

"So far what I know doesn't make sense, but I'll keep working at it."

"You know, boy, there's usually a good reason to cover something up. And this is a clear case of that. Freezing the amputated limb, hiding the body. Confusing as hell, I'd say."

"Maybe they were up to no good at the time."

"Wouldn't surprise me."

"Well, if I don't get too busy, I'll look into it some more, see if I can find out what they might've been doing."

Doc laughed along with Dal, at the idea he might be too busy to investigate further. "When you get a spare minute you do that, and let me know what you find out."

Dal nodded and said goodbye. The leg and body being buried near Treman's place was definitely done for a reason, and he decided to check that out some more before bringing it up. Truth was, he'd like to learn more about the man who had mysteriously appeared earlier that year and moved into the old shack that had been empty for years. No one seemed to know who he was and it was about time someone found out.

Stiff as a board at her desk, hands clasped in her lap, Jess waited impatiently for the visitor to leave. As soon as the door closed behind the man she popped into Parker's office.

"Who was that?"

With a baffled expression he glanced up from a story he was editing for the paper. "Who?"

"The guy who just left?"

"Oh, uh, his card's there on my desk. A detective from out west somewhere. Why?"

She searched through the scattered papers and came up with the card. "Mark Burnside, LVPD? Las Vegas?"

"I think so." Parker put down his blue pencil and twined fingers under his chin. "Wait, he's looking for your Steve, isn't he?"

"He said Steve Wainwright, didn't he?"

"You seem to know." He gave her a wry grin. "Eavesdropping again?"

"It's what I do. This man is wanted for assault and second degree murder? Is he sure he has the right man?"

"What's going on? Could this be your Steve? Thought he was a cop."

"He was, but not anymore. Might be him, though." She barely whispered the admission, not sure if she should go ahead and tell Parker about the note Tink had found and her own suspicions. He already knew her history, why not get it all out? Besides, if Steve had fled whatever crimes he'd committed and come here, someone ought to know.

"There's no way it could be someone else by the same name. Not in a million years would a coincidence like that occur. Too bizarre. Steve turning to crime is also pretty bizarre. Yet he did all but threaten to kill me."

Parker pinned her with one of his dark-eyed stares that dared her to be evasive or lie. "Same guy? Are you sure?"

"Steve Wainwright? Same name. No way it can be a coincidence."

"Stranger things have happened."

"Not to me." She dug the threatening note from her pocket.

He read it, glanced up. "This isn't signed."

"It's from Steve. Who else would it be? And it's the second note I've received. The first one came here. You handed it to me your very own self."

"But I didn't read it. It was a threat too? Well, let's see just who might be angry with you. There's that piece you wrote last month about the baby that died because the ambulance went to the wrong house. And the threat from the fellow who took a shot at a helicopter flying low over his marijuana patch and you wrote about his arrest. Didn't he accost you in the parking lot at Walmart and tell you to keep your fucking nose out of his fucking business, to quote him exactly? Oh, and don't forget the guy who hit you over the head with his notebook at the school board meeting and told you to mind your own business. Shall I go on?"

"So I've made some enemies. Still, first the notes, then some guy comes in asking about Steve. Same name."

"I think you're making too much of this, but if you're scared, stay in town with Tink for a week or two while they get this all cleared up.

They'll find this guy and it won't be your Steve." He raised his eyebrows. "Or you can come stay with me."

"Oh, great. Just how would that look? No, I'm not afraid to stay in my own home. After all, I now have a gun and a dog. That's double protection if ever I saw it. Now, why did you call and ask me to come in today?"

"Oh, yeah. I nearly forgot. Do you know anything about a man missing from the bed and breakfast?"

She widened her eyes to look innocent. "Someone else missing too?"

"Don't give me that. I know you too well for it to work."

Not sure just how much he knew, she would only admit to what he said aloud. "Okay, I heard something about it. How did you find out?"

"I was at the Red Bird for supper last night and Bob and Betsey Black were there. Having a night out, I guess. Surely she must get tired of feeding folks at the B&B. Said everyone went to Fayetteville to attend a show at Walton Arts Center and eat out over there."

"And so?"

"And so, I found out that one of their guests has been missing for three days. Were you planning on doing a story on that or what?"

"Well, no. Not yet. You're never going to believe this."

"Try me."

"I think... I mean, it's complicated. The guy is registered as John Brown and Tink thinks he may be a hit man."

"She what?" He almost shot out of his chair. "Good Lord. What does Mac say?"

Eyes gazing at the floor, she murmured, "He doesn't know." She didn't dare meet his glare with that reply.

"So, we have a deputy investigating a crime and the sheriff doesn't know, and a reporter not writing the story and her boss doesn't know.

Hit men, missing men, a dead body minus a foot. Hell, what's going on around here anyway? Tell me. Is there any chance this missing person is the dead guy they dug up out at Treman's?"

"I don't think so. I think he's Steve. The guy from the B&B, that is." While he spluttered, she hurried to explain. "If you'd just look at the lists Tink found stuffed in a drawer in his room, you'd see why I think that."

He stared at her and she began to twist around in the chair. "Well?"

"Well, what?" She twisted some more.

"Where are these lists? I'd like to take a look at them."

She leaped up, went to her desk, and dug them from her backpack where she'd stuffed them when she changed clothes. Dropping the wad on his desk, she sank back into the chair before her shaking legs dumped her there.

While he read she allowed her gaze to roam around the room, from last year's calendar still on the wall to a stack of horse breeding magazines piled in the corner and on past shelves stuffed with old newspapers.

Parker cleared his throat and she looked back at him. "What's this Diamond House and Lover's Leap reference? Didn't you write stories about those places?"

"Yes, and I also told Steve about them when I was with him. When I was young well, Rick Granger and I, uh, played at the Diamond House and if you remember it was back then that the woman jumped off Lover's Leap. I told him about that too. How would just anyone from out of town know about those two things? It's Steve. He's here and he's threatened me."

For some reason she held back telling him the full truth about the Diamond House. He probably figured that out on his own.

"Someone could've read your more recent stories about the two places."

"I don't think so."

Parker studied the notes again. "Why has he checked off Rick Granger? We usually do that when something's been taken care of."

"I know. But Rick hasn't lived here in years. Last I knew about him, he was in Virginia going to law school. Or was it North Carolina? I can't remember now."

"You knew him? So this list is all people you have a close connection with. And this Rick?" He raised his eyebrows and held her with a stare.

Guess she'd better come clean. "We were just kids, but he… he was the first boy I made love with and it happened at the Diamond House."

"Okay, you're about to convince me. But let's do what ought to be done and talk to Sheriff Richards about this. Let him begin an investigation. Tink is not an investigator, she's a jailer. And it's beginning to sound like this entire mess is related."

"I know, but she wants to prove she can solve the missing man."

"Surely you realize that if this is all related that's dangerous for both her and you."

"I guess so."

"Okay, then. Call Mac, tell him about it, and give these lists to him. Does he know about what happened out in California?"

"No. I can't tell him. He'll be so disappointed in me. If it comes out I'll have to move somewhere else. Dal doesn't know either, so please can't you keep it quiet?"

"I suppose so. You should tell him. But don't be ridiculous about moving. If everyone in this business who made a mistake had to run away there'd be no newspapers or reporters."

"Men were shot, some badly."

"You did not shoot them. My God, when the story broke, it was their responsibility to cancel the scheduled raid. They went right ahead with it, so sure they could handle whatever repercussions there might be. Granted you shouldn't have written the story, but they should've at least altered their plans."

"So if I'd been working for you then, you wouldn't have printed the story after I wrote it?"

He tapped his pencil in a rat-tat-tat on his desk, then squinted up at her. "I'm not really sure. I'd like to think I would've held it back till after the raid."

Unconvinced, but having no further argument, she slumped in the chair.

Parker slapped the desk top and she flinched. "But that's behind you and done. Now, go find Tink, and you and her get hold of Mac, let him handle this. Then let's all go home and have a nice holiday weekend, or at least what's left of it."

She hesitated in the doorway. "Parker, do you know that Treman guy?"

"Not really. Heard a bit about him. Why?"

"I don't think he's exactly who he pretends to be."

"Well, then, you're a reporter, check him out. Isn't that where they found that dead guy?"

"Uh-huh."

"Good Lord. This is more confusing than a wad of knotted fishing line. Use your charms on your boyfriend and see what you can find out."

"I went out there to interview this Treman and he wouldn't let me take his picture, though he was polite enough. Almost too much so. And besides he's way too good looking under all the dirt, and a bit too smart for the way he dresses and lives. Claims he's an electronics expert."

"Sounds like a story to me. Just be careful. Don't forget a body was found at his place. What does your deputy friend think?"

"I'm not sure. Dal isn't thinking real good right now, and I'm not sure what's up with him."

"Well, you take care. See you Tuesday. Have a good day off."

Because of Parker's admonishments she drove by Tink's to straighten out that misunderstanding. Her car was there, but no one answered the door. Using her key she opened the door. The main room was a mess, and she backed out quietly, afraid someone might still be in there.

Back in the Jeep, she pulled out her phone and called Mac and Dal. Something terrible must have happened to Tink.

8
CHAPTER

Dal took Jessie's call while at the Red Bird, the best place to learn more about Treman, including a last name which he either hadn't heard or didn't remember. Right away he learned it was Ledger.

"You know, like that movie feller who died?" This from Fudge, which surprised Dal. The man didn't act like a movie fan. Fudge smiled at Dal's puzzled expression. "The wife rents stacks of movies and it pays to sit up and watch 'em with her, and then talk about every one of 'em afterwards, if you know what I mean."

Theron, who sat with them, eating apple pie and drinking coffee, laughed and nodded. "Do know. 'Deed I do."

 When Dal's phone buzzed Jessie's name came up and he rose. "'Scuse me, I'm going outside to take this. Be right back." By the time he listened to her frantic report about finding Tink's apartment tossed and her car in the drive but no Tink, he was in his SUV and flooring it, siren blaring.

She waited at the bottom of the stairs that led to her friend's apartment over the triple-car garage. When he bailed out she ran to meet him. "I knew better than to go in."

He slipped his .45 from its thigh holster. "You wait here, you hear me? Did you get Mac?"

"Yes, but he's clear on the other side of the county."

"Okay. Stay here."

He moved silently up the stairs, hugging the side of the building, back against the clapboards. With his left hand he turned the knob, shoved the door open, and darted inside, his gut warning that a bullet could find him. After sweeping the small apartment and checking the closets, he returned to the living room, heart slowing to a normal rhythm.

The place was a mess, and though Tink had a reputation for being a lazy housekeeper, she couldn't possibly be this bad.

Whatever they were looking for they hadn't found it. Disappointment hung in the room for him to pick up on. Could be why they took her with them, though he didn't sense her fear. Right now he didn't trust his perceptions.

Footsteps sounded on the stairs. He swung around, finger off the trigger to point the weapon, though he sensed no danger. "Step inside, hands where I can see them."

"It's us, Dal. Me and Tink. She was at a neighbors."

The small deputy bounced in right behind Jess. "I didn't lock up cause I was only running down to borrow an egg to make some cookies. We got to talking." She halted. "Oh, my Lord."

Dal holstered the .45. "Would you check around, easy like? See if you notice anything missing."

She poked here and there for a while. "Not in here. What about the other rooms?"

"They hit them all. It's such a mess you may not be able to tell if anything is gone. Just check important stuff."

In a few minutes she returned, eyes wide. "If they took anything I can't tell. My MP3, the bedroom TV, a few pieces of good jewelry. All there."

Jess pulled Tink into the corner, whispered something to her.

"What?" He didn't intend to sound so grouchy, but what was their big secret?

"Nothing." Both women spoke in unison.

"Then what are you whispering about?"

"Tell him, Tink, or I will."

"Tell me what? Come on, ladies. We've got a dead man. This is no time to play games. Jess?"

"Okay. She has been investigating the disappearance of a man staying here at the B&B. She found some things in his room."

"But I gave them to Jess, so they couldn't have found them here."

He held out a hand toward Jess. "Could be what they were looking for. Give 'em here."

"I can't."

"What do you mean, you can't?"

"I left them in my desk at the office. They're nothing but some lists that don't make any sense." She glared at her friend.

"Is that true, Tinker?"

"Uh, yes."

"So, let's go get 'em."

"The office is closed. Parker went home."

"Jess, what's going on here? You know better than to take evidence from a crime scene." He clasped her arm, stared into her face. "I know you have a key to the newspaper office."

Big fat tears spilled down her cheeks and she pulled out of his grip. "It's none of your business. It's private. And it's not a crime scene anyway."

"Something Tinker found in a stranger's room who has mysteriously disappeared is private to you, so important you're crying, and it's none of my business?"

"Yes, that's exactly true. It has nothing to do with the dead body." She wiped her face with both hands.

"We have a missing man. You're saying it has nothing to do with him either." It wasn't like Jess to cry even when cornered. Why wasn't she fighting back?

"But… well, it has nothing to do with you, either. Tinker is working the case." Again, the tears. Damn if he could deal with a woman who cried, especially this one.

"Jess, please stop crying. I'm trying to help you out here, but it's getting pretty hard to do. Let's just get this cleared up before things get any worse. When Mac comes back, he's gonna have a walleyed fit if you're holding something back. Not to mention what he'll do when he finds out Tink has been 'working a case.' And to tell you the truth, I'm getting close to it myself. Believe me, my day has not gone very well so far, and the two of you are not making it any easier."

Jess held her hands out, wrists together. "Then I guess you're just going to have to arrest me, 'cause what I have is my private property and none of your business. Slap on the cuffs and take me in. That's all I have to say."

"Ah, dammit, Jess. I'm not going to slap on the cuffs and take you in. Come on, let's lock this place up and I'll get someone to come in and fingerprint it. Show me the room where this missing man is—was staying and let's lock it up too. These two are officially crime scenes till we get this sorted out. Come on, ladies. Tink, if you need some things, go get them, but don't touch anything in this room. We'll wait for you."

"Where am I going? To jail?"

"No, you're going home with Jess. Now get a move on before I change my mind. I'll leave it to Mac to sort out. Just don't leave town." He tried out a grin, but it didn't happen.

"But—"

"Now." He pointed at her and she scurried into the other room.

Out on the balcony, he touched Jess on the shoulder. "What's going on here, honey?"

"I can't tell you. You'll hate me."

He put an arm around her shoulder, pulled her close. "There's no way I could hate you."

She shuddered. "Oh, yes there is. Believe me, there is."

For a while he stared out across the yard and continued to hold her. What the hell had she got herself mixed up in? A breeze swayed limbs of the huge maple trees, sending shadows dancing across the sunlit lawn. A peaceful late summer afternoon. Too bad he didn't feel that way inside. There might be something she could say that would make him, if not hate her, at least walk away from her. What could these two be hiding? He despised secrets, and most especially between him and someone he cared for. It always reminded him of the terrible secrets Leann had kept, secrets that had caused her death.

He'd tried so hard not to care for Jess, but that hadn't worked out too well. Now he dreaded what he might learn when she finally told him the truth. Dammit, he should've known better than to get attached to her.

A vibration against his chest dragged him away from his musings and he pulled thephone from his pocket. Jess went inside.

"Dal? This is Doc. I think I know who our dead guy is. The one without a leg."

"The only one we have at present?"

"That one."

"Okay. When do you plan on telling me?"

Laughter. "Thought you'd want to know how I found out first. Sort of proud of myself over that."

Dal sighed. You couldn't stop Doc once he got started, so he played along. "I'll bite. How'd you find out?"

"On my computer. You see, there's a website where people who are looking for lost relatives or friends can list them with a picture. I thought, what the hell? So I checked it out and sure enough there was our friend. A picture and the description that includes a birthmark I found on his right hip. His name is Marcus Woods and he's been missing for six months. His wife is looking for him. They live in Wichita."

"Well, I'll be damned, Doc. That's a good bit of detecting. Mac will want to notify them and the Wichita Police Department. Could you text me the contact information?"

"Text? Hell, I don't know how to do that. Got me one of these flip phones. You got an email address for Mac?"

"Send it to me at bear ninety-nine at grace dep dot com."

"Oh, hell yes. Now that's funny."

"What's funny?"

"Never you mind. You know exactly what I mean."

Dal couldn't help but chuckle. "Thanks, Doc. Appreciate you." He clicked off just as Jess walked out with a duffle bag, followed by Tink with another bag.

You'd think she was going on a month-long vacation. He led them down the stairs without comment, still fuming over Jess's refusal to tell him what was going on between her and Tink.

"Where's this missing guy's room? Just you, deputy. Jess, you wait in your vehicle."

A frown creased her forehead, but she obeyed, marching away from him with long, angry strides.

He followed Tink inside the B&B, up a wide flight of carpeted stairs along a hall overlooking the foyer. She opened a door halfway down on the left. When she started inside he took her shoulder and held her back.

"You wait out here till I check out the room. Where did you find these private things of Jess's?"

Tink flushed and shrugged.

"Oh, so that's the way it is. You know you could lose your job over this if you keep covering up evidence. I know Jess wouldn't want that to happen."

"Don't make me tell you. Ask her, and if she agrees, fine. She's my best friend."

He went inside, checked out the small room and bath, then bent to go through a trash container. There weren't many places to look and he finished quickly. The room had been thoroughly cleaned out. He stepped into the hallway. "Where's Betsey?"

"Probably in the kitchen."

"I want to ask her a couple of questions. Why don't you go on out and wait with Jess?"

She nodded and headed for the stairs.

"And Tink—don't go anywhere. This guy could be laying hurt or dead somewhere and there might be a way to find him from what you two are withholding."

"No, there's not."

"And you're willing to bet your job on that?"

Again, she refused to answer him.

"Okay."

He found Betsey in the immaculate yellow and white kitchen, surrounded by the fragrance of cinnamon and baking bread. She was a pretty, plump woman, whose sweet face now appeared worried. He introduced himself.

"Could you tell me if you cleaned the room?"

"No, I thought about it, but decided he might return. Then I thought if something bad had happened you'd want it left the way it was. What do you think?"

"I think you're a very smart lady, ma'am." He smiled at her and she smiled back, her dark intelligent eyes sparkling. "We're going to investigate this. As soon as we finish fingerprinting the room, it'll be okay for you to rent it out."

"That's a relief. I appreciate it. Thank you."

He told her goodbye and went outside to join the two women, sorting through his mind for something to say to change Jess's mind. She was stubborn, but he couldn't see putting her in jail. Mac wouldn't like that at all.

After Tink crawled in her car, Dal leaned down into the open window of the Jeep. "Know anyone by the name of Marcus Woods?"

"Nope. Who is he? Not the guy who's missing from the B&B."

"No, but he is our dead guy. And you know what you said about Treman? Well, I think you're right. There's something suspicious going on with him, though your assessment that he might be a hired killer is a bit over the top. I'm going to try to find out some more about him. Funny, we've got three mysterious men in town. I think you know more about one of them than you're letting on. We will get to the bottom of this, and you'd do better to tell me what you know before we do."

She leaned toward him, kissed his cheek. "Maybe he's an undercover cop, if that helps any. And he could be looking for this other guy who may be a hired killer." With a grimace she started the Jeep.

Nearly choking on her ridiculous suggestion, he ducked out of the window and watched the two of them drive away. An undercover cop? Why did she think that? Six months was a long time to remain under in a place like Cedarton, and for what? Surely not worth it to catch a few meth dealers. A hired killer? Where did she get that idea? Did she know something and this was her way of cluing him in? Or was she just trying to steer him away from this missing guy and the unknown items Tink had found at the B&B?

At the stop sign for Highway 23 Jess pulled up next to Tink and signaled her to roll down her window. She did.

"Let's go get a pizza and rent a movie to take out to the house."

Tink nodded. "Lead the way."

At Mike's Pizza Place, they sat in a booth waiting for their pizza.

"Are we going by the paper to get those lists?" Tink fiddled with the napkin holder, lining it up precisely with a container of hot pepper flakes on the center of the table.

"Don't have to. I have them in my backpack."

"You lied."

"No shit. Besides, what'd you want me to do, let him have them?"

"You gonna explain to me why they're so important?"

Jessie frowned and stared down at the table.

"What's going on? We been friends since you came here. This can't be so bad it'll break us up. Or you and Dal, for that matter."

"It's bad. Really bad. Especially for Dal and me."

"Then if you can't tell me, you ought to tell someone so they can help you out. You don't need to be carrying bad stuff around all by yourself."

"I have told someone, so you don't need to worry about that. It's hard to tell just anyone. Even harder to confess to someone who's trusted me."

"And so that's why you don't want Dal to know. You love him. And me, why can't you tell me? I'm your best friend."

"He'll hate me. So will you." Hot tears streaked her cheeks. She used a napkin to wipe them away, steadied herself. Dammit, she wanted to stop crying and figure this out.

The young man behind the counter called their number and they both stood. Tink took the pizza box and handed over a bill. Outside, Jess chose a movie from Red Box, stuck it in her backpack, and they went to their respective cars. While they were inside the sun had disappeared below the horizon. A fingernail moon hung in the western sky. Evenings were warm with a tinge of fall. It was like sensing something one couldn't quite place. A look, a smell, a feeling. Funny how you could taste fall by taking a breath. That was sort of true about danger, too.

By the time they reached her cabin, dusk had chased daylight down the small valley. Tink trotted from her car up onto the lighted porch and hunched away from the creeping shadows, waiting for Jess to unlock the door and let them in. A lamp burned on the table just inside, the same table that contained the .38 Jessie had purchased the previous year after she was shot.

She still had nightmares about that evening, entering the dark house, hearing the shot but remembering nothing else till she awoke in the hospital, Dal at her bedside looking like he'd been run over by a truck. Shaking off the memory, she pulled open the drawer, took out the revolver, and held the thing down at her side.

"Stay right here till I look around."

Tink uttered a frightened squeak. "Did you see someone?" Her whisper sounded loud in the quiet room.

"Nope. Just being careful. Wait right there."

Tink nodded. Not once had she reached for her own gun, holstered at her side. Jessie couldn't remember her ever using it since they'd met. Mac might be right about her not being suited for the field.

No one hid in the house, nor was there any sign someone might have been there. Jessie put the gun back in the drawer. Tink sat on the couch, pizza box open on the coffee table. Its fragrance filled the small room.

"Can I get plates and drinks out now?"

"Yes, I'll help."

For a while neither said anything. They each ate their first slice before Tink spoke.

"My brother shot a man once. He was stealing some of our cows and my brother went around the far corner of the barn. There the fool was, trying to make off with two cows and a steer."

"Did he kill him?"

"Nah, almost missed him he was so scared, but caught him high in the shoulder. Did you ever shoot someone, Jess?'

"Heavens no. What makes you think that?"

"Well, it must be pretty bad if you can't tell anyone about it. And the worst thing I could think of was that."

"I'm afraid there are worse things. Like betrayal."

From out of nowhere for no reason she could fathom, a tear escaped the corner of her eye and she swiped it away. This bawling every whip-stitch was getting old. Somehow, she had to stop. But she wasn't sure she knew how to do that. Not without coming clean in order to erase the painful guilt from her system. And if she did that she would lose Dal. She might as well let Steve do as he wanted because losing the man she loved was not an option.

To shut up before something slipped out, she grabbed another slice of pizza and took a big bite.

Tink gave her one of her stern looks. "Okay, but why don't we look at those lists again, try to figure out what they mean?"

Swallowing, Jess grabbed up the movie. "I'd rather watch the movie, take our minds off the fact that we may be in jail this time tomorrow."

"I may be, but neither Mac or Dal would put you in the slammer. You they love."

Jessie slipped the movie into the player, picked up the remote and plopped back down on the couch. "This one should be good. Bradley Cooper. Almost as sexy as Brad Pitt."

In the corner, the ugly little pit bull barked upon hearing his name.

"Oh, yum." Tink stared at Jessie, snickered, then laughed so hard she hugged her stomach, tried to speak, but couldn't get anything out. Jessie joined her because it was hard not to, though she had no idea why Tink was laughing. Finally, Tink wound down, pointed across the room at the dog. "You... I get it. He's a pit bull and you named him Brad. Brad Pitt." She broke apart again.

"About time you figured it out."

"Well, I can't help it. Jokes don't always make sense to me."

Halfway through the movie Jessie threw a bag of popcorn in the microwave and they sat together on the couch washing down the snack with icy cans of Pepsi and admiring Bradley Cooper's sexy smile and gorgeous eyes.

Dal left the two women and returned to the sheriff's station where he sat down at the computer and searched several sites in an effort to trace Treman Ledger. No luck there, but that didn't surprise him. For a few moments he tapped his fingers on the desk top, wrestling with himself. Then he typed in Jessie West and waited. The pages that came up only told him what he already knew. Then when he was almost ready to give up, he clicked on one more page and found reference to an article in an obscure magazine called *Rats*.

Curious what that had to do with Jess he went to the site. A photo of a young woman who resembled her was shown among others in the masthead along with several scurrilous titles. All appeared to be written about the people in the photos. The magazine was probably one of those yellow rags filled with lies and innuendoes about legitimate personages. Still, he couldn't stop himself thumbing through to the article entitled "Sex Can Get You Killed" about a west coast reporter who slept with an undercover cop, then wrote an article revealing the secrets he told her prior to a raid. The article caused the wounding of several cops. Neither the reporter nor the cop were identified. Probably all lies. But why was it included by Google when he typed in Jessie West?

He hit the print button, not sure why he was doing it, and shut down the site. The telephone rang and when he picked it up it was Mac.

"I need some backup out here on County Road three-sixty-four and Highway twenty-three. There's a cow stuck in the muddy bank of a pond and some old boy raving about shooting the old cow and putting her out of her misery. Not the owner. There's some rope in the storage room. Bring it out here and let's pull this poor old cow out."

Dal chuckled. Just the thing he needed to take his mind off this problem with Jessie. Nothing like playing cowboy to forget all his troubles. If the missing guy didn't turn up by Tuesday morning first thing, they'd look for him for a while, but without any evidence of foul play, the fool was of age and could disappear if he wanted to. There was no evidence the break-in at Tink's had any connection with the man's disappearance. Besides, there was plenty to do, what with Marcus Woods and his severed leg and emergencies like a cow stuck in the mud.

He grabbed his hat, screwed it down on his head, and went to the storage room. After pawing his way through piles of stuff including a pair of spurs, three packages of foam coffee cups, and assorted snack room supplies, he found a coil of rope, looped it over his shoulder, and took off. A new young deputy manned the desk near the front door and Dal told him where he was going in case anyone came looking for him, and pushed through the door into the parking lot.

Overhead the evening shimmered with pinks and golds and purples that bled into a cloudless azure blue sky. Reminded him once again why he'd come here. Climbing in the SUV he pictured a cow stuck in mud up to her udder and the struggle it would be to pull her out. This would be fun. And something he could tell Jessie about. He also wanted to show her that article about the reporter who looked so much like her. Way too fancy, made up to the hilt, hair in a upswept do. Couldn't be his country gal. A good wind-up to the disappearance of a hired killer, an undercover cop living next to a hog pen, and someone tossing a deputy's apartment. Maybe this day would end on a brighter note after all.

Mac's unit was nosed partway into a ditch at the crossing of the two highways, one no more than a dirt road. In the corner pasture a huge pond reflected the streaked sky. And in that pond, her head and neck sticking out of the water, stood an enormous red cow. She must've weighed more than a thousand pounds. Halfway to her, water over his thighs, Mac stood, hands planted at his waist, staring back toward the road.

Dal bailed out, ducked through the barbed wire fence, and headed toward his boss, trying not to laugh but not having much luck. "Stuck in the mud, are you?"

"'Bout time you got here, son. I was beginning to think I was gonna be up to my ass here overnight. And wipe that smirk off your face. Ever lasso a critter?"

Dal dropped down in the grass on the bank and tugged off his expensive snakeskin boots. "A few times. You?"

"When I was a kid I took to rodeoing for a summer or two. Wasn't much good at it, though. You wanta give it a try first? I'll be your backup just in case you can't do it."

Dal waded into the pond, the muddy bottom squishing around his socked feet.

The cow swung her head, stared at the two men, then let go with a pitiful bawl. She obviously had little trust in her rescuers.

"What happened to the gunman?" Dal worked the rope into a noose and swung it over his head a couple of times. Just to practice.

"Aw, he left out when I called for backup. Think he just wanted some excitement."

"Not his cow?"

"Naw, belongs to his neighbor. I got the feeling they don't get along too well and he thought he could use this as an excuse to shoot the poor critter."

"Mac, why don't you get out of the water? When I get her roped, then you can take the other end and tie it to your bumper. Easier to pull her out that way."

"That's assuming you can get it over her head."

Dal studied the situation a bit more. "You know, the angle we've got here we could break her neck. She's really stuck. Why don't you go around yonder to the gate and drive to the other side of the pond, pull her out that way. And don't worry, I'll get her on the end of this rope if I have to swim out and place it there."

Mac high stepped his way out of the pond. "Wish we had someone out here with a camera, 'cause I got a feeling this is gonna be one hell of a show."

"Wouldn't surprise me." Dal muttered the words, gave the rope a few solid whirls, and let go. The loop settled over the back of her neck, then fell pretty as you please down over her nose. He gave it a tug and had her. "I'll be double damned."

About that time the cow decided she'd had enough of standing in the mud and threw her head around, humped up, and dragged Dal onto his face. Water flew in all directions. She thrashed and bawled and kicked. Meanwhile, Mac was still fiddling with the barbed wire gate. Damned if he'd let go, Dal came up for air, wrapped the rope around his wrist once, and hung on.

Eyes rolled back in her head, the cow lurched two or three times and was nearly to the opposite bank when Dal lost his footing and went to his knees. She dragged him slipping and sliding across the muddy bottom and up onto the grassy bank, where she lowered her head and took a great bite of green grass. Chewing as if nothing untoward had happened, she eyed him first, then Mac, who by that time was out of his vehicle laughing so hard he couldn't stand up straight.

Hatless and bootless and soaked in muddy water, Dal untangled both hands from the rope and slipped it off over the docile animal's head.

"Laugh, you old fool. You tell anyone about this, I'll tie you up with this rope and leave you in the storage room all weekend." There was no way in hell Mac could keep this a secret. Might as well prepare for the kidding that would follow.

"Better wade out there and get your hat." Mac managed the words between great bursts of laughter.

"Aw, hell." The fine silver Stetson, paid for out of his own pocket, bobbed around in the churning pond. He scrambled to his feet, jumped back into the water. Taking tall sucking steps, he made it back to the bank, shaking the bedraggled hat. Now it'd have to be cleaned and blocked again, if they could even save it.

"Come on, son. Git in my rig, I'll take you back to your'n. You look like you been rode hard and put up wet."

"I reckon I have." Dal climbed in with Mac, both of them ignoring the globs of mud and brown water they were depositing all over the sheriff's car.

"Let that kid, what's his name, the one who hotwired one of our cars, let him clean up this mess." Mac slitted a quick glance toward Dal, then laughed so hard he couldn't start his car.

"Laugh on. You don't look much better, you old fart."

"No. Don't reckon I do."

Dal hopped out and opened the gate, closed it behind Mac's vehicle, then rode around to the crossroads where his was parked. He looped the rope and threw it in the back of his SUV.

"Aidan. Aidan Smith."

"Yeah, that's him. Say, did you learn anything about the leg or the feller it belongs to?"

"Oh, yeah. Doc went online and he found him. Marcus Woods from Wichita. Been missing for over six months. Don't know much more yet. Figure Monday we can begin to trace his movements, maybe find out who wants to kill him. I think he's related or friends with whoever did it, so all we really need to do is talk to his wife and find out about any kin he's got here."

"How do you figure that?"

"Because, he trusted who it was. Wasn't the least afraid of him."

Mac whirled his hand around in the air "Oh, you mean you learned it from that magic thing you do."

"Yeah, that magic thing." Wait'll Mac heard what Tink had done and that Jess had helped her keep it a secret. The fur would fly.

9
CHAPTER

After Tink went to sleep on the other side of the bed, Jessie lay wide awake in a dapple of moonlight thinking about the scraps of paper found in the bedside table of the missing man's room at the B&B. She had to figure them out. With the stealth of a cat, she slipped from the bed and the room. The backpack sat on the floor at one end of the couch. She reached down for it, and Brad barked one sharp retort, sending her into a shaking frenzy. Getting used to him in the house wasn't easy.

"My goodness, dog. It's me. You don't bark at me. At the bad guys. Go after them, not me."

In the dark, toenails clicked across the wood floor and a wet tongue licked her hand.

"Okay, you're forgiven, now go back to your post and keep watch."

As if he understood, Brad clicked away.

Fingering the lists from an outside pocket, she dropped to the couch, flipped on the table lamp, and flattened them, one after the other, on the coffee table. Okay. There was 'Diamond House' and 'Lover's Leap.' Even after all this time, she recalled the conversation between herself and Steve when they got on the subject of good places to get rid of bodies. He'd told her about a place there in California, an old mine of some sort that had a bottomless cave in it. That they discussed such things was disturbing now that she looked back.

"Probably piles of bodies down there." He'd said it in a chiding way, but her skin crawled thinking of it. He kept it up. "No one would ever find them. You can throw in a rock and count to sixty before a sound echoes back up at you."

"Okay, enough already." Trying to outdo him, she'd told him about Lover's Leap and how below the overhang, trees were so thick all the way to the bottom of the deep chasm that a body could lay down there forever and never be found. "Still some places where no human has ever set foot in that wilderness."

He doubted that and told her so. "There's no place on this planet like that. At some time or the other man has walked everywhere."

"Well, you just haven't been in the Ozark wilderness."

"So, dare I ask why they call it Lover's Leap?"

"Oh. Some poor stupid girl, ditched by her boyfriend, went out there one night, left a short note under a rock, and jumped off."

"Sounds like an old wives' tale to me."

"No. My second cousin's mother-in-law's nephew knew the boyfriend."

"Yeah, right." He leaned forward and kissed her, ending the discussion.

They had hurt each other so much after that and she let go the memory.

Came back to the next thing on his scrawled list. A real puzzle. Diamond House. The rock house with diamond-shaped colored glass inset above all the outer doors and windows was a memory she could not remember sharing with Steve. And there was a good reason she hadn't—

fear that he'd suspect something she didn't want him to know. And the really scary thing was it included Rick Granger, a name on his list. This was getting too frightening.

Once when her family was back in Arkansas for a visit, and she was around sixteen, she'd gone to see Rick, an old childhood friend, and the two of them drove out to Diamond House. Hand in hand, they thrashed through the thick saplings grown up until the abandoned place couldn't be seen from the road not fifty feet away. Inside, where it was cool and quiet, they'd kissed, then ended up lying in each other's arms on the sloping wood floor. Making out like crazy. What the kids today called hooking up. Rick had a condom in his wallet that had been there so long it had indented the leather with a circle. Just lucky it was even any good.

She was a virgin, curious what all the fuss was about when it came to sex. She found her answer on that warm summer afternoon when Rick slipped her clothes off slowly, pausing to kiss every inch of her skin as he uncovered it. He'd begun with her face, treating eyes, earlobes, nose, and mouth as if each were sacred treasures. By the time he uncovered one breast she was hot and eager. His lips closed around the nipple, tongue licking savagely, and she thought she would go out of her mind. The lower he went, the hotter and more frantic grew his kisses, him acting as if he couldn't wait for the next taste, all the while taking his time to savor each one. The world spun, grew dark. Lights flashed in all colors, her ears rang. And she wanted everything that very moment, afraid she might die first.

At the vee of her thighs, his panting breath hot against her skin, she had his pants open, bare flesh rubbing against his hard-on like a crazy woman. When he asked her to put the condom on for him, she thought she would faint. To actually touch his penis, hold it while she slipped the rubber over the smooth skin, rolling it up to his balls. This was not something she had ever done. Oh, sure, she'd wrapped her fingers around a penis or two through denim when making out with a boy, but never anything so erotic as he suggested.

She fumbled with the damned thing, frantic to figure it out and put it on him. He kept calling her sweetie and giving her instructions between nibbling her flesh. She could barely make out his words for the noises they were both making.

At last she got the idea. His reaction to her slipping the cool prophylactic over his hot, hard, primed-for-action member and unrolling it slowly, was frightening to her. She thought she might be hurting him, the way he carried on. By the time she opened her legs to him, she was so close to her first true orgasm she barely made it till he plunged deep into her with a joyous shout that left no doubt about his gratification. The pain was instantaneous, unexpected, and killed her joy for a few moments.

He was good though. He soothed her with kisses in all the right places, his lips, tongue, and hands leading her away from the pain and back to enjoyment. She would always be grateful to him for teaching her to enjoy sex. He also set a high bar and until Dal, she hadn't found someone so well versed in bringing her to one orgasm after another while making wild, passionate love. At last she truly knew what all the fuss was about. Before he finished she was exhausted and could not move when he rolled off to her side. She lay there, staring out a broken window into the thick tree leaves, breathing heavily, fingernails digging into her palms.

Even when she could finally speak, she didn't. It would have ruined everything. Instead, she turned toward him, ran her hand up his muscled thigh and over his hip, stopped there to outline a small birthmark, then moved on. His smooth skin rippled under her touch and he made a sound down in his throat.

She whispered, "Thank you."

Still she did not want to talk to anyone about the experience they'd shared. Somehow discussing it would ruin her memory of the day she learned to truly enjoy sex. She had never seen or heard from Rick again, but he held a special place in her heart. It wasn't until she met Dal that she again felt that exquisite pleasure that sex offered. Though neither wanted to admit it, love had been added to the mix. Because much as she'd enjoyed Rick teaching her what true sexual pleasure was, Dal reinforced that and then some.

Nothing was ordinary about making love with him. Every time she was near him, all he had to do was look at her and she wanted his hands and mouth on her. The crazier the situation, the more dangerous the place, the more she craved his body. Maybe committing to each other would ruin things, or maybe it would make things better. She wasn't sure, was leery of taking the chance. Things were awesome the way they were.

Time to get back to the list. No more places, just four names. Parker, Mac, Dal, and Rick.

It wasn't possible Steve knew about Rick, and his name coupled with the Diamond House on the list was a puzzle. Rick must have told someone, but still that didn't explain Steve knowing about it. No one, positively no one, knew about that glorious summer day she'd spent at the Diamond House with him. She'd never told anyone, and they'd gone back to California the next day. As far as she knew Steve'd never even been to Arkansas, let alone her hometown. So, what could he have somehow learned about her and Rick that would threaten her? Even so she was convinced that the man who had gone missing from the B&B was

Steve, and he was here because he'd found her. And he intended to ruin her life by revealing her terrible past to the people he'd found meant the most to her. All before hurting them.

Oh, God. And then, after he did that, what was he going to do? Throw her off Lover's Leap? That's the only sure thing she could read into the list.

She hugged herself and shivered, not sure what to do. If she told Dal and Mac they would not only know her dreadful secret, but they would put her under lock and key, and she didn't want that, yet she doubted her ability to handle Steve alone.

Did Treman Ledger have anything to do with this? And what about the dead body? Were they all connected? Ledger arrived about the same time as Doc, so he might not be in the mix, but she had a feeling he was in it up to his lovely pecs. Did she dare go to Dal with all this and take the chance she was right? He'd find out everything about her past. Best if she could put an end to it without him ever knowing. That might be impossible with his ability to read her intent and just about everyone else's when he took a notion.

While that ability was something he'd tamped down in order to remain the private person he'd come here to be, he could ramp it back up. And if he got too suspicious about what she was hiding, he'd read her mind. No, it was best to let him investigate the killing and now the disappearance without taking part. He hated when she butted in as a reporter, but still he would be suspicious if she didn't. How could she convince him she had other things more important to occupy her time? And further, that she'd lost the lists. He'd never believe that.

Her mind going over and over her choices kept her awake.

Tuesday morning she would go to Parker for a favor that should take care of keeping her busy elsewhere. But if Steve found her in the mean-while, he was just angry enough to kill her.

Monday morning Dal called to talk about Kathy and Dave's barbe-cue. Were they meeting there or what? She agreed to do that. As it was a regular event in all their lives, she thought nothing of it. He might be pissed at her, but this wasn't, after all, work related. It was for fun.

"I'm bringing some killer turtle brownies. About two?"

"Yep. Wait. You cook all of a sudden?"

She laughed. "Not really. I just have to open boxes, melt some cara-mels, stick it all in the oven. Found the recipe online and decided to try it. Scrumptious. Helps me act like an ordinary woman. Figured it was about time I learned to do something in the kitchen besides—you know."

"Enough said. I know what you do best in the kitchen. And in the woods, the shower, in old storage rooms. . ."

"You sound better this morning."

A slight pause, but not enough to make her wonder. "Slept good last night. I take it your night went well too."

"Yep, nothing untoward happened. See you in a while."

Not one for phone amenities, he had hung up.

Dallas stared at the cell phone for a few seconds before slipping it into his pocket. She sounded aloof, even a tad miffed. Probably still thinking about his demand she turn over the information Tinker had given her. Lately they hadn't been getting together as much as he'd like. His fault, most surely. Maybe they could spend the night together. Mend some fences. All this crap about her keeping stuff from him could probably be settled with a little bit of talking. It couldn't be too bad, and he missed their sexual play.

Today might pave the way. No talk about work, just have a blast with the Spaceys, eat too much, drink too much beer. All the usual stuff. Still, with this crowd, talk almost always came down to discussing the latest cases. What the hell was getting wrong with people? Even out here in this place where the worst that ever happened used to be cousins knocking each other around, a few B & Es, some husband clocking his wife. Crops of marijuana. All bad to be sure, but Christ. He didn't want to think about what had happened with the burning car. Two guys killing someone, sawing his leg off and burying it in a hog pen, the rest of him in the woods, then burning the car, which was probably stolen. Why couldn't he get a handle on this one?

Damn, he hadn't been thinking straight. The body was buried a few hundred yards from the leg, which had been kept frozen. Which must mean the guy was killed in Treman's shed, his leg cut off and stuck in a freezer, the body hauled to the woods nearby in the car they later burned, and buried. Then Treman's shack set on fire to hide the evidence of the murder and so they'd find the leg. It didn't really matter whether the body was found or not.

Why in hell do all that? What was the point? Why at Treman's? The actual crime scene could be anywhere in the county, but he'd bet it was at Treman's. Not likely he was involved or he'd not have done the chopped-off leg thing right in his own yard. It was probably a message to Ledger. If they didn't find forensics pointing to the killers they might never make an arrest. The only lead he had was the burned car and whatever he could glean from the spot the two set it on fire. Within sight of his trailer. It had to have been burned because it was used to move the body. Twice he'd been at the scene and all he got was a lack of violence or fear. Just the two fighting. Nothing else. He'd assumed that was because he'd lost his ability to read the scene.

This was a good one. Was it possible that the men who burned the car had nothing to do with the murder? He was getting nothing of value at the gravesite or where the car had been burned. The car had no clues, the fire had destroyed everything. He needed to check out the site of the burned shed one more time in case he was right and that was the scene of the killing.

He stared some more. What if they wanted the body found at a specific time for some reason? Thus the entire setup. From the fire at the shack to the discovery of the leg, then the body, then the burning of the car. Hell. If a body without a leg sent a message, it would be *you can't run from me (us).'* Something to think about.

He found the phone in the seat of his recliner, dialed Doc's number. When he answered, the connection was filled with static and the sound of running water.

"Who's this calling me on my day off while I'm trying to catch a trout?"

"Sorry, Doc. You can see who it is on your phone."

"Yeah, I forget that new-fangled stuff. So I guess this is business, deputy. And on a Sunday to boot."

"A question, that's all. How long would you estimate the body has been buried?"

"I guess you mean our murder victim. Maybe three, four weeks."

"And did you find any forensics on it at all? Anything out of the ordinary? I know you look, even though—"

"Hold on there, boy. You said one question and I'm wanting to toss my fly back out over the heads of some mighty fine looking browns. I'll go over the blamed body again if you'll wait till Tuesday. The term Labor Day does not mean we labor, in case you wondered."

"Sorry, Doc. Yes. I'll talk to you then."

Dal hung up.

Mac had sent the paper a carefully worded release that stated the victim had been identified. He withheld a name and the bit about the handsaw, but everyone knew most of the story. It seemed the Wichita police couldn't locate Marcus Woods's wife at the address she'd listed online in the missing report. But it was old. She'd posted it almost five months earlier. Her phone was disconnected, she'd quit her job at the local Safeway, and moved out of her apartment.

And Jessie was wound up in that disappearing man and the lists she refused to hand over. She didn't seem interested in the murder. How odd was *that*? There was definitely something going on there. Hopefully, the missing guy would turn up and it would come to nothing. Tracking down Marcus Woods's past was enough to do without looking for a man who might have just decided to disappear and start a new life elsewhere.

Tuesday he'd drop in at the newspaper and have a talk with Parker. Withholding evidence of a possible crime was not something her boss would tolerate. She'd be furious, but what the hell?

Meanwhile, he'd try to forget it all and have a nice visit with his friends. There was always the story of the cow he and Mac had rescued from the mud. Maybe he and Jessie could make up.

He stepped out of the shower to the ringing of his phone. A call on a holiday didn't bode well. Maybe it was Jessie or Burt. He picked up the cell. No such luck. It was Mac. So much for his day off.

"Yeah, boss?" His gaze wandered to the window that looked out over the creek. A fire, something burning. "What the hell?"

"Dallas, you there? What's going on?"

He blinked. It'd been a vision. Nothing. Except someone hollering his name. "I'm here, Mac. Sorry. What's up?"

"I got a call from WITSEC in Wichita this morning."

"WITSEC? Shit, don't tell me our dead guy was one of theirs."

"Okay, I won't tell you that, because you guessed right."

"What was he doing in Witness Protection?"

"He was supposed to testify in a trial out in LA against some cops in cahoots with a big drug trafficking ring. Guess he was either undercover DEA or someone turned by the DEA, didn't get it straight. But this was so big a bust, the investigation had been going on for years. They hid him out till the trial. It was scheduled for last month, then he disappeared. They've been hunting for him ever since. That's about all they say. Pretty close-mouthed."

"How in hell did he end up here dead?"

"You got me. They're sending some investigators to look at the case. Just a heads-up. They won't be here till tomorrow sometime. We'll give 'em what we got and step back."

"Okay by me. I want no business with drug traffickers, the DEA, or US Marshals."

"Let's just hope if this was a drug hit that they've left town. We don't need those ole boys traipsing around down here. God, what if they decide to get into the drug trade right at our back door?"

Dal clenched his jaw and stared out the window some more. That happened, he'd go Rambo on them. The thought went through his mind along with a memory he could not suppress. Leann with a needle hanging out of her arm. A dark alley, bullets cutting him down. It would not happen again. Not here. Not as long as he could help it.

"Son, you there? You okay?"

"Nope, I'm not okay. Goddammit, Mac." He swallowed hard, couldn't catch his breath. When he finally could, words tumbled out. "The sons of bitches. They aren't getting this place. It isn't going to happen."

"Take 'er easy. They got their man, chances are they're hundreds of miles away from here by now. There ain't enough money around here for drugs like they pedal."

"And so that makes this all right? This killing of a man with enough guts to stand up to them?"

"No, it don't. But you and I, we need to stand down on this one. Let these guys handle their own mess."

Dal sighed and ran a hand through his wet hair. "Yeah, you're right. I'm going over to Kathy and Dave's. Meeting Jess and Burt and Tink there. Why don't you join us, Mac? Relax. Dave's famous barbecue. Forget all this at least for one day."

"Think I'll just stay out here on the river bank catching trout and enjoying my so-called day off. Thanks, Dal. You okay? You sound a little stressed."

"I'm just fine. Don't worry."

"Take 'er easy, then. See you later."

Dal hurled the phone across the room. It landed in his recliner. Damn good thing, too. He'd already broken two of the blamed things. The department wouldn't look favorably on replacing yet another one.

Jessie finished off a cup of coffee, picked up the plate of brownies, stuck her wallet and phone in the pockets of her jeans, and ran out to the

Jeep. It'd been a while since the gang had gotten together at Kathy's and it was perfect weather for an outdoor barbecue. Sunny, temps in the 70s, a gentle breeze. Being around Dal all day would be hard because he'd surely want to ask her about the lists. If only they could keep it social she'd be fine. Otherwise she'd steer clear of him.

Since she was so obsessive about being on time, she was the first to arrive. Kathy and Dave were in what they called the 'yard.' They kept a large section of the woods surrounding the house mowed. Smoke floated lazily from the charcoal pit near a redwood table with benches. Chairs were scattered around in no particular arrangement. Jess placed the plate of brownies on the end of the table beside an apple pie still warm from the oven. Baked beans, potato salad, and a green salad were set out along with two pitchers, one of tea, the other of lemonade. The cooler on the ground nearby would contain beer. On the grill were ribs that Dave was busy brushing down with his own aromatic sauce and corn on the cob wrapped in its husk.

"Oh, my goodness, it smells heavenly." Jess rushed to hug Kathy.

"If the remainder of our guests don't arrive soon, we'll start without them." Kathy smiled. "I'm going to run and get the bread out of the oven."

Two cars pulled up at the same time. Dal crawled out of his unit and Burt and Tink climbed from his.

Kathy appeared with a pan of rolls while the others greeted each other. "You're just in time."

Burt rubbed his hands together. "I could smell it all the way out to the highway."

"Well it's ready, so get your place at the table." Dave loaded a platter with ribs and another with corn, balancing them expertly and depositing both on the table.

"Beer in the cooler, or ask for tea or lemonade. Let's eat."

Dal sat at one end of the table and Jessie at the other. Tink and Burt tucked in next to each other opposite them.

Kathy stood beside Jessie for a minute. "Scoot over, girl, so I can sit here where I can pour drinks."

Without remarking, Jessie picked up her plate and moved toward Dal but left a space between them. His puzzled expression gave her pause. She wasn't mad at him at all. In fact she wanted to be near him. But with what was going on, it wasn't a good idea.

Not at all.

He raised his eyebrows in her direction but didn't say anything. It was like they'd never met and were sizing each other up for the first time. Kathy must have noticed something odd going on between them.

"Let me introduce you." She laughed, then did so, as if they'd never met.

Dal went along with it, nodding in Jessie's direction. "Pleased to meet you, ma'am. Do you live in these parts? Thought I saw you the other day with one of the ugliest dogs I've ever seen."

She nodded, smiled. "That's Brad. Left him home for fear he might take a bite out of anyone who didn't treat me real good."

"Pretty woman like you surely can't worry about being treated bad. If you'd move over closer to me, I could protect you from any smart mouth might be in the crowd."

Tink and Burt burst into laughter and even the quiet Dave was amused.

She lowered her eyelids for a moment, not sure how to handle this. As everyone was trying to treat the matter lightly, she would do the same.

She held out her hand. When he took it, shivers ran up her arm. His touch always did that to her and there was no way she could stop it.

He must've recognized her reaction, because he kept hold of her for a spell, then gave her one of his killer smiles. "Guess we'd better eat before everything gets cold. Then perhaps you can tell me more about yourself."

Things would be okay just as long as he didn't ask about the missing lists, and he didn't. In fact, he steered clear of talking about work at all. Except for the story about him and Mac getting the cow out of the mud. Technically, that wasn't work.

Everyone was laughing hysterically by the time he finished telling it.

"I don't know how Mac felt about it, but to me it was the most important call we've had all week. That poor old cow is probably still gossiping to her pals about how she did all the work and we just got dragged around in the mud. And you know what? She'd be right." He clasped Jessie's hand. "That reminds me. That rope I borrowed from you a while back, we used that to drag that old cow around, or vice versa. It's in the back of my car. You might want to remind me, I'll throw it in your Jeep before you leave today. Could be you'll need it."

What she could possibly need the rope for she had no idea. Before she could reply, Burt, who had only been on the job a bit over a year, was laughing so loud everyone joined in.

He finally sobered up. "How often do you get weird stuff like that? I remember last year when someone threw a doll in that old abandoned well and we got that frantic call that a baby was down in a well. That near scared me to death till we saw it was a doll. Everyone was so relieved we laughed and joked about it the rest of the day."

Kathy rose to clear the dishes and Tink and Jessie got up to help. In the kitchen Jess loaded the dishwasher while the other two put away food.

"I thought maybe we'd make some homemade ice cream later. It'd go good with the pie and brownies. We could get the men to turn the crank. What do you think?"

"Sounds good to me," Tink said.

Kathy made up near a gallon of cream, milk, eggs and sugar, poured in a good splash of vanilla, and tasted the mixture. "Mmm, perfect."

Tink watched wide-eyed. "I thought you couldn't use raw eggs."

"Oh, I wash all my eggs with soapy water. The salmonella they talk so much about is on the egg shells, not in the eggs themselves. Besides, ice cream isn't good without eggs right from the henhouse and milk and cream straight from the cow. You can either wash the eggs well or heat the mixture in the microwave as long as you don't leave it in till you've got scrambled eggs." Kathy picked up the jug. "I prefer just to wash them as we gather them from the hens, then there's no worries.

"Jess, if you'd get the ice cream freezer out of that bottom cabinet, and Tink, grab that quilt folded up in the utility room. I'll carry the mix and we'll be all ready. The cooler is full of ice and Dave took the salt out earlier."

The men were deep in conversation, lolled in chairs in the shade of a sprawling maple, each with a can of beer. A breeze shook leaves loose from a nearby walnut tree, a warning that summer had come to an end.

Jessie set the freezer down beside Dal. "Guess who gets the honor of turning the crank?"

She sank near him on the quilt they would use to cover the freezer when the ice cream was ready and he reached for her hand. She pulled away, pretended to tuck her hair out of her eyes. His expression of confusion sent a pain through her, but she didn't give in. If things went bad with Steve, Dal would hate her. It was best to prepare herself and him for that now, though it hurt like crazy to think of losing him.

He and Burt fit the insert in the freezer, and layered in ice and salt. "This means Dal gets to turn first."

"Be glad to." Casting one last frown toward Jess he grabbed the handle and went to work.

Sunday she would ask Parker if she could do a series about the growing homeless problem in Grace County. They had talked about it several times. That would leave Parker to work with Dal on the murder and eventually whatever Steve stirred up. The man missing from the B&B was Steve Wainwright. Had to be. And he was out to make her finally pay for what she'd done. She was as sure of that as she was that the sun would not fall from the sky. Thinking about it was driving her crazy.

For a while conversations darted between the women discussing a new television show they enjoyed and the men discussing sports. All grew quiet, then Kathy spoke up.

"Dal, did Doc ever get back identity on the body?"

"Sure, but it's—"

She held up a hand. "I know, an ongoing investigation. Come on, we're friends here and no one is going to say anything."

"I can't really tell you much because of involvement from other law enforcement. But I can tell you Doc is inventive." He kept right on cranking the ice cream. "We got nothing on fingerprints, but the old fart used the Internet to do a search on a missing persons program and we were able to identify him through a small birthmark on his hip that popped up on that site. A woman looking for her husband. And that's all I can say for now. It'll probably all break next week."

Beside him, Jessie gasped.

Dal eyed her. "What is it? You turned pale as a sheet. You okay?"

Kathy rose and went to her side. "You sick, honey? What's wrong?"

"Rick. It can't be." She could barely speak above a whisper.

"Rick who? What are you talking about?"

She shook her head. "No, dammit, no. It's Rick and Steve killed him."

Not sure he understood her outburst, let alone what caused it, Dal went on his knees next to her. "Who is Steve? Who is Rick? What's going on?" He lifted her chin with a finger. "Look at me, Jess. What in the hell are you talking about? What do you know about this? How did you come by such misinformation? Next thing we know, you'll be writing a story about the murder, naming a Steve and a Rick, neither of which were involved in the murder."

"Don't you look at me like that. Rick Granger has a birthmark on his hip. Steve Wainwright is the missing man from the B&B, and he's here to get back at me for what I did. That's why Rick's name was on the list and checked off, 'cause he killed him. I thought he was going to blackmail me to those on the list, but he… he's going to kill them. And it's all my fault." She broke down, sobbing hysterically.

Dal came to his feet, glared from her to Tink, then back again. "What do you know about this, Tinker? The two of you messing about with this could get you both in deep trouble if not killed. You have no idea what's going on here. I want this list, now."

Kathy, who'd had her arms wrapped around Jessie, looked up at him. "Dal, cool off. Can't you see she's upset?"

"Not nearly as upset as she will be when this blows up. You need to keep her here, not let her go home till I call and say it's okay. You understand me? This is serious shit."

Dave rose, went to stand beside Kathy. "Okay, Dal. We'll do that, but you don't yell at my wife. You got that?"

Suddenly, the only sound was Jessie's soft crying. Everyone else stared speechless at Dave, who rarely said much of anything, and when he did it was in a soft voice.

Dal was already on his way to his car, Burt on his heels, Tink trotting along behind. The barbecue was over. In his fury, Dal opened the back of the SUV, tossed the rope to Burt.

"Put that in Jessie's Jeep. Tink, you bring me that list, you hear?" Fear for Jessie's life fed his anger till all he could do was climb in his car and drive off.

He hammered on the steering wheel. All reporters ought to have their computers smashed to bits. Ever last damn one of them.

10
CHAPTER

All day Tuesday was hectic, getting everything done at the paper to get it over to Harrison for printing. It was after midnight before Jessie dragged herself home, wondering if holidays were actually worth it. Might be better just to work them.

The next day Jessie dragged herself out of bed in time for lunch. Tink was working the late afternoon shift, which explained why she found her sitting on the back deck bathed in sunlight, eating a salad and drinking a cup of tea. Feet up like a rich wife who had nothing better to do. Jessie had to work and so did Tink so remaining at Kathy's didn't make much sense, since she and Dave would be at the college every day. They had left Kathy's with a promise they'd stay together and be careful. It would all sort itself out.

"I've got to go to town," she told Tink. "Want to catch Parker before he gets wrapped up in something." She hadn't slept much. Dal had upset her with his anger. But he wasn't going to tell her how to live her life, and she sure wasn't going to cower in someone's house like a refugee.

"You going to take a copy of that list to Dal?" Tink peered up at her through her eyelashes.

"I don't have much choice. Besides, I blurted it all out yesterday anyway. The boar hair's in the butter, as they say." She lowered herself in a chair next to her friend. "I don't think he'll ever forgive me when all this is over."

"I'm not sure what 'all this' is, but I'll probably be the last to know. I've got a feeling Dal will forgive you anything."

She touched Tink's arm. "I hope you're right. We'll talk about it tonight. I'll tell you everything. It's about time I did."

Tink nodded. "That's good. I'm going to stay here for a while. It's so peaceful. All I can hear are birds singing and the creek chattering. But I'm going back to my place when I get off work tonight."

Jessie leaned down and kissed her on the cheek. "Just be careful. Remember, if you think anyone is messing with you, call Mac. Don't go in. I'll come by from work."

"Yes, Mother."

No sense in bringing up why Tink wouldn't come back out here when her shift was over. She couldn't do the drive. The country was just too darn dark. A phobia like that must be miserable to deal with, and though the guys teased her a lot, Jessie wouldn't. As for her plans to keep looking for the missing man, Tink would probably call that off, considering Dal's outburst.

"Let me know if you need help with your investigation, would you?"

Tink stared at her for a minute. Probably trying to judge just how she meant that comment. At last she nodded.

When she arrived at the paper, she went straight to Parker's office. "Could I talk to you for a minute?"

He glanced up from reading the paper. "Sure. What's up?"

"I had an idea for a series, and wondered if it'd be okay if I got started on it for next week's issue."

"Sit. Tell me about it. Whatever it is, it'll have to be put on the back burner till all the excitement about this murder is settled. And while you're at it, tell me why you aren't chomping at the bit for this story, as grisly and mysterious as it is."

"Oh, I don't know. There's not much happening there. Mac is sending releases and you can do that, no sweat. I want to do something more creative on the homeless kids in this county, maybe a series with interviews from parents and kids. There are way too many and I think if people really knew about all these kids going without food, they might begin some sort of program."

"School's started so there is a program. They're feeding them breakfast and lunch. Do you have any stats to back up your presumption? I haven't seen bands of homeless rug rats running around town." His gaze caught hers, pinned her in the chair. "I can't believe you aren't working on a story about a leg buried in the mud out at Treman's place. That's right up your alley. Your pictures are super. Go on over and charm that good-looking deputy you hang out with and get us a good follow-up story. I've got a meeting to cover tonight, plus three stories to work on. Do what you do." He shooed at her with one hand.

"But—"

"I really don't think you want to *but* me this morning. I went home at two this morning to find a sick mare. I've got to run home soon to medicate her. May have to call the vet out if she doesn't improve. If you and Dal have had a spat, fix it. Now go. Trail him around. Get me a continuing story on this murder for the front page. By the way, you look dreadful."

"Thanks a bunch." Because they were close, she knew better than to argue with him when he came down that hard. Her worries about Steve seemed to have slipped his mind, or he thought it really wasn't an issue to be concerned about. He could be right. Dear God, she hoped he was. She sighed, rose, and went out to pick up her backpack and go find Dal.

The new young guy was at the front desk at the sheriff's office, manning phones and walk-ins. She couldn't remember his name, so she raised a hand in greeting.

"Hi. You know where Dal is?"

The kid stretched to look, as if she hadn't already seen he wasn't at his desk.

Damn, did she have to help train this guy? "Check your list there. If he signed out it'll tell where he was going."

"Oh, yeah." The kid flushed and grinned. "And who are you?"

"I'm Jessie West."

"Oh, yeah, the reporter."

"Oh, yeah."

"Says here he's taking personal time."

"In the middle of a murder investigation?"

The kid shrugged.

"Is Mac here?"

"Mac?"

"The sheriff. I think you need to pay more attention to what's going on around you. How long you been here?"

Her tone must've got on his nerves because he swelled up like a toad frog. "Listen, when they tell me you're my boss, then maybe I'll listen to you. Otherwise, it's none of your business how I'm doing my job." His voice rose until he was on his feet yelling by the time he finished.

What was she doing, jumping all over him this way? Not like her at all. It was turning into a lousy day before it even began.

Mac came through from inside. "What the tarnation is going on out here?"

Jessie and the kid both blurted out their explanations at the same time, till no one could understand anything.

Mac held up a hand. "Okay. Start over. Colby, you go first."

Colby, that was his name. Unusual. Colby had flushed a bright red, till his face almost matched his hair.

"Sorry, sheriff. She got to bossing me around. Didn't mean to lose my temper."

"Women are that way, son. 'Specially this one. Might as well get used to it. They tend to have this need to tell men what to do."

"Mac, that's not true." Jessie had cooled down some, but was still annoyed. "However I do apologize. I'm looking for Dal, and he, uh, Colby, said he took some personal time. I asked for you and he didn't even know who I was talking about. Even you would've been pissed by then."

"Now, now, Jessie, watch your language. What's got you so riled up?"

He was one to talk. On occasion he turned loose with some choice words, but why bring it up now and add fuel to a rapidly burning fire?

"Okay, sorry. Just having a bad start to a worse day."

"Sounds like you're both sorry. Colby, why don't you go do a walk-through of the cells, make sure no one needs anything." He turned to her. "So what did you need? I've already sent Parker a release on the murder and I don't have any more to say on the subject."

"You said last week that he'd been identified. Has his family been notified so we can say who he was?"

"I said I have nothing more to say. Read my release."

"Has his body gone down to Little Rock yet? Can I talk to Doc."

"Jessie, girl. Why don't you go take some pictures or make up a story or something?"

Boy, everyone was in a piss-poor mood this morning. Considering what she was facing with Steve, it didn't set right—him goading her like that, coming so close to her real fear. Rather than start something, she slammed out the door, leaped in her Jeep, and squealed tires across the parking lot. No matter how much she loved Mac, he couldn't tell her how to do her job. She drove to the mortuary, parked on the street, and sat behind the wheel for a while to cool off before jumping out and going inside to find Doc.

She treaded quietly 'cause there might be a service going on at the moment. Doc handled almost all the funerals in Cedarton and the surrounding area. Otherwise folks had to go to Harrison or over to Fayetteville. Most preferred to use Doc's mortuary.

However, she found him sitting behind a desk in his office furiously going through a stack of papers. She rapped on the open door rather than barge in on him.

He looked up, opened a drawer, and dropped the file inside. "Come on in, young lady. What can I do for you? Hope you're not here on business."

Eyeing his wry grin, Jessie couldn't help grinning back. At least someone was in a good mood. Doc was always able to calm folks down. Probably 'cause so many of his clientele were laid back, so to speak. But why had he tossed that file in a drawer so quick when he saw her?

"I just wanted to see if I could get a quote from you on this latest murder. Or maybe I could ask you a few questions."

"Well, now, I'm not—"

"Come on, Doc. It's surely not classified. Just some good ole boys getting into a fuss and going too far. After all, who, other than a redneck, cuts off someone's leg for the hell of it?"

He looked startled. "As a matter of fact you'll need to talk to the sheriff. That's all I can say. " He held up both hands, eyes sliding to one side to peer at the drawer where he'd put the papers.

Interesting. Definitely something there she needed to see. If she could get her hands on those, she'd just bet she'd have a story. "Okay, I'll leave. Wouldn't want you to get in any trouble."

She drove around the block and parked behind the large building beneath a row of overgrown hedges that would conceal the Jeep from nosy passersby. Sooner or later he had to leave and when he did she'd get a look at those papers he hid away.

Crap, she'd forgotten to leave the list on Dal's desk. Now she'd have to deal with his temper, when he came back from his so-called personal day. And what was that all about?

Wednesday morning Dal got as far as the square before what was bugging him took over. What he needed was a day off work. To get stuff sorted out. At the station, he locked his utility belt, weapon, and cell phone in his locker, then told Colby he was taking a personal day. At home he changed out of his uniform into jeans and a tee shirt, dug around in the junk drawer in the kitchen till he found what he was hunting for, walked out to the storage shed and dragged the rarely-used mountain bike out that Ina Mae let the renters use, and pedaled out of town. All without really thinking about what he was about to do. But he had to do it in private with no interruptions. Thus the bike and not his patrol unit.

Red Rock camping area was a primitive place popular with hikers and bikers. It lay deep in the wilderness high on the mountain northeast of town near an entrance to the hiking/biking trail.

About five tough uphill miles along the highway, he stopped at a sign for Red Rock, near a lookout on a ragged bluff that hung precariously over a deep ravine. He walked the bike into the woods between the trail and the highway, covered it with dead limbs and weeds, then started on foot down a narrow animal path that clung to the cliff-side. Rocks and gravel slid from underfoot. Several times he had to grab a handhold on boulders on the upper side when his bad leg threatened to dump him over the edge. Sweat had soaked through his tee shirt when he finally reached a rock finger that pointed into space with nothing visibly holding it there. No wider than the couch in his living room, it afforded a panoramic view of a hundred-eighty degrees. With great care he settled his butt on a huge boulder protruding from the mountainside where he removed his shoes and socks and tee shirt, took two containers the size of snuff tins from his jeans, and limped to the end of the rock.

In the woods behind him something rattled through dead leaves left over from last year. He paused, peered over his shoulder, but decided that wasn't a good idea considering where he stood at the moment. Probably just a squirrel. Catching his balance, he stared across the mountain peaks, jade green speckled here and there with early fall colors. Toward the horizon distance deepened the shades to a hazy purple. Heights never bothered him and he stood for a long while, gathering the beauty of the peaks.

The sight filled him with a reverence for life that he embraced, then steeled himself for the battle at hand. Ready to fight the evil that had taken over his spirit he turned inward. With his right hand he dug out a tin, opened it, and dipped two fingers into the red powder, slashed across his forehead and both cheeks.

After replacing the tin in a pocket, he opened his arms wide and chanted the formula for killing one's enemies, calling upon the Red Man to assist him. The Cherokee words bounced around the peaks and echoed back. Chants that asked the gods from the heavens above, the earth beneath, and waters below to banish the enemy who haunted him. It had been a long time since he'd taken part in such a ceremony and he was a bit rusty.

His leg sent a familiar painful sensation up into his hip and shot across to his spine. With gritted teeth, he finished the sacred formulas, removed the second tin and slashed black powder beside the red, then repeated words that meant death to his enemy. On knees that trembled he backed up and dropped once more to the boulder, to sit with his legs folded crosswise in front of him. Addressed Grandfather in Cherokee.

"I need your help. An evil blackness has entered me from the burning car and I can no longer find the spirits I seek to help me do my job. Instead, they punish me, taunt me, remind me of my wrongdoings. I am no longer deserving of this gift. Tell me what I can do."

He listened intently, but the mountain breezes carried no messages, nor did the singing of the birds nor the chatter of the squirrels. Hands open, he laid them in his lap, palms up to capture any sacred formula that might befall him. After a long moment of gazing across the magnificent panorama, he closed his eyes. The sun's heat moved over him. Sweat ran in rivulets down his back. Still he did not move.

From overhead came the scree of a red-tailed hawk, its shadow swooping across the valley far below. One hand shading his eyes, he located the bird against the vivid blue of the sky, soaring on thermals.

Its broad, rounded wings were a rich brown on top and pale below. The short, wide tail, streaked belly, and dark bar between shoulder and wrist on the underside identified it as a large female. Seen from this distance it might fool some into thinking they were seeing an eagle, but only till an actual eagle came along. He knew the difference.

Darkness found him returning from the heights of the heavens, the depths of the earth, and beneath the seas where time meant nothing. Where he searched for the pain and suffering he must endure to cast out the darkness from his soul.

He let out a breath and slumped forward. All was still for another instant before the crickets, frogs, and other night critters took up their songs again. The morning sun awoke him, his bones cracking when he straightened his aching chilled body.

"You slept well, my grandson."

He jerked around, gazed into the face of his grandfather, who squatted nearby. "Did you find answers to your questions?"

"I am not sure. I am afraid not."

"Perhaps you need to remain here, clearing your mind and heart and soul. It is a dilemma you face. One that has nothing to do with your gift but rather with your confusion, your guilt. You seek to live in a perfect world, one where there is only peace and no sorrow. Yet you carry that sorrow within your soul, a guilt that weighs heavily. There is a saying, that the soul would have no rainbow if the eyes had no tears. But we must not shed tears all our lives grieving for things from the past for the rain passes and we are led forward. Life is not yesterday or tomorrow, but today."

"That's the problem. I can't seem to move from mourning Leann's death to find a way to live. Every time I think I'm getting over the guilt, it comes back to haunt me again. There have been way too many tears."

"Then perhaps you should enjoy the rainbows from those tears and thank the gods for giving you a new life. Walking in the past and the present will tear you apart."

The old man was right, but being right and doing what was right were two separate things. He gazed at the wrinkled leathery skin that stretched over his bones, the long white hair caught back in a thong, the eyes pale with age that had beheld a long life. This was only his conception of his grandfather, for the old man had been dead many years.

"I saw a red hawk the day before this."

"An untold omen. You must move carefully. Be aware."

"Yeah, especially sitting out here on the edge of this rock." He chuckled at his attempt at a weak joke. His grandfather vanished.

Wearily, he leaned back and straightened his legs. His mouth was dry, his throat parched. This must've been easier for his ancestors than it was for him. All he could envision was a hot shower and a soft bed. God, what had he been thinking? His life was that of a modern man. The answers to his problems were to be found in this world where he had so damned much to lose if he didn't make the right choices. Not in the world he did not understand.

Jessie walked on the edge of a precipice as dangerous as the one he sat on. It would do for him to get to work on this murder and all the strange happenings. She seemed to be up to her pretty neck in dirty secrets. Right now he wanted to shake some sense into her, then take her in his arms so they could both forget the darkness haunting them.

He pulled on his socks and walking shoes, wiped his hands and face with the tee shirt, and rose, sending small rocks sailing off into the treetops below. Probably a good idea to get off this damned mountain before he fell and broke his fool neck.

He made his way carefully up the narrow path, mind searching for answers. The sound came again, from behind him now—more like an upright being walking, thinking, plotting. Hands on his back. Too late, far too late to react, he stumbled, wind-milled both arms. Underfoot the edge of the trail loosened, fell from under his next step. The world tilted and there was nothing but air for his fists to grasp. Head over heels he toppled down the steep incline, thudding against boulders, smashing into trees, tumbling first one way then another, until there was nothing. From within the dark came a voice, a hand reaching out from another place. Not to save him but to drag him into a world where he did not want to go.

All came to a halt, grew silent save for his breathing, the beat of his heart, blood whooshing through his veins. Somewhere in the distance soft chuckles, whispers, voices talking in muted tones. A bright light that moved away and grew dim, vanished into nothing. A void. No color, no light, no life, no sounds. A nowhere place.

He was among the dead. Most surely dead himself.

On Dogwood Street under the shade of immense maple trees, their leaves just beginning to turn, Jess waited, ear buds transmitting "A Heartache Tonight" by The Eagles. Probably pretty apt to the situation she and Dal faced. The back entrance of the mortuary remained closed.

That was okay. She could wait. She was doing what Parker asked, working on the story, the killing. She tapped her fingers on the wheel in rhythm to the song. Trying to forget all about where Dal might be and if he hated her yet. She still hadn't turned in the lists.

The door opened and Doc came out and hustled to a small black sports car. She ducked low so he wouldn't spot her. Felt foolish.

Doc, you dog you. Car like that. Probably meeting some lovely lady for a lunch rendezvouz.

Under the gangly hedge row she waited till he drove away, turned off the music, removed the ear buds, and climbed from the Jeep. Tucking her phone in the pocket of her jeans, she locked the backpack inside, and hightailed it to the door, fingers crossed it would not be locked. It wasn't and she slipped inside, hugging the wall until she could look around and make sure all was clear.

She was here for one thing only. That file Doc had secreted in his desk so fast when she'd shown up earlier. And she dare not take it with her. Pictures with the phone would have to do. The hallway was empty and she scurried to the office, opened the door, and slipped in. No one was around, so she dropped into the chair and opened the drawer where he'd put it when she came in. A fast look told her the file was gone.

"Dammit."

Quickly she sifted through the contents of the other drawers. Where could it be? He didn't have anything with him when he left. Maybe he'd passed it on to someone else. But who? He was the coroner.

She turned the chair and spotted a briefcase snugged up against the wall. Dropped to her knees and lowered it flat on the floor. A combination lock. One of those you had to roll through four numbers. Crap, she'd never get this open. Okay, she didn't know for sure the file was in there. Don't waste time on it.

Footsteps sounded soft on the carpeting outside. On hands and knees, she crawled into the knee hole of the desk and hunkered there, sure her heartbeat could be heard. The door to the room opened, a pair of feet crossed to the briefcase, picked it up, and left. She sat under there for a while, hugging her knees, unwilling to give up so easily.

Across the room sat a two-drawer filing cabinet. A last chance. If it wasn't in there she'd have to give up on this and use other tactics to get a good story. Bottom drawer, manila folders labeled by dates so that she had to finger through each one. Finally, at the very back tucked into a folder with no name or date on it, were the papers she'd only glimpsed earlier. Enough to recognize them though. All she'd seen were the words Autopsy of Mar… Nothing else.

With a muffled sigh of relief she tugged the blank folder out, opened it up on the floor and in the light from the window in the door read the first few lines. This was it. The autopsy of Marcus Woods. The man with the birthmark on his hip? If so, he was Rick Granger, and she might be the only one who knew that. Yet.

Using her phone she took photos as fast as she could, hoping they would be clear enough for her to make out the important stuff, which often was the small print. But she could make it larger.

On the third page, she lost her breath. The header read Drug Enforcement Agency Document with a date of six months ago with much of the information blacked out. A redacted file.

Holy crap.

On the top corner of the page was a sticky note that read: *I meant to give you this file when I saw you in Wichita in March. Make what you can of it.*

What was going on here? And had it really been Rick buried in the woods near Treman's place? Get real. A body with a birthmark the same place as Rick's. Who else would it be? Every page after that had great sections redacted, but she took photos anyway. There had to be some good information. She was running out of time. Doc or someone was sure to come in the room at any moment, so she turned pages and took photos as fast as she could. Out in the hall someone said something, someone else laughed. She froze, dared not even breathe till the footsteps went on past the door.

She had to get out of there and now. With trembling fingers she stuffed the papers back into the unmarked folder, stuck them back precisely where they were, and scuffled to the door, cracked it open, checked both directions and fled. Fear crawled up her spine till she could hardly concentrate. Find the exit, get the door open, not fall down like a goof, get back in the car, and drive away without being seen. If she were caught, she could lose her job, no matter her excuse. She could also get in big trouble considering she was probably stealing classified information. How could there be such a thing in this small town with no one of any importance living here? Even as she climbed into her Jeep Doc drove up from the other direction, parked against the building, got out, and went inside.

Just in time. How close she had come to being caught. When she could breathe normally she sat up straight, started the car, and drove off.

Where to go with this stuff? Back to the office where Parker could return at any moment? No. Home? Maybe safe if Tinker had gone in to work. She glanced at the clock on the dash. Only three o'clock? The day had seemed an eternity. Due for the five o'clock shift, Tinker might well still be there enjoying the quiet of the deck. It wouldn't be fair to give her yet another secret to keep. Dal's? What would he say? No, he was already madder than a rock-pelted hornet's nest. She'd broken the law in more ways than one. And he now suspected she had some really bad secrets he would not like at all.

She could not sit one more moment in the Jeep where anyone could come along and start up with her. Okay, think. One place. A place she hadn't thought of in years. Not till the lists. No one ever went there 'cause the only people that even knew about it anymore were dead or gone from this place, save herself. It would be quiet, peaceful, safe, and she could think. And maybe remember precisely what had gone on between her and Rick. She had everything she needed in her backpack. Her laptop, water, pens, paper, phone. Even a couple of packs of granola bars. First she'd need to transfer the jpegs from her phone into the laptop so she could work with them. Decide what to do with them.

Checking to make sure no one was around who knew her and could tell anyone where she had gone, she made a quick U-turn and headed out of town. At Weaver Road she turned left and followed the dirt tracks, seldom used now that the lake cut off the route, and at a thick grouping of cedar trees, pulled off the overgrown road and deep into the trees.

Backpack over her shoulder, she tromped through the woods, deeper and deeper into the thick overgrowth. The Diamond House lurked beneath kudzu vines, covered so completely she had to take out a pocket knife and hack away enough door covering to hunch and make her way inside.

Since she and Rick came here so long ago, the floor had rotted through in places. The kudzu, as was its habit, had totally covered even the roof. She could imagine that when it rained only a few drops would drip through. The gloom didn't reveal much, but she was able to find a corner where the floor still held good. There she slid down, opened the backpack, and laid out everything she would need. The laptop had a seven-hour battery and had been plugged in all night. That should give her plenty of time.

Computer on, she opened the phone, plugged it into the machine and began to transfer the photos she'd taken at the mortuary. Waiting gave her time to think.

What was she doing? She was probably in deep trouble for a story she had written several years ago that got people hurt, and here she was about to do the same thing again. No telling what she would find out about Rick and his alias Marcus Woods. But Parker had told her to do it, hadn't he? Still, what she had to think more about than anything else was what would Dal think? Her relationship with him had been slippery lately, and he never had trusted the reporter side of her. Now he might never speak to her again. But that was already a definite possibility.

As the download continued, her thoughts whirled. She would see what she had, then decide if it would hurt anyone or reveal any secrets. If it would then she wouldn't use it. She would take it to Parker and let him make the decision. What had she done with those lists Tinker had found in the B&B room? The ones Dal so wanted to see. To her mind they proved Steve was in town, here to get back at her for what she'd done. How ironic that would be if this story she was working on would somehow be tied to him. And Rick too. Wow. It was mind bending.

She dug around in the backpack, dumping most everything out before she found them. One read Parker, Mac, Dal, and Rick; the other had two places scribbled on it: the Diamond House and Lover's Leap. She hadn't forgotten those, but she didn't recall that the paper was torn from a pad, which might mean whatever was written on the previous page would be indented there. That was a trick they used on television mysteries all the time, but she'd never tried it. Worth a try.

A pencil in the bottom of the backpack had to be sharpened and she used the knife she'd hacked away the kudzu with. Once sharpened, she placed it on her own writing pad and rubbed the lead back and forth on the first list. In one corner was what appeared to be doodles that made no sense, but right under it were MW and RG followed by a question mark. Okay, if it had to do with the lists, then Marcus Woods and Rick Granger were easy guesses, though they didn't have to be correct. Who was she kidding? But even if they were, what was the story behind the deception?

How could Steve Wainwright have any knowledge of Marcus Woods or Rick Granger unless the missing man, the lists, and the murder were all connected? Seemed a big reach, though. Go a step further. The missing man registered as John Brown, an alias if she'd ever heard one. She jotted her own notes on a fresh sheet of paper while the computer and phone continued to do her bidding.

John Brown is Steve Wainwright. She copied the lists to her notes, then added the two sets of initials. She then drew lines from Rick to the Diamond House to Steve, then from Steve to John Brown. The tick beside Rick's name could only mean one thing. Steve had taken care of him. Killed him. Her stomach heaved. But how did he know Marcus Woods was Rick? Her thoughts went round and round.

The phone finished the uploads to the laptop, she opened them with her media program and brought them up on the screen. The first few pages were the results Doc had come up with, followed by pictures of the body and injuries. The gruesome stump where the killer(s) had removed the lower half of his right leg along with several angles of the removed leg and bare foot.

She was busy reading and scrolled down to fill the next page. Photos of the thigh and hip of that leg. And an oh-so-familiar birthmark, though she had only seen it once. Once a long time ago, while lying naked in this very house making love to a man she would never see again. Not until this moment. To make sure she bumped up the view for a closer look.

Whispered, "Oh, my God. I was right. It's Rick. Marcus Woods is Rick Granger." Her buried hope it wasn't true dissolved.

Tears in her eyes for that long ago lost moment in her life, she stared unseeing across the gloomy room. Confusion crowded out the sorrow. Who? Why? When? How? At least four questions that needed answering.

This time, though she would do everything right. She picked up the phone to call Parker, then Mac and let them know. It would mean confessing to stealing the files from Doc. How would she explain that? Ah, well, she could come up with something. The phone told her there was no service.

One thing she was absolutely sure of. Steve was coming after her and he'd killed once. Would he do it again, this time to her?

11

CHAPTER

Mac glowered at his cell phone, punched the front desk button. A man's voice answered.

"Who the hell is this?"

An audible swallow. "Colby, sir."

"Well, Colby *sir*, have you seen Deputy Starr or that reporter Jessie West anywhere?"

"Not since this morning, uh, sir."

"What about Tinker Mattawan?"

"Yes, sir. She came in about five minutes ago, sir. Said she'd be on the job shortly."

"So where is she now, son? And stop calling me 'sir.'"

"Yes, sir."

"Well?"

"Oh, sorry, sir. I mean, sorry sheriff."

"Could you answer my question?"

"I would, S… sheriff, if I remembered what it was."

"Where is Deputy Mattawan?"

"Uh, I'd imagine she's in the ladies room. Combing her hair, sir. Dang it. Combing her hair because she complained when she came in about the wind messing it all up. So—"

"Well, at least you're a good detective."

"I am? Thank you."

"Tell her, when she gets her hair combed, I'd like to see her for a moment. You can hang on to the desk a while longer, if you don't mind. Oh, and Deputy Colby—did you say what your last name is?— if you don't mind pulling another shift, I need someone to fill in for Deputy Starr while he's gone."

"Be happy to, sir. Son of a gun. What unit shall I take?"

"Come see me after Deputy Mattawan returns from my office and shows up to take over for you. Which you will tell her I said to do, please. Then I'll tell you what to drive and where to drive it and what to look for. And you'll introduce yourself."

"Yes, sir."

"Son, were you in the Army?"

"No, sir. The Marines, sir."

"And I don't suppose there's any way I can get you to stop calling me *sir*, is there?"

"Well, I'm trying, sir, but—"

"Where did you serve?"

"Afghanistan, sir. I mean, just Afghanistan. Two tours."

"Son, you have permission to call me *sir*. And I'm pleased to have you on the job here."

"Thank you, sir."

A huge smile on his face, Mac hung up. Now if only he could figure out what in thunder happened to Dallas and Jessie, he'd be happy. There was a slight chance they were together somewhere, but he couldn't imagine either of them neglecting their work, even though they did tend to have some hot and heavy get-togethers pretty often.

A rap on the door frame, and he looked up to see Tinker standing there looking a bit shame-faced.

"Come on in. Sit."

Her expression was apprehensive. Normal, probably, but she might've been up to something more with that so-called missing B&B client. So far he'd pretended not to know about it, just to see where she'd take it.

"When did you last see Jessie?"

Her eyes widened in surprise. "I thought—er, she left right after noon going to work. That's when I last saw her."

"Did she say if she was going straight to the office or what."

"No, but I thought she was."

"Do you know what story she's working on? Would she maybe have been meeting Deputy Starr somewhere?"

Tinker gulped. "I'm not sure. She was—I mean, I thought she was going to do a story from the press release you sent over there on the murder."

He nodded. "Okay, I'll call over there, see if she's shown up. I called a while ago and she wasn't there. Thanks, Deputy. You can tell Colby to come on in and I'll tell him which unit he's taking out and where he'll be patrolling."

Tinker stopped in the doorway, lifted her shoulders, then turned to glare at him with fire in her eyes. "The young guy you just hired is going out in the field?"

Mac shot to his feet. "We will not have this discussion again, Deputy Mattawan. And if you don't like the way things are handled around here you are free to resign. Under my watch women do not patrol. It's a man's job, a dangerous one at that. Be damned if I'll go to a woman's funeral."

"When was the last time a deputy came under fire in Grace County? Or even had a fight with someone? And we've never had to have a funeral, thank God."

"Dismissed, Deputy." No sense reminding her he had been under fire recently. He wasn't actually a deputy. She would call that to his attention. This could go on all day with Tinker involved. So he held his ground in grim silence.

She stared at him for a long moment, then took off her badge, stomped to his desk, and dropped it there. "Then I quit."

"Your prerogative. It's customary to give a two-week notice so I can make arrangements for someone to man the phones and your desk."

"Two weeks, then." She grabbed the badge, stuck it back on her belt, and took long, angry strides down the hall to the front desk.

He covered his mouth so she wouldn't see him smile, then stood in the door watching the two young deputies. He'd lost count of how many times Tinker had quit. Colby hopped up and rolled the chair around, held it so she could sit down.

"I don't need your help. I can hold my own chair."

The new young recruit looked as if he'd been slapped. Jaw set, he kept his eye on Tinker and marched to Mac's office.

"Don't pay her any mind." Mac chuckled. "She has four brothers and has always thought she's one of them instead of a dainty young woman. A wonder she didn't sock you."

Colby grinned and rubbed his chin. "Sure glad she didn't, sir. She looks like she packs a mighty wallop." He stood Marine straight. "Name's Colby Brewster, sir."

At least he didn't salute. Mac walked back behind his desk. "Good to meet you, Deputy Brewster. Sit. I remember you now. You were among the last bunch that came in to apply for this position. There must've been a dozen or more. Hope everyone got a job somewhere."

"Me too, but I'm pleased you chose me for this one."

"Where you from?"

"Marshal, Arkansas. Born and bred."

"Small town. How come you came back after serving?"

"Missed it. Always thought I wanted to live someplace else, till I went over there. Two tours and I was ready to come right back here. Couldn't get on the department over in Harrison, no openings. So this is close enough."

"Hmmm. Glad to have you. I need someone to patrol the southeast corner of the county today. Let me show you." He rose and went to a large map on the wall, pointed out the roads that crisscrossed the section he spoke of.

Colby took out his phone, shot a few pictures of the area from the map, and put it away. "No problem. Am I looking for anything or anyone in particular?"

"Just anyone kicking up a ruckus. You see anything that looks dangerous or strange, you don't walk into the situation alone. You understand me? Don't play hero. Put yourself where you can watch and call for back-up. You got that? Lots of black holes over there. No service on your cell. Got it?"

"Yes, sir. Hide, watch, and get help. Goes against my grain, but you're the boss."

"Damned right I am and I don't want any heroes on this job."

"Whatever you say, sir."

"While you're patrolling, keep an eye out for Deputy Dallas Starr's SUV. It's got the number one on the doors and the roof. Your unit is number six. That's your call as well. Keys are out in the hall on the wall. You take care, you hear?"

"Yes, sir. I will. What should I do if I spot number one?"

"Just let me know, that's all."

"Okay, and thank you, sir."

Mac watched the tall young man march off. Good country stock. Couldn't beat a Marine on the job. Reminded him of someone. He swiveled the chair, stared out the window into the past, back when he walked and talked like that young man. Till he'd been in country long enough to learn some bitter lessons. Vietnam and a war they'd been trained to lose. Vietnam and the day he'd watched his best friend die. Die for nothing but politics and folks back home who didn't give a damn. Kept telling himself they died for each other, those boys. Still did.

He shook away the memories, rose, and went out to talk to Tinker. Didn't want her to quit, hated she itched to go into danger. He ought to let her go, but he just couldn't bring himself to do it.

She watched him with a wary eye, like maybe he was going to yell at her or something. He smiled to ease her mind, but she looked away. Not going to make up so easily.

"Has Deputy Starr called in or been by?"

"No, haven't heard from him."

He hooked his thumbs in his belt and gazed out the door a while. "Not like him."

"He's been moody lately."

"Oh? Hadn't noticed."

"Men don't."

"Don't what?"

"Notice lots of stuff."

"I suppose. What do you reckon is wrong?"

"You might ask Jessie. He's pretty close-mouthed though."

"Would if I could find her."

"It's Tuesday. They're running every which way to get the paper out. Maybe Parker knows where she is. Funny, she's usually over there working. She must be out on a story."

Tink turned her gaze toward Mac, then quickly away. She knew something she wasn't saying. Eventually he'd find out, though. He always did.

Jessie gathered up her notes, carefully folded the two valuable slips of paper from the B&B, put everything in her backpack, and picked her way over the rotted flooring to the door of the Diamond House. Above it, patches of sunlight snuck past the kudzu to shimmer through the glass diamond. No one had ever figured out who built this place and why they put a glass diamond shape above each of three outside doors plus some of the windows. She'd searched a lot of history, interviewed plenty of people, but never learned the answer. In fact, most of the folks she asked about it didn't even know the house was there, overgrown as it was. The owner of record was unreachable. That in itself was strange.

Leaving behind yesterday's ghosts, she tore her way through the creeping vines and thick saplings. When she reached the Jeep, she was sweating, and paused to drink from the water bottle in her backpack. Where should she go first, the sheriff's office or the newspaper? Perhaps if she wanted to keep her job she'd best get back to the paper. At least pretend to write a new story from Mac's latest release.

Before her belly kissed her backbone she'd stop at the Red Bird and get a hamburger to go. The usual crowd filled the small café so she sat at a table with Theron and Fudge. Naturally they got to talking while she waited for her burger and fries.

"Ole Dal's car broke or something?" Fudge forked up some meatloaf, waited for her reply.

"Don't reckon, why?"

"Seen him riding one of them bikes out toward Red Rock earlier."

"Bikes? You mean a motorcycle?"

He drew a circle in the air with his knife. "Nope. A bicycle, like kids ride, only with all them extra gears."

"That's odd. Did he say where he was going?"

"Never spoke. Was concentrating mighty hard on something. Figgered I'd let him be. Knowing how he is."

Ruby brought her order in a paper sack and set the drink down beside it. Jessie excused herself, paid at the cash register and hurried out to her car. Where in the world was Dal going on a bike? Red Rock? He didn't bike or hike or camp. Better leave him be. He was pretty upset over this latest killing that he couldn't seem to read. Probably needed some space. She drove on to the paper, took her meal inside and, against Parker's orders, ate at her desk while working on a dull story taken from Mac's press release. There'd be another release, hopefully, before next week's paper so she didn't try to finish it.

If Parker noticed, he didn't say anything. Just glanced at her, then left. She remembered where he was going, and a good thing too. He usually didn't just take off like that. Sick horse, needed medicated. He had mentioned it earlier. Everyone was acting really weird today, doing things they usually didn't do. Must be something in the air.

Wendy leaned out around the corner from her desk. "You're sure quiet today, Jessie. Anything going on?"

Jessie laughed. Evidently she too was acting weird. "Ah, it's just a crazy day. Lots on my mind." Like being in possession of classified material. Yeah, there is that.

"Let's take a break out in the sunshine for a while. It's gonna be a long day and I'm about cross-eyed reading these correspondents' articles."

Funny, she'd finished her hamburger without even tasting it. So she carried her Coke outside where she and Wendy leaned against the Jeep in the sunlight and gabbed about nothing in particular. Well, almost.

"I nearly forgot," Wendy said, out of the blue. "There was a guy in here looking for you while you were gone earlier. I was so busy I hardly paid any attention, so I come close to forgetting. Sorry."

Oh, crap. "Did he say who he was?"

"Nope. Tough looking fellow. Had a mouth on him. Like he was pissed off or something. Said to tell you when you came in that he'd see you real soon. He didn't sound like he thought you'd be too happy about it. Couldn't get a name out of him."

For a moment Jessie had trouble swallowing the mouthful of coke. Finally she got it down. "Did he ask where I lived or anything?"

"No, and I wouldn't have told him if he did. Didn't like his attitude."

"Like what kind of attitude?"

"I don't know. Just a smart ass, you know? Wanted to know if you were any good at your job or if you caused any trouble here. Stuff like that."

"What did he look like?"

"Um, scruffy. Real bright blue eyes. Could've used a shave and a haircut. An odor like he could stand a wash. At the time I wanted to tell him to clean himself up. He might have been handsome if he did."

Steve? The bright blue eyes fit. So did the scruffy, but only when he was undercover. Far as she knew he wasn't working for the law in any form. Well, shit.

"Did he say where he was going?"

"Just said he'd wait for you. I asked for his name a couple of times, but he just acted like he didn't hear me."

It must be Steve. She had to get everything done and get on over to see Mac. It was time she came clean about this mess before she got herself hurt or killed. As soon as Parker got back she'd tell him what was going on and what she was going to do, then she'd go tell Mac. But one secret she would have to keep for now, and that was her possession of copies of the Marcus Woods—or Rick Granger—papers. Upset over Rick's death, she couldn't help but wonder what in the world he'd been involved in that brought it about. What she needed was more time to try to figure out the redacted papers and why Doc had them. And she wanted to talk to Rick's dad, Bud Granger. He was strangely missing from the Red Bird today.

Parker returned and put everyone to work. "I'm going to have to sit up all night with that sick mare, so let's get this stuff done. Have to get back soon. Left the neighbor kid there keeping her on her feet."

She caught him before he drove off. "I'll go home with you and help if you'd like."

He sat behind the wheel a minute, then nodded. "Okay, I appreciate that. Just have to medicate her regularly all night and make sure she stays on her feet. If she lays down we could lose her. Vet says she acts foundered, but I left all the feed shut up tight. You sure you're up for it? Tomorrow will be a helluva long day no matter how we look at it."

"I'll follow you over in my car. I finished that story. There wasn't much in the release."

"Okay, good. And, Jess, I really appreciate this. I'm dead tired."

"Well, this way you can sleep a few hours after you show me what to do and I'll stay up with her. You know I love your horses."

He regarded her with deep brown eyes, then nodded. "Okay, then see you there in a few."

By morning, the mare was showing some signs of recovery. She no longer wanted to lie down, instead was moving about in the corral. Parker had risen about one and Jessie curled up on his bed. He awoke her at eight and they ate breakfast together.

Every once in a while she looked up to find him studying her, a soft expression on his face. She would smile, then go back to eating.

Finally, he stood.

"Think I'll take a shower. Feel grungy. I'll bet you do, too."

"I guess." He didn't leave and she laid down her spoon. "What?"

He held out a hand, those brown eyes saying so much. She rose and went to him, put her fingers in his warm grip. This had been coming for a long while. Curiosity walked up and down her spine, played with her erogenous zones. He was the exact opposite of Dal. Tender, soft spoken, polite, shy in ways that made her wonder what making love with him would be like. It looked like she was about to find out.

He led her through his bedroom to a large bath with a walk-in rain shower that was larger than Dal's entire bath. He ran his fingers through her hair and down one side of her neck, lifted her chin.

"Are you sure? It's been a long while for me. I may disappoint you." His voice rasped, nudged her desire to be caressed, petted.

She kissed his palm, still lying along her jawline. "I don't think so."

His lips closed on hers, taking his time as if he were memorizing every line of her mouth. On her toes, she slipped her arms around his neck, nestled against him. He wasn't as muscled as Dal, but firm enough. Be good to stop comparing the two, but she couldn't help it. He cupped her buttocks and pulled her closer. Their lips never moved apart while he worked her jeans down over her hips. Following his lead she unfastened his belt and unzipped his pants.

Amazing how slowly they went about this. By now, Dal would have had her stripped and been naked himself. And she liked that about him and the way he made love. But something about the heady anticipation with Parker built a fire that engulfed her with desire. A flame that teased at her, ignited a passion that made her dizzy.

He must have felt the same, for he moaned and ran his hands up under her blouse, cupped her breasts so they rested in the curve between his thumb and fingers. Steam from the shower filled the room, and he leaned down, breath hot and moist where he nibbled through the lacy bra. She gripped her thighs together, squirmed at an orgasm that teased erotically. They weren't even under the shower yet and she was about to come. Tiny noises escaped her throat when he slipped both hands behind her back and unfastened the clasp of the bra, slowly lifted the straps off her shoulders and moved his lips and tongue and teeth from lace to flesh.

Needing to move on, yet desperate to keep his mouth right where it was, tasting her like she was candy, she worked his pants down to release his erection and wrapped her fingers around it. Mmmm. Nice. Hot, hard, and ready.

His reaction, to bend her backward, suck at her breast and moan, was all she could take. Her insides were going wild while he worshiped her mammary glands.

"I want that inside me. Could we do that?" Her words came out a bit shaky.

"Oh, God." The words hoarse against her skin.

"Come on, let's shuck these clothes and get in the shower. Okay?" By now snakes crawled all over her.

"Uhm, yes. Okay. You sure you want to do this?" Funny thing for him to say while she gripped his cock.

"If you do. Yes."

"What about you and that deputy?"

"What about us?"

"I thought you—"

"You want to do this or not, 'cause he has nothing to do with us. It's different, that's all. I like you a lot."

"And I like you. I just don't do this very often anymore. In fact I haven't—"

"I don't need to know all that. Come here, I'll help you get out of your clothes. I like undressing men. I'll show you what to do if you're worried about that. Too late to quit now, buddy."

He laughed, sounding a bit embarrassed.

"Let's get out of our clothes. It'll be a lot easier then."

They moved somewhat awkwardly into the adjoining bedroom where he sat on the edge of the bed. "Shoes, I need to get out of my shoes."

She dropped to her knees, let the bra straps slip off so she was naked, then took off his shoes and socks, and finished pulling his pants off. Dark hair curled over his chest arms and legs. She was accustomed to Dal's nearly hairless body, and ran her fingertips over Parker's chest. His eyes were closed, his expression one of supreme enjoyment. Leaning forward she bit at his nipples, taking her time moving from one to the other.

A groan rumbled up from his throat. Slowly she moved down the center of his stomach, separated his knees and lightly kissed his erection, touching it with the tip of her tongue.

"Good Lord." His muscles jerked.

"Now, into the shower and I'll show you a few things you may have forgotten, since you don't do this very often."

And so she did, making sure to go slowly since he'd set that pace. It was nice, not being so frantic. Exploring each other with hands and mouths until finally he backed her up against the wall and eased inside her so slowly she gasped with delight. When she could take it no longer she hooked her legs around his waist and shoved hard as she could.

He got with the program, gathered her close, and moved in and out, increasing the pace slow and easy. How he kept it up so long, she couldn't imagine, but she came over and over before he finally climaxed. He buried his face in the curve of her throat, and clung to her, gasping as if he'd run a mile. At long last he quieted, cupped a hand over the back of her head, and wrapped his other arm around her waist.

"That was beautiful. Thank you." Whispered in her ear.

What a strange man. She'd never been thanked in such a way for sex.

On top of that, he then grabbed a wash cloth and soap and bathed her from face to toes, taking so much time that she grew hot again. On his knees, he looked up at her when he'd finished washing her feet, his face even with her stomach.

"Would you like me…?"

She nudged his head forward. "Yes, I would."

By the time they finished pleasuring each other further, the water was cold.

She would never look at him the same again.

In his jockeys, he sat on the bed and watched her dress. Because he was enjoying it so much, she did a little dance between slipping into each garment. On the edge of the bed beside him, slipping into her shoes, she suddenly couldn't think of anything to say.

"Now what do we do?" He stood, dragged out a clean pair of jeans and a knit shirt, and put them on.

"I don't think I know."

"Well, you've got the deputy, and I've got… uh, celibacy I guess."

"Parker, there's not a woman comes into the office who doesn't wish she could go to bed with you."

He flushed. "You're kidding, of course."

"Not at all. Tell you what. The next available female who enters, ask her out just for coffee. Bet you money she'll go with you. Then if you like her, go to the next step."

He glanced at her with a half grin. "Ask her to take a shower with me?"

"No, silly." She laughed, then caught him looking at her with that same burning expression that put her in the shower with him. "I have to admit you give one hell of a shower. If you look at her that way right there, she just might crawl in there with you."

"I've been married three times. I fall for someone, I want to marry them. If we didn't work together I'd ask you right this minute to go to the court house and marry me. Nope, it's better I stay away from women. Though, don't get me wrong, I'm pleased that we did this. I'll never forget it."

She kept her mouth shut, but wished he'd find him someone he could love and live with and be happy. For whatever reason, he must be difficult to live with. Working with him showed her some of the reasons why. He was a real slob, and too particular about other people's habits and opinions.

It was getting dark when they left, him to return to the paper and her to head home. In the car, halfway there, she suddenly remembered what she had planned to do that afternoon. Confess to Mac and tell him about Steve and why he was here. And tonight she'd planned on poring through the papers she'd stolen photos of at the mortuary. Parker was right. They couldn't keep this up and work together. Maybe she could get to that soon as she got home.

Her phone rang while she was gathering her backpack and keys to get out of the Jeep.

It was Mac. "You seen Dal at all today?"

"Nope, why?"

"He's nowhere to be found and his unit is parked at his place. Ina Mae says she saw him leave out on a bicycle earlier today. A bicycle? What do you suppose he's up to?"

"I have no earthly idea. He's been sort of strung out lately. Not figuring out much about the dead body has him in a quandary. Fudge did tell me he saw him headed up to Red Rock on a bike. I thought maybe he'd been enjoying too much of his crop. You know Fudge."

"Yep, I do, but it's not something I discuss or like to think about. Red Rock, huh? Well, he's a grown man, but still, it's pretty rugged up there and if he gets off on some of those hiking trails he could be at the bottom of a ravine. With no cell service, we'd never know."

"Mac, you don't seriously think he could be in trouble?"

"Not yet, but he don't get back or get in touch soon, I'm gonna go looking for him.

One of the things we encourage folks to do is go into the wilderness in groups or at least in pairs. How many times have I heard him preach that? And what does he do? Takes off on some rattly old bike, doesn't tell us where he's going and he does it alone. But that's just like him. You'd think he was addlepated or something."

Dal could be a little boy, the way Mac carried on but she could see his point. Still, if there was anyone who could take care of himself it was Dal Starr. Like last year when those hoodlums had trussed him up in the back of their car, he'd not only broke loose, he'd taken one's gun away from him and shot the other one with it. And he'd only been out of the hospital a few days when they grabbed him. No, she wouldn't worry too much about his safety.

Brad met her at the door and zipped out between her legs. She'd have to quit going off and forgetting she had a dog. Poor little bugger. He could stay outside during the day, but she needed to remember to put him out when she left for work.

Hours later, the phone rang waking her from a deep sleep. She turned over to see the clock read 4:33. It was plumb dark outside. When she hit the button to answer, a voice began to jabber at her.

"Who is this?"

"Colby Brewster. Tink asked me to call you."

"At four-thirty in the morning?"

"She didn't say a time. No, she said the park ranger found a bicycle hid in the brush up on top of the mountain near the trail access at Red Rock, and called the sheriff's department to see if anyone is missing in town. She wants you to come down there. She broke into the deputy's locker and found his weapon, his phone, his equipment belt." He paused.

"Wait, down where? What deputy?"

"The sheriff's station. Number One, uh, Dallas Starr. I thought it was illegal to break into someone's locker."

"Technically it is. Where are you?"

"Almost there. She wants me to come in and take care of dispatch so you and her can do something. I couldn't understand what she said there."

Oh, crap. What in the world was going on now?

"Has anyone talked to Mac?"

Silence, then static. "I don't think so."

"Well, someone better or he'll have a cow. I'm on my way."

No telling what was going on with Dal. But he ought to be home by now. What was wrong with him? Going biking on a dangerous hiking trail. Oh sure, he could take care of himself, but if he fell off a bluff or something he could be hurt real bad.

12
CHAPTER

Dal opened his eyes, or thought he did. Black as night so he couldn't see. Where had he been last? Not home. What the hell? Where was he? What was he doing here? He couldn't move. Intense pain. Arms and legs. Chest. Back. Paralyzed. His brain froze. The thing he had most feared, ever since the shooting. In Dallas.

Had it all been a dream? Jessie and the job. Arkansas? And here he lay in some care home. A coma. Could be. But he was waking up. That was good, wasn't it?

Still. Paralyzed. His head hurt, pain radiating from behind one ear. Couldn't even raise a hand to feel it. Find out how big it was. Was it bleeding? Something had him pinned down, but down to what?

A slight breeze dried the sweat on his face. An owl hollered who and waited for a response. Nothing. Poor lonely fellow. He could relate. But it was a good sign, that owl. A sign of wisdom. Something else, but he couldn't think.

Share some wise, old buddy.

This was ridiculous. Maybe he was tied to a bed in a hospital. The way he hurt, that's where he ought to be. But something poked at his hip, the pain so bad he couldn't be lying in a soft bed. Besides, in a hospital there'd be lights. There'd be those funny pinging sounds of equipment, and the squish squish of nurses' shoes on tile. Not a breeze and an owl hooting.

First off, the thing to do was start with one part of his body, move it and go on till he'd tried out every inch, see what would move and what wouldn't. Obviously there'd been an accident, but where was he? If he could remember something about the day or the evening it would help. Only thing he knew absolutely was it was night. Nearby frogs croaked, and a pleasant sound he couldn't place. Frogs. Water. A creek.

My God, he was outside but where? Definitely not that alley in Dallas. Not a hospital in Dallas.

The owl spoke again. Not ready to give up. Some thought they meant death. Don't think about that shit. This ain't nothing. You've been through worse.

At least his brain was working a little bit. He knew who he was. At least who he thought he was. Yet what had happened? His thoughts turned circles till they made absolutely no sense. Nothing would come from his mouth, no sound at all.

Jesus, his head hurt.

A rustling nearby. A glow. A face. Someone was here.

"Grandson, you are in trouble. Can you not move?"

"I can't move." The words, garbled, hoarse. And he was imagining someone. No, not someone. A head floating about, glowing in the pitch dark. He was in bad shape.

The head moved closer. Feet. Moccasins. "Who are you?"

"I am Grandfather. You are far away from any help. Will your instrument summon for you?"

What the hell was he talking about? His instrument?

"The thing you call upon someone with."

"Phone. Phone." Saying the words pained his mouth and he tasted blood. "Please."

"Yes, that is it. Do you have it or did you lose it in the fall?"

"Fall? Where did I fall?" It was so hard to speak. It was worse to breathe, to think, to try to move. The mountain. Not a dream after all.

"You are not as sure of foot as I. You were not so clumsy as to step off a trail. Someone else was there. I think perhaps they pushed—"

"Grandfather, my head hurts too bad to listen to this. I'm not a Cherokee warrior like you. I can't... can't—"

More rustling nearby. So thirsty. Tongue dry, mouth dryer. The water, so close. A stream? Would he dare drink from it? Depended on where he was. That was a laugh. He'd have to get to it before he could drink it.

Once more, he tried to move, even just a little. One leg would not move at all. What if he'd broken it? But the other one finally twitched to one side, sending a roaring pain upward to explode at the base of his skull. Stupid to be relieved that he'd fallen off a mountain. Still, there it was.

A grunt from nearby, more a growl, loud and scary. So ferocious he would've run given a choice. He chose to close his eyes and deny everything. Much better in the black, fuzzy nowhere.

"It is a black bear, Grandson. He will not hurt you."

Jerked back to reality. Reality. That was some joke. Did he tell you that?

There was something badly wrong with him. Hallucinating, paralyzed, mute or nearly so. And possibly brain dead. On his way to the land in the sky.

Something cold nosed his bare arm. Snuffled a hot breath. Made its way down his body with little grunting sounds that sounded friendly. Dal let out a small breath. Waited. What might happen next? He wished to stop his heart from pounding so hard, so loud.

Go on your way, friend bear. I will not, cannot hurt you. Just get me out of here. Someone get me out of here.

"Rest. Someone will come." A feathery touch across his cheek.

No, come back. Don't leave me here alone. The words would not come from his mouth. His mind passed to another place, leaving behind the pain, the anguish, the terror. The bear, Grandfather, the frogs, the sound of water, trembled away. Peace engulfed him, cradled his aching head, bore him away.

Jessie drove like mad till she arrived at the square, then braked and skidded into the parking lot at the sheriff's station, leaped from the Jeep and ran inside.

Tinker stood at the window behind the desk inside the front door. "Did Colby tell you what's going on?"

"I'm not sure. Why don't you try?"

Tink paced, threw her arms upward. "Okay. Got a call from the park ranger who told me there's an abandoned bike up along the hiking trail at Red Rock on the mountain."

"Got that much. Start from there." Dal? Surely not.

"Don't you see? It probably belongs to the guy who is missing from the B&B. He's gone hiking and is lost up there somewhere."

"Tink, why did you call me? You need to call the ranger back, tell him someone is missing, and let him arrange for a search party to leave as soon as the sun comes up."

Her friend stared at her. "I thought we could go. This is my case."

"Not in the state park, it isn't. Let the rangers handle it." Wait, bike abandoned. What if it was Dal? Oh, sure. Fudge, the local marijuana grower and dealer and user, said he saw him riding up the mountain on a bike yesterday. What if it was him? Now she was ready to go up there herself. Dal had been acting so strange, no telling what he'd been up to. She'd never even seen him on a bike and he takes one out on that rugged mountain trail? He must really be in trouble to want to be that alone.

First, call him. Phone in hand, she plopped into an empty chair, punched in his number. It rang, then his voicemail came on. "Dal, call me as soon as you get up, would you?" She tried his cell. Same result.

Now what? Suppose that was his bike. She grabbed Tink's arm. "You stay right here, I'll be back in twenty. Doubt Colby can get here before that. If he does, just wait. I've got to check something. Be right back. Don't go anywhere."

The last she said while pushing out the door, with Tink yelling "Wait, wait," after her.

She made it to Hidden Holler Trailer Park in twelve minutes. All was dark save the safety light on a pole in the center of the cluster of mobile homes. Dal's vehicle was nosed up against his trailer. She hopped out, sorted his key out on the ring, and went inside. It didn't take long to learn he wasn't there. Short of breath and more than frightened, she ran back to the Jeep, hurried down to Ina Mae's and pounded on her door till a very ruffled old woman in a flannel nightgown finally answered.

"What the thunder is going on out here? Can't you come see me at a decent hour?" She flipped on the porch light and peered up at Jess, white hair standing on end to reflect the glow. "Oh, Jessie, it's you. What's wrong? What's happened? Do I need my shotgun?"

"No, Ina Mae. I have a question. Was there a bicycle stored in the shed here? One that maybe Dal rode off on yesterday?"

"Yep. Dallas rode out of here yesterday on it. Didn't see him come back, just figured he did. Why?"

"He's not home. Can we go see if the bike is back, real quick? Please."

"Let me get my shoes on."

"Wait, is the shed locked?"

"Heavens no, child. Why would it be locked?"

In a few seconds Ina Mae returned properly shod and carrying a flashlight. She started out across the yard toward the shed, with Jessie running along behind. "We could take the car."

"Nonsense, it's only a short ways out there."

The old woman shuffled along, with Jess wishing she'd hurry. She finally shoved open the shed door, flashed the light beam all around.

"Well, looks like there's no bike in here. Why would Dallas ride a bike when he has a perfectly good car sitting up yonder?"

"I don't know, but I'll find out." Jessie didn't feel right running off and leaving Ina Mae to get back to her house alone, so she walked along beside her, itching to get going. Just as she reached the Jeep her cell rang. It was Mac.

She settled in the seat, prepared to go through everything one more time. Maybe then she could get her own search party organized.

With the phone on speaker she spilled everything she knew and some of what she suspected, holding back Tinker's information about the missing man. It was up to her friend to confess that. Winded, she stopped for a breath.

Mac's tone was incredulous. "Can you see out the window that's it's dark? So, number one, this is ranger business unless they ask for our help. Number two, we can't do anything in the flat-out black night whether they do or not. Number three, why did Deputy Mattawan call Deputy Brewster in from patrol? Just who in tarnation is running my department, anyway?"

"But Mac—"

"If he's still among the missing at daylight, we'll notify the rangers so they can begin a search. We'll offer assistance if it's needed. Meanwhile everyone needs to go back to what they are supposed to be doing. Solve this murder. You, I can't boss around, but I can tell you to stay out of my deputies' business and mind your own."

"Okay, you don't have to yell."

"It seems I do." A click and he was gone.

Boy, talk about waking up grumpy. Mac was an expert at that. Still, the last time Dal pulled a disappearing act, Mac had a conniption fit. Maybe he got used to him going off and decided it was nothing to worry about. She felt different.

Back at the sheriff's station, she filled Tink in.

Looking worried, her friend tramped another round in the small office. "We've got to get out there, see what happened."

"It's dark, very dark up on that mountain. I doubt you want to go there till morning. So, you just call Colby, tell him Mac wants him to stay on patrol wherever he is supposed to be, and you sit here at this desk till your replacement comes in."

"Okay about the dark. But what are you going to do? Call your boss and ask his permission for you to go up there? He'll let you do just about anything you want, the way he looks at you."

"Where did you get that idea? First place, I don't have to ask him what I can do on my own time, and Lord knows the middle of the night does belong to me." Was it possible she and Parker transmitted their feelings to everyone? It was just a one-night thing. Neither could afford to have it get around that they had slept together.

"Oh, come on. I have a feeling if Dallas Starr was no longer present it wouldn't be long before the two of you hooked up."

"Well, you're wrong. Dal and I are tight." She held up crossed fingers. And if he didn't show up and soon, she'd see to it they had every law enforcement member in the state looking for him. And have Mac looked at by a doctor, cause he wasn't acting right at all.

"I'm going up there. I know I can't do anything till the sun comes up, but I don't think they can stop us from taking part in a search and rescue."

An expression of dismay on her face, Tink plopped down in her chair. "Well, after sitting up all night I won't be worth much, but I'll be up there soon as I'm relieved here. Mac can fire me if he wants, but he can't tell me what to do on my own time either. Can he? Besides, I quit once already."

Again? She wouldn't reply to that.

Actually, he probably would, whether he should or not, but Jessie kept her mouth shut about that.

She drove home, head spinning with possibilities. In the kitchen, helped by Brad who followed her every step, she dumped her backpack, refilled it with bottles of water a handful of health bars, the box of Wet Ones, ibuprofen. She stopped, turned a few circles. Tried to imagine the worst so she'd be prepared. The idea of Dal lost or hurt in the wilderness remained with her. It wasn't cold at night yet but maybe that space blanket she'd picked up at a flea market 'cause she thought it was cool.

She found it in the back of the linen closet, rolled it into a small, tight bundle, and stuffed it in on top of everything else.

It couldn't possibly be Dal. It just wasn't something he'd do. Biking through the woods? Nah. Yet, where did he go on that bike and why wasn't he back? Still, whoever it was, it would make a heck of a story, so she'd be there all the way, taking pictures, interviewing searchers, and eventually interviewing whoever was lost, if they lived through it. Maybe it was Tinker's missing man, and maybe he wasn't Steve. Things were so confusing at this point it was better not to assume anything. At the last minute she grabbed her computer. It was a long time till sunup and she was still a reporter.

In the car, her mind took up earlier thoughts. Whoever left the bike had gone that far, then started hiking the trail. Maybe it wasn't the one Dal had ridden out on. It was a popular trail, beginning north of Cedarton and twisting through the wilderness down to Mount Nebo and on into the Ouachita Mountains.

The drive up the mountain in a night so dark it was like being afloat in space left her time to think. No landmarks stood out. Music blared on the CD player, to only accomplish the feeling of dread and loneliness. Headlights were smothered by a heavy fog so she slowed to a crawl. To add to the depressing setting, thunder rolled over the mountains and fat raindrops splatted the windshield. Not a good time to traipse around in the woods looking for someone who might not even be in trouble. There was still no answer on Dal's landline or cell. Wherever he'd gone off to, he would have returned by now unless he was injured.

Convinced the man missing from the B&B was Steve, she could easily be tracking him down only to meet whatever fate he had in store for her. On the other hand it was like Dal to go where he pleased without informing anyone. He'd done it before when he took off to St. Louis and Mercy Hospital last year because he didn't want anyone knowing about his back. Still, it was the abandoned bike that bothered her. What if Steve had learned about her relationship with Dal, followed him, and thrown him off a cliff? Seriously? Get real, Jessie. If Steve did attack Dal, it would more likely be him who went off a cliff, not Dal. But Steve would come for her and her friends. That much she knew about him. After all someone had already killed one of the men on the list. Rick Granger.

Every once in a while Dal did something out of character. In truth, he could very well have ridden off on that bicycle and decided to bike the trail for a while. He was mighty upset over the problems he had with the burning car and the body. He just couldn't get a handle on either of them. She wasn't sure if he was frustrated because he couldn't read them, or if it was because what he read turned out to be wrong. The only way she could find that out would be to figure out what Mac knew about the murders.

She hammered at the steering wheel. All those pictures she took of the papers she found at the mortuary were in her computer back at the house. Shouldn't she be studying them instead of wandering around in the middle of the night in the fog and rain? Better to try and find out more about her childhood friend, Rick Granger, and how he became Marcus Woods. And what was he doing lying on a slab in the morgue? What a story this could turn out to be. Ironic that her biggest story yet would explode in the papers while Steve combed the state for her in order to seek revenge for another big story. She deserved punishment for what that had done to Steve. But this one, no. It was a story that needed told. A hometown man and how he somehow became an undercover agent. And further, why he died a terrible death and who killed him.

She rounded a curve, the tires skidding in wet gravel. She was on top of the mountain. Flashlight in hand, she climbed from the Jeep into a steady rain, and waded knee-deep soggy grasses to reach a rock sign that read, Ozark Loop Trail—Red Rock—Eighteen Mile Mark. If the bike had been found near the trail and close to the road this was the spot, for the two veered away from each other here. Beyond the sign she flashed the beam around until a red reflector caught the light. Only a few more steps into the edge of the woods, she found the bike. Lying on its side. Nothing else. Some clue.

Propping the flashlight against a tree, she cupped both hands around her mouth and yelled for Dal. Once, twice, three times. Rain came down harder, wetting her face. The echo of her own voice bounced around, eerie and isolated. There was no use straining to see. The rain melted the fog away, but became the enemy of sight and sound.

Forlorn and wet and cold, she climbed back into the Jeep, started the engine, turned up the heater, and leaned back to wait for daylight.

Blind, wet, and cold, Dal struggled to open his eyes. Nothing. Panic then terror embraced him. He was back in that alley, full of bullets and waiting for the final head shot. Yet he'd been down that road many times and pain had never been a part of the nightmare. Panic and terror, yes, but not pain. This was not the nightmare, but the trauma itself. If he had hurt before, now he was in agony. And if he did not somehow crawl to his feet and escape this place, he would die. And he did not want to die. The possibility crept over him, a black cocoon that threatened to take away his last breath.

"Grandson? Can you move?"

"No… yes… I don't know."

"Do you recall the tale of the warrior sorely wounded by his enemies? How he hears the wolf's howl and how the wolf comes to him, licks his wounds. Over and over he continues to return and lick his wounds. Each time before the wolf leaves him, he tells him not as in a dream, but face to face, that he must keep up his courage, for he will soon be healed and return to his home. Soon he is able to sit and it is not long before he is found and restored to his people."

"A myth, Grandfather. Besides, there are no wolves here."

"Ah, do not be so certain of that, Grandson. Now close your eyes and you will soon awaken to the howl of a wolf. Believe in him, welcome him, and he shall heal you."

Crazy old man. He would die here.

And there was nothing he could do at all.

He drifted off, perhaps this time to enter the Darkening Land. A howl in the distance stirred him into consciousness. For a time he was foolish enough to await the arrival of the wolf who would lick his wounds. Then he came to his senses, opened his eyes to moonbeams, and the movement of fairies… no, not fairies, for they did not exist. Fireflies, their flashing so bright they lit his skin. The storm had passed. At least for that, he could be grateful. That he was alive, not so much. He was soaked through.

Again the howling. A rustling in leaves and standing over him, gazing down at him, the golden eyes of a white wolf. She stepped close, and licked his face and neck. Soon she had worked her way along his arms, and even though he wore clothing, her tongue brushed his flesh as if he were naked. And it felt soothing, healing. After she left, he fell into a deep sleep, and once again awoke to her licking him.

"Grandfather, are you here?"

"It is time you rose and returned to your people. And time for you to forgive yourself. You have paid much and she still haunts you."

"No, Grandfather. I cannot forgive myself for letting her get hooked on those drugs. I should have saved her. I spent years on the streets saving other people, and it never occurred to me I was needed at home to save the woman I loved. I will never pay enough for that mistake to be forgiven."

"She forgives you, you know."

"She is dead. Dead. How can she forgive me?"

"Because her spirit seeks peace and she is sorry she hurt you so much. Until you stop punishing yourself, her spirit cannot find solace. She is waiting for you to let her go." Grandfather spread his arm to indicate the surrounding trees.

Above his head, through branches shedding colorful leaves down around him, the sky lightened. A rainbow arched across the heavens and a fireball streaked through the opening.

"It is a sign."

The next breath he took dragged in cool, clean air. Dare he hope he was free of guilt and bitterness? He did not believe in signs, still the glorious beauty of such a sight touched him to the core.

He moved his legs. Short, jerky movements filled with excruciating pain, but they moved. After more struggle, he used one arm for one would not work, to push himself upright. A groan rolled from deep inside his gut. Muscles tightened across his belly. More pain. Sitting, he took in his surroundings.

He was very near the rim of a bluff, his feet so close to the edge he scooted backward to keep from sliding off. Surprised that he could move, he experimented some more and was able to get a bit further back from the sheer drop into a canyon. Pain sent shards of darkness through his vision, but he tamped it down. He had been here before. He could do this.

How close he had come to death. A few more feet and he would have plunged to the bottom of the rugged ravine. His body would probably never have been found. Grinding his teeth, he grabbed a sapling and dragged himself still farther from the edge. Every muscle, every bone, even his teeth, ached, but he could move. Little at a time he worked his way above a larger tree where he could lean back against it and rest.

"Well, Grandfather, I reckon that wolf showed up after all." No reply.

Had it been real? Surely not. No more than wild ass dreams, the result of tumbling head over heels halfway down a mountain. Probably had a concussion, maybe even a broken bone or two. He couldn't tell yet, the pain was so severe as to feel like he might've broken every single one in his body. Yet he could move. Maybe within another day he would be able to work his way up the incline from tree to tree, until he finally reached the trail where someone would come along who could help him.

Settled against the rough bark of a large oak tree, he patted his pockets for his cell phone. Most of this area had no service, but he needed to know. The phone was gone. Maybe he'd lost it in the fall. Not that it mattered.

Perhaps Mac or some of the rangers were already looking for him. He allowed himself a wry chuckle. It would have helped if he'd told someone where he was going.

The DEA papers she'd copied to her computer told a story that sent chills down Jessie's spine. Names, dates, and places were blacked out, but the story was there. At least for a nosy reporter who didn't give up easily.

The main character in the story, Rick Granger, had been turned by the FBI and became an informant for the DEA against a drug trafficker. How a boy from Arkansas ended up involved with drug traffickers was a good story in itself. She had to fill in the blanks since the FBI or DEA did not write their reports in a story-like way. But it didn't take much imagination to put it all together.

Rick's best friend was involved in dealing drugs and introduced Rick to that life. Because of his ability with accounts, he was quickly put to work, probably for his best friend's father. He was arrested for some sort of crime and was turned by the DEA. He had no choice. It was that or go to jail. Then he was sent back in as an informant. To help put a stop to the movement of drugs throughout the west coast. Six months ago the trial against the boss using Rick as one of the star witnesses, found him guilty. He was sent to prison for life and because of constant threats against his life, Rick went into Witness Protection and became Marcus Woods. So why was Marcus then reported missing by his wife? No answer to that here.

She might never figure out the names of all the players, but it wouldn't be too hard to get online and find trial reports. Small town boy makes good in the drug business, then is murdered for testifying against his old boss. She could interview his father, Bud Granger, who lived alone since his wife died, and some people in town who knew him.

The thing was, did she want to write this story? She came home to get away from this type of dangerous reporting. Stuff that could hurt innocent people. Bud Granger would never get over this coming out into the open. He had other children. How would they be affected? And the bottom line. Did she want to put herself in danger? Someone might decide to shut her up, permanently. What, if anything, Steve had to do with this was anyone's guess. She couldn't believe he was involved at all. But what a wild coincidence if he wasn't.

Someone rapped on the passenger side window and she startled. It was close to light enough to make out features, and she squinted to see the face framed by a hoodie.

No luck. A man, that was for certain. Nothing else was, though.

She slipped her hand into the console where she kept her gun, then smiled. He made a motion like rolling the window down and again looked extremely friendly.

She was having none of that, not with Steve on the loose. "Take off the hoodie."

His bent elbow came up, smashed into the glass. It shattered, shards flying into her cheek. The pain brought tears to her eyes. She grasped the gun, brought it up like Dal had shown her.

"Stop, now, or I'll shoot you."

"No you won't." He yanked the hoodie off so it hung down his back.

"Steve." Her hand holding the gun went limp. How could she shoot this man she'd once loved with all her heart? "What do you want?"

"You ought to know what I want, Jessie. I want to ruin you like you ruined me. Let's give that a try, shall we?"

Her tongue moved, she was sure it did. Nothing came out. It crossed her mind that she should scream or pull the trigger.

She could do neither one.

"Not so easy to kill another human being, is it? Oh, I forgot, you have other ways to cause that."

"How did you find me?"

Finally, she did have a voice, shaky though it was.

"I have a story to tell you, but we're going somewhere else."

No, she had to stay here. Find Dallas. Appeal to Steve's cop side. "We can't leave here. There's a man down there. Lost, hurt. I have to find him."

"Oh, so you've turned to saving men now. Besides, I'm sure he's dead. He fell a long way. Head over heels."

Around the curve in the road, headlights cut the murky light. Someone coming. She held her breath. Turn his attention in another direction till they got closer, then make a break. He wouldn't do something with a witness. She pointed off down toward where the bike lay.

"See there? His bike. He left it there nearly twenty-four hours ago. He ought to be back by now. Something bad's happened, I know it. Wait, how do you know how he fell? Did you—oh, my God. You—you pushed him."

"No telling what might've happened." He peered through the broken side window.

The headlights grew closer, the nose of a truck in full view now. Slowly, she moved her left hand toward the door handle. The gun still in her right, like he knew she wouldn't shoot him. But he was wrong. If he'd truly pushed Dal off that mountain, she would most certainly shoot him. But he could be mocking her. Leading her on.

He must've heard the noise of the truck's engine, for he twisted back toward her, one hand coming down on top of hers. She yanked the door handle, kicked it wide open, and struggled against the grip he had on her. He was trying to keep his hand around both the gun and her fist.

Her finger, wrapped around the trigger guard, was squashed tight. The truck was right on them, the man driving it staring in their direction. She opened her mouth, screamed at him to help her. Surprise contorted his face. He looked out the windshield as if searching for someone to help, then the vehicle darted off down the road, tires spitting grit when his foot depressed the accelerator.

"No, come back." She wrestled ineffectively with Steve, still trying to escape and run, though he could easily catch her using the Jeep.

"Stop, Jessie. Just stop. This is the day you pay for what you did and there's nothing more you can do about it. Your friends will all pay too. A couple already have."

She sagged against the back of the seat, gazed at him closely for the first time. He looked older, tired, lost. "Please, Steve. Don't do this."

"It's already done." Hate hardened his steel gray eyes.

"What are you going to do, kill me? You loved me once, surely—"

"You loved me, but you loved your work more. You've nothing to bargain with here. I lost my job, my friends, my family looks at me like I'm a pariah. You deserted me as well. So that's what I'm going to do to you."

"Steve, please, help me look for Dallas. He's down there. He has to be hurt or he'd be back. Then you can do anything you want to me. Anything." His grip on her gun hand relaxed and she flexed the finger. It slipped onto the trigger.

He sneered. "Honey, I can already do anything I want to you. Your poor Dallas is a big boy, he can take care of himself. You won't be seeing him again, anyway. He's at the bottom of that gorge. As for Parker, what do you suppose happened to his horse? And Mac's been acting awfully funny, too. Why do you suppose that is?"

"How did you...? I didn't... You're *lying*." The barrel of the gun. Where was it pointed? Impossible to see. What if she shot herself? Dear God, what if she shot him?

"Didn't what? You went home with him, stayed the night. What do you call it?"

"Spending the night with a friend." Lips clamped between her teeth, she pulled away from him as much as she could. Tightened that finger's grip.

"Jesus Christ. Is that what you called it when we were fucking?" He grabbed the back of her head, pulled her so close all she could see was his eyes. His hot breath smelled of licorice. She'd almost forgotten that.

Remembering sent her back to the days they were together. She always accused him of using it as a breath mint. He thought that was funny, and they ended up rolling around on the floor. She squeezed her eyes shut to block the memory, but it didn't help. His mouth on hers, his hands cupping her breasts. He loved her breasts, said they should be immortalized like Rodin's The Thinker so men forevermore could admire them. Wonder what he thinks of them now. A Picasso nightmare, perhaps.

Now he was her nightmare. He was pulling her hair out by the roots. She sucked her gut in as tightly as she could, gritted her teeth till she tasted blood, and squeezed the trigger.

13
CHAPTER

One hand clutching a tree, feet braced against the upper side of a boulder, Dal pulled and shoved at the same time. Pain blurred his vision. The left arm dangled, useless. Muscles screamed in agony. He hung on, managed another few feet. Every breath sent lightning strikes through his ribs. Cracked them, probably not broken. He knew what that felt like. The steep incline at his back, he paused and stared up at the lightening sky. Sucked in some shallow breaths. Something was bad wrong with his left arm. The bones ground together when it moved. Definitely broken. A knot on his head hammered a message. Time to upchuck.

Oh, and by the way, there was a unicorn peering from the brush. Glad I got to see that. Always halfway figured they were around somewhere. Someone who converses with ghosts and spirits, and yes, there is a difference, should have seen more than unicorns. How about a few dragons soaring up there in the blue? Come on, give me a goddamned show.

A good time later, no idea how long, the world tilted back to normal and the pain settled down to a dull roar. What would happen next? Had to get moving. Might shove himself past the sapling he clung to and on up the incline. Maybe he could reach that cluster of bushes. They had stout trunks, more like small trees, and if he could crawl in among them he could stretch out and rest. They would keep him from rolling back down the hill. Wouldn't do to have that happen, after all this hard work. Damn, there wasn't a muscle or bone that didn't hurt.

He twisted enough to see his watch. The crystal was cracked, stopping the hands at 1:23. That would be in the dark of night, actually morning. A shimmering blue sky told him it was daylight. Eight or perhaps a bit later. Someone would be looking for him by now. Mac and Jess, maybe Tink and Burt. But thanks to his self-assuredness, they wouldn't know where to start. For who would expect him to go bicycle riding in the most remote park in the state? Who would expect him to go bicycle riding period?

If he ever got out of this, he would give up old habits, like stubbornness and stupidness. If there was such a word it fit him to a tee. He'd even check in and out with not only Mac but Jess. About now, she'd be pissed off at him good. Too bad he couldn't read her mind long distance, or send a message that way.

How thoughtless that he left furious at her and let her know it. If he didn't make it back she'd never know how he really felt. But none of that. He would make it back.

The pain subsided enough that he could contemplate his move from the sapling to the next stop. He heaved with both feet. Had to get one—make that the good leg—propped against the sapling in order to push himself upward. Small rocks scattered from underfoot and tumbled down the mountain, rattling noisily. But he had a foothold. Just as he was waist high in his next goal, and wondering why the hell he was doing this, a gunshot reverberated across the peaks. Impossible to tell precisely where it came from. Above him, that was for sure, but to his right or his left? And how far away? He couldn't tell.

Technically guns and hunting weren't allowed in the state park, but often that law was broken out of sight or hearing of a ranger. Somewhere up there was the road, and probably a poacher shooting at a deer out of season, not someone searching for him. Stretch as he might he could not see the bench where it circled above the hiking path. He had a long way to go. He tried hollering again a few times in case the illegal hunter might hear. No results.

After he got his breath, he shouted one more time. Might be better to yell fire, like the old joke, but instead he shouted help, paused a few seconds, then hollered again. It hurt his head like someone was banging on it with a hammer, so he had to wait longer before trying again. When he received no hello in return, he lowered his face in one hand and shuddered. Had to get hold of himself. Must have a concussion. Eyesight was blurry, he was dizzy, and nauseous. Oh, and there was that unicorn again. Curious little bugger. A sure sign of head trauma.

Where the hell was Grandfather? He could help him out a bit about now. Blackness crashed around him, and the next time he opened his eyes, the sun was higher. He'd passed out again. One eyelid offered a slit through which he could see above and off to one side a small overhang that sheltered a flat spot. Dying for a drink of water. But the creek was below and one way he didn't want to go was down. If he could make the overhang he could rest. Or perhaps pass out again. Whatever worked.

227

Seated in the car next to Steve, Jessie shuddered against the ring-ing in her ears. As soon as the gun fired, she released the weapon. The stench of gunpowder was followed by an acrid odor. It left a bright taste on her tongue. Jesus. Something else smelled like fresh meat. She gagged. Blood. Hot blood spread across her chest. Had she shot her-self? No pain, but maybe....

Steve let go of her hand, slumped forward. She'd shot him. Her teeth chattered and her stomach roiled. Sweat poured down her face chased by cold chills. Shock probably. It wasn't every day she shot someone. Check that. She never had shot anyone. What if she'd killed him?

Unable to move, to think, to do anything. Steve lying against her. Hot, sticky blood on her hands and arms. Soundless tears drenched her cheeks. Do something, idiot. Something.

"Steve? Are you okay?" A stupid something to ask. No reply anyway.

Against her shoulder the faint beat of a heart. He was alive, but bleeding to death and no way to get help. She could try though. Slide out, grab that bicycle, and ride it to the first house. There would be a telephone. So move. Move.

He was heavy, but she dragged herself from under the weight, eased him down on the seat. Shook him. Listened to that small voice one sometimes heard. The one that expressed the true feelings we all learned to suppress because they were evil.

You shouldn't have shoved Dal off that mountain, you bastard. She didn't shoot him on purpose, she didn't.

"Steve. Steve. Listen to me. I'm putting my jacket over your wound. You hold it tight there and I'll be back, I promise. I'm so sorry." Sobs jerked from her throat. Tears all but blinded her. Tears not for herself or Steve, but for Dal, who had suffered a terrible penalty for what she'd done so long ago. What if he was down there dead? What was it her grandmother used to say? Your chickens have come home to roost. And Parker's horses, and what had Steve said about Mac. She ought to just let him lay there and bleed out.

She staggered across the road and through the weeds. Hauled up the bike, straddled the seat, and kicked off. One thing you never forgot was how to ride a bike.

The wind in her face dried the tears, leaving stiff trails on her skin. It was downhill and she flew into that wind. Faster and faster. Never mind the fear that clogged her throat. If he died she would be a killer for the rest of her life. If he died a piece of her other life died with him. If he lived, maybe he would forgive her. But she would never forgive him for killing Rick and Dal.

Oh, God. *Dal.* She wanted to scream and never stop. Instead she let out a breath and sucked in another. A phone could get him help too.

A house, up ahead on the left. Small, sort of dilapidated. What if no one lived there anymore? They had to, absolutely had to.

A vehicle coming, honking, pulling up beside her so she couldn't turn.

"Get out of the way. I have to get to a phone. Get out of my way."

They were both stopped, her still screaming at him. He crawled out of the truck. Something written on the side, she couldn't read it through her tears. He wore a uniform, all khakis. Had her by the shoulders, his mouth moving. She could hear nothing but a roaring, a terrible, awful roaring.

"Don't you understand me, a man is dying. Back there. Have to get to a phone."

He pried her hands loose from the handlebars, still moving his mouth like maybe she could hear him. Fool. Stupid fool. Let me go. I shot him. This time her mouth moved and nothing came out.

His arms caught her when she slumped, unable to remain upright. She regained her senses riding in the truck, and then he pulled up and stopped beside her Jeep. A man inside bent over Steve. Now she could rest. They would take care of him. Something else. Yes. Dal, down the mountain. Had to tell them, make them understand.

Some more men arrived in pickups and on four-wheelers, others in a bright yellow truck, then still more in a fire truck. Everyone piled out. All talking amongst themselves and wandering around.

Someone do something, please.

They put Steve on a stretcher in the back of one of the pickups and hovered around him. Milled about talking to each other. Low conversation, serious stuff 'cause a man lay dying.

Up from the valley a siren wailed. Long before it came in sight the flash of lights painted surrounding trees, red like a never ending scream. Dust rose along the road that climbed the mountain. She breathed a sigh of relief and let her body slump further down in the seat.

Something urgent tapped at her memory. A thing she should do. What was it? Darkness closed in around her.

A different world greeted her when she opened her eyes. A world of muted sounds. A room she didn't know. And then she remembered. Fear laced fingers around her heart and she began to yell.

Dallas lay under the overhang, exhausted, thirsty, hungry, and frustrated. Up on the road, vehicles came and went, as did people. He shouted till he was hoarse. Dug around for rocks to throw, but had no power. Damn, what a fool he was. Coming down here unarmed on a bicycle, for

God's sake. No one could hear him, and the way up from here was steep, craggy. A climb fit for an expert. He'd never make it. The effort so far had completely exhausted him and increased the pain in the arm. It was broken for damn sure. Battered, bruised, cut, and concussed, he laid in the soft loam under the bluff and listened for the sound of even one human voice. Nothing. Everyone was gone, so shouting in the descending silence made no sense. He could die right here. Not the first time in his life he'd experienced that threat, but it didn't make it any easier to face.

He drifted into a vision of Grandfather sitting beside a campfire and went to sit beside him. The old man told him a myth about brother rabbit and he relaxed. A peaceful place to be.

In the hospital, Jessie's shouts attracted plenty of attention. Nurses, aides, even a doctor showed up. At first she could make no sense. It was as if she spoke into a bottled vacuum. Probably her own fault. She could scarcely understand her own words.

The doctor snapped orders and one of the nurses left, returned with a hypodermic filled with a milky fluid.

"No. You don't understand. We left him out there to die. You have to call the sheriff, tell him."

One of the nurses patted her arm. "No, they brought him in. He's going to be okay."

"Get that needle away from me. I don't mean him. I mean Dallas Starr. He's a deputy, and he's down there somewhere, maybe at the bottom of the mountain. Someone has to go get him. Or call Mac, tell him I need to talk to him. Do something. Don't just stand there staring at me like I'm naked or something. And do *not* stick me with that thing." Their faces faded, the room disappeared.

She woke with a start, sat up in a darkened space, only one dim light burning. All the shades drawn. She wasn't hooked up to anything, just lying there. And no one had done anything about Dal. Absolutely no one. She swung her legs off the bed. Stood. Wavered a moment using the bed to balance herself. A cold draft on her behind. Crap, she wore a hospital gown. Of course, because Steve's blood soaked the clothing she wore.

Oh, God. Please. Don't let him die, and get me the hell out of here.

Bare feet on the cold tile floor. Shoes, she'd have to have shoes. Frantic, she searched the room. On hands and knees she found them under the bed. Enough, that would do. She had to go find Dal. No more trying to talk someone else into doing it. What had they done with her Jeep? And the keys? And her backpack with all her stuff in it?

Think. *Think.* She smacked her forehead with the heel of her hand. Went to the closet in the room. There on the floor was the backpack. Made sense her keys would be in it. She pawed through every pocket. They weren't. Dammit, now what? Wait, she kept a spare. Her racing mind wouldn't access that bit of information. But it was with the Jeep. The clock above the door read close to twelve. Hope to God it's noon and light outside. Get out of this place.

Slinging the backpack over one shoulder, she eased the door open and peered in each direction. One way nurses huddled around a central station. The other way, an exit sign. She went for it, acting like she belonged. A door opened onto a staircase and she took it. At the bottom painted on the side of a door was the number one. All things being equal, this was the ground floor. Once again, a cautious move. The stairs exited toward the rear of the hospital, which only had two floors, but there were no doors to the outside. They were up front. So, she would have to parade down the hall and through the lobby dressed in a gown with her bare butt sticking out. That would never do.

A hallway to her left and she took it. Doors led to rooms, then one said supply closet. She eased it open. Cleaning supplies. Back out into the hallway and the next one was blank. Inside shelves held folded scrubs in several colors and sizes. Grabbing one from a stack marked M—she hoped that meant medium and not male—she wrestled her way out of the gown and into the pants and shirt. An okay fit, though she wouldn't win any fashion shows.

Again in the hallway, she put the backpack on over both shoulders and head high, walked through the lobby and out the front doors.

Once outside she leaned against a bench and took deep breaths till her head cleared. Lord, she'd almost fainted with fear someone would stop her. Now to find the Jeep. Good thing the parking lot wasn't too big. She paced through the rows until in the one farthest from the building and right on the street sat her car. No use taking up a convenient parking slot.

Now, where had she put the key this time? Under the rear bumper? Nope. Under a front fender? Nope. Boy, she was really getting paranoid someone would steal the ten-year-old car. At last she found it in a mag-netized holder beneath and behind the driver's side door. Someone in the hospital had the keys to her house and vehicle, but she didn't have time to worry about that now. She'd eventually get them back. And she kept a key to the house under a rock next to the back patio so she could get in.

The clutter in her mind needed stopping. She couldn't think, or be rational. Staring out across the highway, she took deep breaths to calm herself. Then she slipped out of the backpack, climbed in the seat, and started the car. No one would help her. Mac thought she was crazy and wasn't worried about Dal. What was it Steve had implied, something he'd done to Mac? Tink and Burt had gone off on a secret search for the missing man, who was right now in the hospital recovering from surgery or dead. Too bad she didn't know which but there wasn't time to find out.

Once she found Dal, she could call and learn if Steve were dead or alive. But first things first. She headed back out toward Red Rock. Ten minutes later she parked where they'd found the bike, grabbed the heavy backpack, and hurried down the path to the hiking trail. She was wearing Sketchers so they should hold up for the hike.

The trail followed an old bench around an outside curve and disappeared into the miles and miles of thick Ozark National Forest. A wooden handrail kept clumsy hikers from tumbling off the rugged drop to one side. Down the incline a narrow footpath led off the trail to a flat rock hanging out over the valley. Not part of the hiking trail but something that would attract a man like Dallas. He'd want to stand at the very tip and lean forward. Just to see if fate had something dangerous in store for him.

A sob jerked her chest. Little did he know what fate awaited him because of her.

A small sign marked the path as hazardous. Huh. Didn't take a sign to convince her of that. But it needed to be checked out. Between where she stood and the lookout rock, one side of the foot path dropped off precariously.

She had to go out there, see if there was any sign he had fallen into the deep hollow. The ground was riddled with small loose rocks and roots from trees growing on the upper side. Easy to trip or go sliding. Nothing to hold on to. Navigating it was about as threatening as one of the Wallenda's high-wire acts. Easy to fall, even if you weren't pushed. Just past the jagged shelf a piece of the walkway had broken off. She stopped, gazed down into the shadowy tree tops. It wasn't quite so steep here, looked like someone had recently slid down to the next bench, bending and breaking saplings and plowing through underbrush.

She cupped her mouth with both hands. Shouted his name. Dal, then Dallas, then back to Dal. Paused to listen to the sound of her own voice. A red hawk circled above, his shadow flicking over her, a loud scree greeting this interloper in his territory. But no human voice replied.

Where are you, Dal? My God, where are you? Tears overflowed and she swiped them away. Stupid. Crying would not solve anything.

She closed her eyes, and there he was. That dimpled grin when he tilted his head and teased her. The way he held her when they danced. His hand sprawled over her head when she awoke beside him in bed. The time he almost died. She sucked in a sob. Dammit, girl. Get on with it. She turned to step out onto the rock where she'd have a better view of the terrain and heard something. A sound that didn't belong with the bird songs and scolding squirrels and leaves rustling under the passage of lizards and armadillos.

A voice. Was it simply her imagination? Holding her breath, standing oh so still, she strained to hear, to sort out the normal noises of the forest. And there it was again. Faint, feeble, but definite. Someone was down there. Way down there. Maybe answering her call in jest, more likely calling for help. Yes, it was that one word. Not her imagination.

High out here in the open, she just might get a signal on the phone. If it was in the backpack. She couldn't remember. She backed off from the edge, squatted, and eased off the heavy pack, dug in the outside pocket where she usually kept it and pulled out the phone. Little good it did. No service popped onto the screen. She rose and crept back out to the edge, stood on the highest point, looking nowhere but at the screen.

The height could be dizzying if she looked down. Still no service. She turned, held it out in front of her and two bars popped up.

Quickly she hit #2 for Mac and listened to the ring, lips moving, "Please, please, please." If he didn't answer, she was going to ban him forever from her list.

His voice. Yes!

"Mac? Someone has fallen off the trail out here where they found Dal's bike. Please, get help. Please hurry." There, fast as she could, before the signal disappeared, she said what was needed. Heard nothing in return. Waited some more. Said his name a couple of times, but the bars had flicked off.

Had he heard her? Would he believe her after all that had gone on yesterday and today? Hard to say. She'd give him a little time, then if no one came, she'd figure out a way to climb down there.

Stowing the phone, she went back to the spot where someone's feet had skidded through the leaves and stones, leaving a scuffed path. She knelt there because if she stood another moment her trembling knees would send her over the edge too.

"Dal, Dal, if you're down there, help is coming. Someone is coming." She didn't yell the words, just said them in a normal tone as if he sat beside her.

Even if it wasn't Dal, it could be anyone, someone needing help. Was she just imagining it because she so wanted to find him? To know, at least, that he was alive. Or to be right? After a while, she tired of sitting there squinting into the thick forest and went back to the Jeep. She dragged out a pad and pen and wrote down what was going on. It would be a good story if and when they rescued whoever was down there. Or even if it turned out no one was down there and it was all her imagination. Steve could have lied just to upset her some more. She so needed to have the busyness of writing it all down. While she waited and trusted Mac to believe her, bring people who could get down there.

What would she do if no one came? Go down herself?

She might. She just might.

Though Dal strained to hear more all was quiet. The voice must be his imagination. But he'd heard his name called, clear as a bell. While he sat beside Grandfather staring into the campfire's flames. So very sure he had passed into the next world.

Jessie called him, and he wanted to go to her. After a long struggle to open his eyes did he see or only imagine a moss-covered overhang? Or make a sound with one last effort to shout her name? Lying still, breathing heavily. The scent of last year's leaves and the moist soil thick in his nose, he imagined her in his arms. Her warm breasts pressed against his bare chest so he could barely think straight. Until all he wanted was inside her, a moist sweetness closing around him.

If anyone could find him in this place, it would be Jess. Odd to think how much he trusted her to do so. How close they had become despite his pushing her away at every chance. And how pissed off she was at him this very moment. He'd laugh but it hurt too much. All he wanted more than anything was her giving him hell, those crystal blue eyes flashing, her stubborn chin poked out.

Jessie paced up and down the road. No one was coming. They'd had time to get here. Well, to hell with all of them. She pawed around in the back of the Jeep. There was a rope in there somewhere, Dal had flung it in there Sunday when he left the cookout in a fit of anger. But was it long enough to do any good? One end protruded from the tangle and she yanked it out, looping in over one shoulder till she had it all. Starting back to the trail, she stopped, returned to the car and grabbed her notes, fastened the book so the notes hung outside the closed window, wrote **HELP** in large dark letters so whoever noticed it would read it, then ran back to the trail.

On the upper side, she tied the rope around a good-sized tree. Found the other end and tied it around her waist. Before taking that first step off the edge, she tried backing up holding the rope in both hands, yanked hard two or three times. Her hands weren't going to like this, but it wasn't the time of the year for gloves to be in the vehicle, so she gathered the excess rope to play it out. Placing her feet in the scuff marks where Dal, or someone, had skidded off, she inched her way down.

Backing down a mountain hanging on to a rope looked easier when someone who knew what they were doing did it. Like in a movie. Feet slid in the loose leaves. The rope burned her palms. Her heart lurched into her throat. There were better ways to do this, but damned if she knew them. Fall and the rope would stop her descent when she reached the end. Or at least one would hope so. It could be painful and she might crash into a tree or two. Break her damn fool neck, is what was about to happen. Stop thinking and do.

Funny how time likes to fool around with people. It could pass lazily while lying in the sun, or fly by when racing to meet a deadline, or crawl like a slug on glass when going down the side of a mountain tied to a danged rope. Should she call to him again, or concentrate on the descent? Women are supposed to be good at doing two things at once, but all she could think of was hanging on and keeping both feet under her.

She halted to check the skid marks he'd left, saw they had veered off to her right a bit and leaves and rocks were torn up pretty bad. He'd started to tumble. A couple of hops in that direction and she continued moving. The rope tightened and held her in place. She'd reached the end. Okay, don't panic. Hang here till you get your breath, then call out. Find him and get to him. Pray to God, or whoever was up there pulling all these cruel jokes, that he was conscious and could answer. And that she could reach him. He might be another fifty feet below her. He might be dead.

Then what?

One problem at a time. She called his name, first in a trembling voice, then increasing the volume to frantic. Frantic to hear something. Anything. She waited, so still the beating of her own heart thudded in her ears.

"Jess? Jess, I'm here."

She dragged in a grateful breath. "Where are you? Keep talking to me."

All he could do was repeat her name. Weakly, and finally nothing.

Definitely below. Off to her right shelves of jagged rocks protruded from the incline, so common in the Ozarks. If she could swing that way, maybe she could use them like a ladder to get down to him. They might not be able to climb out, but she did have water and food and the first aid kit to help him till someone showed up. If no one did, then at least they'd be together. To the end.

Lord, what a fateful thing to think of at such a time.

Palms on fire, hot and wet with blood, she clung to the rope, took a sideways step, then another. Slipped. Thanked God she'd tied it around her waist. Above her the coils snagged. Halted her movement. Bracing both feet, she whipped it into the air and it came loose, dropping her a foot or more. The stop jerked her hard, cutting into her waist till she almost vomited. Dizzy and sick, she hung on tight, tried to get her bearings.

"Jess, are you still there?"

"Yes, I'm here, but I'm above you. I can't see you."

"I'm under big slab of rock." The words weak, barely discernible.

"Okay, just keep talking. I'm coming." Maybe. She'd reached the ragged slabs. The only way to go down them was to untie the rope. Crap, that would be scary.

No more words from below.

Be careful. Concentrate. Find a foothold and handhold before you untie the rope. Damn knot pulled tight. Fingers so weak she could hardly hold on. What if she let go, would she swing back and forth banging into the sharp rocks? Had to get her weight off the rope so she could untie it. Balanced on a wide step-like rock with both feet, she hugged the cliff facing and let go, pried at the knot, working blindly. It was a forever effort, but at last the only thing tethering her dropped away leaving her clinging to the steep rock wall. And there she was, for one terrifying moment plastered so tight she could not move. Feet planted, fingers clinging, she hung there. Safe but frozen in place.

Dal wasn't talking. Hadn't in a while. How long ago she wasn't sure. She'd gone deaf concentrating on the death defying feat of getting down to him with nothing to keep her from falling. There was still the descent, and be damned if she wanted to take it in one great plunge. Cheek pressed into a jagged rock, she felt for lower handholds so she could then find a step for her feet. Each time she searched open space for a new hold her stomach lurched, threatened to come up into her throat.

This progress seemed to last for an eternity, but she kept going, her gaze always to the right where she'd last heard his voice. A chunk of rock broke off under one foot and she was left dangling by three points, listening to the shards of broken stone tumble away. Exactly where she could easily end up. The next step and her eyes grew even with an overhang. Could it be where Dal was waiting? If he'd climbed back up more or less the route he fell, that's where he would be. For just to her left was where he'd skidded down leaving a clear trail. Her heart sank when she shouted and got no reply. Maybe he wasn't here at all, but much further down. How could she keep this up?

A little farther, just a bit more, and she should be able to drop under the shelf. And if he wasn't there? Cross that bridge when she came to it. The final foothold broke off and she was left dangling, legs flailing, holding on with both hands. Time to turn loose. One breath, then two and she pushed away from the wall and let go. She fell, stretching to one side. For a long moment she imagined plunging to her death, before landing in the soft loam with a solid thud that knocked the wind out of her. After several minutes getting her breath back, she opened her eyes. There he was a few paces in under the slab of rock, lying flat on his back, eyes closed. Not moving.

"No, no, no. Honey, no." She crawled to his side, afraid to touch him. Yet she had to.

Under her fingertips the flesh of his cheek was cool. "Hey, tough guy, don't you die on me." A whisper 'cause she was afraid to speak the words too loud.

Still no reply. She placed the shredded palm of her hand over his heart. His chest rose and fell. Teeth caught her lower lip, she let the tears flow, and to hell with it. Swiping them away, she kissed his swollen eyelids.

"Come on, you. Look at me. I'm here to save your crazy ass."

"I knew you'd come." Though he didn't open his eyes, he uttered the words under his breath.

"You did, did you? You hurt anywhere? Is your back okay?"

Tough to look at him. The skin on his face was shredded, bruised and bloody, both eyes still black from breaking his nose a few days earlier. He shivered. What was left of his tee shirt and pants was smeared in mud and bits of gravel and grass.

"My poor baby." She could hardly bear to look at him or touch him, yet couldn't stop doing so.

Cold, he was cold. Help him. Unstrapping the backpack, she opened it and dragged out the space blanket. Spread it over him, tucked it gently around his legs, hips, torso.

He screamed when she reached his arms, the left one spread awkwardly at his side. "Oh, I'm sorry." His other hand reached out to her and she took it, held it to her lips. He was going to die, right here, with nothing she could do. Nothing. For a long moment she couldn't move, just knelt there and held his hand, soaking his skin in her tears.

He groaned one word.

"I brought water. Lay still till we're sure you haven't hurt your back."

His only response, the repeat of the word water.

Lying on his back he'd choke if she poured it in his mouth. Her mind ran in frantic circles. Settle down, think. Help him. Save him. A piece of cloth. She yanked off her tee shirt, soaked a portion till it was dripping, then held it to his lips. He sucked it dry, would hardly let her have it back. She repeated the process over and over till he stopped taking the cloth. Stopped doing anything.

Oh, God, no. No. She placed her ear over his mouth, felt tiny puffs of air. He'd passed out, was still breathing.

"I could kick you for doing this. You could've died down here." Her words spewed out, fury overcoming fear. She ached to tell him she loved him, but didn't.

Digging around in the backpack, she found the first aid kit, opened it, and gently cleaned the bloody knot behind his ear with antiseptic Wet Ones. Scrapes on his hands and face needed attention and she cleaned them. With an easy touch she checked out the rest of his body, replacing the blanket as she went. One knee had a great gash that had bled down his leg. Best if she could finish it while he was out. It was bound to be painful.

While she worked on a scrape down his shin, he groaned and struggled to sit up.

"Best if you just lie still. I'm sure you have a concussion."

"More water please." He sounded better, but that could be the water.

She propped his head, poured three ibuprofen into her palm, and gave them to him with water from the bottle. By the way the earth was churned around him, he'd obviously moved around a lot, crawling up here at some point. Too late to worry about injuries to his back. More than anything else, she wanted to take him in her arms, but was so afraid she'd hurt him.

"You've been out here a while. Are you hungry?"

"I don't know. I guess."

"I have some protein bars."

"Jess, thank you."

"You're welcome. What for?"

"I knew you'd come."

"Oh, you did? I ought to knock you silly, doing this." She focused back on cleaning one of the cuts on his leg. I've been so scared."

He touched her with his fingertips. "Sorry. Oh, God, there's that unicorn again." His hand fell away. He'd passed out again. She slid down beside him, a great sob quivering through her.

What if no one came? How long would it be before someone stopped to check her Jeep and read the note?

Off in the trees a whippoorwill called and another answered from far below. And the sun slipped behind the peaks to the west without making a sound.

14
CHAPTER

Tink blustered into Mac's office. She'd had enough and no longer cared if he fired her or never let her in the field. Well, maybe not that so much, but lately he'd been sort of weird. He was getting old and grouchy and forgetful, but still.

"When did you last hear from Jessie? She disappeared from the hospital and has been gone all afternoon and I can't rouse her on her cell."

"Good evening to you too. You have late shift today?"

"Yes, I do. Has she called you?"

"Someone did, but I couldn't hear them. You know how Jessie is. I called the hospital, talked to her doc. He said she was okay, just left without checking out. You know good and well she's off trying to root out stuff on this murder. Hopes to solve it before we do."

Too impatient to argue with him, she stuck out her hand. "Let me see your phone."

"Why would I do that?"

"If the call got through, the number will be in there."

He squinted his eyes. "You're just trying to see who all has called me."

"Why would I give a crap about that? I just want to see if that was Jessie or Dallas calling."

Grumbling, he dug the phone out of his pocket and handed it over. "Danged things, next they'll be cooking supper before you get home and turning on the TV to your favorite show."

She clicked through the incoming calls till she came to one from Jessie's number. Held it in front of him. "This the one? See the time with her number?"

"I reckon that's it."

"And what about Dallas?"

Mac shrugged. "I have to presume he's with her. Keeping an eye on her while working the case."

"And does he answer his cell?"

Mac kicked his chair back and glared up at her. "Since when is it unusual to get in a… what do you call them places where you can't use those doo-dads?"

"Phones, you mean? Dead zone."

"Yeah, that. And not be able to make calls or take them?"

"Mac, she shot someone who tried to shoot her. She'd be more than a tad upset. Looks like you'd be looking for her to get a statement as to what happened. I want to go up there and check out the area where it happened. She was with that guy for a reason. We don't even know who he is or what he was doing with her."

"I asked her to come in as soon as they released her so I could take a statement. It is strange she hasn't done that. So, okay, I'll go. You're supposed to be on the front desk. Who's out there now?"

"Burt said he'd handle it while I talked to you. He just got in. His shift is over, but he's still in the station. I want to go with you. I think something bad has happened up there. Parker is worried about Jessie too. It's been too long since we've heard from her. I just know she went looking for Dallas. Come on, Mac— er, sheriff, please."

"Oh, for goodness sake." He waved an arm. "I'll take the whole danged bunch if it'll get you to hush up about this. I just figgered she went home to get some rest and Dallas is with her. They stay glued together most of the time."

Tink studied the old man for a long while. What was wrong with him? He ought to be investigating the shooting, talking to Jessie about her part in it. Checking out this guy to find out who he was. Wouldn't surprise her if he wasn't getting a bit too forgetful. It'd be a shame if he was showing signs of that Alzheimer's. She had no idea who to talk to about this, but someone ought to know.

"Let's just go on up there," she said. "Did someone bring her car down? If they did, where is it now?"

"I don't know. It's after five. I believe you're right, she ought to have checked in with Parker by now, if no one else."

Burt appeared in the doorway. "Phone call for you, Mac. I couldn't figure out the buzzer."

Mac picked up his phone. "What line?"

"Oh, uh, not sure."

"The one that's lit." Tink turned to Burt. "Let's call the rangers up at the park. Mac and I are going up there where they found Jess and that fella she shot. She's left the hospital and no one knows where she is. I think she's looking for Dal. She thought he might've fallen off the trail, though that seems unlikely. Since there's no cell signal up on the mountain, I want them to know what's going on before we leave here."

Burt nodded in agreement and led her to the front desk. She found the landline number of the ranger station and punched it in, spoke to an Eli Perkins. After she told him what was going on and hung up, Burt said he wanted to go along.

"Shall we wait for the sheriff?" He glanced down the empty hall.

"Probably. He's still on the phone."

Mac hurried into the lobby, hat in hand. "That'll have to wait. Treman called and said someone just tried to gun him down. Y'all go on and check on Jessie. I'll just bet you'll find her at home sound asleep from some of those pills them docs do love to give to everyone, whether they need 'em or not. Have her stay put and I'll catch up to her for a statement. That feller didn't die, did he?"

"Nope, he's alive. Does that mean I can go with Burt?" Tink met Mac's glare with a smile.

"Oh, go on then. Find someone to man your desk first, though."

It took way too long to finally clear things up. Then when they crawled in Burt's unit he said, "Let's go by her place first. Mac may be right and she's there. Save us a trip up the mountain."

Made Tink want to kick something. "It's almost sunset. If we do and we don't get up there those rangers won't want to search till daylight. It's already been way too long." She reached for the door handle. "If you don't want to go straight on up there, I'll go myself."

"Get on back in here. We'll go together. I don't want you getting caught out in the dark anyway."

She settled back in the seat. "And just so you know, I'm going to try to get help about that dark thing. I'm tired of it getting in the way of things I want to do."

"That's good, that's real good. It's lucky it's still Daylight Savings

Time. Maybe we have daylight to figure out if anyone's lost off the trail before the sun goes down."

When they came in sight of the trail entrance a pickup from the Ranger Station was parked behind Jessie's Jeep. Tink nearly jumped from the car before Burt parked.

"See, I told you. That's Jessie's car. I knew it. Didn't I tell you?" Without waiting for him to reply, she raced to the opening that led to the trail.

Two men in uniform stood near a narrow track. One of them turned when she approached.

"Did you find anything?" She gazed up at him. "You Eli?"

He nodded. "Just found this note on the Jeep. Says help, but reads like she was writing an article or story about going down a rope to look for someone called Dal. Then we found this." He indicated a rope tied to a tree and lying across the narrow path. "I believe she might be down there, but we've tried hollering and got no reply."

Tink picked up the rope. "Then I guess someone needs to go down there and see."

The two men glanced at each other. The shorter one finally spoke. "Wadn't she the little gal they hauled to the hospital this morning? Shot that feller? And now you think she's down yonder looking for this Dallas character? You know neither of us is trained in mountain rescue. Truth is, we'd probably just create more bodies to rescue."

"Bodies? You don't think she's laying down there dead, do you?"

Eli shrugged. "No one is answering us." His angular features revealed a mix of sadness and fear.

"Well, for crying out loud. What are you going to do about it? Just stand around jawing? Seems like there's been enough of that already."

"Nope. Harold's gone to get that ole boy who lives down the road.

He's good at climbing, 'bout like some mountain goat. He'll scoot right on down there and check it out. We never had anyone do this since I come here."

The short guy, who hadn't introduced himself, chimed in. "Me neither. Hell, most I've done is hike the trail to look for lost folk. Never had to go down no rope, nor anything like that before. They was that fellow who stepped too far back out on that rock and fell plumb to the bottom. We didn't get in on that search, though. Mashed him up pretty good, I hear tell. Dead, he was."

"Who is this *Harold*? And who's the climber?" Burt had finally joined them.

"Harold delivers snacks to our machines up at the station. He was there when y'all called. Anyway, he was coming back this way and said he'd rustle this ole boy out and send him up here."

"You sent a snack delivery man to get this ole boy, someone you don't even know, to rescue Jessie? Good grief." Tink couldn't believe what she was hearing.

"Jessie? That who's down there?" Short guy glanced off down the side of the mountain. "That'd be that pretty reporter lady? Sure looks like someone took a header all right, tore up the ground pretty bad. May be scooping them up when we get down there."

Tink sucked in her breath. "Oh, my God. Burt, *do* something."

"I'm going down there." He shucked out of his uniform shirt to reveal a white tee, and started pulling on the rope. "It's not hooked to anything at the bottom. I'm going to lower myself down. See what I can find. It'll be dark in a while."

Eli got real nervous. "Sir, I'd rather you didn't do that. You fall and splatter yourself all over the mountainside, we're likely to be in trouble."

She'd had all of this she could take. Getting up on her toes, she glared into the face of the shorter of the two rangers. Only because Eli was too tall to challenge eye-to-eye.

"You are an idiot. Those could be my friends down there, and if they aren't they're somebody's, and you talk about them like they're 'splattered' all over the place? Don't you guys have to take classes in how to behave around civilized folk? I ought to smack you around a little, till you learn how."

Shorty backed up a few paces, glanced at Eli, and spread his hands, as if surrendering.

"Sweetheart, it's okay." Burt put an arm around her shoulders. "I'm going right down, but you need to cool off. I know you're upset."

"You're darned right I'm upset. I'm afraid for her, but I don't want you going down there. Have you ever climbed a rope, down or up?"

"Well, when I was a kid, but not lately."

The idea tore her in half. Losing Burt was not something she wanted to contemplate. Before she could get any further with the thought, a motorcycle roared up, slid to a stop, kicking up a dust cloud that pinged gravel on the parked vehicles. A man climbed off. He gathered lines and other paraphernalia from the back of his bike and strode toward them.

"This where you'uns need a climber? I'm your man. Name's Nick Snow, and no jokes, if you please."

One look at this guy and Tink felt much better. He wasn't very big, maybe five foot eight or so, and had muscles just about everywhere you looked. Not like those weight lifters, just the kind that spell out strength.

The two rangers showed him where it looked like someone had fallen. He started assembling his gear, first fastening a line much thinner than the rope, to the same tree. From his belt hung what looked like spikes on chains. He fastened a light to his head and handed Eli a yellow walkie-talkie.

"I'll let you know on this. Just keep it on. "Might be down there till after dark, but don't you worry none. If there's anyone to bring up, I can do so if they're moveable. If not, I called the first responders from the house, told them to bring mountain rescue equipment and that I was going on down 'cause we're losing daylight." He glanced at Tink. "Now, ma'am, don't you worry none. I've done this plenty of times. I'll get 'em up here."

She nodded. Be sooner if he'd quit talking and get to it, but she didn't say anything. Just nestled closer to Burt, mixed feelings stirring around making her sick to her stomach. How do you pick between those you love when something like this happens? Risk Burt cause he might save Jessie? Darn good thing this guy arrived when he did. Nick Snow. Not a name anybody would forget very soon.

A gust of wind lifted her hair and sent a slight chill through her. Nights already turning cooler. Summer definitely on its way out. Fall always reminded her of the dead and dying. Everything flaring in bright colors, then shriveling up to nothing. The chill turned into a shudder while Nick Snow disappeared over the rim of the drop-off. What if Jessie and Dal were hurt real bad, or worse dead?

A hand shaking her shoulder roused Jessie, and when she jumped Dal groaned awake. A man with a light on his forehead knelt beside them, his features in shadows. It wasn't dark yet, but dusky under the slab of rock.

Relief flowed through her like warm water.

"You two okay? Got any broken bones or the like?" The light jiggled when he talked. "Name's Nick and I'm gonna get you both ready to get out of here."

Dal folded his good arm across his forehead. She touched him. "We're getting out of here. How do you feel?"

"I'm alive. Arm hurts. So does everything else."

Keeping a hand on him, she turned to Nick. "I think he has a concussion and his left arm is broken. He's pretty beat up. What if he's bleeding inside?" She trembled at the thought, her voice shaking.

Nick watched her intently till she finished. "Don't you worry none, ma'am. We're gonna take care of him. You look pretty good. Did you both fall, or were you the one who shinnied down that rope?"

"I am, I mean I did. I couldn't leave him down here alone, not knowing if he was dead or alive, or hurt real bad." A terrible fit of the shakes passed over her and she hugged herself, letting tears flow.

Nick patted her awkwardly on one shoulder. "I can walk you up outta here 'fore they come down to get him, if you'd like. You seem pretty shook up."

"No, no. I'm not leaving him. You get him out first, okay?"

"Jessie, go on." Dal's voice was weak, fading "…outta this hole."

She took his hand, held it to her lips for a moment. "I'm fine."

No big deal, shooting someone. Not compared to maybe losing Dal. The idea had carved a huge hole around her heart, darkened her spirit, and she couldn't turn loose of him. Not till they had him up and out of here. This she couldn't admit out loud, because him and her, they didn't admit that kind of crap to each other. Sentimental garbage. Not worth speaking of. 'Cause if you did, if you even let stuff like that pass your lips, then you were bound. And once that happened anything stupid you might do would hurt the both of you. And she was just plain good at being stupid. It was like when you became one then life turned dangerous on you both. She and Dal, they couldn't chance that. It would ruin what they had. And what they had was each other, and they both knew it.

A great deal of noise interrupted her scrambled thoughts while she sat there holding the hand of the man she cherished beyond anything else in her life. And that right there proved something she and Dal both worked so hard to deny. Whether you admitted it or not, when you got to feeling that way about each other, well you were bound. And that's all there was to that.

Nick spoke into the walkie-talkie, touched her shoulder and rose. "They're here. They'll be coming down with a stretcher to take him up, and I'll walk you up right behind him. You okay with that?"

"Uhmm, yes. I am." She had the shakes so bad she could hardly talk. Surprising how she was starting to fall apart. Now that everything was okay, she could let go the constraints that held her together.

Two men came down the mountainside with the stretcher. She had to turn loose of his hand then.

They put a brace around his neck, moved him to the board and onto the stretcher, and strapped him down.

"See you," he whispered, clinging for another minute to her before letting go.

She dropped to her butt, fastened her arms around both knees, and began to rock.

A gloved hand on her shoulder. "Ready to go up, ma'am. You okay?"

"Uh-huh. I'm fine, just falling apart a little bit. I shot a man. Not sure if it was today or yesterday. Did you know that, Nick? Did you know I once loved him, and he loved me? And now he's trying to shoot me, but the gun went off and he—uh. And then I find out he—uh—Dal is missing, maybe hurt or dead. It's just been one heck of a day or two. Seems like more."

Nick squatted in front of her. "It's hard, that. I've shot people, never anyone I loved, and it ain't a easy thing to get over. But you will, after a spell. Especially if you keep on doing what you love, being with folks you love who love you, and think of all things beautiful, as much of the time as you can." He rose, his soft voice changing tenor. "Now, let's get you up there with him. They can transport you together. And, ma'am?"

"Hmm?"

"I can guarantee you of one thing. You hang together, you'll get over this. Believe me, I know. Just don't let go each other." He took her elbow. "Okay?"

She let him help her to her feet. "Yes, fine. Thank you."

He placed her in front of him, fiddled with the line some, and she had no idea what he did, but he told her to put her feet on the slope and start walking, he'd do the rest. And he did. His muscular body tight against her back, they went up that incline easy as you please.

At the top he unfastened her, then himself from the rigging. An ambulance waited on the road.

Tink grabbed her. "I was so scared when you didn't come back."

Burt wrapped his arms around both women, didn't say anything.

One of the first responders trotted over. "You want to go with him? He's asking for you. Someone can bring your vehicle down. Should we leave it at the sheriff's or take it out to your place?"

"Just leave it at the hospital, if you don't mind. Thank you." She turned to thank Nick, but he was on his bike, kicking it to life. Why had she never met him before? Maybe she could get an interview. Quite a guy.

Two EMTs accompanied her to the ambulance and helped her climb in. She sat beside Dal and laid an open hand on his belly, careful to scarcely touch the torn flesh. The inside reeked of hospital scents. All she wanted was to go home with Dal and go to bed with him. Hold on tight as she could. He lay so still with his eyes closed. The mountain had done a job on him, battering his face and head, arms and legs. Blood smeared his torn clothing.

"Dal, you okay?"

"Sure as shootin'."

He sounded drunk. Panicked, she glanced at the EMT, recognized him as Mike Healey. Dal had talked about him, said he was a nice guy but had a thousand-yard stare from serving in Special Ops. Wasn't sure where and when.

"He's fine. I gave him something for pain. He took a hell of a beating tumbling off that mountain. Amazing to me he was even conscious. Tough old boy, you ask me."

"He crawled more than halfway back up till he found that overhang."

"Doubly amazing, then. He could've broken his neck, he definitely should've broken more than he did. His vitals are fine. We'll check him out though. Make sure everything's okay."

The ambulance driver had opted not to run flat out with the siren blaring. Still, the sharp curves gave them a rough ride.

Healey leaned down over Dal. "You stay awake now, you hear me? Don't want you noddin' off and missin' anything."

"Wouldn't want that." Dal mumbled, squeezed her hand. "Saved my life, she did. Come down a rope. Didn't know you could come down a rope. Knew you could come down, uh, well you know."

Relieved that he could try to tell a dirty joke, she laughed.

Healey smiled. "He's gonna be just fine."

Probably not when he found out she had shot Steve and how it had all come about. But that could wait for another day. And when that day came, he might just tell her to take a hike. For he never knew all the truth about what happened out in California that sent her running home to Cedarton. There wouldn't be any way to keep it secret any longer, now that she had shot Steve. God help her.

Tink rode back down the mountain with Burt at the wheel. Darkness chased them and she tried to hold it together. Until she figured out this fear of the dark, she'd never get to do some of the things she wanted. Mainly, working night shift on rotation with the other deputies. Like for instance, this night. Mac said someone was shooting at Treman and she yearned to join him out there. Take part in a shootout. Investigate this really interesting case.

So far there was a dead man buried near Treman's, part of his leg in the hog pen near the shed. Then there was the man who tried to shoot Jessie and was now in the hospital, a guest missing from the B&B, and now someone shooting at Treman. It was like a circle connecting the same crime to all of these weird events. One thing for sure, it was perking up little old Cedarton.

Static on the radio and Mac came on. "Burt, you down off that mountain yet? I need backup out here at Treman Ledger's place. You drop Tinker off at the office so she can man the desk and pick up that new boy, the Marine. Hell, forgot his name."

"Colby. Will do. We're almost back to town. Jessie and Dal were off down the mountain and they got 'em both out. They're on the way to the hospital, but they'll be okay."

Mac signed off without comment.

"What's wrong with Mac lately? He's acting a bit off."

"Hadn't noticed."

She shrugged. "Did I hear a shot in the background before Mac signed off?"

"Sounded like."

"Well, let's get our butts out there. Taking me by the station is a waste of time. Radio Colby, tell him we need backup out there. He can figure out what to do. The boy's not dumb."

"But it's darker than pitch out there, and it'll be darker when we get on out of town."

"Then I'll just cringe in the car. Come on, Burt, let's go."

"Mac will kill me if I take you to a gunfight."

"Mister, I'll kill you if you don't. Some choice, huh?"

Burt didn't say anything for a minute, then he sighed, hooked the radio mic and talked to Colby giving him the rundown on all he knew, then directing him to Treman's.

The further out of town Burt drove, the worse Tink shivered. All the lights were behind them. Here and there a rural resident had a security light in the yard, but those didn't cover much more than the immediate vicinity. Her phobia grew full-blown before she heard the shots. Hunkered in the corner of the seat, she made herself as small as possible, arms wrapped around her knees.

Burt braked to a halt when the sound of gunfire increased. "You stay right where you are, just like you are. Hear me?"

Muted by terror, she could only nod, which of course he couldn't hear. He might, however, have heard her teeth clacking together or failing that the slamming of her heart against her chest.

After he disappeared, she obeyed him for a while. Another patrol car roared up, parked near her and someone jumped out, visible for an instant in the dome light. Colby. All the other deputies were either at home in bed or out patrolling the county. Guns continued to pop, someone hollered, shooting paused, then began again.

She closed her eyes tight, imagined being involved in a shootout, then imagined what the guys would say, most especially Burt. She'd qualified on the shooting range, so by God she was going. Teeth gritted she slipped out of the car and, remaining low, pulled her .40 from its holster and headed for the action. Fear and adrenaline drove her through the damn dark. The phobia could just wait till she had time to deal with it. For now, she was needed by her fellow officers. The dark didn't have bullets.

Parker emerged from the shadows of the emergency room where Dal and Jessie waited for a doctor. Dal lay on a bed and she sat beside him holding his bandaged hand.

"Is he going to be okay?"

"Uh-huh. They took X-rays and an MRI and cleaned up his wounds. He's beat all to hell, Parker. We're waiting for the doctor to come back and tell him the results." Her eyes filled and he came close, laid a hand on her shoulder.

"You've been through a lot these past few days. You need to get them to take a look at you as well."

"After they fix him. Oh, God, what am I going to do?"

"About...?"

"Steve, the shooting, Dal, and what he'll do when he learns everything."

He kissed the top of her head. "Listen to me. If he loves you and he's worth two cents, he'll stick with you through this. If he doesn't, well then he's not much of a man. As for the shooting, from what I know about it, you'll come through okay. They'll not charge you with anything, I'm sure."

"It's not what I'm worried about. I shot a man I once loved. He was right to want to get even with me for what I did. I deserved all that happened to me, but I deserved more and never paid. His life was ruined and I started it."

"Look at me." He knelt and turned her face. "A good man does not try to kill the woman he once loved. A good man does not blame her for everything when it was a snafu from the start. He broke the code when he told you what was going down. Then when the paper came out with the story, the higher-ups added to the mess by going ahead with the raid and planned arrests after it was common knowledge. Yeah, you should have held back on the story, but you're not solely to blame for those men getting shot. You made a mistake that cost you your life as you knew it. So this fellow needs to get up on his feet and start over, just like you did. Instead he comes after you, tries to kill you, for God's sake."

She leaned into his shoulder. "You're a good friend, Parker. I'm sorry about the other night, I was just—oh, I don't know, maybe trying to see if I'm worth anything at all. I love Dallas so much, but what we have is so complicated by the baggage both of us come with. It's so stupid. But that's the way it is. It's like we use each other, then toss each other away. Deny our feelings."

"Well, honey, we'll get all this straightened out. Then the two of you can go back to doing whatever it is you do, 'cause it seems to make you both happy."

"I hope you're right. I really do, but I don't see much chance he'll forgive me for what I've done. It comes too close to what was done to him and his wife. On top of that he still loves her."

"Jessie, that you?"

She bent over Dal. "It's me. You're going to be okay."

"Are you?"

"Sure. I'll admit it isn't every day I shinny down a rope, but hey, never a boring moment, huh?"

"I'd like to go home now."

She smiled and kissed his cheek. "I know you would, but let's wait till the doc comes in and ask him. Meanwhile, I'm right here."

Parker touched her shoulder. "I'm gonna get out of here. By the way, I dropped by your place and picked up that ugly mutt of yours. He was pretty glad to see me. Found the kibble and I'll keep him at the farm till you can come get him."

"Thanks. I forgot all about the poor dog. See, this is why I don't need a dog. Can't even remember I've got one."

"You take care. Everything's going to be all right."

Parker was gone before she replied. She'd forgotten to ask about his horses. Steve had caused that as well, unless he'd been lying about it.

Soon after Parker left, the doctor came rushing in. "You were right about your ribs, Mister Starr. They aren't broken, but they're going to hurt for a while. I want you to remain overnight so we can monitor you. You do have a concussion. Miraculously all your innards are in place."

"His innards? Gosh, doc, I love it when you use medical terms." Jessie smiled with relief.

"What I do to make patients laugh when their ribs are bent or broken."

"Kind of you." This from Dal.

The doctor turned to her. "I want you in the other cubicle, stripped down, young lady."

"Doctor Jones." Jessie put a hand over her mouth in mock surprise.

"While your young man is getting a room, I'm going to check you over. There's blood on your clothes so I know you need some medical attention. And you needn't worry. You're safe in my hands."

She rose to obey and all hell broke loose. An uproar outside in emergency. A head poked through the curtains.

"Doc, we've got two coming in with multiple gunshot wounds. One is the sheriff. It looks real bad. They're reporting a DOA at the scene."

"Okay, let's get this man upstairs to his room. We'll be needing all our space down here."

Dal swung his legs over the edge of the bed and sat up. "I'm gonna help."

"No, Dal. You can't get up. They'll take care of things." Even as she told him that she had the urge to run out into the melee of the emergency room.

"The two of you can't do anything down here. Now go."

A large aide entered, went to Dal's side. "Just lie back down here. I'm taking you up to your room."

For a minute it looked as if Dal would bolt, but the noise level from the room beyond the curtains and the pain he no doubt was experiencing must have convinced him he had no business out there. He laid down and let the aide wheel him out of the cubicle with Jessie following along.

Mac shot? Someone dead. What in the world was happening to this nice quiet town?

15

CHAPTER

The next few days were horrendous. Jessie ran from one place to another interviewing people for news stories on the shootings.

The town had never seen so much excitement as the gun battle between Treman, Spider, Mac, Tink, and Burt. Because word sped around town like wildfire, the story changing with each telling, she had to make sure she collected all the right information. Mac had been shot in the arm but was doing well. The man known only as Spider, who actually owned the place where Treman lived, was dead. It remained to be seen who had shot him, bullets were flying everywhere. Tink was afraid she'd done it, but that hadn't been confirmed. Jess hoped to learn the truth with the interviews, but knew there would be forensics to prove whose bullet had done the deed. She'd filed an initial story to go in the paper that went to print the day after the shooting, but it only contained a few facts about the entire affair. No real explanations from those involved. Certainly no interviews or forensics results. She gathered more of the interviews and the story promised to be long and detailed.

Meanwhile Dallas remained in the hospital where she visited as often as she could. Late one evening, exhausted and sleepy, she sat in the chair by his bed. He appeared to be asleep and she held his hand. The swelling in his face had gone down but he was still so battered. Unbidden, tears poured down her cheeks.

"Jess? Don't cry."

She jumped. Had almost dropped off herself. Peered at him. His eyes were closed.

"I'm gonna be okay." Well, that was weird. His lips hadn't moved, but it was definitely his voice. Her imagination, maybe? So how did he know she was crying? The tears were silent.

"I felt them on my hand, Jess."

The hair on her neck stood up and she shivered in the warm room. Some weird stuff happened around him, but this, well it was brand new. Mind meld? Despite everything, she giggled. *Star Trek* and Mister Spock. She was way too tired and had obviously been dreaming.

With a sigh, she rose, kissed his forehead, whispered good night, and turned to leave the room.

His voice followed her out. "Good night, Jess."

After tossing in her bed till dawn, she drove to town to keep her appointment for an interview with Mac. One arm in a sling, he leaned back in the chair behind his desk at the station.

When Treman called and said someone had shot at him when he went out to take a leak, I immediately called for backup, responded, and approached the scene with my gun out. The only light came from the window of his trailer and I hollered the house. It was so blamed dark I figgered whoever shot at him and missed wouldn't hit me either.

He hollered back and they shot again, this time breaking the glass.

"Put that blamed light out," I said through the broke window.

*He did and at that point I yelled that I was the sheriff and who-
ever was shooting should stop. That's when I got shot in the arm.
Whoever was out there didn't give a hoot I was a lawman.*

*How it happened is all of a sudden, a gun goes off right over my
head. That fool Treman had shot through the window, immediately
that guy shot back and hit me. So I'm laying on the ground rolling
around and groaning. Treman musta seen the flash or something,
'cause, bam, he got that guy broadside right in the gut.*

*We found Spider sprawled out in a pool of blood. You'll have to
talk to Treman about how he made a shot like that. I don't know. But
I 'spect he saved both our lives. What got into Spider I have no notion.*

Interviewing Treman was somewhat surprising. Since he claimed he
didn't have a phone, she went out to the trailer on the Saturday after the
shooting. Brad was in the Jeep before she could climb behind the wheel,
so she let him go along. Unsure about the situation, she wasn't looking
forward to talking to Treman. Considering the state he was in the first
time she showed up at his place, she approached with dread.

He opened the door to her knock and she could only stare. His long
dark hair was clean and combed and pulled back in a clip. He wore a
blue knit shirt, not new but clean, jeans only slightly wrinkled, and tan
leather moccasins. The most surprising thing was he looked and smelled
good. Tall and handsome, he smiled and stepped out on the stoop and
pulled the trailer door closed behind him before she got a good look.
Clearly he didn't want her inside. Too dirty or secretive, one or the other.

"Let's sit out there on the bench. It's a beautiful day." Gone was the accent he'd used the first time they met. The one that made him appear to be uneducated and non-communicative.

I lit the lamp when it got dark and had just sat down to supper when a bullet nicked my ear. Came so close I heard and felt it pass. Stung like a hornet. Made a neat hole in the window.

Now, I've been shot at more than a few times, so I don't hesitate to get the hell out of the way. I dropped down to the floor, called Mac, and then crawled over to where I kept my guns. Fetched the nine, then decided I'd need the rifle as well, so hanging on to both of them I went back to the window. Thought I would just lay there and let whoever it was shooting at me dictate the next move. I didn't think he had any grenades or flash-bangs. Laying on the floor was a safe bet.

The guy must've come a bit closer 'cause I could tell the next shot came from right out behind that big old oak tree in the side yard. He was taking his time, but it was hard to figure what he was shooting at. He could no longer see me. I wanted to blow out the lamp, but if I got up to do that he'd have a good target.

Mac showed up and got shot at so I just reached the rifle up there and knocked the lamp off the table. Kerosene went everywhere and it caught, but I was able to smother the fire real quick. Then I went to the window, which he'd broken out earlier, waited for him to fire again and when he did I saw the flash and I got him. Just like that.

"That was quite a shot, Mr. Ledger."

"Call me Trey. That's what I'm called at home."

"Where's home?" Odd how he'd dodged her compliment.

He grinned. "Oh, just out west."

"Out west." Another dodge.

"Uh-huh."

She studied him for a long moment. He peered up at the sky, then down at his feet. "I'd appreciate it if you didn't put any of this in the paper just yet. About me, I mean."

She rose, fumbling for her backpack and stuffing recorder, pad, and pen in it. "Damn all these people who want to confide in me, then tell me I can't write it. What the hell? I'm a reporter, for God's sake, not some priest or psychiatrist or something. I hope I never again hear the word confidential or off the record. Tell me, why did you agree to talk to me?"

He sported a crooked grin. "Don't get so hot about it. I figured if I didn't it would just make you all the more curious and you'd insist on writing about me in your article. It's important that you don't do that, and I can't tell you why."

"So, you expect me to make up something about the shootout? Even Mac wouldn't ask that of me. I'm tired of secrets. I don't want to know anything I can't put in the paper. I've had enough of that."

"You talk to Mac before you write this story. I know he issues releases on crime related incidents and that's what you print. Would you just do that, please?" His smile didn't hide the fact that he was adamant.

Before she could reply, he went on. "Tell you what. In a few weeks when this is all settled, I'll come back here and give you a story that'll be much better than this one. What do you say?"

She stared hard at him. If it weren't for her past and all that resulted from that first big story, she would've told him to get ripped, but knowing what she already knew, it could be really important for the whole story not to get out yet.

"Okay, that's a deal. But don't you run out on me."

He held out a hand, long graceful fingers clean as could be. "Shake, then." His next smile was genuine.

When she approached the Jeep, Brad, who'd been perfectly comfortable taking a nap, stood in the seat, barked twice in reply to her mutterings, then raised to his hind legs and poked his head out the open window.

With Burt and Tinker still waiting to be interviewed, she called her friend and arranged for the both of them to meet her at the Red Bird. Might as well get this done over burgers and fries. The notes would keep till Trey returned to give her the real story.

At the cafe Brad waited in the car. He'd been in this situation often enough to know he'd end up with a juicy burger when Jessie came back.

The couple waited at a table in the far corner where they'd have some privacy. Weaving through the crowd, greeting everyone with a wave and smile, she reached them and dropped into a chair. The backpack went on the floor where she dug around until she had her pad and pen. Too noisy to record in here, but these two would have very little to tell her, since they didn't arrive on the scene till most of the excitement was over. What she wanted mostly was their reaction to the entire episode. A short quote from each would do. Then she could get back to the paper and contact Mac. She just might give him hell.

"Hi friend. How are Dal and Mac?" Tink was fairly beaming. Something going on there between these two, no doubt.

"Dal is so sore he can barely walk. Guess he may come home tomorrow and then he'll be chomping at the bit to get back to work. I may have to tie him down in a day or two. Doc says two weeks, Dal says two more days is all he'll do. As for Mac, he's on the job at the station. If he wants to go somewhere one of the guys takes him. We're all concerned about his condition. He's forgetful, short-tempered, and occasionally depressed. I'm hoping we can get him to go to a neurologist and get checked out. You can imagine how that'll go over."

Wanda came and took their orders. When she left Jess turned to Tink. "How about the two of you? You look extremely happy. Tink, I might add, is glowing. What are you up to?" It didn't take a mind reader to figure this one out. Either they were getting married or they were going to live together.

"I'm going to a shrink about my phobia. As soon as I can get rid of it, Mac's gonna let me go in the field, but with a partner." She grinned hugely at Burt.

Well, so much for her mind reading abilities. "And Burt is your partner? I thought that was a big no-no, putting life partners together on the job."

"Oh, it is. Burt isn't my partner at work. Colby is. He fought beside some women in Afghanistan. Said they were as brave as some of the Marines he knew. I'm sure that's an exaggeration, but it does mean he trusts me. 'Course I have to stop hiding in a corner every time I'm in the dark."

Wrong again. "Well, that's wonderful. Good luck to you." So, these two weren't ready to commit yet either. Must be something in the water.

Wanda brought their burgers. "I'll have a patty fried all up for Brad when you leave." She grinned at Jessie and left.

While they ate she got her quotes for the article.

Burt was first. "When I heard the gunfire I was afraid they'd shot the sheriff. I asked Tink to remain in the car while I approached the scene. By the time I arrived, it was all over. That was one heck of a shot Treman made. I don't think I could've done it."

"It was pretty dark. Did you see him make the shot?"

"Well, he was in the trailer, Mac was on the ground. The gun shot came from inside the trailer. Had to've been him."

Tink came next. "Going onto that scene made me realize if I wanted to be part of the Grace County Sheriff's Department, I had to get over this fear of the dark. I'm ready to do something about it."

Good stuff, the personal touch. Just what she needed to complete the story. No one knew why Spider fired on Treman, now known as Trey. Well, not that they would say. Trey probably did. No one knew who killed Marcus Woods or why, or if they did they weren't talking. Trey's not-for-publication comment probably meant he knew who did.

She might be the only one who knew Marcus's true identity and she wasn't sure quite yet what to do with that information. It was frustrating as all get out for a reporter with stories to write. She'd do whatever Mac and Trey wanted. She had some other people to see who would probably never be featured in any of her articles.

First she went to the paper only to find a release about the incident from Mac lying on her desk. Itching to work on the entire series, which Parker said could run for at least three issues, she wrote a story from that for the current week and left it on Parker's desk for editing and headlining.

She drove home, took a long shower, then sat on the deck watching the sun head slowly toward the peaks to the west. Somehow she had to get her head straight. A chill wind came up and chased her inside where she poured herself a cup of coffee, drank it standing at the bar. In the bathroom she brushed her hair loose, touched her lips with a bit of color, and changed into a western blouse the color of her eyes. Time to go to the hospital and visit Dal.

Eventually she would have to tell him about Steve, the whole sordid story. Not till he was recovered though. At least give him that. She was on the verge of disappointing him, of hurting him, of losing him. God, what a mess. But it was time for her to pay for her sins.

He sat near the window, watching the sky. The last ashy gray faded to black and stars flashed to life. He heard her, spoke without turning.

"Beautiful, isn't it? I thought for a while I might never see the sky from this land again."

She moved to touch him, leaned down and kissed his cheek. Lately he'd taken up speaking more like his ancestors. The fall and his brush with death had done things to him, made him more idealistic.

Seated next to him, she took his hand. He laid it over her thigh. "Pretty shirt. Be good to go dancing in."

"Soon, I hope."

"I don't know. Every time we've tried something has interrupted. They told me I can go home tomorrow. About time. I was about to pull an escape."

"I was about to help you. I've missed you."

"Missed our battles?"

She laughed. "Well, that and other stuff."

He tweaked her breast. "You mean stuff like that?"

"Yeah, like that." Should she tell him about that first night he was here? When he'd spoken to her in her mind or in a dream, she wasn't sure which.

"Jess, I know I promised not to do this, but playing with your boob let my guard down. You mean when I felt your tears on my hand and asked you not to cry? You heard me, didn't you?"

Squeezing his hand tightly, she nodded and let her gaze meet his. "How do you know that?"

"We connected. Well, our spirits connected. Jess, you saved my life at the risk of your own. I never thought I would say this to a woman, to anyone, ever again, but we became one, so now…." He shrugged, never stopped staring into her eyes.

"Do you really believe that? You read my mind, then I read yours?"

"Yes." He went back to looking at the night sky, now ablaze with the glitter of stars.

Now what was she going to do? All this time she'd been preparing to tell him something that would tear them apart forever, and he says something like that. All she had to do was tell him she loved him and never think of anything else again.

"What is it, Jess? You don't want to be one with such a nice guy? Such a tough guy?"

He was shirking it off now, making light of it. In case she wanted to? Or he wanted to.

"It's okay. I won't do it again. I promise. So, what time are you picking me up tomorrow? Or do I need to get someone else?"

"Of course not. Did they say what time?"

"By noon, if all goes well, but you know how that is."

The next day she left him at his trailer with a promise to return later in the day. Ina Mae was available if he needed help in the meantime.

It was suppertime when she returned. After knocking several times, she tried the door. It opened and she went in, afraid she'd find him on the floor. But the place was empty. Moving to the sliding glass doors, she saw him navigating the creek toward her, stepping from rock to rock. If he fell he'd reinjure something. Ribs, arm, leg, back. You name it.

Arms folded under her breasts she went out on the patio to watch. Once he was across and coming toward her, she went down to meet him. The bank itself wasn't the safest place to wander about in his condition.

He saw her, smiled in that way he had when he knew he was in trouble, then waited for her to take his good arm and accompany him back to the trailer.

"Can't leave you alone for five minutes, can I?"

They sat on the couch, each sipping a beer before he replied.

"What? I just wanted to take another look at the scene."

"Get anything else?"

"Not really."

After he finished his beer, she rose. "Isn't it time for those bandages to be changed?"

The worst of his injuries were still healing. She went to the kitchen to get the ointments and gauze. "Let's go sit on the bed. You'll have to take most of your clothes off anyway."

He glanced up at her. "And…?"

"We'll see."

With a wide smile he started for the bedroom. By the time she got there, he was sitting on the edge of the bed, his shirt in a pile on the floor.

Without commenting she knelt and took his moccasins off. Since the accident he hadn't worn his boots, said they were too difficult for him to put on and take off. On her knees, she moved between his legs to unbuckle his belt.

"Raise your butt up."

He did so and she tugged his pants down.

"Aren't going to take my jockeys too?"

"Oh, you want me to? This could lead to something we might not ought to do."

"Let me be the judge of that."

With a nod she pulled the jockeys down too.

By the time she had replaced the bandages on his legs, he had a hard-on. She touched it. "Looks serious. Might call for extra attention."

"I'd say it does."

"I'm afraid I'll hurt you."

"It'll hurt more if you do nothing."

"Okay. Why don't you scootch up and lay down?"

"Sounds like a plan to me." His movements were slow and painful, but he finally managed to get flat on his back. She stood at the foot of the bed where he could see her and removed her clothing, one piece at a time. Slowly so he could enjoy the show.

"You're driving me insane."

"Coming, dear." Carefully she placed the bandages and medicine on the far side of the bed, then bent one leg over him, still wearing panties and bra, leaned down and gave his erection an open-mouth kiss, then crawled over.

"Ah, God, woman, did you have to stop there? I'm going nuts here."

"Bad pun."

"Unintentional."

"Must take care of the doctoring first." She removed the bandage around his knee, applied ointment to the wound, and rewrapped it. "There, isn't that better?" She tapped on his penis. "Does that hurt?"

"Damn, I didn't hurt that. What're you gonna do, wrap it up?"

The look on his face was priceless and she couldn't help but laugh. "Poor baby."

"I am gonna get you for this. You know I will."

She kissed him deeply, tongue to tongue, a gentle nibble on his lips, then back inside again. His one arm encased in a cast, curled around her waist and he pulled her close, continuing the deep kiss despite his groans. His ribs were still sore and she didn't want to hurt him, so she pulled back.

"Sweetie, let me finish this for you. I'm afraid we'll go a bit crazy and you'll get hurt."

"I wish you would."

She trailed kisses where she could find unbroken skin till she found her target and did as promised while he lay back and enjoyed himself. Both hands wrapped in gauze and several fingers patched with Band Aids, he could do very little for her. She lay next to him for a long while before she rose to finish tending all his wounds.

"That was good, so good," he murmured. "I just need one more thing."

"Men. Never satisfied. What is it you need, sweetie?"

"A taste of those beautiful tits."

"Tits? You dare call my breasts *tits*?"

"Okay, breasts. I'll call them anything you want if you'll just let me kiss and play with them."

Though this would start something else altogether, she gave in. His warm, moist lips around her nipple renewed the enjoyment she'd experienced giving him release, and she was in no hurry for him stop. Satisfied, she lay beside him, his hand on her breast, and fell asleep.

The day after the paper went to press Tuesday night, she went to visit Steve Wainwright to begin her penance. She'd spent nights with Dal to make sure he took care of himself, all the while terrified he'd interrogate her about the shooting and Steve and the lists he still hadn't seen. So much was hanging over her head that it was time she started cleaning it up. She was exhausted at having to live that way.

In the process, maybe she could find out who killed Rick Granger aka Marcus Woods and why, and also who Trey Ledger was, and why Spider had tried to kill him. It was tricky, like a tangled skein of yarn that had so many knots it might never be unraveled. Right now, with Mac and Dal both on the injured list, she had a better chance at figuring this all out.

She hated the smells and sounds, even the ambiance of hospitals. But then, who didn't? The patients and their needs should come before the visitors and their dislikes. It wouldn't be proper to take Steve a gift, so she went empty-handed. Waited in the door of his room long enough to study him. Though his appearance was wan, he looked much the same as she remembered. A typical cop face, if there were such a thing. Square jaw, stubborn chin, wide set eyes that could stare right through a person. He'd taken to cutting his hair shorter than he once wore it, enhancing that cop image.

Turned away, gazing out the window, he didn't see her till she moved around the end of the bed into his field of vision.

"Jesus, you've got a lot of nerve. What are you doing here, anyway?" With care he shifted a bit in the bed to better face her. Grimaced.

"I… I'm not sure why I'm here. To put an end to this, I suppose."

"Oh? And how do you propose to do that? Shoot me?" Jaw clenched, muscles bunched in his face.

"Funny. You know that was an accident and only after you pulled that gun on me." Not wanting a fight, she backed off, began again. "I'm not sure yet. Talking usually helps. And failing that, perhaps you could shoot me." She hadn't meant to say that, it just came out. He had appeared very willing to pull the trigger and end her life.

"I would if I had a weapon. You bitch. You shot me."

"With a gun you had pointed at me. Steve, please, can't we get past this unfortunate situation and go to the crux of the matter?"

"The crux of the matter? You always did like to use writerly phrases, like you were better than me. I trusted you, I loved you, and look what you did. How can you think for one minute that I'd forgive you? How could you even believe we could discuss it?"

"I don't know. You came here for some reason. To kill me? I'm sorry for all that happened. I was young and stupid and all I wanted was to make it in the big time. What a story I had. You gave it to me and I used it, and I'll regret it the rest of my life. But I need you to take some responsibility and forgive me, or at least stop stalking me."

"Oh, that's a good one. I'm stalking you now, is it?"

"Well, you came to my hometown years after all this was behind us and you started finding my friends, making a list of them. For all I know you killed Rick. You marked him off the list. You tried to kill Dallas. What were you going to do? Kill everyone who loves me?"

"What the hell are you talking about? What *list*? Who is *Rick*? I came here for a reason that has nothing to do with you. I didn't even know you were here till I saw you get in your Jeep on the square a few days after I arrived."

She stared at him. How did he expect her to believe such nonsense? He always could lie, but men who worked undercover lived with lies most of the time. "Oh, come on. What a wild coincidence that would be. You can stop lying now. It's all coming apart. Why are you here, then?"

"That's none of your business, but I can swear to you, it wasn't to hurt you. Oh, the minute I saw you, I knew I could do what I came for and take care of old business at the same time. It was beautiful. I could take you somewhere, out in the woods or over to Lover's Leap and drop your body where no one would ever find it."

She tucked that mention away for later. He'd slipped, bringing that up.

"I'll admit, I became obsessed with ways to pay you back, but that only after I spotted you on the street."

She lowered herself into a chair by the bed. This was going to be a long conversation and she was determined to get a promise that he would leave her friends alone, go away and not try to kill her again. She didn't expect him to forgive her, not with this attitude.

"You sent me a note at the newspaper. Tell me, Steve. Where have you been staying while you're here?"

"Why do you ask? What I'm doing is none of your business."

"Well, were you at the Five Bees?"

"Sounds like a really sweet place to stay, but no, never heard of it."

She ignored his attempt at a pun. "Where then?"

"What's with this desire to know where I'm staying? You want to sneak in some night and stick a knife in my heart? Well, I can tell you, you've already done that, in spades."

"When are they letting you out of here?" She rose, prepared to leave feeling sad and incomplete. He would always hate her, and as long as he did, she would have to look over her shoulder. Anything could happen that would put him in the mood to come after her again.

"I don't know, but it'll be a while. You can rest easy for a few days yet."

He didn't know he could be charged with attempted murder. Strange they hadn't already done that, but she didn't want to be there anymore. He could never admit he came here to hurt her, maybe even to kill her.

Without saying anything more, she left.

Dal prowled the trailer. Didn't take too damn many steps to get from one end to the other. He stopped at the sliding glass doors and peered out at the creek and beyond where the car had been burned. Still picked up no lingering violence. All he felt was the message that he hurt in places he never knew he had. Even the hairs on his head sent a jag of pain to his brain. The trick was to work it out. Worry about the other shit later. He slid the door open, eased down onto the patio. Just doing that felt like it had when he'd climbed back up that mountain. Muscles screamed, joints objected, and the torture ragging at his chest continued.

He opened his mouth, pulled in a lungful of air, held it, then let it out. Damn, that hurt. At the same time it felt good to be alive. When he thought what could've happened to him on his fall down the mountain, he blocked the possibilities. Tried to think of anything else but that. The nightmares were there to deal with. Finding Jess beside him each night helped more than anything else.

Bent like an old man, he paced the length of the patio and back again, mind racing. She had come down a rope to get to him. He'd never forget that. What courage that had taken. There were times he wanted to gather her close, kiss her, and tell her how he really felt about her, that he loved her. But then he'd come to his senses. This business with the man in the hospital worried him. How long should he wait for her to come clean before he faced her with it? Back inside. God, that step was agonizing. Be damned if he'd ever take another hike in the woods. He stood in the center of the kitchen when she drove up.

She came into the trailer flushed and carrying a bag of groceries. He limped to her side. "Should've hollered, I'd a helped you with those."

She smiled up at him. God she was pretty all fresh and sweet. Didn't need any paint on that face. It was perfect the way it was.

"It's okay. Just one sack and it doesn't weigh anything."

When she set it down on the table, he peeked inside, pulled out a box of protein bars. "You really like these?"

"They're okay. I like to keep them in the backpack for emergencies. Never know when someone is going to fall off a mountain."

"Oh, yeah. Well, I hope you brought something for when I'm kicked back in the chair."

He didn't get to say more, she wrapped her arms around his waist, didn't squeeze but held him for a while, her head laid on his chest. "I'm so glad you're okay. So glad."

He patted her shoulder. "So am I. You saved my life, truly saved my life. I coulda laid there and died."

"Shh, let's not talk about it, okay? I want to talk to you about something else. Let's make sandwiches and eat first, though. I don't know about you, but I'm starved."

Out of her embrace, he leaned for a moment on the chair back, then unpacked the sack of groceries, handing them to her to put away. They sat at the table and made sandwiches, opened bottles of iced tea to drink with them.

When they finished, she cleared things away. Took his hand in hers. "Let's go sit on the couch. We need to talk."

From the expression on her face, this was serious. What he had feared was finally coming to pass, and he didn't want to hear it.

16
CHAPTER

For a long time Jess sat beside Dal on the couch and held her tongue. She could lose this man right here, right now, but she would not lie to him even by omission. Not anymore.

She took one of his bandaged hands in both hers, holding gently. His gaze locked on hers, the deep green eyes almost black. From hope or passion? Maybe a bit of both. Sunlight filtered through the trees to cast shadows across the window, an occasional leaf trailing down. Even as she struggled to open her mouth, tears filled her eyes. How would she get through this? Would she hurt him too much to be forgiven?

He searched her face. "What is it? What's happened? Are you okay?" All questions with a hopeful tone. "Don't ask me to probe."

"I have to tell you something and I don't want you to say anything until I'm finished. Then whatever, just give me a chance to explain first."

He swallowed so hard she heard the click in his throat. Shook his head slowly like he didn't want to hear, yet his silence told her he had to.

So she began at the beginning and told him everything just as she had spilled it to Parker. That she had betrayed Steve to get ahead in her career, that he had threatened her life. "I know how you feel about reporters who don't care who they hurt with their stories, how you were nearly destroyed when Leann died and they turned you into a bad cop, even accused you of being a drug dealer."

He pulled his hand from hers and she didn't try to stop him.

"Please, let me finish."

Glancing toward the window, he said, "Go on." Wooden words, harsh and unforgiving.

"He came here and tried to shoot me." She shrugged. "I deserved to be punished, I know that, but surely not the death penalty. I didn't mean to shoot him, but he didn't give me a choice. He was going to kill me."

Nothing.

"I love you, Dal. I know you don't want to hear that either, but I do love you. I would never, never betray you that way. If I could go back, I would not betray Steve in that way either. I was stupid, driven, hell, I was anything you want to call me. I tried to get him to forgive me, but he won't. He still has every intention of hurting me, maybe killing me. Worse, he pushed you off that mountain, and so that's on me too." The ache in her throat muffled her next words, words she wanted to suppress, but that would break her vow not to lie to him by omission.

Dal's eyes widened, he shook his head so hard he closed his eyes against the pain. She laid a hand on his thigh and he flinched, but let it remain. A good sign? God, she hoped so.

"Please forgive me for not telling you this. I don't want to lose you. What we've had—"

He stared at her, finished the sentence. "—is nothing. Nothing. I could never have been with you for one minute had I known this." His effort to stand was thwarted and he cursed under his breath, planted his hands on either side, and struggled once more to rise. Failed.

She stood. "Stay where you are. It's okay, I understand. I'll go. I'm so, so sorry. If there's anything I can do to get you to forgive me, I'll do it." She sucked up a sob, turned and fled to the doorway where she paused. "Please take care of yourself. I couldn't bear it if anything happened to you. I'll try to make this right, I promise. I promise." The last words came from so deep inside she almost didn't get them said before running down the steps and to the car.

All the way home she could barely make out the road for the rush of tears. Her stomach ached with the pain of losing him. For almost three years they had been lovers, friends, best buds. She wanted no one but him. Though prepared to do penance for her mistakes, this hurt way more than she ever imagined. Dal would never forgive her, and worse, she would never forgive herself.

Over a week later Dal climbed gingerly from his car and limped into the sheriff's station. After two weeks of daily walking and giving in to some rehab at the hospital everything still hurt. But he could manage it, and needed to get back to work. Anything to stop dwelling on what had happened between him and Jess. When he wasn't cursing his own stubbornness he was cursing her foolishness.

Mac had preferred to wait for him to return to work to get back to the unsolved cases. Most especially, who killed the one-legged man? He'd come to think of him that way.

So many questions on the agenda: find out who the heck Marcus

Woods was and why someone would want to kill him and how long he had been in Cedarton and what was he here for and who were the two men who moved the body and burned the car? Most important, why did they cut off his leg and call attention to it like they had? He hammered himself with these questions to keep from thinking of her betrayal. For she had done to him precisely what she had done to Steve Wainwright.

Reaching his desk, he dropped into the chair. It'd been more than two weeks since she had risked her life to come down that rope… but no, he refused to think of that part… since he had been shoved off the narrow path and almost died on the mountain. Still he wore out at the drop of a hat. The inbox on his desk was full and much as he disliked paperwork he would clean that out first. All the while his mind could go over those questions and come up with some answers. Anything. Please, anything to keep his mind off her. The sky blue eyes, the dusting of freckles across her nose, the sun-streaked hair that tickled his chest when she… goddammit, *stop*.

With grim determination he worked his way through reports from the deputies who were involved in various facets of the cases and started his own file into which he would enter his findings. There was a report from the Spaceys detailing the digging up of the body and he went over that, not discovering anything he hadn't already known. Something did jump out at him, though. He paged through the other reports. No, it wasn't there. How could everyone have missed this? There was no cause of death. The amputated leg was supposed to have been postmortem, but maybe it hadn't been. Maybe he bled out when his leg was cut off? He didn't know, but something ought to be listed as cause of death.

Mac wandered through with two cups of coffee and set one on his desk. Propped his butt up on the corner.

"Thanks. Say, where's the cause of death on Marcus Woods?"

"Hell, don't ask me. The Spaceys usually chime in on that, or Doc. Maybe they're waiting for it to come back from Little Rock. The ME down there has final determination. He may be backed up."

Dal nodded. "Then it's just been missed or delayed. I'll call them."

"Good idea. Anything else that might help us solve this thing?"

"Not yet. We may need to get fresh eyes on this. How about Colby? Could he maybe take a look at the reports?"

Mac sent him a questioning look. "How you feeling, boy? You still look wiped out. Maybe you hadn't ought to be here."

"Doctor said I could come back to desk duty and it looks like I've got a lot of that." He gestured to the inbox.

"Okay, son. Just take 'er easy. That was a hell of a fall. You're lucky you survived."

"Yeah." He set his jaw, not wanting to go further in that discussion.

Mac went on his way and he concentrated on the paperwork. If Mac knew about his breakup with Jess, nothing was said.

When he picked up the two-page printout from the in box he only glanced at it at first. The man in the photo looked familiar. It was Steve Wainwright. He couldn't help reading the story about why Wainwright had been fired. How an undercover plan to bring down a drug lord had gone bad because of pillow talk with a reporter who broke the story prior to the raid. Eight men were wounded, and they were fortunate no one was killed. There was also a copy of the article in question by someone named J.J. Stone. Jess West, once J.J. Stone.

The last thing he wanted to do was read any more. Yet, he couldn't take his eyes off the next page, had to see it all through to the end. So he read "Sex Can Get You Killed", an additional story about a West Coast reporter who slept with an undercover cop, then wrote an article revealing the secrets he told her prior to a raid. This one, about Jess. Why did he continue to read it? Because he could not take his eyes off the words. The article caused the wounding of several cops. Neither the reporter nor the cop were identified in the second story. Of course it was J.J. Stone. *His* Jess. A month ago he would have thought it all lies. Those yellow rags never printed the truth. He was surprised one of those involved wasn't identified as an alien from outer space just to juice it up some more. He stared at the two pages for a long while before he remembered how it must've gotten to his desk. He was online checking up on Jess before she shot Steve. Clicked print and was called away.

God help him, he must've known it then but couldn't admit it. He wished with every ounce of energy left him that he had never met her, never touched her or let her touch him. Damn her to hell. If he had to he would leave Cedarton, anything to escape this gut feeling like he had been stabbed with burning hot blades. Over and over.

He wadded the print-out into a tight ball and threw it in the trash basket next to his desk. Time to get busy, forget about her, and solve these obviously connected crimes.

He picked up the phone and called Mac.

The gruff-spoken old man answered.

"Mac, this Marcus Woods, have we anything further on him?"

"Oh, yeah. Funny you should ask. I was just gonna call you. We received results on his fingerprints from the state police. Sent them over just now. Turns out he was a local guy. Name of Rick Granger. You know Bud Granger? His son. Believe that? Odd, always liked old Bud. He'll be devastated. Someone will have to notify him soon."

"Odd. Wonder why the alias."

"You got me. Boy's been gone from these parts for ten years or more. Also got results from the staties on the bullet that killed Spider. It doesn't match any of ours. It does, however, match Treman's weapon. Witnesses agreed, said he hit Spider with one hell of a shot in the dark. Reckon it was true."

"Figure he had to have night vision glasses of some sort to make that shot in the dark." Dal remembered something Jess had said. Swore Treman was an undercover agent of some sort. Had to be a wild guess 'cause where would she get that kind of information?

"Mmm. Something to think about. Much as I hate it, I'm going on out to the Granger farm and talk to Bud about his boy. Too bad we didn't have the prints back 'fore Doc sent the body to Little Rock. They'll probably want him down there to do an ID. Goddamn government. Fingerprints should be enough, but they always want more. While I'm gone, why'nt you call Doc? He says he found a birthmark on Marcus uh, er, Rick's body You might want to verify that 'fore we go any further. Bud would know.

"Don't suppose you've gleaned any more information from your spirit guide, or whatever the hell he is. We could use a break about now. I'm all but ill-confused over this whole situation. We don't get this figured out, we'll have the staties all over us like fleas on a hound."

Dal's phone rang and he told Mac goodbye. When he connected he heard a voice he hadn't wanted to hear ever again.

"Don't hang up. This is strictly business. I've got something I think you'll want to take a look at. Do you want me to drop it off with Tink and she can bring it to you?"

"Yes, that would be best."

He didn't hang up and neither did she. The dead air hanging between them was filled with his disappointment. His gut ached with the desire to work with her again, trade arguments on who was right and who was wrong. After fighting like badgers, they'd go to bed and make love with a wildness that filled his heart and soul.

"Dal?"

"Jess?"

Their voices overlapped. More silence, then he said, "What is it?"

"Some papers from the DEA. About Marcus, er, Rick and, I think Treman and Spider, but I'm not sure. I wish we could—"

"—well, we can't. DEA? Shit, Jess, where did you manage to get those?"

"Best I don't tell you."

"I'll just bet. Don't you ever learn?"

Pause for a couple of beats. "My job is to dig out the truth. That what you want me to stop doing?"

"Okay, let's not get into that. Why are you sharing them with me?"

"Because your job is to find whoever's stirring this up, getting people killed." Her breath resembled a sob and his heart jerked a beat.

"Jess?"

She didn't reply for so long he thought maybe she'd gone. Finally she replied. "Yes?"

"You alone at the paper?"

"Yes, it's Friday. No one's here."

"I'll be there in ten." He didn't wait for her to reply. Just grumbled himself out of the station, past the front desk where he left word where he'd be, across the parking lot to the patrol unit, and all the way to *The Observer*. Called himself every name he could think of and just kept right on going. To her. To Jess. Like he didn't have good sense.

And, of course, he didn't.

She waited for him like a girl on her first date. Heart fluttering, stomach rolling over, nerves tingling all the way to every erogenous zone.

Tires crunched on gravel, a car door slammed, the front door opened. She rose. "Dal, lock the door, please."

No reply, but in a few seconds he appeared in the doorway from the tiny lobby. And stood there, eyeballing her from beneath the brim of his Stetson, thumbs hung in the pockets of his snug jeans, that one hip cocked.

She rose, started toward him. He held up a scarred palm.

"Stay there. Where you are. I left the door open."

Throat clogged, she nodded and waited. When he remained silent, didn't approach, she gulped. "You came. There's no way we can stay apart."

"Hush, girl. Just hush. I'm working at this awful hard, but don't try to convince me. I gotta do it myself."

One corner of her mouth tilted up. She couldn't help it. It was so, so Dal that she could hold the smile no longer and it spread. He was going to forgive her, it would just take a while was all. Maybe a long while. But they were in the same room.

"We got ourselves a doozy here. You got something, I think I do too, so let's do the usual but keep it strictly business. Then, when we figure it all out, we can go our separate ways."

It wasn't the solution she'd hoped for, but at least they'd be working together. It would give her a chance to earn his forgiveness. "Okay. Could you come on in now?" She moved to the receptionist's desk and snagged the comfortable chair for him. He lowered himself slowly. Still hurting. She could rub down those aches and pains, make them feel better, then they could make long, slow love. She squirmed and tried to settle the itches she wanted him to scratch. She loved him so much it made her shiver all over.

Okay, behave yourself. You're a big girl, so act like it. Which was exactly what she was afraid she would do. Big girls love sex, don't they? Love making love in all the ways possible.

"First the list." He pinned her with a stare, held out a hand, waited while she dug around in her backpack and came up with the slightly wrinkled paper.

He took it, glanced at the names with lifted brows, then folded it carefully and put it in his pocket. "Now, what is it you want to show me?"

His lilting voice didn't settle her down one bit, but she reached for the sheets she'd printed from the pictures she took at the mortuary. Handed them to him and leaned back to watch his reaction.

One page widened his eyes, the second gained a disbelieving glance in her direction, the third brought out some words he seldom used. He went through every page without further comment, then laid them on her desk.

"Where'd you get these?"

"Some guys visited Doc. They definitely looked like Feds of some kind. When they left he had them and I got a quick look, so he went out to lunch and I snuck in and took pictures."

"But you left the file right where it was?"

"Of course, it looked too important to steal. They'd have been all over all of us, maybe stuck us in a cell and withheld food and water till one of us talked."

"Well, that's a bit of an exaggeration." His eyes actually twinkled, but he blinked and shut that down. Quick.

"What do you think they are?"

"First place, they aren't officially redacted. Someone took a black marker to them. See how wavery the marks are? Probably the men who shared them with Doc. They only wanted him to know enough to not poke his nose in any further. See here, Marcus agreed to testify against this trafficker. Looks like the trial prep was going to take a long time, so they put him in witness protection."

"So someone found him. I know, er, knew him. He's Rick Granger. You've met his dad. Bud Granger. Eats at the Red Bird, or he did. I haven't seen him in a while."

He shuffled through some more of the papers. "How did you know it was him? This Granger guy, I mean."

Okay, here goes. She bit her lip, turned away to look out the window. "Once, a long time ago we, uh, we made love. We were kids. I saw the birthmark on his hip. Doc or someone, I don't remember who, mentioned it after he was killed."

He acted as if he hadn't heard the words about her and Rick making love. Just went right on. "I'd guess, since his body showed up here, that for some reason he came home. That's a death sentence for anyone in WITSEC. Mac got the ID today on Marcus and said he would go tell Bud his son is dead. He can find out if the boy came to see him in the past few months. That'll give us a start."

"Wait. Cutting off his leg was telling him he couldn't run anymore. But he was dead, how did that send him any message?"

"It was really to the DEA and witness protection. These drug traffickers are good at such nonsense. Makes 'em feel so damned self-important. Think they can get away with anything." He folded the papers and rose from the chair, face flushed with fury.

"Hey, wait. Where you going?"

"To see if Mac has left. Thought I might go with him to see Granger."

"A lot to pile on him all at once, isn't it?"

The phone rang and at the same time Dal limp-hopped out the door and slammed it on her words.

Tempted to let the phone go to voice mail, she started across the room. His car roared out of the parking, tires spitting gravel against the front windows. At the receptionist's desk she picked up the phone.

"Observer, this is Jess West."

"Trey Ledger here. You going to be there for a while?"

"Well, I suppose so. Why?"

"I'll be there in twenty."

"Wait, what….?" He hung up.

Back at her desk, she dropped into her chair. What in the world could he want? She pulled up her copies of the DEA document, hit Control P, and went to the printer to gather the sheets and staple them together. Flipping the first page over, she held it to the light to see if she could make out the words blackened by a marker. Got nothing she could read. Maybe on the original, but probably not. These guys were real careful.

Back at her desk she sorted through her notes and didn't hear the door open. Footsteps clunked on the hardwood floor and she looked up to see Trey Ledger standing at the counter peering through the window between the waiting area and the receptionist's cubbyhole.

"Okay if I come on back?" Without waiting for a reply, he pushed open the half door, strode to her desk, and dropped into the chair Dal had left empty a few minutes earlier.

"It's time you and me talked."

"It's I."

He tilted his head and gave her a wry grin. "Pardon?"

"I. It's you and I talked. Drop the you and you wouldn't say me talked, would you?" He made her nervous as hell but this babbling had to stop. Hard to believe she'd even said such a thing.

"Well now, I never thought you was a grammarian, but then since you write all those purty stories, reckon I ought not be surprised." His eyes hard as pebbles in a stream regarded her.

He'd dropped into that hill boy accent so easily she might have been talking to someone else. She didn't much care for the expression on his face either. Still, might be better if she got along with this guy. He could well be their killer or at the least know who was. He had shot Spider, though in self-defense.

"Sorry. It's automatic. By the time I finish helping with the editing around here, every grammar mistake crawls up my back. I apologize. Now, where were we?"

"I wanted to talk to you about where you got some of your information in your last two stories."

"I thought I attributed everything I wrote. Could you be more specific? If the information isn't in the paper, I may not be able to tell you my source."

"I think you probably can."

The harsh demanding tone in his voice startled her and she glanced up. He held his jacket open to reveal a revolver in a shoulder holster.

"What? You came here to shoot me if I don't come clean?" Though she was shaking inside, she gave the words a joking quality.

"Aw, look. I didn't mean to threaten you. This is just a friendly discussion. I need some information, you can probably give it to me."

"Well, that's a little bit better. Ask and we'll see if I can help you out or not. But first, I'd like to know just who you are. You've been living out there at Spider's place for what, six months now. Dressing like a hillbilly, acting like one too. Then someone buries a severed leg on your property and sets fire to your place, and now you're mister clean-cut guy. That seems pretty suspicious, if you ask me."

"Who do you think I am?"

She chuckled. "I told Dal I thought you were an undercover cop, but now I'm beginning to believe you're a hired hit man."

"Ah, that's a pretty good one." His laughter sounded anything but humorous. "You're pretty brave, accusing me of that with no one here but you and me."

"Am I? You still haven't asked me what you want to know."

"Did they identify the body that was sent to Little Rock earlier?"

"Not officially." That was only technically a lie, but she wasn't about to tell him when no one had told Bud Granger his son was dead. Not that she was aware of, at any rate.

"Then who is he unofficially?"

"Name is Marcus Woods. That was in this week's paper. His wife reported him missing several months ago. They lived up in Wichita. Again, this was all in my story. I'm insulted you didn't read it."

He rolled the chair up tight against hers. "Okay, pretty lady. Enough of this horsing around. It's time you realized that we are alone in here and I am serious as hell."

He had her pinned into a corner where her desk butted up against the table that held the printer and she couldn't get away. Fear took the place of bravery. His expression and tone told her he was not kidding around.

Though he was officially restricted to desk duty, when Dal found

Mac had already left for Granger's, he drove out to join him. It was time this mess came to an end. Mac's patrol unit was parked in the long circular drive in front of the sprawling ranch house. Dal stepped out, put his hat on, and started the difficult walk to the front porch. Off to the right and back of the house was a barn and corrals. Two men stood near the fence, one leaning on the top rail, obviously distressed.

Dal cut across the immaculate lawn, and halfway to them wondered at the advisability of the walk. His knee objected first, then his back. Breathing past the cracked ribs brought him up short to lean against the trunk of a sprawling oak. He'd almost made it.

Mac must've seen him coming, for he met him there under the tree. "You're supposed to be at your desk. What's going on? You okay?"

Between shallow breaths Dal told him about the papers and why he was there to speak to Granger about his son's whereabouts for the past few months. "If he was in WITSEC and came to visit his Dad for any reason, those assholes knew it and identified him. They'd a had someone watching him. Classic behavior when WITSEC is involved."

Mac frowned and scrubbed at his jaw. "You're absolutely right. The man's pretty broken up, but we need to find out if the boy's been out here. You okay to finish this up, or should I?"

"Let's both do it." Giving up midway wasn't an option. Dal straightened and together the two of them went to join Granger, who still leaned against the board fence. As it turned out, Rick had been in touch with his dad only a week before his death. Because the older man had been diagnosed with cancer after Rick went into WITSEC, the boy felt he had to pay him a visit.

"I don't have very much longer and Rick knew that much." Bud wiped his eyes and went on. "He called from his cell phone, asked if I'd seen anyone odd hanging around. Who looks for odd people? I told him no and he came out, walked through the woods where he figured he'd be safe, and spent an evening with me, slipping in after dark and leaving around midnight. I don't sleep much, and so we stayed up talking."

Mac glanced at Dal, then asked, "When was that, Bud?"

"Let's see, it was about a month or so ago, maybe a bit longer. Time passes so fast, but I think that's about right. I never saw him again. Lost my Betty last year, now this." He massaged his eyes with thumb and fingers.

Mac thanked him, repeated the nearly meaningless words of being sorry for his loss, and told him there might be more questions later. The old man nodded his head, then stared out across the pastureland filled with grazing cattle.

"Probably have to sell the place before long. Girls don't want it and I haven't got too much longer."

A knot grew in Dal's throat, thinking of the loneliness of such a situation. "If there's anything we can do, Bud, please let us know, would you? And we're plumb sorry about your loss." He tipped his hat and followed Mac back to their units.

He leaned on the roof of his car to catch his breath before opening the door and sitting down.

Mac bent down. "Who do you reckon killed the boy? Got any ideas?"

"A few, but I need to talk to this Steve character as well as Trey Ledger. There's a connection between the two of them, perhaps it includes Spider and Marcus, er, Rick Granger."

"I agree, they're all tied up in this, but there's one or two haven't come to the surface yet. Let Bud alone for a few days, but we have a lot more questions for him. I expect the marshals to descend pretty damned quick. Probably still out there trying to find their way here."

From somewhere out in the pasture a cow called its calf and was answered with short little bawls.

Mac stopped in mid turn. "Let's get back to the office. Didn't find out what you was doing out here."

"Getting some information from Jess and she told me about Marcus being identified."

"Yeah, well, all this folderol only confuses things more. I tell you, boy, if we don't get this solved and quick them staties and marshals will be all over it and we'll be left holding our bare asses in both hands just to prove we know where they are."

Mac raised a hand and walked away.

Despite himself, Dal laughed. Pain knifed through his ribs and was gone. At least he was getting better. Bright sunlight slashed through the window, blinding him when he steered the car around the driveway and headed back toward town.

First thing he was going to do was try to decipher the meaning of the names on that list Jess finally handed over. His being one of them was disconcerting to say the least. Damn thing resembled a kill list, which meant whoever pushed him off the mountain probably sent it. And had no doubt killed Rick Granger. He'd be coming after the rest of them, including himself. Had Jess shown the list to Mac and Parker or Steve, the man she'd shot? And why did the mysterious Brown leave it when he disappeared from the B&B? He wished he had Jess in on this. She had so many answers that would save him a ton of time.

Wherever his mojo had gone, he wished it would return so he could get a handle on this. That was something he never thought he would want. It took all he could muster to drive past *The Observer* without going in, plopping down at her desk, and having a talk about the case.

A car sat in the drive next to hers, but he didn't recognize it. Lots of people visited the newspaper.

He drove on by without turning his head to look at the window of the building where Jess was. And it filled him with sorrow. A huge chunk had been cut from his spirit and he might never get it back.

17
CHAPTER

"Sit back down." Trey whirled from staring out the window when Jess jumped from her chair.

Be damned if she'd sit there and let this guy do anything he wanted to her. The best route would be out the back door that opened off the storeroom. If she ran real fast. Evidently not fast enough for she only made it as far as the door into the small room. Once used as a darkroom, it was still not well lit. His fingers clamped her upper arm before she saw him.

"Come back over here. I have something to show you. Don't struggle, I'm not going to hurt you." He plopped her in her chair. "Where were you going?"

The conversational tone surprised her. He reached under his jacket and she huddled into the chair, expecting him to take out a gun. Instead he held a leather case that he flipped open. She stared at the badge and ID for a long time and he let her while he smiled.

"US Marshal? Am I under arrest, or what? Is that thing real? It can't be. You don't look like a marshal. Well, today you almost do. You sure don't look like that guy you pretended to be all this time."

He handed her the leather case. "It's real. I'm sorry I had to stay undercover till we found out for sure our witness is dead. Goddamn, why did he have to come home and reveal himself? Soon as he did, he signed his own death warrant."

"So Rick was in WITSEC. We sort of figured out that much, once the body was ID'd." She wrinkled her nose and handed the badge back to him. "Never saw one of those before, so am not sure, but don't see why you'd misrepresent yourself to a member of the press. Oh, wait a minute, you already did. What I really don't get is why did you come on so strong when you first walked in here? You scared me half out of my britches. I really thought you might kill me."

"Sorry. I'm told I come across that way sometimes. Didn't mean to scare you. I was only here to keep an eye out for our witness."

"Well, you didn't do a very good job of it, did you?"

"Guess not. Never lost one in protection before. Trouble is, he didn't remain in protection. Didn't have the sense God gave a goose over how to hide out on his own, so it's on him. Coming home was his big mistake. That's how they got him. It's all these damned deep woods and him sneaking around like he thought that would help. All it did was lose me long enough for someone who knew the back trails to grab him. I'd sure like to find out who did this."

"Then you ought to talk to Dallas Starr. He's in charge of the case and can bring you up to date."

"You know what? I can't do that."

"Whyever not? He'll cooperate. He used to work undercover in narcotics in Dallas. He gets all this stuff, even if us hillbillies don't."

He laughed, pulled a rolling chair over close by her desk, and sat down. "It's not that. Not at all. I've come to you 'cause I'm supposed to leave here. My witness is dead, so my job is over. I'm not very popular right now. I'm not a detective either. They'll send one, someone with a gift for rooting out killers. But I'll be damned if I can leave till y'all catch the killer. It would drive me nuts. If I go to your sheriff for information, he'll surely get in touch with my people at some point and they'll learn what I'm doing. I put in for some personal time, so, well, you can see my problem."

"So, you want me to keep you in the loop, so to speak."

"Exactly. I figured out right quick how close you and this Dallas are. All I want is to know who killed my witness and how the hell he managed to do it with me right here all the time."

"You know what, this sounds like something I'd be good at. The problem is, I've got a situation to iron out that just wouldn't work with me lying to Dallas and Mac."

"I'm not asking you to lie, just keep me in the loop."

"Without telling them? That's lying, as far as I'm concerned."

He appeared so distraught she felt bad. "Just tell Mac you want to be kept advised on the investigation. You never know about him. He's an old codger who does what he wants most of the time, and he gets results."

"I can see you're not going to be any help at all. You expect someone else to lie instead of you. Isn't that just as bad?"

"Well, not really. If he decides on his own to lie, it's not my doing then, now is it?"

He studied her with an amused expression on his face. "You and this guy Dallas have a thing going?"

The unexpected change of subject caught her off guard. "That is none of your business."

"Figure you do. Must be hard, him being a cop and you a reporter. The two don't exactly mesh, do they?"

"You don't know the half of it. Look, let me help you out by showing you the story I've written for the upcoming week's newspaper. It has a lot of information in it not yet revealed. It's all been okayed by our sheriff because it's still a case under investigation. Then if you have questions I can answer, I will. Let that be the end of it. If I'm asked about you, I'll tell the truth as I know it. Best I can do."

He stuck out his hand. "Deal." Again those long delicate fingers, like you'd expect on a piano player, certainly not on a man who held a gun for a portion of his living. Liking this guy was easier than she'd thought it would be.

She printed out her article for the current week's paper. "This still has to be edited by my boss, but it's basically what'll be published in the paper."

Last month a body was found near the home of Treman Ledger. The previous day a fire destroyed Ledger's home on Cedar Creek Road. According to the Grace County Sheriff's office a partial leg was found in the remnants of that fire. Later Doctor Weston verified that the leg belonged to the body. The murder, the first one for Grace County this year, is currently under investigation.

A second death occurred in connection with this case when Ledger was returning to his trailer, which replaced his destroyed home. Sheriff Richards said that Ledger was fired upon by Spider Grafton. By the time the sheriff arrived, Ledger had returned fire and shot and killed the assailant, who owned property in the nearby area.

Richards stated, of the gun battle, "It was so blamed dark I figured whoever shot at him and missed wouldn't hit me either.

"He hollered and someone shot again, this time breaking the glass.

"'Put that blamed light out,' I said through the broke window.

"He did and at that point I yelled that I was the sheriff and whoever was shooting should stop. That's when I got shot in the arm. Whoever was out there didn't give a hoot I was a lawman."

According to Sheriff Richards, Ledger returned fire and the gunman was killed. No motivation for the attack on Ledger has been uncovered, according to the sheriff's office.

Deputy Burt Sample arrived on the scene after the shooting. He had the following to say about Ledger's return shot: "That was one heck of a shot Treman made. I don't think I could've done it."

Though no connection has been found between the two events, an ongoing investigation of both incidents continues, said Sheriff Richards.

Cutlines: Photo 1 – This human foot was found sticking up out of the mud following the fire at Treman Ledger's home early last week.

Photo 2 – Crime scene tape blows in the wind where it marks the discovery of the body, and is visible from the site of the Ledger fire.

Trey read the article and cutlines twice, a frown wrinkling his forehead. "This is no help to me at all. It tells nothing of value, just repeats what's already been reported."

She smiled at him as sweetly as she could manage. "And I can't reveal anything that Mac doesn't put on the release. He allowed me to use the quotes from my two interviews to update the story."

"It sounds like to me you know a whole lot more than you're telling."

Again she grinned. "Oh, does it? Well, I'm taking the fifth, and believe me I know the value of keeping my mouth shut. You want anything else, go talk to Mac. He may tell you more, since you're a lawman, though like I said…."

"Yeah, I know. He doesn't like Feds."

She raised her shoulders, able to joke now that she knew he wasn't the bad guy and probably wouldn't torture her for answers. "Afraid that's all I can do."

He hadn't asked about the shooting between her and Steve. Maybe he didn't see a connection. Parker had written the story for that week's newspaper. Steve had admitted he opened the feed bins where the horses could get in them. One mare later died and he was still tending another sick horse who might not make it.

As far as she knew, Steve had been charged with attempted murder, but that was still up in the air. Once the trial began, she would be called to testify, not only about his attack on her, but what he'd told her about pushing Dal off the mountain, and leaving the feed bins open to founder Parker's horses. As far as she was concerned, he'd killed Rick Granger, but he hadn't exactly confessed to that as yet.

Everyone was sure that the people Granger was going to testify against out in Kansas City had a hand in that, and maybe they were right. If so, they just beat Steve to it, because he put him on the list.

There hadn't been so much excitement in Grace County since she'd returned to Arkansas from California. Maybe never. It was almost too much to bear. She hoped these incidents didn't warn of times to come on a permanent basis for the small, normally peaceful town. She missed Dal so much it hurt.

Dal awoke with a raging headache, slit his eyes against the sunlight shining through windows above a ratty couch. Where was he? Familiar stuff. He'd fallen asleep in his recliner, lap filled with notes he'd scribbled. His left arm, encased in a cast, rested on the chair. For a moment the words he'd written made no sense at all.

Shit, he really *had* knocked himself silly in that fall, hadn't he?

He dug the phone out of his pocket, punched the number for Jess. Here he was, reaching out to her because he trusted her, because he needed her, because he loved her. To hell with everything else. Because he forgave her anything and everything.

She picked up. "Dal?" Whispered.

"Hi." Not whispered, but a small sound.

"You okay?"

"No."

"I'm coming."

He dropped the phone on the floor beside the recliner and let his head roll back against the leather. Hammers pounded the inside of his skull, leaving behind dents he might not fix. He closed his eyes and fell off that damned mountain. Rolling, tumbling, hitting trees and boulders, sailing through the air, grabbing for something, anything to stop the plunge through space. Sucking air like there was none left. What about the next thing he hit? A huge boulder. A tree. Would it kill him? A hand on his shoulder stopped the plunge toward death.

"Dal, honey. Open your eyes. I'm here."

A cool cloth on his forehead, another swiping gently over his cheeks and mouth. He opened his eyes, saw her through a blur, said her name, took a deep breath. For a moment he was lying under that bluff, her tending to him. Crying.

"Dal, talk to me. Do you need to go to the hospital? What is it? You need to talk to me."

"Jess? I'm trying. I fell… I fell off that damn mountain and I thought I was going off the bluff down there. I keep seeing it. Living it."

From the arm of the chair, his hand lifted, reaching for her. She took it, kissed the knuckles. "You're home now, though. Do you know where you're at?"

Why was she asking him such a foolish question? "What's that over in the corner? It's not a unicorn, is it?"

"That's Brad. He insisted on coming. I hope you don't mind. He likes you a lot. What's this about a unicorn?"

"I saw unicorns for a few days after I came home. And Brad's being very polite."

"He promised me he would if he could come along. He gets lonely there by himself."

"He can play with the unicorn."

"I'm going to call Doc Weston. He can come right over."

"No, don't. I'm okay. I'll do anything you say, just don't put me back in the hospital. It's lonely there. Everything is white and it smells and when someone dies you can hear the machines stop working. For an instant I'd think it was me that died."

"I don't believe you'll do anything I say. That would be the day. But I'll stay with you, no matter what. Still I'm worried. Did you go back to work today? In the field?"

"Uh-huh, we went to Bud's to tell him about Rick. To tell him his son was dead. He has no one left. His wife died and now Rick. No one wants to be alone. I. Don't. Want. To. Be. Alone." His forefinger tapped on his thigh with each word.

She kissed his cheek, his mouth, his other cheek. "You aren't alone."

He nodded up and down, then cringed. "Goddamned head hurts. I am alone."

"You need to forgive yourself, Dal, and you need to forgive me."

He pulled her hand to his heart, spread it there. "I forgive you, Jess. I do."

"Okay, that's a start. Now, say you're not alone, then let's work on you forgiving you. Then maybe I can convince you of that. We all love you. Mac and Tink and Burt and me. The Spaceys. Heck, there's too many to name."

"Okay, I'm not alone. But that forgiving shit. I don't know about that."

"A step at a time. You're sounding much better. How's your head?"

"Hurts like hell. Some pills in the kitchen cabinet above the sink."

She slipped away and panic swam around him like a shark till she returned with a glass of water and two of the pills in the palm of her hand.

What was going on inside his brain? He wished he knew. After a while, him sitting still and her on the floor next to him, head leaned against his thigh, the hammering between his ears lessened. He spread the fingers of one hand through her hair.

"Feeling better?"

"Yeah, feeling sort of foolish too. Acted like a ten-year-old."

"I think it's probably normal after what you've been through. It scared me, though. You're so tough. When you come apart it's a fearful thing to watch."

"Sorry, I didn't mean to scare you."

"If you hadn't called me, though, I'd be pretty pissed. Everyone needs someone sometimes. You been having nightmares about the fall?"

"Ah, not so bad."

"Uh-huh, now you're back in your tough mode."

"Reckon?"

"Hungry?"

"Of course. I been sitting here trying to figure some of this stuff out that's been going on around here, and haven't reached any conclusions at all. It's pretty baffling."

"Well, let's eat, then we'll work on it together… unless you can come up with something better for us to do. Feel like going out, or want me to run get us something?"

He wrestled his way out of the chair, took a deep breath. "Good God, don't ever fall off a mountain."

She raised on tip toes and kissed his jaw. "You know what? You stay right here and I'll go get something. Hamburger, fries, and a piece of apple pie sound about right?"

"Does it ever."

"I'll be right back, then." Her hand drifted down his arm and he twisted his fingers through hers. "What?"

"I don't want anything to happen to pull us apart. We can get through this, and if you need to talk about it, I'm ready to listen."

She nodded. "When I get back. Stay in that chair, don't get up and wander around."

Relief washed through her like a spring breeze. Laughing at Brad who hustled into the Jeep like he knew what came next, she climbed in beside him. Dal's wanting to talk about her and Steve gave her hope they could settle this thing. She started the car and backed into the lane, her mind drifting to Rick's bizarre death. They had all they needed to solve the murder. It was just a matter of putting all the pieces together. Convinced of that, she drove alongside the lowering sun that flashed through the surrounding trees like a gigantic strobe light.

By the time she returned, the vehicle filled with the fragrance of burgers overpowered by French fries and apple pie, it was nearing dark. Her headlights had little effect yet, but beneath the trees shadows settled in, hiding the ground. Something white flashed in and out across the creek. A man? Because there weren't any white animals in these woods. What was a man doing darting through the trees near the trailer park? Better question. Who the heck was it?

She parked close to Dal's trailer, gathered their meal, and went up on the porch, stopping for a last look around. Brad barked toward the trees, then nosed up to the door. Not easily frightened, she didn't cringe from things that go bump in the night, but she was cautious. She saw nothing and heard no one, so she shoved her way inside.

Dal sat where she'd left him, as he'd promised. She broke a beef patty into a plate on the floor and Brad dove in. All the food piled on a tray she carried it to Dal. Sat down on the couch with hers. He hadn't turned on any lights, so she leaned over and snapped on the lamp on the end table. The room still kept its shadows, but some were gone. They ate in quiet companionship, and when they finished, she gathered everything and disposed of it.

"I can't make much out of this." He tossed the sheaf of DEA papers down on the coffee table between them.

"Me either. But if he's not lying, Trey Ledger is the marshal sent here to watch the Granger home in case Rick showed up after he disappeared. But I have a question. I thought the immediate family was usually offered the chance to be relocated when one member went into protection with Witness Security." She went on to tell Dal about her visit with Ledger and what she had learned. Then added, "That is, like I said, if he's telling the truth."

"Did you believe him?"

"He really didn't give me any reason not to, I just got this under-the-skin feeling, you know? He was pretty much in a hurry or I'd have asked him why the wife advertised online when Rick went missing from WITSEC. Looks like that put a bullseye on his back."

"Do you think Ledger could be the one who killed him? I suppose that's possible. But not if he's really a marshal." He finished off the last of his fries.

She held hers up. "Here, want mine? Someone did kill Rick. Could be someone hired by those drug traffickers."

He took her fries. "Thanks. Where did Doc get those papers?"

She didn't answer right away. It hadn't occurred to her that the entire thing could've been contrived. But why? She asked him aloud why.

"I'm not sure yet. But I'm getting a really antsy feeling over this business. Let's separate this stuff down a bit. See what really makes sense."

She licked salt from her fingers and grabbed her backpack, took out her pad and pen. Waited.

"Okay. Marcus Woods has been definitely identified as Rick Granger?"

She nodded. "I knew him when I was younger." She flushed. In for a penny. "He had a birthmark on his hip. So even though WITSEC wiped records of his fingerprints and other forms of ID, I could vouch for that."

His grin told her he was handling that okay. "Sort of a wild child in your youth, huh?"

"Well, not really. I was sixteen and still a virgin until that time, so not too wild."

"What, ten years ago? Hell, I didn't know teenage virgins existed ten years ago."

That was a relief. But there were still lots of things for the two of them to hash out. "Well, we did. Scattered here and there, at least. So, what does this prove?"

"Not much, yet. I think we need to go back and talk to Bud Granger. How in the world did a country boy from Cedarton become involved with drug traffickers to learn enough to make a deal to testify when he was arrested by the DEA? Bud may have some answers to that."

"Then do you feel up to starting there?"

"You mean going to talk to Bud? Yeah, maybe tomorrow, if you'll come with me."

"You trust me not to spill everything we learn?"

He stared at her, the lamplight glimmering in his green eyes so he looked a bit like an animal peering from a moonlit hidey hole. "Yes, I do."

"Don't suppose it would do any good to call the Marshals' service and see if they have a Trey Ledger? His ID and badge looked authentic."

He chuckled. "Bet you can get one online just as good. That's probably not his real name though I'm not familiar enough with the agency to know if they change IDs when they're undercover. Besides, the Feds are not anxious to share anything with a rinky-dink sheriff's department." Before she could object, he held up a palm. "Not that I think Cedarton is rinky-dink, it'd just be their opinion."

"Well, I guess it is, really." She laughed.

"You think?" He gripped his temples between thumb and fingers. Enough of this.

She put down her notebook, rose, and took his hand. "Come on, let's go to bed. We can work on this some more tomorrow."

"I'm glad you suggested that. I'm ready." With a groan he pushed himself from the recliner using one good arm and swayed on his feet.

"Hey, careful." She encircled his waist and he allowed her to support him into the tiny bedroom where he collapsed onto the firm mattress. Together they undressed him, wrestling with the awkward cast. After he fumbled his way under the covers, she took her own clothes off and crawled over him so she'd be on the far side of his broken arm.

It was the first time in a long time she could remember going to bed with him and just curling up together and falling asleep, but it felt pretty good. The fear she'd lived with the last few days that he would never forgive her, never hold her in his arms again, faded into the darkness that closed around her.

Sometime during the night she awoke with moonlight shining on her face. His left arm lay across her breast, her one leg tucked between his two. His eyes were open, staring at her.

"Hi. You okay?" She touched his cheek.

"Uh-huh. You know what I woke up thinking?"

"No, what?"

"How you cleaned my eyes and when I opened them you were looking at me in a way I'll never forget, your tears pouring but you weren't making a sound."

For a moment, she was puzzled. What was he talking about? Oh, yes. When she'd found him on the mountain. She'd opened the pack of Wet Ones, fingers trembling so badly she couldn't hold on to them. His poor face, battered and dirty, bruised and bleeding. And her thinking that he was dead and how terrified she'd been.

In the moonlight, she smiled and kissed him. "Go back to sleep."

He massaged her breast and the next thing she knew it was morning and he had maneuvered himself till his head lay on her belly and his left arm rested across her bare thighs. His breath was warm between her legs. The position was so intimate she lay very still, not wishing to awaken him.

Pretty soon he stirred, kissed her tummy, then rolled off and onto his back to reveal one hell of a boner.

She laughed. "Doesn't that hurt?"

"Which that? Most everything does."

She wrapped her fingers around his stiff penis. "That."

"Oh, damn, that feels good. Why don't you mount up, or something?"

"You sure? There's not much of you that isn't bent or broke."

"Surely not my dick. Is it damaged?" He made at lifting his head to check.

"I take it your headache is gone."

"It's not this head that aches." One finger touched his temple.

"Smart ass."

He moved enough to nibble at her breast. "Please stop talking and do something."

"Do something, huh?" Astraddle of him, she was careful to support her weight with her knees when she lowered herself to take him inside ever so slowly.

"Ah, that's so good."

"Everything okay?"

"So far, so good. You might want to do a bit of moving about."

He twitched deep inside her and she clutched her muscles tight several times, an orgasm thrumming.

"Heavenly." He gasped, struggled to lift his hips. "Shit."

"Just lay still, I'll do this." She rocked forward and back several times, and he groaned. She stopped. "Does it hurt?"

"No, come on, do it again. Faster. Harder. Hurry."

And so she did, till they both came with shouts of passionate joy that could well have been a mixture of pain and pleasure.

They took a shower together, the cast covered with a plastic bag, and she washed his back, and then the parts he couldn't reach with just one arm. The bruises had faded and most of the cuts were scars. Tracing them with her fingertips, she marveled that he hadn't died out there that night.

Later, both dressed in jeans and tee shirts, they drank coffee and ate stale honey buns. She checked him over with delight. He was a damned good looking man.

"You still feel up to paying Bud Granger a visit this morning?"

"Feeling better than I have in a while. Let's get to work on this. It's time we figured out what the heck is going on."

"Well, it's a beautiful day. Want me to drive?"

He held up the cast. "Guess it's not against the law for me to drive one-armed, and I could do it, but maybe you'd better."

The phone rang and she was closest, so she picked it up, miming 'it's Mac' before speaking. "Good morning, Mac."

"Well, I guess you two have made up, either that or one of you killed the other one, in which case I'll send a deputy out."

"Not nice, not nice at all. We were just discussing going out to question Bud Granger about his son's past."

"When were you going to tell me about it?"

"Right this minute, Mac. This very minute."

He laughed. Sounded like he was feeling a whole lot better. "That's good. Tell Dal to drop by the station when y'all come back and bring me up to date. I've got some Feds to meet up with this morning. Maybe we can trade information, though I doubt I'll learn near as much as they do."

"Okay, will do. Anything special you want us to ask Bud?'

"Nah. You can play it by ear, I trust the two of you. Got another call. See you later."

Outside the door, the sun shone brightly. The air so still falling leaves drifted lazily down to carpet the green grass with brilliant patchwork designs. The shadow of a high-flying hawk darted across the ground, her scree cutting through the stillness.

He shaded his eyes and looked up. "Did you know that 'dark-morph' hawks are all chocolate-brown with a warm red tail? 'Rufous-morph' are reddish-brown on the chest with a dark belly?"

"No, I did not, and I thank you for letting me know. Next time it comes up in a conversation, I won't feel dumb."

It felt good to laugh and have him join her.

They were no more than out of the house when the inside phone rang. Over one shoulder she carried the backpack and held his elbow with the other hand to make sure he got down the steps. "They can call back or call the cell." She remained beside him to the Jeep where Brad had called shotgun.

"Okay, dog, you gotta ride in the back today." Dal pointed to the rear seat, Brad barked and obeyed, allowing Dal to climb in front. His phone rang and he dug it out of his pocket.

"Mac, what's up?" He tilted his head, listened intently for a full minute, then said, "Well, that's a hell of a note. Where do you think he'd go?" Again the intense listening. "Okay, yeah, we're on our way to talk to Bud. She's with me. I'll make sure she does. Okay, holler if you and Burt need any help." He hung up, glanced at Jess. "Okay, come on. What?"

Feet planted, she remained outside the car door. She didn't have to ask.

"Steve left the hospital against doctor's orders about an hour ago.

Mac and Burt are going after him. Mac thinks he'll stay in town till he finishes his vow to get back at you. Wanted to make sure you're with me."

Arms wide, she gazed at him. "I thought he was under arrest. Was last time I heard."

"Oh, sorry. Mac said he had a setback a couple days ago and they put him back in for observation. Someone misunderstood and didn't handcuff him. Guess I thought you knew that."

"Then I guess I'd like to go with you when you talk to Bud. I'm not comfortable wandering around alone with Steve loose. He wants to throw me off Lover's Leap, and that doesn't sound like much fun."

"Jess, he what?"

"I thought I told you that."

"No, but it explains that on his kill list."

"One thing's for sure. Eventually, this is going to be a good story. I'll be thoughtful with Bud. The man is sick, and I understand that."

He touched his hip. "You know what, I feel naked without my gun. Think I'd better go back in and get it, what with Steve being out there running around somewhere."

"You wait here, I'll get it." She leaped out and ran inside, found his utility belt and lugged it out to the car. "This stuff weighs a ton. Don't see how you carry it around all the time."

He laid it on the seat between them.

18
CHAPTER

The farmhouse had an empty look when she braked to a stop. A pickup was parked beside a small barn to the west. Another larger barn sat about five hundred yards to the east. Cattle and horses grazed in sprawling green pastures. Beside her in the car, Dal listened intently, heard nothing coming from inside any of the structures. Still, he could no longer trust the instincts he'd grown accustomed to working under.

Dangerous.

He opened his door and stepped out, eyes focused on the front windows while he fastened on the .45 and buckled the utility belt.

Everything looked far too normal. Something was wrong. A twinge ran up his spine and he smiled with no humor. You're back, you bastard. He settled his shoulders, ready for the battle.

"I don't think anyone's home." She stepped out. "Stay here, Brad. Stay." The small dog looked disappointed, but lay back down, nose on the seat between his front paws.

With one hand Dal signaled her to wait, took the porch steps slowly, rapped on the door, and from habit stood to one side waiting for a reply or a bullet. When there was neither, he rapped again. "Bud, you in there?"

Jess moved to the window and peered in. "Dal, something's wrong. I can see feet and legs on the floor behind the kitchen door."

He rattled the knob and the door creaked open. Vestiges of violence slammed into him like a gust of wind on a quiet day. Scrambled menace and fear, broken by surprised pain and disbelief.

"Stay back, Jess. Let me check it out." He palmed the .45, took a deep breath. "I'll be careful. You get on your cell and call 9-1-1, ask for an ambulance and backup. And do not come in. Okay?"

Dread for her safety pressed against him. She would come in because she couldn't help herself, but she would do as he asked first. Perhaps that would give him a chance to find out what had happened inside before she set foot in there. Maybe the old man had died suffering a lot of pain. But he that wasn't near all of it.

He slid around the door frame and crouched behind a huge recliner facing the television across the room. From there the feet and legs were visible. Breath caught in his throat, he watched for movement. Nothing. The air reeked with the stench of death. That's all this feeling of imminent danger was. The poor old man's death. Dal's legs cramped and he scrambled to the wall between the living room and kitchen where the body lay. Rested there to overpower the pain.

Bud probably had a rifle around somewhere. Someone would have it by now if they were in the house. He turned his back to the wall and searched the room for a gun cabinet or wall rack. Nothing. It must be in another room. For a long time he listened, sensed only silence. Opened his mind to random thoughts, found nothing.

Jess stepped into the doorway, saw him, and started across the room.

He gestured at her to hurry to him and she did. Had he tried to get her to leave, she wouldn't have. Damned good thing he knew her so well.

She hugged up close to him, said in his ear, "What's going on?"

"Stay here, you understand? Please wait till I tell you it's safe."

Her nod and staunch expression alerted him. Determined that she could take care of herself often put her in danger. Nothing he could do about it. He moved into the kitchen where the body lay. Checked out every corner, keeping the gun at the ready. A typical bachelor's mess. Dirty dishes, cluttered counter tops. No closet or pantry. One door to the outside, another opened into a bedroom. He went to it, took a quick look around. Moved back to the body before seeing the blood pooled beneath it. He'd bet his bottom dollar this man didn't die of cancer. Looked like Bud Granger, but he wouldn't move the body. Touched a pulse point and felt nothing. The body was still warm. Backup would soon arrive with what they needed to treat this like a crime scene.

"Jess, would you go to the Jeep and get your camera? I need you to take some pictures. Okay?"

"Yes, okay." The sound of her footsteps crossing the hardwood floor, out the door and down the porch steps. Good. She was doing exactly as he asked. And a moment later, he was sorry as hell.

Shouts from outside. Brad barking without stopping.

He rushed to the door. A tall blond man, one arm around her from behind, a gun under her chin. For a split second, just that flashing moment when adrenaline told him to get the hell out there and shoot the son of a bitch, then good sense took over. To get close enough to take the guy out, he'd have to cross the open yard. A perfect target. He'd be no good to her dead. Couldn't shoot the guy from here. This was why cops didn't partner with someone they loved. Couldn't think straight, do what was best. A danger he would get himself killed for her, then she'd be next.

If she'd done what he asked, then several deputies were on their way, but who knew where they were when the call went out? Mac had gone looking for Steve Wainwright. Maybe he ought to walk out there, let this guy take him too. At least she wouldn't be alone. He listened for a long moment, hoping to hear sirens, but there was nothing. If the ambulance was out on another call it could take some time for it to show up as well.

Time to do something.

"Well, shit." He pushed open the door, crossed the porch and headed toward Jess, now behind the wheel of the Jeep, the guy still pointing what looked like a 9mm Glock at her head. If the bastard made her drive off, then he couldn't do anything for her. This had to stop here.

"No, Dal," she shouted. "Go back, please. He'll kill you."

That wasn't what he worried about. He took a few steps, the .45 hanging at his side.

"Dal, is it?" Looking at him, but not taking the gun away. "You were supposed to be dead. Tough guy, huh? Drop that gun on the ground before you take another step. Then get your butt on over here, pretty boy. It's time the three of us had some fun together."

Without dropping the gun Dal limped across the yard. "You don't want to do this. Let her go. Right now you're in enough trouble, but you'll only make it worse."

"I said, lay that weapon down now, or I'll shoot her."

Hoping to God he'd made the right choice he got as close as he dared, then dropped the .45 in the grass, held his good hand out to his side. "You must be Steve."

"And you must be Dallas Starr. It's time we met. Jessie, shut that god-damned dog up or I'm gonna do it for you."

She reached in the back seat and grabbed Brad, dropped him to the ground. "Git, Brad. Go on, now."

The pit bull, not accustomed to being shouted at by this human, tucked his tail and ran off a ways. He sat, watched for a minute, then made up his mind and came barreling back. All the human shouting in the world would not have stopped him. He leaped over her lap and grabbed the gun hand of the man before he turned his attention from Dal.

Brad's teeth sank into the man's wrist, blood spurted. Jessie screamed and so did Steve. Dal fell toward his own weapon. Couldn't get to his feet, so scrambled closer on hands and knees and aimed at the struggling man and dog. No shot there. Maybe he wouldn't need one. That dog turned vicious real quick. Despite Steve's attempt to dislodge him, the pit was in it for the count. He refused to turn loose. Blood ran from Steve's face as well as his wrist, which he flung around, dog and all, without much result.

The gun went off in his hand, the bullet going through the windshield. Jessie rolled out of the Jeep, landing close to Dal, who then lunged onto the car seat. Still off-balance and one-armed, he couldn't bring the .45 around. Excited by the action, Brad shook Steve's gun hand like a dirty rag and the weapon flew to the ground. Brad kept up his attack and Dal punched the barrel of his gun into Steve's belly, so close the guy's breath washed over him.

"Feel that? Stop struggling, now, or take my word I'll shoot you. Now, dammit."

Jessie rose, spoke in a shaky voice. "Steve, this fellow who just dis-armed you is Brad the pit bull."

The expletives that spouted from Steve were quite inventive, but produced no results at all from humans or dog.

Dal had done all he could. There was not one ounce of energy left in him. If he hadn't outweighed Steve, who was still recovering from a gunshot wound to the gut, plus had a dog and a woman as backup, he'd never have won this battle. He sprawled against Steve, the .45 barrel still poking into the man's gut. A man who had given up his struggle.

This was as embarrassing as hell. Last year Ina Mae had used her shotgun to rescue him from the bad guys. Now, he had help from a flea-bitten dog and a woman to subdue this bad guy.

Brad may have turned loose, but he stood over Steve baring his teeth. With a gun in his belly and an angry pit bull on guard, Steve gave up. Dal couldn't convince his sore body to move and Jessie remained right where she was. They were stuck there till someone showed up.

Jessie took in Brad's scowl and the dirt and blood smeared on Steve's face, then turned to see how Dal was doing sprawled across the bottom half of this dangerous felon. She burst out laughing. After a while the laughter was catching, at least where Dal was concerned. He was totally wiped out, but by God he could laugh. Brad braced both feet on Steve's belly where he'd already been shot once, and growled, as if daring the man to enjoy himself.

"I'm gonna bleed to death if you don't get this blamed dog off me. Never did like dogs anyway."

"Well, you shouldn't have jumped in the middle of this, hmm Dal?" She only stopped laughing long enough to reply, then started in again.

"I do hope you called the cavalry, Jess, 'cause I'm getting mighty tired of sprawling here holding on to this piece of shit. They don't come soon I'm gonna have to go ahead and shoot him. You, buddy, should've stayed in the hospital where you belonged and not come out here to stir up trouble."

She glared at Steve, then glanced toward Dal. "Oh, I called them all right. Just hang on for a bit longer. There'll be deputies all over the place. What I want to know, is, did you kill that poor old man in there, Steve?"

"I'm not answering any questions. I want a lawyer. I want a doctor." He turned to Dal. "Has she told you her nasty secret? I'll just bet she hasn't or you wouldn't be fool enough to stay around her."

A Grace County Deputy Sheriff's patrol car slid to a stop in the dust nearby. Out jumped ex-Marine and recent new-hire deputy Colby Brewster. "Just what in the name of all that's holy is going on here? Uh, sorry, sir. Didn't recognize you there for a minute."

Dal responded with evident relief. "Glad you're here, deputy. This man is under arrest, if you'd be so kind as to handcuff him and put him in your unit."

Colby leaned back on his heels and laughed. "Sorry, sir, but this is a strange way you have of arresting someone. Is this a Grace County thing, or do you personally enjoy doing it this way?"

"Deputy, I'd really appreciate it if you could assist me in getting up. It seems my legs have gone to sleep restraining this vicious outlaw."

"Be glad to. I was wondering which one of you I should undo first. Looks like any one of you comes loose, this fella may make a break for it. And if you don't mind, I'm leaving that mean dog to one of you. He just might take a chunk out of me." He finished getting Dal to his feet. "I can't rightly handcuff him till you do that."

"Brad, that's a good dog." Jess crawled off Steve, who had given up any sort of struggle. "Come on, sweetie, turn loose of the bad man. It's okay. You've got a hamburger patty in your near future." She removed Brad, now wagging and licking. Colby clamped on the handcuffs, and Jess went to Dal, who looked as if he needed to sit down somewhere.

Collapsing in the jeep's seat, Dal waited till Colby had Steve locked in the back of his SUV before calling him over. "I'm afraid we have a homicide inside. You need to handle this like a crime scene and I'll be in there as soon as I can manage. Okay?"

"You bet, sir. I'm sorry to have treated this with so much humor. I didn't realize we had a killing, sir."

"Hell, that's okay. The old man was dying of cancer. Why that piece of crap over there had to kill him is beyond me. And it's better to laugh than cry anytime. Do you know if Mac is on his way?"

"He told me to take care of it. He's still looking for that guy who escaped from the hospital."

"That's him, there in your SUV, so you might let Mac know. And go inside and check the body. I'm pretty sure Bud Granger is dead, but you might want to double check. I wasn't functioning on all burners. Thought we were coming out to ask him some questions about his son, the poor fellow we found murdered a few weeks ago. Guess we won't find out anything from him."

Jess took Dal's trembling hand in hers. He'd had entirely too much excitement for someone whose doctor hadn't yet released him for this kind of duty. She wasn't anxious to watch him have a meltdown right here.

"Don't you think it would be okay if we went on back to your place for a while? Colby can handle this."

He stared through the bullet-cracked windshield for a minute, then leaned back onto the headrest. "I'd like to stay a while if you don't mind. I'm getting some vibes and would like to go inside and sit in the kitchen with the body till Doc gets here. Would you go with me?"

It was the last thing she wanted for him or for herself.

She held his hand to her lips for a while. "Of course, if that's what you want. Please don't do too much, though. I know you don't want to end up back in the hospital."

"You'd make a good mother."

The unexpected words did something strange to her feelings, and she glanced at him to make sure he wasn't deriding her. His eyes were soft, his expression loving. Dear God, what was going on here? Never had he said something so very personal regarding anything close to a serious relationship. It must just be what he'd gone through lately. He couldn't mean it in the way it sounded, and she certainly did not want to take it that way. Marriage didn't appeal to her, and having babies was even further from her mind.

"Just behave yourself for your own good, is all I meant."

"I know, I know. Let's go inside where I can commune with ghosts for a while." With him back on a lighter subject matter, she relaxed.

They went in together. Back in the swing of things, she took the photos he'd asked her for earlier while he sat in a kitchen chair to, as he put it, commune.

"Jess, could you do me a favor and lend me your recorder, please? Mac will want this information." He sat in silence for a while, then began to dictate into the small digital machine. "Two men visited Bud Granger earlier. Said they were US Marshals and wanted to know all about Marcus Woods aka Rick Granger. Bud said he hadn't seen his son in years, had no idea how he got mixed up with drug traffickers. Didn't really believe it, since his son never took drugs. They asked questions about if he kept double books and where the extra copies might be. Bud didn't know. One of them smacked him around a bit, then someone is coming. They have to leave in a hurry, declaring they'll come back later, ransack the house and barns, find those books.

"Steve comes busting through the front door. He and Bud have a fight over Rick. Where is he? Kill the son of a bitch if he can find him. He fucked Jessie once a long time ago, and he wants even. He's wild and crazy, says everyone who's ever touched her life will pay, then she'll be last. He'll teach the bitch to treat him like she did. She ruined his life, now it's her turn to have hers turned upside down. Gonna take her out to Lover's Leap and the two of them jump off together. Two shots, a lot of cursing, then Steve runs off. Bud is still alive. Mutters something like, 'Least he could've done was put me out of my misery.' The door bursts open, one more shot. All is deathly still."

Jess had tried her best not to listen to Dal's voice restructuring what had been said and done here in this room. It freaked her out that he could do that and she'd rather not be involved when he did. This was not a good time to leave him alone, though, so she gritted her teeth and tried to think of other things. But when he reached the part about Steve planning to take her to Lover's Leap and jump off with her, she couldn't shut her ears.

The man was crazy. Had to be. What sane person comes up with stuff like that? He was nothing like the man she had fallen for. Hopefully they'd put him away so deep he could never get out and find her again. She might owe him a lot, but not her life. Or in this case, her death.

Dal had finally stopped and sat staring beyond the room into some other place. It would take all night to calm him down, and she wouldn't dare leave him alone. This was no way for him to have to live. She had been so happy when he appeared to have lost this weird ability to read violence left hanging over a crime scene. Now it seemed to have come back with a vengeance.

"Jess, you okay?" He touched her shoulder and she jumped.

"What? Yes, of course. As okay as I can be knowing that man out there planned to commit double suicide with me. He must have hated me so much. And who can blame him? After what I did."

Dal took her hand in both his. "You don't deserve what he's tried to do to you. Enough is enough, and you've more than paid. He was as much to blame for what happened as you were. You need to let it go. As for him, he's become unstable, and I would bet he would've become this deranged killer had you never met him." He kissed her hand. "Darlin', we've both done unforgivable things. We desperately need to be forgiven. Can we do that? Forgive each other and ourselves. Can we do that for each other?" His green eyes darkened with a familiar passion. His words freed her from a guilt she'd carried for so long. Like it had been physically jerked from deep inside her and flung into the wind.

She touched his cheek with the tips of her fingers. "I hope you're listening to your own words. The same right back at you."

Colby stepped inside. "Sir, Doc is here. He said he wouldn't come in till you okayed it. Thought he might interrupt something."

Keeping her hand, Dal rose, glanced down at the old man whose features reflected none of the pain he had suffered, but rather appeared at peace. "No, I'm done in here, deputy. Thanks."

Jess walked out beside Dal. "Do you think Steve actually killed Rick?"

"I think he was capable of doing it, but I'm not sure he did. He wanted to take the credit because that's part of what he came here to do. But he's so erratic and unpredictable it's doubtful that he would've done it like it was done. He would've simply killed Rick and left him there on the spot. Not left the clear message that Rick couldn't run anymore. Not with just one leg. I think we still have to find our killer."

She put an arm around his waist. "He did push you off the mountain, and he meant for that to kill you. It still sends shivers through me when I think of you falling all the way down to that drop-off. You are lucky to be alive."

He climbed into the passenger seat next to her, scooping Brad up and putting him in his lap. "I don't think luck had much to do with it." Brad licked his face. "Okay, buddy. I like you and all, but please keep your licking to hands, if you don't mind. I know where that tongue has been."

The dog turned a couple of circles and lay down in Dal's lap, issuing a huge sigh.

Dal laughed. "Guess he's had a hard day."

She keyed the ignition, backed up and headed down the road. "Let's go to my place, if that's okay. I want to work on this story. My laptop is there, and I'd also like to check some things online. You know, you could come into this century and get WiFi at your trailer."

"I'm beat, Jess."

"I know you are. I have a bed, you know. You can take a nap or whatever you want. No one will bother you. I don't feel comfortable leaving you alone."

He leaned his head against the side window and closed his eyes.

She rubbed his thigh. Let her thoughts wander. If Steve didn't kill Rick, then who did? And why? Clearly, there were people who would want to kill him if they knew where he was. But he was in WITSEC living in Wichita, then all of a sudden he disappeared, his wife didn't know where he was. When she put his picture and name on that site online, someone must've recognized him. Someone out of his past? Or the men he worked for who he was going to testify against? How could she have been so dumb?

She needed to try and find his wife. After sitting on the bed beside Dal till he fell asleep, she went to her laptop and Googled Marcus Woods, found nothing of any value. She moved to the white pages for Wichita, but he obviously had an unlisted number. Then using the slightly illegal gray area to search, she cross-referenced Rick Granger with Marcus Woods, checking electrical, heating bills and phone service. She got a hit through KG&E, found an address and phone number for Marcus. Picking up her cell phone, she called the number, got voicemail, and hung up.

What if the woman hadn't been notified of his death yet? Just because she knew who the dead man was, did anyone else? She couldn't remember. If Trey was telling the truth and he truly was a marshal, he'd know. But if he was lying about his own identity and she contacted him, he might feel she was getting too close to the truth.

Back on the computer she went to Facebook and typed in Treman Ledger. Nothing. She tried Trey Ledger, got a couple of hits, but neither were him. Foolish to think a US Marshal would have a Facebook page, anyway. She needed someone who could get into some law enforcement sites. Doc could help, but he was probably still out at Granger's. Damn it, she wanted some answers now. Ledger had a cell phone, but that didn't help 'cause she didn't have his number. Online, she learned that there was a Marshal's office in Fayetteville, so she called the number.

A man answered, saying his name was Adam Clinton. He actually even sounded helpful—atleast at first.

"I'm looking for Trey Ledger. I was told he works out of your office. Could you put me in touch with him, please?"

"If you could tell me the nature of your business, I could have someone help you."

Okay. "I met someone who told me he's a US Marshal, and I'm wondering if you could tell me how to find out if what he says is true."

"If you would give me your name and phone number, I'll have someone call you shortly. Could you tell me this gentleman's name, please?"

"Maybe you could just tell me this. Do marshals work under cover?"

"Ma'am, I'm sure someone here could help you. Is this person threatening you in any way?"

"Uh, no, I don't think so. It's just, how do I know if he's a real US Marshal or not? How do I tell if his ID is fake?"

"If he told you he's working undercover, then identified himself as a US Marshal, then I would presume he is not a lawman. You say his name is Ledger. Trey Ledger?"

"Yes."

"My advice to you is to report this to your local law enforcement."

"I'm reporting it to you."

"What is your name and address and phone number? Someone will be in touch within a few days."

Oops. She hung up. Not that it would do any good. He already had her number on Caller ID, which meant, should he desire, he would have every piece of information ever collected on her. She hadn't done anything wrong, but felt guilty nevertheless. She might end up having to explain herself to some burly Marshal somewhere down the line. Or they might consider her a harmless kook. They would know she was a reporter, and that would be enough to write her off.

As for asking Mac or any of the other deputies, they couldn't or wouldn't help a reporter dig up sensitive stuff for a story on a crime under investigation. She'd just keep poking around. That paper Doc had that she copied, the redacted one, might have more in it than she'd found so far. She dug it out, sat on the couch, and went to work studying each page with a flashlight. It didn't help.

"What you doing?"

"Dal, I didn't hear you get up. Feeling better?"

He walked barefoot into the kitchen and poured himself a cup of coffee. "Want some?" He held up the pot.

"Yes, sounds good. Thanks. I was looking over these papers again, hoping to find something that might help with this story I'm struggling with."

He brought two cups of coffee, one by the handle held in the fingers sticking out of the cast, placed them on the table where she had some of her notes and sat down beside her.

"What's the angle?"

"I really wanted to tell a story about Bud and Rick, but I'm not sure where to start. Probably best if I just wait for Mac's release on Bud's death and go ahead and follow that killing till it's solved."

He sipped, studied her over the rim of his cup, green eyes solemn. "The story about Bud and Rick, that would be more of a feature than a news story, wouldn't it?"

"Well, sounds like you've been paying attention."

"I always pay attention. Sometimes I don't do anything about it."

"Why not?"

"Sometimes stuff is just too tragic to think about. Don't you feel sometimes that people's lives are best forgotten? Some people just do dreadful things and ruin their own lives and those of their families. Those stories ought to just be let lie. That poor old man, his son obviously doesn't care that much about him and takes off, he loses his wife, then gets cancer. Bad enough he's all alone, someone comes along and kills him, just for the hell of it. Can you think of anything sadder?"

"I guess not. Who do you think killed him? Steve?"

"Steve was here first, he shot the old man, then must've heard them coming and ran off. It wasn't a fatal shot. Bud was still alive when someone else arrived. From what I heard probably someone hired by the man his son was set to testify against. They panicked, thought he knew something. When he didn't learn anything, he shot him twice more. Probably afraid he'd identify him. If that's the case, then he's known in the area. Steve must've been hiding in the woods when we drove up. He waited till you went out alone to jump you. Hell, who knows? Some people kill for no reason at all, but there was a reason behind this."

"So you don't think Steve killed him?"

"No. He didn't kill Rick either, though he sure as hell wanted to. Is really angry that he didn't have the pleasure." Dal glanced at her. "How do you suppose he found out about you and Rick and your summer fling so many years ago? And why in the world did he think it would punish you to kill some guy you had sex with more than ten years ago?"

"I have no idea. I can't remember telling anyone about that day."

"Did you keep a journal or diary that he might have found while you were with him?"

"Oh, my God. I did. I mean, not while I was with him. When I was a kid. I was lonely a lot and after that summer I began to keep a journal. I'd forgotten all about it, don't even know anymore where it's at. But I would've had it out in California. I remember thinking how romantic that little tryst was and writing all about it in a journal my mom gave me for Christmas a couple years earlier. I hadn't ever written in it till after we went back home from visiting here when I was sixteen."

"Well, if you wrote it in a romantic way, Steve probably read it and thought you were in love with this guy. Maybe you even thought you were, back when you wrote it."

She rubbed his shoulder, then leaned over and kissed him on the cheek. "I guess I did. Now I know that wasn't anywhere near love."

"And how do you know that?" He turned and cradled her head with his right arm.

"I don't want to scare you off, and I don't expect any more from you than you're ready to give. But when I saw you laying under that bluff, beat to hell, I ached so bad inside I could hardly stand it. I knew then I would do anything to keep you from being hurt. That if I could I would take your place. I never wanted to feel that way about anyone 'cause it's so damned scary, but there it is. Now don't go getting all—"

He lifted her chin and kissed her, a lingering tender kiss such as they had never shared. After a long while he pulled away, eyes gleaming with unshed tears. Flushing, he glanced across the room, batted his eyes several times, and cleared his throat. "Well, okay then." His voice was hoarse.

Neither of them had said they loved the other.

"You know what? I think I'm about to starve, how about you?" She shifted the notes and papers from her lap, stacked them on the table. "Want me to go get something or do you want to go out?"

"How about a big thick steak? We could go to the Blue Door in Harrison, if you want. My treat."

"You mean, you're actually going to feed me?" She stood and laughed. "Maybe you'd better put on some shoes, then."

He rose, reached down for her hand and the window on the other side of the living room shattered into thousands of pieces, followed by the echoing boom of a big gun.

Brad yelped and scooted under the couch. Dal hit the floor on both knees, cursed, and pulled her down with him.

"You hit?" She rubbed her hands all over him.

"No, you?"

"Huh-uh. Now what?"

"Well, I don't think it was a stray bullet from a hunter's rifle. Stay down. You still have that revolver in the drawer over by the door?"

"Yes."

"Well, mine is in your bedroom, so it'll have to do."

She grabbed his tee shirt by the tail. "Dal, don't go out there. Stay here and let's call Mac. Please."

He untangled her fingers from the cotton fabric. "I'll be careful. You call 9-1-1, I'm gonna take a quick look around."

Even as she dialed the number, she began to cry. Why did he always have to be so brave, so tough? Just once, why couldn't he hunker down with her and wait for someone else to come save the day?

The door opened, then closed, and he was gone. The echo of another shot sounded, then nothing.

19
CHAPTER

Evening shadows crept from the trees surrounding Jess's cabin, but the open spaces clung to the dying light. Dal kept low and hugged the building. Squatted into the corner where the side deck connected to the house, he fired in the general direction of the first shot. Then he held up. The little .38 didn't have enough range to hit anyone hidden out there in the trees, but that wasn't what he wanted.

Just once more, you son of a bitch, and I'll know where you are.

He waited, stared into the distance.

Nothing. Silence hung like a heavy fog.

About the time he decided the shooter had moved on, Jess came flying out the door and across the yard yelling his name.

Hell, no. "Over here. Get down. Now."

Another shot rang out and she tumbled head over heels, then lay still.

Jess. Dear God, *no!*

Adrenaline poured through his weary body. Firing in the direction of the shot, he ran to her, fell to the ground on his broken arm. Pain flared, blossomed like a ton of explosions. Seeing stars, he fired again, crammed the revolver in his pocket, and using one arm, dragged her and himself across the yard into the shadows afforded by the house. Sprawled there, holding her across his lap, he ran his hand over her starting at the top of her head. The way the arm hurt, he must have re-broken it. No time to worry now. He'd reached her thighs, no wound yet. She muttered something he didn't understand.

"Jess? Are you hit? Where?" His heart liked to thundered out of his chest. Sent jags of pain through his damaged ribs till he could hardly breathe. He was shattered into a million pieces. Maybe this time he wouldn't heal.

"What are you doing? Why are we laying on the ground?"

Terror for her melted away. She was okay. He gathered her close and rocked, unable to speak or breathe for the mix of fear and agony that closed off his windpipe.

"Dal, are you okay? Are you hit?" Gentle hands touched him.

A gasp dragged air into his lungs. "No, no." He buried his face against her breasts. Damned arm throbbed. Damned ribs ached. Damned legs cramped. His brain flashed through horrors of the night she was shot, memories of being covered in her blood, of knowing she was dead. But she breathed now, safe in his arms. All he had to do was calm down. Talk to her.

"We should leave this place. Go away somewhere peaceful and not do what we do anymore. Jess. God, I thought you'd been shot again. Why did you come out here like that?"

His tears dampened the front of her shirt.

"I thought. I needed. I wanted. Oh, shit, can't talk straight. We're both okay. Okay?" Her disjointed words reassured him.

If he didn't get up off the ground and soon, he would be stuck there forever. "Come on, Jess. Let's get inside and call the station. I want someone out here to go over the ground where those shots came from. And besides, I can't crouch here like this any longer. It's killing me. God, I thought you'd been shot."

"No, I tripped over something. Good damn thing, too."

Together they struggled to their feet, kept to the shadows. He grabbed the edge of the deck to stay on his feet. Staggering against the side of the cabin, he made it to the steps and up onto the porch, with her close behind clasping his waist.

At the door, he slumped against the frame. "Remind me never to go hiking in the woods again. I'm fed up with this. It's like my muscles are on fire when I try to do ordinary things."

She supported him to the couch. "Is tackling me in the yard ordinary?"

"I hope not." At last they both could joke about the experience.

She dropped down beside him. "Who do you suppose that was shooting at us? Couldn't have been Steve unless he escaped from jail. That only leaves a few people mad enough and dumb enough to shoot at a deputy."

"Unless there's someone we haven't considered carrying a grudge, I'd imagine it was one of those yahoos come in here hired to get rid of Rick. I can't see anyone else doing something like this."

"Or someone who's shown up here in the past few months. Maybe someone waiting for Rick to show up?" She peered at him.

"My brain aches. I don't want to think about it anymore. But you may be right."

"Me, neither. I guess neither one of us feels like going out to eat, but I'm hungry. I think I've got some frozen lasagna in the freezer we could nuke."

With a pathetic whine Brad crept out from under the couch on his belly. Must have been the mention of lasagna. He licked Dal's bare toes as if apologizing for wigging out on them.

Dal scratched the pit bull's ears. "And they're not even bloody. Cowardly brave dog. Frozen lasagna will be better than nothing." He leaned his head back on the couch, chest jerking with each intake.

"Your ribs still bothering you?"

"Ah, they're okay. Come here, you." He encircled her in a cautious embrace and nibbled at her neck, then hung on, head resting on her shoulder. Too exhausted to do anything else. Things he wanted to say rattled around in his brain. That's where they'd have to stay. He never meant to ever fall in love again, not after the pain of watching the love between him and Leann destroyed by her addiction. And if he admitted it, his devotion to his job played a part. Did he love Jess, or were they just using each other to heal old wounds? If so, maybe that wasn't such a bad thing. One thing for sure, it felt good having her around.

A fist pounded on the door. Dal jumped and Jess let out a startled sound. Brad yipped and went back under the couch.

"I think he has PTSD." Dal released his hold. "You stay right here. I'll see who it is." He picked up the gun from where he'd dropped it on the couch and went to peer through the window. "It's okay, it's Colby and Tinker. We didn't call them yet, did we?"

"No, I don't think so."

He swung the door open, gun still in his hand.

"Whoa, man. Would you put down that weapon, sir?" Colby hadn't drawn his gun, but he had a palm planted on it.

Dal grinned, feeling silly. "Sorry, we weren't sure who it was. Someone just took some shots at us and we're a bit nervous. Come on in." He laid the .38 down on the table top by the door. His arm was beginning to give him fits and he hugged it close to his chest.

"You okay?" Tink studied him from head to bare feet, then did the same with Jess. "You both look like hell. Have any idea who it was? Hey, guess it wasn't that Steve fella, huh? Congratulations on that one."

"Thanks. The real hero is over yonder under the couch shivering." He sank into one of the big chairs in the central room. Everyone took a seat. Jess went to the kitchen, a side portion of the central room separated by a waist high bar, and started a pot of coffee. The pleasing fragrance helped settle his nerves. When she returned she flipped on some lights. Brad came sneaking out from under the couch, inspected Colby's polished boots and Tink's brown shoes, then went to lay beside the front door.

"Brad definitely does not like gunfire, in fact I think he's gun shy. The last guy who shot a gun around him ended up in handcuffs." Small chuckles relayed from Jess around the room as if everyone was doing their best to get back to normal.

Something she'd said a moment ago poked around in Dal's brain, though he couldn't quite dig it out. Eyes locked on her, he spoke to the two deputies.

"I'm hoping you can search out in the woods where the shots came from and see if there's any evidence at all. I'll walk out with you and show you where it's at."

"You don't look like you ought to be walking anywhere." Colby gazed out the window. "Besides it's getting dark. Let's wait till morning, I'll come out and do a search pattern over there. If they left anything, we'll find it."

Relieved that he didn't have to hike out across the yard, Dal relaxed.

Tinker sat next to Jess. "You okay, girlfriend? You're sort of grassy and dusty." She plucked a colorful oak leaf from Jessie's hair.

"That tends to happen when you roll around in the yard while someone takes pot shots at you." Jess shuddered with the words.

"They actually shot at you? You're sure they weren't just shooting at something out in the woods? Hunters maybe?"

Dal gave her a long quizzical look. "In the dark? No, they were shooting at us all right. Wait. Who called it in? What did they say? We were going to when you knocked on the door."

Tink glanced at Colby. "Do you know?"

"Nope. Some man called the station direct, not 9-1-1, said he'd heard some shots fired out this way and since hunting season's closed, he figured he ought to report it. That's all I know. Mac is manning the phones now they have Steve in custody. Anyway you know how it is in these woods. Folks target practicing, taking pot shots at some feral animal bothering their cattle or something like that. We didn't take it too seriously till we got out here and realized the shots had been fired near here. Thought maybe you guys were practicing."

Dal rubbed his shoulder. "Only thing we were practicing was dodging bullets. Did Doc have anything to say yet about Bud Granger's death?"

Colby leaned forward, elbows on his knees. "Yep. He was shot three times, two different guns."

"Which shot killed him, does he know yet?"

Colby looked confused, and Tink answered the question. "Well, you know, Doc doesn't really do that stuff, though he generally has an opinion before he sends the body down to the ME in Little Rock. Haven't heard it yet though."

"I forgot y'all don't have an ME up here. Does he usually share this kind of thing with you? Doc, I mean." He looked directly at Jess. "You being a reporter and all."

Jess stared at Colby. "Another one of those. Dal, would you please explain how things work around here to this newbie? I'm gonna nuke some dinners. Dal needs to eat. If you want to stay we'll share with you. Just frozen lasagna, nothing fancy."

"Naw, we gotta get back. I'll explain things to 'this newbie' for you, Jessie." Tink cocked her head toward Colby. "I wasn't privy to anything they discussed, but I can call you later if I find out anything."

Jessie paused, a sharp knife in one hand, the lasagna package in the other. "No need. I imagine Mac will have a release out tomorrow on Bud's murder. I wish all this gunplay would end. Or these people would find someplace else to wage their war. I'm getting sick of it. I want to go back to writing about all the fun stuff folks get up to here in Grace County. Like growing a little weed or hot-wiring a deputy's car and parking it on the dam. Or maybe the good stuff, like winning college scholarships. This murder and mayhem needs to stop."

"I think we're all agreed on that." Tink stared at the floor for a minute. "I heard today that Steve Wainwright is the missing man from the B&B. Made me feel silly that I even wanted to be bothered to look for someone who came here to harm my best friend. We shoulda caught him and put him in jail right away before he could have done so much damage."

Jessie laid the knife on the bar, slid the lasagna in the microwave, and set the timer.

"Well, we're gonna get these people raising havoc around here. Believe me, we will." Dal rose. "If you'll excuse me, I have to answer the call of nature. See you guys tomorrow." Brad followed him down the hallway.

Tinker and Colby bid him goodnight, then Tink turned to Jess. "You lock stuff up out here tonight and keep that pea-shooter handy. Call if anything crazy happens. Take care of each other. He looks bad. You gonna take him to the doctor in the morning?"

"That's exactly what I'm going to do. He gets any worse, I may just call the first responders to come out and haul him in tonight. Stay safe, you two." Jess backed up against the door until the sound of the car leaving faded into the night. Then she took a couple of plates out of the cabinet, and poured two glasses of tea over ice.

Only when she came back into the central room, did she notice that her gun was gone from the table. Dal must've taken it when he went into the bathroom. She put the plates on the table, along with the iced tea, set out butter and took a partial loaf of sourdough bread from the freezer, removed the lasagna and stuck the bread in.

"Don't tell me I can't prepare a meal." At the sound of her voice Brad trotted back into the room. "Ah, bet you'll like lasagna, won't you? Where is that man?"

She crept down the hall to the bathroom, tapped on the door. No answer. She called his name. Still nothing. Sorry about this, honey. She cracked the door open to see Dal sitting on the lid of the toilet, eyes closed and a thoughtful expression furrowing his face.

"Honey, are you okay? What is it?"

He jumped, opened his eyes. "I think I know who's been tearing shit up around here lately, and I don't like it one bit."

She moved to him, cradled his head against her tummy. "Won't this wait till morning? You look so wore out. And you need to eat something."

He glanced up at her, his eyes glistening as if he were about to cry.

"Aw, honey, let's get you to bed. I'll bring the food in to you."

"I'm okay. That lasagna smells good. Maybe you could give me a hand getting up and we can eat."

He leaned on her so heavily she staggered under his weight and deposited him in the big, comfortable armchair. "Sit right there. I'll bring it to you."

When she returned with supper, he was examining the cast on his arm. She set the tray on the side table and ran her fingers over the crack that zagged all the way from his elbow to his wrist.

"I'm afraid you've broken it. The cast I mean. You eat. I'm going to call Doc. He can come the fastest and he'll know right away if you—"

"No, don't do that. Call Mac and have him send Les out. He's an EMT, he'll know. I don't want to bother Doc. I think—I mean, I guess he's got enough to do. I don't want to make a trip to town if it can wait till morning."

"Why don't I just ask for the first responders? They can take you to the hospital if you need a new cast."

"Please, Jess. Just do as I ask, would you?"

His tone was a bit on the impatient side and annoying him was the last thing in the world she wanted to do. "Okay, sure." She placed the tray in his lap, arranged the food so he could start eating, then picked up the landline. Half the time the signal on the cell was iffy. No sense taking a chance being cut off midway.

Mac answered the call, which was odd, but Tink had said he was manning the phones. All the deputies must be in the field.

"Y'all okay out there? Tink radioed in that you were, but she's a bit concerned about you. Maybe you need to bring Dal in and let someone take a look at you both over at the hospital."

"Mac, he's asked if you could send Les out with the responder unit."

She turned her back to Dal. "I know this is a lot to ask, but could you do it? He's really upset and hurting. I don't want to force him into something right now. Please? If Les wants him to come in, I think he'll agree."

Dal called out from his chair. "Hey, don't go talking about me where I can't hear you. Just ask for this then come eat with me. Okay?"

"Okay, sweetie. Mac, I'm gonna hang up now. Please do this." She pressed the disconnect before he could argue with her.

There was something she was going to ask Dal, but she couldn't remember what it was. All she wanted was to get him taken care of. Seeing a big strapping healthy man like him knocked flat was disturbing. He'd been well on his way to recovery until this latest set to. She laid the phone on the table, then remembered what it was. The gun. She wanted to ask him if he had it.

She turned. Head leaned back on the soft cushions of the leather chair, Dal had set the tray on the side table and fallen asleep.

Behind her, Brad leaped up from the floor, barking furiously. She turned, Dal startled awake as the front door swung open ever so slowly.

A familiar figure stepped through the opening, hands out palms down. "It's just me. Didn't want to bother you if you were asleep. Looks like your dog did that, anyway."

"Jesus Christ, Doc." Dal rubbed his face, focusing on the old man. "Next time, knock."

"I thought the door was locked." Frowning, Jess moved to Dal's side. "Hush up, Brad. Now." The dog stopped barking. A weird silence settled around them like something left unsaid hung in the air.

"Tinker must've not pulled it plumb shut. Want me to lock it now?" Doc peered around the room.

"No, that's okay." Jess moved toward Dal.

Something strange was going on here.

He reached out, touched her arm. "Would you mind getting me some ibuprofen from the bathroom?"

"Of course. But I think there's some here in the kitchen cabinet."

"Dammit, Jess, would you go into the bathroom and get those? They're buffered." His dark eyes motioned. What was he trying to tell her? Get out of the room? She nodded, scurried around him and down the dark hallway into the bathroom where she left the door open a crack to watch and listen to the two men. The gun had mysteriously disappeared from the table top. Doc had obviously hung around outside till Tink and Colby left. And now Dal didn't feel at all comfortable with the nice old man in the room.

What she'd said earlier came back to her. The two people who had most recently come to Cedarton besides Trey Ledger, who was a US Marshal, and Steve Wainwright, who was in jail, were Doc and Colby. No one knew anything about them, not really.

Was Dal thinking the same thing? If so, he'd made friends with Doc, unusual for him, and he would hate like hell to think he was involved in the killings. And everyone liked Colby, though they were just getting to know him. Mac was notorious for taking in strays, so no telling what the new deputy's background was. Trey's claim that he was undercover for the Marshal's service was a stretch as well.

Well, Jessie, why trust anyone? Safer that way. Right?

All along she'd had Trey pegged as the troublemaker, the shooter, the killer of Rick Granger. But then she remembered something she'd seen after she came away from Doc's with photos of the papers he'd hidden from her view. And reluctantly put it all together.

A sticky note stuck to the corner that she'd only glanced at. The memory returned. Scribbled on it, I meant to give you this file when I saw you in Wichita in February. It was signed in a scrawl she couldn't read. But that didn't matter. What did was that Doc was somehow connected to Marcus Woods and his disappearance from WITSEC.

"You feeling rough, boy?" Doc asked after Jess slipped away to the bathroom, a puzzled look on her face. "Sit. I'll take a look at that arm. I believe you probably re-broke it taking that header across the yard."

Oh, shit. Dal shook his head and dropped back into the chair. Though he hated it, he'd about figured out that Doc had come here to keep an eye open for Marcus Woods aka Rick Granger after he left WITSEC to come visit his dying father. The old man had witnessed the earlier gunplay else why know so much about it? Maybe he'd even been involved, though the idea that Doc could fire a gun with any reliability was doubtful. And this person had to be working for the drug traffickers. What better way to keep an eye on things while waiting for Rick to show up? Away from WITSEC's protection, he'd be easy to get rid of. But how did they distract Trey? Or did this go deeper than that? Was Trey simply a decoy for the real Marshal supposedly keeping an eye on Rick?

Les was coming, and Dal needed some way to warn him about what was happening. He wouldn't come in gun out and clearing the rooms, 'cause he had no reason to. If Doc was involved, well, hell, that was just plain disappointing. He liked the old man, a hell of a lot. Didn't like too many people that much.

Didn't hardly see how Colby could be involved. The former Marine didn't strike him as someone who would kill a man, then cut off his leg to freeze before burying him. Besides, he hadn't been here then. Or had he? Doc must've done that with someone's help to bury the body and burn the car. Tinker didn't take that .38 from the table. It had either been Colby or Doc.

Was Doc here to make a clean sweep? And what had he done to the bodies of Rick Granger and Spider before sending them off to Little Rock? Enough to cover any involvement of the traffickers? As for poor old Bud, that body was now at Doc's morgue. He could do just about what he wanted to change the cause of death. Talk about a convenient setup to cover three murders. Send in a fake retired coroner.

"Figured it out yet, Dallas?" Doc shot a harsh gaze his way. "Hate like hell it had to come to this. I liked you, boy, and I'd rather have stayed out of this part, but once you and that pretty little gal started poking around too deep, you sealed your own fate. Why didn't you just stay dumb? None of this much mattered anyway."

"You crazy old coot. Didn't much matter? You murdered a man who was trying to do right, another one who was just a dumb redneck who wasn't sure what he'd stumbled on, and then to make it worse, killed poor old Bud Granger who never did anything bad to anyone. And, oh, yeah, you tried to kill me and Jessie and I understand one of Parker's horses is dead, the other real sick. All because of you and stuff that doesn't much matter. For God's sake, Doc.

"How could you even rationalize hurting Jessie, even in your wildest dreams? Let her go. She hasn't figured it out yet. Just leave her be."

"Can't do that, son. Sorry. Truly, I'm sorry. I grew right fond of you and our talks. But had you died in that fall off the mountain, I wouldn't be here tonight. God, boy, who toughened you up? That shoulda killed you."

Dal studied the old man in silence. What the hell? Everyone knew

Steve Wainwright had shoved him off that mountain. Now Doc talked about it like he'd been privy to it.

Out of the corner of his eye something stirred in the darkened hallway. Jess, giving up on finding the pills in the bathroom and coming back. He had to do something and quick before she stepped right in the middle of things. And she would. Nothing could keep her from barrel-assing right in here once she saw Doc's gun and heard what they were talking about.

Drawing on every ounce of strength left to him, Dal came up out of the chair, pain fueling his fury, and slammed Doc in the middle with his right shoulder. Hit him so hard he drove him across the room and into the waist high bar. The gun Doc held went off, shattering Dal's hearing in the confines of the small room. With frantic fingers, he clawed along the top of the bar until they closed around the knife Jessie had used earlier to open the lasagna. He would drive it into the man's gut for what he'd done.

But he just didn't have what it took. Doc guessed what he was up to and kicked him in his bad leg, the toe of his boot contacting the bone with a crack. At the same time the old man twisted away from the knife blade so it sliced deep into the flesh alongside his belly. Probably hurt like hell and blood went everywhere. Didn't put him down, though.

Dal's leg buckled and he went to one knee still holding the knife. Darkness closed over him. Hot blood flowed, the knife handle slickened, and he lost his grip. He hung on to consciousness long enough to hear Jessie yelling, cursing, to see her slam into Doc, to feel himself crumpling to the floor.

Jessie wrestled with the pudgy little man, anger driving her. The knife came free and she curled her fingers into the wound and tore at it till he screamed, whether with pain or rage, she couldn't tell. Hoped it was a lot of both. Doc held on to the gun, but was having a hard time aiming at anything. It went off, knocking the lamp onto the floor and she continued to claw at his torn flesh while her ears roared from the blast. Brad came from under the table, grabbed Doc's ankle and bore down. Mouth open in a yowl she couldn't hear, Doc tried to kick the dog, lost his footing on the blood-slick floor, and went down.

The front door banged open.

"*Look out, Les, he's got a gun!*" Jessie screamed, down on her knees pawing at the struggling old man.

"So do I." The voice did not belong to Les, in fact she didn't recognize it at all. "Kindly let go the old man and behave yourself or I'll be forced to shoot you, Jess. Much as I'd hate to. Be a hell of a way to greet each other after all these years."

Faced with that demand, she released Doc and scrambled backward, slipping and sliding in the rich, coppery blood that continued to spurt from the old man's wound.

"You might want to sit over there beside your fallen hero where I can keep an eye on both of you. Though you neither one appear to pose any danger." He high stepped into the center of the room. "Good God, it looks like a slaughter house in here."

Jessie crawled to where Dal lay and touched his face, leaned over to make sure he was breathing. Glared toward the stranger, but he wasn't a stranger, not really.

"But you—I thought you were—Doc said…."

Rick laughed. "How else was I gonna get those bastards off my trail but die? And how convenient to have a retired doctor for a friend. Now we have to decide just what to do to clean up this mess."

Dal groaned and made an effort to sit up. Jessie continued to stare at the man who had, once a long time ago, taught her about love on the floor of the Diamond House.

"What the hell is going on?" Dal's befuddled gaze took in the man standing in the center of the bloody floor holding a wicked looking pistol, then swung toward Jessie. "Who is this? Where'd all the blood come from?"

"All in due time, if you behave yourself. And you'd better put a leash on Jessie there along with that dog. They've already caused enough trouble to get shot."

Seeing Dal was functioning, Jessie came up off the floor, scrambled for Brad who was pretty bloody himself. "What're you going to do, shoot all of us? And how will you explain that? Not even Doc can put a spin on that stupidity. Things have gotten out of hand, here, Rick. Can't you see that? A deputy is on his way, there's a Marshal in the mix somewhere, and here you stand, ready to commit murder again."

"Jessie." Dal interrupted her.

She whirled. "What? I'm not going to let him kill you and me without a fight."

Instead of arguing with her, he climbed to his feet, though shakily, and studied the man holding a gun. "So you're Rick Granger. Your Dad would indeed be proud of you about now."

"Shut up."

Dal stared at him for a moment, then glanced down at Doc, who, freed from Brad's grip, lay on the floor bleeding profusely. "I think your friend down there may be in trouble. That knife must've hit a bleeder. You going to include him in your head count?"

"I said shut up." One quick glance in Doc's direction and he paled.

Clearly Granger was not happy with the situation, in fact appeared a bit confused as to his next move. Take care of his bleeding partner or tend to business. If he could keep him talking till Les drove up, maybe he could cause enough disturbance to warn the deputy. These guys couldn't both have arrived on foot. So where had they parked? What would Les see as he came up the long lane to the house? How could he get Jessie out of harm's way? That was his first concern.

"Jess, could you help me?"

She took a quick step toward him.

"Hey, you stay where you are."

"I thought you told me to go stand next to him. Can't you see he's hurt? Some asshole pushed him off a mountain."

"Yeah, that asshole was gonna take care of him. Just shows you can't count on someone else to do your dirty work for you. And so, here he is, still in one piece. Well, more or less."

Jess slipped under Dal's outstretched arm, snugged hers around his waist. He leaned his head on hers. Whispered in her ear. "You be ready to get the hell out of here. I'll take care of myself. You got that?"

She nodded, but he wasn't sure she'd pay him any mind when the time came. All he could do was warn her he had something planned. She'd be able to take advantage of a chance to get out. Her hand slipped into his pocket and he stood very still. His phone was in there. What good that would do her, he wasn't sure, but it might be helpful.

Before he could consider his next move lights flashed across the windows. Someone coming, and it could only be Les. He was an EMT, a volunteer fireman, and a deputy, so he'd be armed. Dal had to do something to make sure this idiot didn't get his way and wipe out everyone in the house. But what it was he hadn't a clue.

20
CHAPTER

The telephone rang. Outside, a truck door slammed. Doc whimpered and rolled over in his own blood. Brad decided at that moment to slither through the mess and take a big chunk out of Rick's pant leg. Rick swiveled pointing the gun, but couldn't find a good target. Les hammered on the door and shouted. The damn phone kept ringing. It was much like a three-ring circus gone wild.

Dal shoved Jessie toward the back door. "Get out of here, now. Hurry."

She stood there staring at him. Across the room, on the far side of the puddling blood, lay Doc's gun. Dal dived across the floor on his belly, trusting the blood to be good and slick. Had to get his hands on that revolver before Les came in and became a target for Rick's 9 mm. At that close a range it would cut him in two.

He slid so far he banged up against the wall, groped around in the mess till he came up with the gun just as Les hollered and shoved the door open. It was all like some stupid slow motion movie. Rick skated around to face the door, arm windmilling, dog hanging onto his britches leg. Doc flopped around like a dying fish. Dal brought up the gun with both hands. Blood dripped off the barrel. He aimed at Rick's gut, pulled the trigger once before the .38 slipped from his grip. The smell of gunpowder, the deafening boom. Penned in the small room, the noise was deafening, the stench mixed with an acrid slaughterhouse stink.

In the open doorway, Les palmed his .45 from its holster, mouth open in what must have been a shout no one could hear. Blood bloomed on Rick's middle at the same moment he aimed the heavy semi-auto directly at Les, who was faster and fired three times. Bam, bam, bam. Rick's went wild, knocking out the windows next to the door. Les didn't miss. Rick dropped across Doc, who had stopped kicking.

For a moment, the only thing moving was Brad, who continued to gnaw on Rick's pant leg, his feet slipping this way and that. Frantic because he couldn't see Jessie, Dal struggled to climb to his feet, shouting her name. His feet slithered and slipped in the gore. She couldn't hear him. Hell, he couldn't hear himself. All he could hear was the thundering echo of all those gunshots clamoring around in the small room.

He crawled on hands and knees through the blood toward the side door where she would be if she'd paid the least bit of attention to him. However, she probably didn't. Even so, if she'd kept her head down she ought to be safe. Christ, what a mess.

A hand clamped his shoulder and he looked up to see Les, shouting something at him.

He pointed at his ears and shook his head. The lanky deputy helped him to his feet.

Heart pounding, mouth dry, Jessie rose from a crouch in the far corner of the central room, and spotted Dal leaning on Les. She raced to him, bare feet slipping so she ended with an arm around each of the two men. They picked their way out of the room into the bathroom and she slammed the door. Her stomach heaved but she held back. God, how she hated to vomit. It was the next thing to dying. The sink faucet looked inviting and she turned it on, splashed her face, then drank the icy well water from cupped hands.

By then her hearing had returned enough to hear Dal's suggestion.

"I think we ought to call someone, don't you?" He dropped onto the stool and she moved to perch on the edge of the bathtub.

Les stepped under the shower head and turned it on. "Hope you don't mind. This is disgusting." He swiped at his uniform front with sticky hands. Stood under the water till the bathtub ran red around his shoes.

"I tried to call with your phone, but there wasn't a signal." Jessie raised Dal's tee shirt to inspect his belly and back. "Are you hurt? You're covered in blood. Take off your pants." She pawed at his belt buckle.

"Jessie, honey, stop. I'm okay." He held both of her hands in his one, the other arm hanging useless at his side.

Brad barked at the door and scratched frantically. "Let the poor little thing in." Jessie grabbed the doorknob.

"Yeah, let him in. He wants to lick our feet." Dal sounded half-wild.

Shocked Jessie stared at him a minute. He stared back. She snickered, then broke into a laugh. He joined her. Then Les chimed in, until they all approached hysteria. It was a long time before they wound down and regarded each other with a bit of dismay.

"I think the best thing to do is burn this house down, don't you?" She shook her head, felt a cold chill that wouldn't stop.

Les climbed dripping from the tub, took her arm, checked her pulse, and felt her forehead. "She's going into shock, Dal. We need to get our hands on a phone."

"Your walkie is on your shoulder, Les. Use it."

"Hell, I may be in shock myself." He thumbed the button and called in, requesting an ambulance, first responders, and deputies. "All you've got, Mac—and I'd suggest you use the patio door to enter. Oh, and Mac? You'd best notify the State Police. This is gonna be one hell of a mess. You're gonna need backup."

A haze hung over Jessie so she didn't understand Mac's reply coming through static on the walkie. All her senses were intact down to tasting the aftermath of the cold water she drank, but it was like being in a dream where she was unable to react. All that blood. Rick changing from the loving man she remembered into a stone cold killer.

And Doc. Dear, sweet Doc. What in the world possessed *him*?

Worst of all, the very worst was what Dal had gone through. This might well drive him back into one of his dark places. Another shiver rode through her and tears streaked her cheeks.

"Let's get her in bed. I can carry her. Can you handle yourself, Dal?"

"Hell, yes. I'm fine. Hunky dory. Nothing to worry about here. I'm gonna get in the shower and get washed off. Feel like I took a bath in it. Take her down the hall on the left is her room."

Without protesting, she allowed the hefty deputy to pick her up, but she watched Dal over his shoulder until he started down the hall. "Les, help him, please. Will you?"

"Honey, as soon as I get you in bed, I'll check on him. Don't you worry yourself none."

Before he had the covers pulled up under her chin, sirens blared, tires squealed. Vehicles left the highway, engines roared to a stop, announcing help had arrived.

In the bathroom Dal ripped the tee shirt down the front, peeled it carefully off his broken arm, then with awkward fingers undid his belt and zipper and took off his pants. Leaning his right hand on the wall on the far side of the tub, he stepped over the rim, closed the curtain, and adjusted the water.

Excited chatter, the tromp of men's boots, groans of disbelief. He heard it all but did not comprehend. The rain showerhead poured hot water over his tense body, propped by the one arm and standing stock still. If he opened his eyes all he saw was blood running down the drain, so he squeezed them shut.

How long does it take to wash away that much blood? All day, a week, a month, a year? He came here for peace and look what he found. What if there was no more peace in this world? What if it was all waiting in the next? A great sob jerked from his chest, the damaged ribs sending jags of pain in all directions. He sank to his butt, leaning his head back against the side of the shower. His tears mixed with the hot water pouring over him. They might never stop.

Someone, he knew not who, found him there, helped him out and dried him off. He did not object, nor cooperate. Wrapped in a huge towel he was loaded into an ambulance.

"Where's Jessie?" He remembered asking that before whatever was in the needle took over. He didn't remember getting an answer.

Jessie opened her eyes to a room that looked familiar. She stretched, gazed out at a silvery dawn. Leaves floated lazily in a slight breeze, the mountainside brilliant with fall colors. She slipped from under the covers to find a robe draped over an old-fashioned rocking chair. This was Tinker's spare bedroom. What was she doing here? Making her way to the bathroom, it hit her and she staggered a bit before catching herself. The shooting, the bloodbath in her beloved cabin, and all that had gone down that night, all came rushing back. Last night? The night before? She had no way of recalling that. Nor could she recall how she got here.

In the robe, she crept into the small kitchen where a note was propped in front of the coffeepot. From Tinker. Early shift. Be home by three. Dal's in the hospital. Your car is out front. Terse with no explanations, but all she needed.

Without stopping for coffee, she found a stash of her clothes in the bedroom, put on jeans and a tee shirt, grabbed her backpack from off the floor near the rocker, and hurried down the steps to the Jeep.

When Dal opened his eyes it was to bright morning sunshine. He lay in a bed, left arm encased in a fresh cast, an IV hooked to his right hand. No one was in the room. He sat up, didn't like what happened. Mostly the room spun, his stomach heaved, and pain lashed through various parts of his body. He lay back down, stared out the window a while, trying to get rid of the bloody visions in his head.

"Hey, tough guy." Her voice, that dear, sweet voice.

"Jess." Relief flooded through him. She was alive, she had survived the nightmare.

She came to him and he reached for her, folded her up against his chest and held her there for a long time, neither of them saying a word.

At last, she broke the silence. "You okay? I mean, besides…." She gestured toward the cast.

"You mean in my head."

"Yes, I guess that's what I mean."

"We need to talk."

"Well, honey, that's what we're doing."

"Somewhere besides a hospital room. Not conducive to getting down to the bones."

"Okay, this sounds serious. When are they letting you out of here?"

"I don't know about the letting. I'm leaving here today. See, I'm all patched up." He held up the fresh white cast. "And I would presume you have nowhere to go, what with what happened out at your place. So, my trailer, tonight. Bring food."

She smiled at him, kissed his cheek. "Sounds like things will be back to normal."

"Yeah, well, we'll see." He threw back the covers to reveal most of himself. Hospital gowns failed to cover much of someone his size.

"Do you need help getting dressed?"

"Nah, I can manage."

"Shirt sleeve over cast, buttons, zippers? I'm good at all those."

He didn't want this, couldn't do it. Wished he were someplace else, that he'd never seen her so he wouldn't have to do this. God dammit anyway. "I'll meet you out there. You go do the food thing. I'll be okay with this. A nurse will help. Please, Jessie, just go."

Her expression came near breaking his heart and he turned away so she'd leave. Didn't turn back till he was sure she was gone.

He had to call someone to come get him and take him home, so he called the one who would ask the least questions. Colby didn't know him well enough to wonder what the hell was going on between him and Jessie. He wouldn't ask questions about all that had gone down out at her place. About the murders, the betrayals, the losses.

When the young deputy dropped him off, her Jeep was parked at the trailer. Ina Mae watched them go by through the window and he waved at her so she'd know everything was okay. She wouldn't come up and ask questions.

At least, not yet.

He slipped in the door. Jessie sat at the table where she'd spread out food from the Walmart Neighborhood Market. A rotisseried chicken, baked potatoes, green beans, and fresh baked bread.

She'd changed clothes. Her streaked blonde hair was pulled back away from her face with a bright colored scarf that matched her shirt, the blue of her eyes brightened by the pattern. Circles bruised the skin beneath. Damn, did she have to be so pretty? So decent? So right for him in every way? Inside and out? This was going to be hard.

She smiled. "You look so good. I'm glad you're feeling better."

"It's been a tough few weeks, hasn't it?"

He didn't go to her, but pulled out a chair and sat across from her at the table. "Looks and smells good."

"Yeah, I slaved over it."

She fixed him a plate, letting him indicate when she'd piled enough food on, then slid it to him so he could manage with one hand. A pitcher of iced tea sat between them, catching the gleam of the late afternoon sunlight coming through the sliding glass doors. She poured two glasses, gave him one.

They ate in silence because he had no idea what to say and it appeared she didn't want him to begin. Intuitive as she was, she probably already had it halfway figured out. God, he didn't want to hurt her, was already hurting himself more than he'd imagined.

After they finished, they went into the living room and sat down across from each other, like they had just met and were feeling each other out.

"Have you talked to Mac yet?" She spoke quickly, like she might steer him away from what he was about to say.

"You mean about the case? No. I don't really care."

She jerked her attention away from looking at her spread fingers. "You aren't curious at all?"

"Jessie, I don't want to talk about that just now. I have to tell you something. You can talk to Mac or Parker and get the lowdown for your story, I'm sure."

"Parker is writing the story. I don't want any part in it."

He studied her closely. "Okay, I get that. So maybe you get why I don't want to talk about it."

"What do you want to talk about?"

He blurted it out without thinking any more. "I'm leaving Cedarton."

"You—when will you be back?" Her cheeks reddened like he'd slapped her.

He shook his head. "I'm not taking R-and-R. I won't be coming back."

"Oh." She picked at the fabric of her jeans, eyes downcast. "I thought we—I mean, maybe I could go with you?"

"I don't think that's a good idea. I'm having—I mean, I'm in a dark place, a very dangerous place."

"That's when we need our friends the most, Dal. I love you, and I know you love me."

"That's just it. When I love someone I hurt them or they hurt me." He tapped his temple. "It's way too bad in here for love. I'm done hurting or being hurt. It's not going to happen this time." He did not tell her the truth, that he loved her so much he had to prevent what he might do to her. What she could do to him. This time, he would not let something like that happen. "I just have to go alone, that's all."

"But you'll come back. I know you will. What about all that forgive ourselves and each other stuff? I thought we—"

"No, please don't count on it."

"Could we—would it be okay if you held me for a while?"

"If I did, we'd end up in bed together. Please don't ask me to make love to you."

"Please don't ask me not to love you. Because I do, and I will. Always."

His insides crumbled as if she had reached in there and ripped his heart out. Exactly what he did not want to deal with. He rose and turned from her. "Please go, Jessie. Please."

"Will you let someone know where you are?" The words broke into tiny pieces so he could hardly understand her. He didn't answer, but went into the small bedroom and closed the door like a whisper goodbye.

She sat alone for a long time.

The sun sank, darkness crept all around her, still she remained there in his place, with his things.

Inhaling his smell, remembering his touch, his smile, the way his cheeks dimpled when he teased her. Finally, she rose and crept to the silent, closed door. Twisted the knob and padded in.

The bed took up all the space and she slipped out of her clothing in the cramped slot before crawling under the covers next to him. His cast-enclosed left arm blocked her. He didn't stir. His legs didn't move when she crawled over them without putting any weight there. He was so banged up. How could she even think of hurting him? This man who had branded her heart, her mind, her soul. Yet, how could loving him possibly hurt him? It wouldn't. It couldn't. It could only prove to him that he must stay with her, that he couldn't rip part of her away with his leaving.

He must've been sleeping, still drugged by the medications. Yet when she drew her arm across his chest and tucked her head into his shoulder, he made that soft little sound somewhere between a growl and a moan of pleasure that always precluded their lovemaking. So she followed through, ran her fingers down into the nest of hair to feel the swelling as he grew to meet what would surely happen next.

Next. First she pictured in her mind his finely sculpted features. Brought her hand away to slip one knee across his flat belly. Warm skin, still healing from the torturous fall down the mountainside. The muscles tightened with his indrawn breath. Before he could exhale, she tasted the moist lips with her tongue. Wake him now. Make sure he wants this.

"Dallas?" Whispered into his mouth, tongue lapping along the velveteen smoothness.

He sucked at her intrusion, lifted his head the tiniest bit to take her in. Inching across his body till she rested on her knees, hairs between her legs feathering into his. A tactile sensation that sent delightful shivers deep inside her before his rising need touched hers to set off an animalistic arousal.

He spread one large hand over her butt, shifted a bit so that he slipped deep inside her. Tilted his head backward and released a huge ah that stirred her soul. Once he filled her to her depths, both rested, as if to hold that moment in time.

She would not let him go. Could not fathom waking every morning to a world emptied of him, his magnificent spirit, his essence. A desperate need rose in her, filled her to overflowing.

"Dal?" She repeated his name several times, the need growing to a frantic passion she could not control much longer. But do this to him so it was as if happening in his dream? No, she would not. Could not.

She shook his shoulder and he turned his head, back and forth, as if telling her no, yet where he moved within told her yes.

"Wake up, tough guy." A rough arousal accompanied by the beginning of movement, a brief stirring.

"God, Jessie. Oh, dear God."

His hips rose, fell, rose again. He went deep, deeper, hard, harder, and she moved in rhythm with him, orgasms matching orgasms. As if neither could stop coming, could cease the reach for something far beyond understanding. Far beyond any human knowing.

When it should have been over, all passion exhausted, her sprawled over him, him limp inside her, the need struck, grew, increased and he flipped her over, never losing contact, he straddled her lap, supported her back with one strong arm and brought her along with him once more.

The only words between them, animalistic sounds until both reached the summit and tumbled down the other side. He collapsed over her, his mouth seeking her breast, where he suckled until he brought her to a wilder, stranger orgasm that had her offering him the other nipple so he would begin again.

Inside her brain screamed, N*ever stop, never stop. If we die in the midst of this torturous pleasure, then it will be all we could have ever wanted.*

But of course, that couldn't be. Exhausted beyond all imagination, she fell limp under him, he rolled off, all but for one leg which captured her, held her long after all else but breathing ceased. Her head lay on his arm. The room smelled of their bodies, of his aroma that she would always know, of her sweat and tears.

Eventually, long after the night sounds faded toward morning, and the early twittering of birds welcomed the silvery dawn light, they pulled away from each other. A slow untangling only hinted at by mutterings of grief.

"I'm sorry," he murmured.

She laid her fingertips over his lips. "Me too. You will come back, I know you will. I love you."

He didn't say anymore and after a while she crawled from the tumbled bed clothes, plucked her things from the floor, and crept naked from the room, an ache so deep she would never be able to soothe it with her own touch. Only he could reach that far inside her.

And he was gone.

EPILOGUE

The story came out the following week on the front page of *The Observer* and in several papers in Arkansas where anyone gave a damn. The Wichita *Eagle/Beacon* called it "Butchery in the Ozarks" when they picked up Parker's story. A west coast underground paper and two online blogs wrote their own versions of what had happened in a tiny Arkansas town, using the title "Slaughter With Grace".

Despite herself, Jessie read Parker's version, ignored all the rest. And she learned what she hadn't known, hadn't even cared to know before that moment.

Trey Ledger verified that he was a US Marshal, but WITSEC didn't lose Marcus Woods. Not technically, at least. So WITSEC continued to rightfully claim they have never lost a protected witness. Doc Weston, a retired ME from Kansas City, helped Rick Granger escape his WITSEC cover in Wichita, ostensibly to visit his dying father in Arkansas. When it was learned Granger had fled, Trey was sent to Cedarton because it was presumed that was where he was going. It was months before Granger showed up. He decided he had other places to be, mainly to get revenge on some of the men involved in the drug ring with whom he'd worked for years. He felt cheated out of his due when the DEA caught him and turned him into an informant, so he headed back to retrieve the funds he felt were owed him. No one learned whether he succeeded in that quest prior to his death in Jessie's cabin.

Steve, once betrayed by Jessie, had been hired out as a bodyguard of sorts within the drug ring and became friends with Granger so when he made his deal with the DEA Steve joined him.

When Granger's wife did not hear from him for several months she reported him missing as Marcus Woods, his WITSEC cover—not a particularly smart decision. Convinced he would eventually show up in Cedarton, the head of the ring of drug traffickers bribed and threatened the mortician in Cedarton to turn the business over to Doc so he would be on hand when and if Granger showed up. He turned the tables on the drug leaders and sided with Rick for reasons unknown. Together they found and killed a homeless man in Fort Smith, brought him to Cedarton and his body was declared to be Granger's. Doc destroyed his fingerprints, faked his birthmark, and shipped the body off to Little Rock identified as Rick Granger/Marcus Woods.

Somewhere along the line, the drug traffickers fought back, hiring Spider to kill everyone involved, but that didn't work out. They had underestimated Trey Ledger's training.

One of the drug-dealing members delivered the DEA papers to Doc at the mortuary—those that Jessie managed to copy. A note on the file placed Doc in Wichita when Granger disappeared.

Sometime after the story broke, Parker secured an interview with Steve and his part in the killings and assaults came out. He had located Jessie, thus offering himself up to help Granger so he could go to Cedarton to help fake Granger's death. Steve saw this as a chance to get back at her by killing Dal and punishing her friends. His final plan, which he was unable to carry out, were to take her to the Diamond House Rick had told him about, rape her, and toss her off Lover's Leap.

However, Parker did not print any of this connection between Steve and Jessie in his story. As the only survivor of the murderous team, Steve was taken back to Kansas City, where he was convicted of assaulting a federal agent, the attempted murder of a Grace County deputy, and the murder of Granger's father as well as the homeless man.

The crime spree was the worst recorded in Grace County, Arkansas.

A few weeks after Dal left Cedarton, Parker and Jessie attended the wedding of Tinker Mattawan and Burt Sample. The couple married in a ceremony held outdoors at the pavilion on the lake.

After a month-long vacation, Jessie returned to work at *The Observer*. She lives in her remodeled cabin outside Cedarton. Sheriff Richards has not hired a replacement for CSI Deputy Dallas Starr. He and Jessie are sure Dal will come back to Cedarton.

Velda Brotherton writes from her home perched on the side of a mountain against the Ozark National Forest. Branded as *Sexy, Dark and Gritty*, her work embraces the lives of gutsy women and heroes who are strong enough to deserve them. After a stint writing for a New York publisher, she has settled comfortably in with small publishers to produce novels in several genres. She enjoys reading mysteries, but it never occurred to her she could write them until Dal Starr and Jessie West emerged from her background in the newspaper business, and the *Twist of Poe* mysteries were born.

Facebook: Author Velda Brotherton
Twitter: @veldabrotherton
http://www.veldabrotherton.com